# THE GLASSMAKERS

# THE GLASSMAKERS

*An Odyssey of the Jews*

THE FIRST THREE THOUSAND YEARS

**Samuel Kurinsky**

HIPPOCRENE BOOKS

*New York   1991*

Published in the United States of America by
HIPPOCRENE BOOKS, INC.
171 Madison Avenue
New York, NY 10016
(212) 685-4371

ISBN 0-87052-901-3

*Library of Congress Cataloging-in-Publication Data*

Kurinsky, Samuel
   The glassmakers : an odyssey of the Jews : the first three
thousand years / Samuel Kurinsky.
      p.   cm.
   Includes bibliographical references and index.
   ISBN 0-87052-901-3
   1. Glass manufacture--History. 2. Jews in glass manufacture--History. I.
Title. II. Title: Glassmakers
   TP849.K87   1991
   666'.1'089924--dc20                                                    91-9370
                                                                              CIP

Printed in the United States of America.

# CONTENTS

# ACKNOWLEDGMENTS

IT IS CLEARLY IMPOSSIBLE FOR AN AUTHOR TO ACKNOWLEDGE HIS DEBT TO everyone who assisted in the execution of his work. A bibliography encompasses but a portion of the body of knowledge from which information and opinion was drawn by the author, who blithely accords thereby his appreciation to those whose life's work was placed at his disposal. The cryptic notes of a bibliography are hardly a measure of the revelations rendered by the works referred to, and the debt to writers who are unknown to the author other than through the title pages of their works is immeasurable.

Nor can one readily render recognition to the scores of individuals from whom the author personally drew knowledge and encouragement in the course of pursuing pertinent information. Some of these individuals must be mentioned, for their substantive input cannot be ignored.

In Italy the author met on a number of occasions with that remarkable, dedicated historian and chronicler of the Venetian glassmaking industry, Luigi Zecchin, who generously allowed the author to tape their conversations and incorporate into his own work whatever material the author needed from Zecchin's vast storehouse of knowledge. The discussions ranged far beyond the limits of the meticulous records which Zecchin had assembled on Venetian glassmaking, a monumental work amassed over a long and most productive lifetime. It is with utmost sadness and regret that the author was unable to benefit from Zecchin's offer of collaboration on researching the arrival of the art into Aquileia, and on the art's arrival into Venice from the Dalmatian coast and the Near East, a collaboration which was compromised by the passing of Zecchin from this world.

Two descendants of ancient glassmaking families of the glassmaking community of Altare, Rag. Marco Grenni and Rag. Ernesto Saroldi gave generously of their time and provided the author with copies of documents, sparing the author from tedious hours of research. Guido Malandra, author of *I Vetrai di Altare*, unselfishly supplied the author with several thousand notations which Malandra had drawn from the archives of Savona and Genoa, many of which were not included in his own monumental work. Special acknowledgment of the author's gratitude to Rosanna Urbani of Genoa is due for her able assistance in uncovering documents of inestimable consequence from the State Archives of Genoa. The information gathered from all of these sources was invaluable to the author and although most of this material relates to events beyond "the first three thousand years," it reinforced the theories which the author had developed. The material will be included in a forthcoming book concerning the next thousand years of the peculiar, symbiotic relationship between the Jews and the art of glassmaking.

Dott. Maurizio Cassetti, Director of the State Archives at Vercelli, Italy, gave unstintingly of his time, and went far beyond the call of duty in personally accompanying the author in his rounds of the area on several occasions. Professor Michael Campo, of Trinity College, who was granted the title of *Commendatore* by the Italian government for his extraordinary contribution to Italian cultural historiography, became familiar with and tendered his valued encouragement to the author early on in the course of his research.

The indominable Professor Machteld Mellink, of Bryn Mawr College, was an inspiration to the author, and although Anatolia, her area of profound expertise, supplied few new facts to the present work, Professor Mellink's quiet encouragement and personal guidance through the ancient sites which abound in Turkey provided the author with a revelatory experience and invaluable background. The seas off the coast of Turkey do, however, contain ancient wrecks which are laded with stores of materials vital to the history of glassmaking. Credit for the revelation of much of this material goes to Professor George Bass of Texas A & M University, the pioneer of underwater archeology, whose work the author was privileged to witness as his guest on the *Virazon*, the research vessel of the Institute of Nautical Archeology. Professor Bass and his proficient assistant and colleague, Cemal Pulak, have rendered not only encouragement but also rescued the author from embarrassment by editing out several errors from the chapters bearing on the wrecks being excavated under their supervision.

In Israel the author was privileged to share experiences with Dr. David Adan-Bayewitz of Bar-Ilan University, whose parallel research in the field of pottery led to the identification of significant pottery-producing industries at the ancient sites of Kfar Hananiah and Shikhim. The author was also privileged to employ the renowned Professor Dan Barag of Hebrew University as a sounding board for the author's radical view of glassmaking history. Professor Barag's cursive but incisive observations went far to direct the author away from the pitfalls which await those who break new ground.

Two Americans, Steven Offerman and Mel Dubin, enthusiastically provided financial support to the Hebrew History Federation Ltd., and thus made possible the follow-up through that organization of several of the peripheral discoveries which the author had made in the course of researching glassmaking history.

The author begs understanding from those whose omission from this acknowledgment should not indicate ungratefulness for their valuable encouragement and support.

Samuel Kurinsky
*New York*

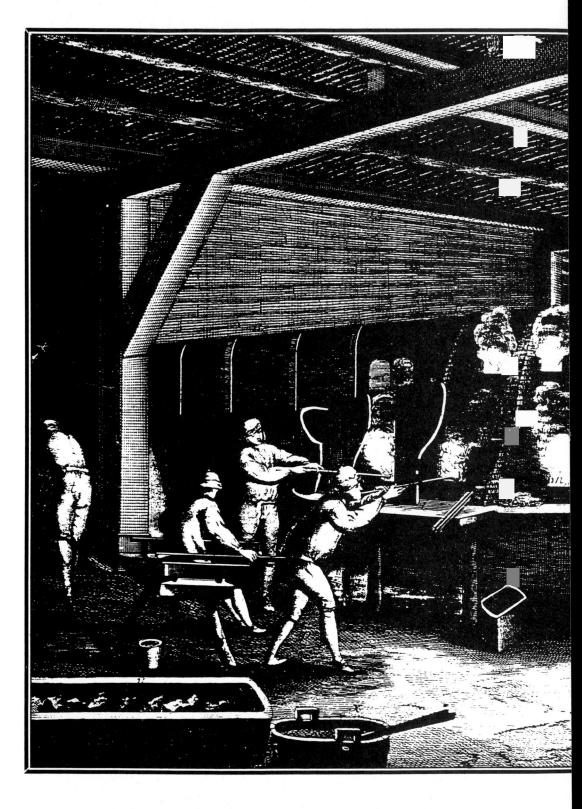

## The Art

*5,000 years ago, perhaps a little more, perhaps less, men of the Chalcolithic Age solved the secret of making glass. Nature did not readily relinquish her secret. Many requisites preceded the event, among which was the engineering of a furnace capable of melting siliceous stone, and fluxes to assist in the process; a furnace capable of maintaining the heat of the mixture long enough to permit it to melt into a new, homogenous material—glass.*

*Verrerie en Bois,* an illustration of a wood-burning glassmaking factory from a work by Denis Diderot (1713-1784) entitled: *L'Encyclopédie ou Dictionnaire Raisonné des Sciences, des Arts, et des Métiers.*

Activity in a 16th century glass factory: glassblowers (gaffers) and assistants at the "glory holes" of a working furnace (left); fritting and annealing furnaces (right).
*George Agricola,* De re mettalica, *Basle, 1556.*

# PREFACE

THE MYSTERIOUS CIRCUMSTANCES UNDER WHICH A COMMUNITY OF glassmakers appeared during the early 12th century in the rugged Apennine Mountains of northwestern Italy lured the author into an investigation of the origin and of the identification of the members of that community. The glassmaking commune appeared in a period for which records are few and information is scarce. The revelations which erupted from the author's search produced more questions than answers, as is inevitably the case with research. Each new discovery opened new areas of inquiry which in turn become subject to an ongoing investigation. The search propelled the author on an odyssey which spanned a good portion of three continents and led him back through 4000 years of human history.

For many years the author was associated with the art of glassmaking as a marketing consultant for various Muranese *vetrerie*. No one associated with the art can be unaffected by it. The drama of vitric production enthralls the observer; the magical transformation of stony silicates into an ethereal material is a spectacular process and the transformation of that material into delicate artifacts by the artistic *tour-de-force* of the masters of the art is an intriguing, awe-inspiring event. The consummate skill with which the masters gather the yellow-hot *metal* (as the molten materials are referred to in the glassmaking industry) from white-hot crucibles, the deftness with which the glowing viscous material is manipulated with the crudest of tools into exquisite works of art, captivate all attendant to the process. It is an art with which one truly falls in love; once bitten by the bug, the effect of the fascination never diminishes; it becomes a part of ones psyche, an enchantment to which all who have been associated with the art will willingly testify.

The process of vitrification is unique among the arts in that it was invented only once in all of human history; the knowledge of that process wound its way out into the world in ever-widening spirals with the people who developed it and passed their knowledge on to succeeding generations. Lithic craftsmanship, potterymaking, weaving, metalsmithing, basketry and, in fact, all other arts spawned independently within human populations and define the cultures of the divers groups of people which compose humanity. These arts were common to every culture within which they ineluctably grew in sophistication in a predictable, evolutionary process. Cultures are measured on the time scale along which these arts evolve; the degree of cultural development is set at the point which those arts attained along that scale. The art of glassmaking is missing among these measures; its appearance among various cultures occurred at times irrespective of and often at odds with the magnitude of the maturity of the cultures in which it appeared.

Therein lies our story. The research into this puzzling history revealed a symbiotic association between the wandering Jews and the art of glassmaking which had scarcely been noted; still further, it exposed gross historiographical mythology and warranted a new ordering of accepted concepts regarding the technological evolution of Western civilization.

This book is frankly and consciously written from the protagonistic position of one who seeks to fill the voids in the substantial and significant contribution the Jews have made to Western civilization and to the world. It makes no pretense of presenting a balanced rendition of history but merely seeks to span the particular gaps that pertain to the Jews and to the art of glassmaking; those gaps are considerable, enough to fill many more such volumes.

Jewish slaves built the Colosseum of Rome and mined the iron and copper of Sicily. Jewish artisans introduced silk agronomy and industry into Europe; they were smiths and dyers and weavers and tanners and shoemakers and tailors and loggers and wagoners; they minted coins for European nobility; they were merchants at the local markets; they formed the core of international trade inasmuch as they were uniquely able to issue a letter of credit in one country and be assured of its being honored in another country months and even years later. They were also the doctors and the accountants; they were councillors to kings. Yes, they were also moneychangers and bankers, occupations whose transactions were placed on record and largely preserved, for taxes had to be paid and they often involved the finances of the various states. The Jews who were involved in financial activity thereby became far more visible than did the millions of Jews engaged in the other mundane activities of which records are sparse and indeterminate.

Kings often implored the Jews to emigrate into their countries, offering extraordinary enticements to gain the benefits of the skills and the knowledge and the literacy possessed by the Jews and lacking in the native populations. Just as often the Jews were discarded, or worse, when disposal of the Jews served the ruler's purposes, or when the Jews, unbudgeable from their democratic and religious precepts, thereby became considered a threat to authority or to rival religions. It was learned, to the author's great astonishment, that glassmaking was deemed a "Jewish trade" from ancient times well into the present era. Unusual enticements were proffered to glassmakers to encourage their immigration into various realms, for it was a secret trade, and only the Semitic migrants were privy to its secrets. It was none other than St. Jerome who complained that glassmaking was one of the trades with which the Semites "captured the Roman world"!

The art of glassmaking appeared during the latter part of the 3rd millennium BCE. The art was associated with the progenitors of the Jewish people, a people who derived in great measure from that Mesopotamian milieu; the spread of the art into both the Eastern and Western worlds may be attributed in no small measure to that common genesis. The path of the dissemination of the art is peculiarly parallel to the dispersion of the Hebrew nation. There are yawning gaps in the histories of both the art and the people, yet it seems that wherever relevant facts emerge, that art and that people merge. When the two histories are placed side by side a parallel pattern appears in which the association between the people and the art becomes plainly apparent.

From their beginnings in Akkadia, westward across Arameia into Canaan, eastward back into Persia and across the desert to China, across North Africa into Iberia, across Anatolia into Greece and Italy, up the Seine-Rhine valleys and across the Hungarian plains, through Germany into the pale of the Polish and Russian plains, Jews sought opportunity or refuge, or were implanted as slaves or displaced persons carrying their arts, science, philosophy, religion and the art of glassmaking with them.

Samuel Kurinsky
*New York*

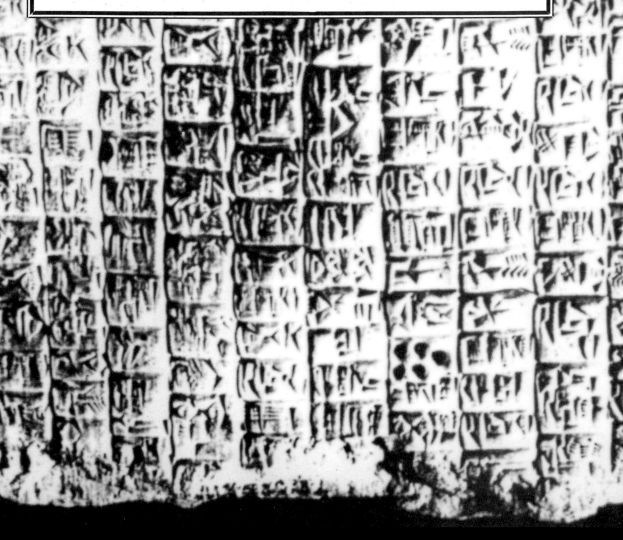

## The People

*Nations multiplied as mankind evolved from hunter to herdsman to farmer. Then a people appeared who leaped ahead; they learned to turn pots upon a wheel and then used the wheel to transport the pots; they learned to smelt iron and make glass. They learned to write, to transmit knowledge beyond the sound of a voice, even from a man long dead to one living. They revered the written word and made it common property. Therein lay the secret of their unique history.*

# INTRODUCTION

CREATIVITY IS MAN'S HIGHEST ATTRIBUTE. CREATIVITY IS THE ULTIMATE exercise of free expression, and because it counters conformity it is anathematic to authoritarianism.

One of the greatest creative leaps civilized man ever took was to conceive an omneitic universe. The revolutionary concept placed the Jews in contraposition to every ancient society but their own; the rejection of the divinity of idols and of rulers set the Jews apart from the precepts of the societies within which they were tolerated, and in conflict with those which felt threatened by the idea that no man-made institution was entitled to divine rights.

The Jews obstinately held to their principles in the eras of paganism and of Christian expansion, and suffered no less thereby. The concept which accords to every individual a personal relationship with the universal spirit of God, which denies that any human has special access to that spirit or can act as an intermediary between man and God, precluded the Jews from accepting the divine authority of any regime. They could not accede to laws which legitimized the arrogation of divine rights by a ruler or a priest or a church. They were in a constant state of philosophical rebellion against the imposition of such constricting concepts upon their own community.

The rebellion against authoritarianism freed the Jews from conformity and placed them in the forefront of humanism. Universal literacy, added to nonconformity, fostered creative expression throughout the Jewish community. Literacy and learning were always synonymous Jewish experiences; the synagogue was the center through which these requisites for the continuity of knowledge were inclusively transmitted to the members of each successive generation. The accumulated wisdom and knowledge of all humanity was thus made accessible to the whole Jewish community.

Language is a repository of culture. The Jews shared a common language, and their shared culture was enriched by the knowledge absorbed from each of the cultures in which they were immersed. The languages of the Jews and of their progenitors of ancient times, Akkadian and Aramaic, were the instruments of international intercourse of Near East civilizations for some of their progenitors of ancient times, Akkadian and Aramaic, were the instruments of international intercourse of Near East civilizations for some 2000 years; Hebrew became the *lingua franca* for the Jews within Western civilizations for an additional 2000 years. The Jews were uniquely intercommunicative throughout the Diaspora. The dispersion of the Jews was both a boon and a bane; their nation was disjoined but their culture was enormously enhanced.

While a unique omneitic outlook sct the Jews apart from other peoples, a common language, literacy and learning bound the disparate Jewish communities together and provided a firm foundation for further creativity. The exercise of this multifaceted creative propensity rebounded to benefit the societies which harbored the Jews and all of mankind. Jewish creativity was not restricted to the written or spoken word. The Jews reverenced work; as slaves and as freemen, as subjects within their own boundaries and as transients within the boundaries of other nations, they performed the basic functions without which civilization would be a shell without substance.

Literacy accelerated the organization of civilization, an impetus which was amplified by a pyrotechnological revolution which propelled mankind from the Bronze into the Iron Age. The progenitors of the Jews, the Akkadians, were at the focus of this revolution; pneumatically drafted furnaces, the basic tools required for the smelting of iron from its ores, were introduced into Akkadia from the Ararat mountains during the mid-third millennium B.C.E. and employed for the esoteric art of manufacturing glass. For almost a millennium these disciplines were practiced exclusively in the Mesopotamian milieu, from which region they spread into the world at large with the migration of its peoples. The Iron Age has been generally acknowledged to have been launched at the end of the 13th century B.C.E. at the time and in the area of the settlement of the Israelites in the hills of Canaan. Iron manufacture, mainly because of its military applications, was absorbed into other cultures and eventually became universally practiced. The practice of iron-making spread quickly throughout the world, and was given an additional impetus in Europe when the Romans tore thousands of young men from *Eretz Israel*, the Land of Israel, to work the mines and forges of Sicily and Spain.

The art of manufacturing glass, however, remained an art whose secrets were secluded among the eastern artisans, virtually all of whom were Jews. Glassmaking employs a technological sophistication which was not surpassed until well into the industrial age. It was an art which required a pyrotechnology more advanced than that which is sufficient for smelting iron; it required a familiarity with a host of minerals and metals employed in the process of glass manufacture and a knowledge of the sources for those materials; it developed skills which were refined by and passed down through scores of generations.

The Jews remained integral to the art of glassmaking over a period of 3000 years, during which time they were also the practicers of many other arts. All creative vocations, physical, mental and spiritual, were esteemed by the Jews. The sages proclaimed that "to work is a great, strong foundation of *Torah* (the Law), a precondition to the study of Torah of greater value than God-fearing." This maxim was vividly illustrated by Rabbi Yohanan Ben-Zakai, who declared that "if a man is planting a tree and is told that the Messiah has come, he must first complete the planting and only then go to meet the redeemer." The *Tannaim* (the fathers of the *Mishnah*, or oral law), and the *Amorim* (the critical rabbinic successors to the Tannaim) not only preached combining work with Torah study, they practiced it. The sages of the great ancient universities of Babylon and Jerusalem labored proudly at various trades to earn their daily sustenance. Teaching was not considered an activity for which compensation was required; teaching Torah was a privilege for which remuneration was redundant. This principle was woven permanently into the body of Talmudic practice: "Torah is not a spade" was the precept practiced by the sages as they eked out a living by creative labor. Prospective scholars were enjoined to engage in even such menial trades as skinning carcasses in the *shuk*, the ritual slaughterhouse, over dependence on public funds.

"God, after all," it was argued, "was the ultimate artisan; it was through his *labor* that the world was created; He earned a rest on the Sabbath, setting an example for mankind." An ancient and oft-repeated rabbinic maxim placed man within the context of divinic creativity: "He who is productive so that the world's work may go on, has a share in God's creation." The rabbinic scholars of the ancient academies dignified their trades; more than 70 ancient sages are known to us as Rabbi so-and-so the cobbler or tailor or as a practitioner of some 30 crafts so listed in the Talmud: "Abba Joseph was a construction worker; Chiyya bar Abba, a carpenter; Yitschak Nappacha, a smith; Abba bar Zmina, a tailor; Abba Hoshea, a laundryman; and Joseph Zeida made fishing nets. The great Hillel was a simple woodchopper who peddled his humble commodity on the streets of Jerusalem before he entered the academy to lecture. Likewise his famous rabbinic opponent, Shammai, worked as a land-surveyor; Yochanan ha-Sandler, as his name implies, was a maker of sandals. Abba Hilkiah was a farmhand, and Resh Lakish was a watchman in a vineyard."

Glassmaking was among the arts practiced by the ancient sages of Judah. The catacombs of Beth Shearim, where many of these great sages were entombed, were tunneled into the very hills on which a glassmaking industry flourished. The wonder of the glassmaking world, the nine-ton slab of glass cast in late Roman times, lies next to those tombs for all the world to wonder at.

The Jews who passed on into eternity left no idols and few amulets to mark their graves. As slaves they may not even have been granted marked graves in which to be interred; as freemen they suffered the indignity of the despoliation and destruction of their cemeteries. The ruins of their meeting places, the synagogues and study houses (those, that is, that were not obliterated or displaced), furnish no statuary to museums with which they can please paying visitors; the simple walls, such as they are, are therefore seldom sought. Nor are golden artefacts likely to be found among their weathered stones; such valued treasures were more likely melted down and made into idolic figures or minted into the money with which the coffers of conquerors were filled.

The mark the many millions made can be measured by the labor they performed. Herein lies their legacy: the baked bricks, the iron implements, the woven fabrics, the leather shoes, the silken purses, the printed books, the blood and bones and stones with which the monuments to their own oppressors were built. All these and more: the healing of the sick, the study of the stars, the rendering of maps, the creation of capital, the counselling of kings can all be counted among the manifold contributions made by those millions to the civilizations they sustained.

The technological endowments the Jews of all ages have bestowed upon human society are sparsely and perfunctorily mentioned. More than grudging references to this contribution are required to assemble the whole of the human story. The layers upon layers of institutionalized obfuscation must be hacked away until the underlying reality displaces the overlying myth. It might be said that in the pursuit of that hidden history too much reliance has herein been placed upon parallels, coincidence and morphological interrelationships. It must be ruefully admitted that such is indeed the case, but we cannot ignore the fact that the dearth of physical and documentary evidence came about not as a consequence of natural erosion but because time and time again the records of the Jewish experience were deliberately discarded and the very evidence of their existence destroyed by human agencies. We are therefore constrained to reconcile the artificial asymmetry of the facts that have trickled down, to compensate for the sparsity of physical evidence and to interpolate whatever circumstantial evidence can be gathered. We are led to rely on the overwhelming weight of that evidence to transform mathematical possibilities into probabilities.

Yet, hidden away in the archives glow rare jewels of light; such illumination was supplied by the document fortuitously found in the Genovese archives, in which a company of Jews headed by *Eliahu Bernol* was officially granted the exclusive right to manufacture glass for a period of twenty-five years in the entire dominion of Genoa. The simple, single, yellowing page speaks volumes to those knowledgeable in the art of glassmaking precisely because of the uniqueness of the art. Only those privileged to the secrets of the art could undertake such work; only those who had apprenticed for many years could perform such work; only those whose progenitors were masters of the art would have been taught the secrets and been trained for such work. The Genovese invitation to Jews to resettle into Genoa after a century of excision and recrimination and the *privilegio* granted to "Eliahu Bernol and his company of Jews" supplies a missing link to the mysterious advent and continuity of the art of glassmaking in the region of northwestern Italy while it raises another set of questions. Eliahu Bernol and his glassmaking compatriots must have been performing their art in Tuscany before their sojourn in Genoa, and must have brought the art to Tuscany from elsewhere. Where is the evidence of that odyssey and what happened to Eliahu and his co-workers in Genova within the 25 years so generously granted to them to cause their disappearance?

The search continues.

CHAPTER 1

# ZAKHUKHIT

## *The Akkadian Connection*

THE ART OF GLASSMAKING WAS BORN IN AKKADIA, THE BIBLICAL SHINAR, THE
home of the tribe of Terach, father of Abraham.

The Bible relates that Abraham was born in Ur, in the land of Shinar.
Yet the existence of such a land, and such a city, was neither known nor
sought until relatively recently, and when found it was hardly acknowledged.
In 1854 J. E. Taylor, the British Consul at Basra in southern Iraq, acting at
the request of the British Museum, was instructed by his foreign office to
investigate the mounds in the area. He did, and digging into a mound known
to the Bedouin tribesmen as *Tel Muqayyar* or "the Mound of Pitch," he
unearthed a number of peculiar tablets. The tablets were incised with rows
of intricate impressions which seemed to have been made by small birds
tracking back and forth across wet clay. Taylor was entirely unaware that
these inscriptions identified the site as that of the fabled city of Ur.

Seventy-five years passed by before anyone became aware of that fact.
Taylor had no scientific background or deepseated archeological interest and
his crude excavation tore away the top layers of ancient structures,
mindlessly scattering bricks over the countryside. The curious tablets and
cylinders of baked clay were covered with inscriptions and titillated Taylor's
interest although he had no inkling of their importance. He forwarded the
esoteric objects to the British Museum where his discovery hardly made a
stir. No one could read the cuneiform writing. The clay tablets were stowed
away deep in the archival vaults of the museum and forgotten.

Taylor dug for two short seasons. Finding neither gold nor gems, nor

1

impressive statues, the investigation ceased for lack of funds, for lack of an interest which would generate the funds necessary to launch a suitable campaign and, importantly, for lack of protection against bands of brigands. The area was infested with fierce tribesmen who fell upon foreigners who dared defy the danger of transgressing their territory. The main effect of Taylor's expedition was to expose an extraordinary, magnificent edifice, a *ziggurat*, to the elements and thereby provide nearby villages with a mine for building materials. Tons of ancient bricks were carted away over several scores of years, each brick stamped with the names of the regal erectors of an ancient civilization: *Ur-Nammu*, the original builder, and the Babylonian conqueror, *Nabonidus*, who, many centuries after its first destruction by invaders, rebuilt the Ziggurat of Ur-Nammu. The massive multi-tiered structure, thus restored by Nabonidus, was again being subjected to dismemberment, to being torn apart brick by brick by the villagers of the surrounding countryside.

The University of Pennsylvania made a feeble attempt to penetrate the area and dig at Ur at the end of the nineteenth century. So little was accomplished that the results of the expedition were never published. It took a World War to bring enough British troops into Mesopotamia to protect prospective archeologists at the sites. A member of the intelligence staff of the occupying British army, R. Campbell Thompson, fortuitously happened to have been a former assistant in the British Museum. Intrigued with the many mounds dotting the countryside, Thompson proceeded to probe into the ancient Mesopotamian cities, *Ur*, *Eridu* and *Larsa (al-Ubaid)*, under the protection of the British forces. A new age of discovery began. "Sixty years ago," wrote Werner Keller in 1955,

> no one would have guessed that the quest for Ur, which is mentioned in the Bible would lead to the discovery of a civilization that would take us further back into the twilight of prehistoric times than even the oldest traces of man which had been found in Egypt....Even before the first pyramid was built on the Nile, Tell al Muqayyar was towering into the blue skies.[1]

The exciting exposure of a civilization which had been considered fabulous Biblical lore shocked the staid, skeptical, scientific world and spurred the British Museum to sponsor a serious archeological campaign. Dr. R. H. Hall was appointed to head an expedition into the area during the winter of 1918-1919. With great and unconcealed excitement Dr. Hall reported that he had unearthed the earliest piece of manufactured glass ever found at the ancient city of Eridu (Abu Sharein), 16 miles southwest of Ur.

> Only one object of great interest and importance has been found in these houses....In the rubbish beneath the pavement, was found a lump of opaque blue vitreous paste which I recognized as true glass. I am confirmed in this opinion by the specialist's authority, Mr. H. C. Beck. Now this piece of glass...is the most ancient piece of true glass known.

The pavement to which Dr. Hall referred was laid in the time of *Amar-Sin*, the third king of the third dynasty of Ur. The date of the glass object was later fixed at between 2047-2039 B.C.E. Both the date and location are those attributed to the tribe of Terach prior to its move to Canaan. Whether it was one of the arts practiced within the tribe of Terach at that time, who can say? The very existence of such a tribe must be taken on faith for the lack of physical evidence of its existence. However, given that the tribe of Terach is, at the very least, a vivid tribal memory based on actual experience, it is clear from a mass of sound physical, philological and historiographical evidence that the art of glassmaking was developed within the framework of the culture from which such a tribe stemmed and spread westward with the migration of peoples within that culture and remained exclusively their property for thousands of years.

The news that these Biblical cities existed, and that the inhabitants may have been technologically far in advance of the Egyptians, long considered the most ancient of civilizations, was met with widespread disbelief. Erudite scientists continued to discount every evidence unearthed in rebuttal to such an upsetting concept. Prestigious students of glassmaking history insisted that the art did not reach Mesopotamia until the Roman, or, as some scholars grudgingly conceded, at best not until the Hellenic period. Items found in Mesopotamian or Canaanite contexts were summarily considered Egyptian imports. New discoveries were constantly erupting which confuted the theory of their Egyptian origin but were insufficient to roil the placid surface of ignorance. As far back as 1811 glass fragments had been noted among the shards and scoria of that fabulous center of ancient civilization, Babylon. Claudius James Rich, rummaging in the rubble of the "City of the Tower of Babel," reported the presence of glass fragments along with other exotic materials. No one was listening.[2]

# THE GLASSMAKERS

In 1849, early in the age of scientific archeology, Sir Austen Henry Layard detailed with evident enthusiasm the intricately wrought ivories inlaid with glass of blue and other colors which he had discovered in his excavations in Assyria; his excitement and wonder became further heightened by the subsequent recovery of glass vessels at the site; in his announcement of the discovery he boldly, unreservedly pronounced that the Assyrians "had acquired the art of making glass" and offered positive proof of the fact:

> Several small [glass] bottles or vases of elegant shape...were found at Nimrud and Kuyunjik. One bears the name of the Khirasbbad King; and to none of the specimens recovered can we with certainty attribute a higher antiquity than the time of the monarch.[3]

Layard continued his excavations. In clearing out a chamber of the northwest palace he made still more startling discoveries; two entire glass bowls as well as numerous fragments of well over a hundred bowls were recovered. Layard's report, published in 1853, put particular emphasis on the vessel which bore the name of Sargon, ruler of Assyria. Sargon's name was clearly inscribed in cuneiform characters along with his title as king of Assyria, both of which were significantly underscored with the symbolically regal figure of a lion. Intrigued with the time-enhanced beauty of the patina of the ancient objects, Layard appreciatively added that the glass "is covered with pearly scales, which, on being removed, leave prismatic opal-like colors of the greatest brilliancy, showing, under different lights, the most varied and beautiful tints."[4]

Both bowls were put on display in the British Museum. The bowl engraved with a lion and the insignia of the "Palace of Sargon, King of Assyria" is a three-inch-high green glass alabastron ground from a single piece of molded glass. The unmistakable Sargon inscription left a few archeologists mildly convinced of the autochthonous character of the glass objects unearthed, but skepticism continued to reign. Some experts sneered. Others found it hard to adjust to hide-bound concepts. The remarks of Alexander Nesbitt, F.S.A., whose book is still quoted as authoritative, was typical of the reaction. Unable to ignore the Sargon inscription, Nesbitt reverts to obscurantism in defense of untenable "classic" historiography.

> Next in date to the earlier Egyptian examples...would appear to be the vase of transparent greenish glass found in the North-west Palace of Nineveh, and now

in the British Museum. On one side of this is engraved a lion and a line of cuneiform characters, in which the name of Sargon, king of Assyria, B.C. 722. Fragments of colored glass were also found there, but our materials are too scanty to be able to form any decided opinion as to the extent to which the art was carried on in Assyria. Many of the specimens discovered by Mr. Layard at Nineveh have all the appearance of being Roman, and were no doubt derived from the Roman colony, Niniva Claudiopolis, which occupied the same site.[5]

Nesbitt's oblique relegation of the glass to Roman times was taken up by other scholars who enlarged upon Nesbitt's cautiously hedged but nevertheless acrid criticism of Layard's conclusion. The obvious discrepancy in date between the Sargon and Roman times was ignored; some scholars refused to acknowledge that the "Sargon" vase was made in Assyria at all. Wilhelm Froehner, setting aside the anachronistic dating, proposed that the inscription was applied to a vessel imported from Phoenicia.[6] The patently tendentious assumption that the Romans employed an eighth century B.C.E. language of which they were completely ignorant to inscribe the vessel in a cuneiform script of which they were equally ignorant passed by these worthy scholars unnoticed. Others, like the equally illustrious scholar Von Bissing stated baldly that the Sargon vase "is without the slightest doubt" of Egyptian origin inasmuch as the art of glassmaking was unknown in Syria and Mesopotamia until the Greek period.[7] The testimony of ancient historians was rejected. Nesbitt obliquely acknowledged, for example, that the legend repeated by Pliny in which the process of glassmaking was accidentally discovered in "Phoenicia" made it seem "very possible" that both the Phoenicians and the Egyptians were connected with the art, but countered by quoting another respected historian of the times to support his stated position: "Sir H. Rawlinson remarks upon this that such an accident is more likely to have occurred in Egypt."[8]

The ostrich-like rationalizations satisfied the community of classicists and became the standard explication of the evidence for many years. The classicophiles, having devoted lifetimes to extolling Egypt, Greece and Rome as the cradles of civilization, also ignored the contradictory evidence being stored away in the British Museum, where artifacts of glass hundreds of years more ancient than the earliest glass items recovered from Egyptian tombs were gathering dust in the archives of that illustrious institution. The myopic attitude of most of the scholars of the time reflected Nesbitt's uncompromising stance: "It is perhaps hardly too bold an assertion that the knowledge of the art throughout the world springs from one source, namely Egypt," Nesbitt flatly stated, and in order to bolster his "hardly too bold" assertion, added that "certainly the most ancient monuments of glass are Egyptian...."[9] Nesbitt did not clarify to which "monuments of glass" he was referring.

Nor were these worthy scholars shaken by subsequent definitive discoveries; examples of Akkadian, Assyrian and Canaanite glassware continued to come to light in increasing quantities, yet the Asian provenance of these artifacts continued to be stubbornly denied, albeit with diminishing vehemence. The classicophiles remained unimpressed with the continuous flow of evidence which made the theory of the Egyptian origin of the art of glassmaking more and more untenable. Professor Dan Barag, in compiling the *Catalogue of Western Asiatic Glass in the British Museum*, notes wryly that even as late as 1942 "Von Bissing did not change his views on the subject in spite of subsequent finds in excavations at Mesopotamian sites."[10]

In 1899, for example, John Punnett Peters could not contain his astonishment at recovering blue and green ceremonial glass axe-heads from a 14th century B.C.E. strata of the ruins of ancient Nippur. It was "a discovery for which I was not prepared," he confessed and acknowledged that the glass was "manufactured by the same methods and with the same excellence as the famous glass of Venice."[11] His startling discovery was among the myriad which were routinely dismissed. In 1913, a century and two years after Claudius Rich had noted the presence of glass fragments in the rubble of Babylon, Robert Koldewey, the archeologist charged with the excavation of Babylon, reported the recovery of glass vessels from an early Babylonian strata, and stated gingerly that glass vases recovered from early Babylonian strata "certainly date back to the same period as Egypt. We need not necessarily regard them as imports."[12]

Not only was the ubiquitous presence of glass in a West Asian context almost universally disregarded, but the basic fact that the pyrotechnology required to produce glass was absent from Egypt, and indeed from anywhere in the world other than Akkadia, did not faze the historians who blithely and blindly stuck to their story. The ability to make glass is predicated on the development of metallurgic pyrotechnology. It was at *Jemdet Nasr* that the earliest use of bronze has been proposed,[13] a site near which Babylon was subsequently established and flourished. The earliest iron artifacts were recovered from the same region, a most significant development inasmuch as iron manufacture signified the existence of the drafted furnaces necessary for the production of glass, whereas the lack of such a technology anywhere else on earth at the time precluded the ability of any other people from producing glass.

The hide-bound concepts of conservative classicists continued to dominate the field for another 50 years. The intransigence of the scholarly world was shaken again with the results of an expedition under the direction of the great Sir Charles Leonard Woolley, launched in 1922 by the University of Pennsylvania in collaboration with the British Museum. Woolley had already distinguished himself in Egypt, Nubia and Carchemish, and his epoch-making excavations at Ur crowned a career of consummate accomplishment. Sir Charles excavated diligently at Ur for 12 years; as a result of his heroic efforts the realization slowly penetrated the obdurate scientific community that Ur, and the other civilized centers mentioned in the Bible, not only existed (a fact which by that time had been generally albeit quietly accepted), but, indeed, were at the heart of a great and ancient civilization.

> We must radically alter our view of the Hebrew patriarch [Abraham] when we see that his earlier years were passed in such sophisticated surroundings. He was the citizen of a great city and inherited the traditions of an old and highly organized civilization. The houses themselves reveal comfort and even luxury. We found copies of the hymns which were used in the services of the temples and together with them mathematical tables. On these tables were anything from plain addition sums to formulae for the extraction of square and cube roots.[14]

Woolley's conclusions were based on the discovery that in the twenty-fourth century B.C.E., coincident with the estimated time of the birth of the art of glassmaking, a great empire was created by Sargon I (not to be confused with the later Sargon mentioned above), the first extensive empire the world had known, consisting of most of Mesopotamia and stretching beyond the alluvial basin of the twin rivers to the shores of the Mediterranean. Agade, the capital city built by Sargon I, lent its name to the province which came to be known under a latinized transliteration as *Akkadia*.

A complex society is evidenced by the buildings, the comprehensive system of irrigation and the tools and implements of bronze found in Akkadia; the artistic sophistication in which the craftsmen rendered their trades bespeaks an already ancient civilization. Akkadia, or, as it was subsequently referred to, Babylonia, the province of the "city of the tower of Babel," proved to be one of the first fountains of civilization as we know it. The objects which, above all others, placed the technological acumen of its artisans far ahead of that of all other contemporary civilizations were the articles of glass recovered from a number of sites, including glass beads, rods and other items from cemeteries and buildings within the city of Ur itself. Some of these glass artifacts date back to the Third Dynasty and predate the object found by Dr. Hall at Eridu.[15] Specimens of blue glass lumps were also discovered in another deposit at Eridu, and these were dated even earlier than the Third Dynasty.[16] At first they were estimated to have been manufactured as far back as 2700 B.C.E. Later, improved methods of dating adjusted these estimates to the twenty-fourth century, and it seems reasonable to place the very beginning of glassmaking to about that time.

Dr. Hall's statement concerning his startling discovery of "the most ancient piece of true glass known" at Eridu remains true for the glass artifacts found in the various Akkadian communities; they are the oldest examples of the art of glassmaking, predating manufactured glass found anywhere else by many hundreds of years.

At this time a discovery was made which should have resolved the question by any standard. A seventeenth century B.C.E. cuneiform tablet was excavated from *Tell Umar* near the Tigris river near ancient Babylon on which is inscribed the oldest dated written record related to the art of glassmaking.[17] Although the site was located in an area then under the control of the King of Ashur,[18] the text was written by a priest of Marduk at Babylon. The Tell Umar tablet was written in the *Akkadian vernacular*. This clay tablet, deposited with the British Museum, bears the formulae for a glass frit and for glass. The word for glass, transcribed into English from Akkadian cuneiform tablet, is *zuka(k)-i*, This is the earliest known appearance of a word which defines manufactured glass as a palpable substance distinct from all others. The Akkadian terms for glass, for precious stone imitations and for the processes involved in glassmaking are matched in antiquity only by equivalent Sumerian terms, a fact which fixes the provenience of the origin of the art to that area even more firmly.

The word derives from the Akkadian *zakû*, which means "be clear". The word is found transliterated into the word meaning "glass" in the earliest known forms of the Semitic dialects, Ugaritic and Aramaic in linear

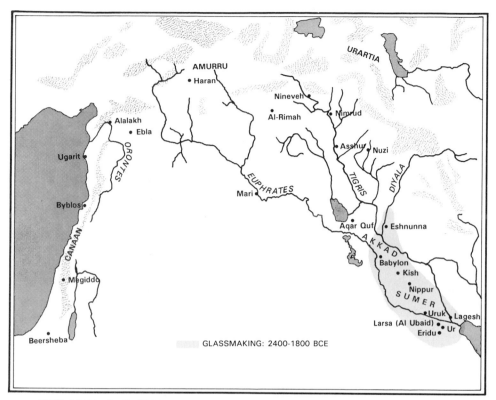

**THE AREA OF THE BIRTH OF THE BRONZE AGE AND OF GLASSMAKING**

The Bronze Age and glassmaking both originated in southeast Mesopotamia. Iron artifacts of manufactured origin (without a nickel content and therefore not of meteoric origin) have been recovered from the same area; some date as far back as 2700 BCE, 1500 years before the formally designated initiation of the Iron Age. The earliest manufactured glass was found in the same area and dates from c. 2400 BCE.

etymological conversions and ultimately ends up as *Zakhukhit* in Hebrew, which translates to "glass" and derives from the Hebrew word meaning "crystal" or "clear." The Aramaic word for crystal, for example is transcribed into English as *zagugita*. The etymology is self-evident. Clearly the Akkadian word included in the cuneiform tablet is a cognate of both the Aramaic and Hebrew words. The people who employed Akkadian, Aramaic and Hebrew, Semitic dialects deriving from a common root language, are none other than the tribes such as that of the reputed tribe of Abraham. Abraham is biblically referred to as being an Akkadian (from "Shinar") and portions of the text of the Old Testament and of much other ancient Hebraic literature are written in Aramaic. The Hebrew language provides an unmistakable linguistic connection to the terms used on the cuneiform tablet. The Hebrew word for glass appears, for example, in the Bible as an example of the most valuable materials. Thus, in chapter 28, we find that Job values wisdom above the most precious of earthly possessions, among which glass is placed: "But where shall wisdom be found?" asks Job, rhetorically, and avers that in value even "Gold and glass [*zakhukhit*] cannot equal it."

Evidence of the symbiotic relationship between the Akkadians and the art of glassmaking is further reinforced by other cuneiform texts found in the library of Assurbanipal (668--627) at Nineveh, an ancient metropolis on the upper Tigris river. Agents of this last of the great Assyrian kings combed through the archives of the then already ancient temples and palaces of Mesopotamia and assembled or had copied a vast collection of treatises on metallurgy, chemistry, medicine and other disciplines. Many of these documents dated back to the Akkadian era.

Assurbanipal left an invaluable legacy to the world. Records which would have been lost to us are preserved in his unprecedented library, and we are left to puzzle out the dates of the store of texts made available to us. Among the ancient texts were detailed instructions for the construction and operation of the different glassmaking furnaces necessary for the round of processes performed in the production of first frit and then glass and for the tempering of the finished products; included is the description of a reverberatory furnace, the earliest such description extant;[19] included are descriptions of the fuels to be employed, details of complicated formulae listing the chemicals required and the precise proportions in which they are to be employed for the production of diverse colors and qualities of glass; included are instructions for repeated heating and fusing with additional ingredients in order to produce glass with differing properties, as well as grinding and molding guidelines; included are detailed instructions for the production of both colored and crystal imitations of highly prized gems; included are instructions as to the burning of the *naga* plant, a plant growing wild in Akkadia, and of the processing of the ashes. The seeds of the plant provided nourishment and the ashes of the burned remainder rendered a requisite alkali, soda.[20]

There is no way of making a precise determination of the age of the original records from which these tablets were copied. It is, however, evident from the archaic remnants left in the language that they relate to a considerably earlier period. It is also deduced from the sophisticated formulae and technology described that many hundreds of years of development were required to arrive at the techniques particularized, to which must be added the age of the documents themselves. The terms employed in these cuneiform inscriptions, as well as those of the seventeenth century B.C.E. inscriptions discussed above, appear in even more ancient inscriptions in other contexts. The advanced mosaic and millefiore techniques employed on some of the earliest pieces found in the various ancient Akkadian and Assyrian sites likewise bespeak several hundreds of years of development. It is a reasonable deduction from these circumstances that much of the information preserved for posterity on the ancient clay tablets from Nineveh could very well have been forwarded from a period not only concurrent with, but earlier than that of the tribe of Terach.

It is clear that the language of the culture within which a product is produced must have a word for that product. Thus we may reasonably assume that since a word for glass existed only within the Akkadian and Sumerian languages during a period of a thousand years that it was only in the area where those two cultures co-existed that glassmaking was being performed. The fact that during that period, not only did the Akkadian and Sumerian languages have words for the product itself but also words which define the product as well as the process by which it is manufactured, the assumption of precedence is reinforced. A philological study of the terms employed in ancient languages concerning glass and its production was undertaken by A. L. Oppenheim, an internationally acknowledged scholar in the field of ancient philology. The results of his masterful study illuminate both the proposition and its corollary, i.e., that cultures which were devoid of terms for glass or its production did not have the knowledge of that production. The etymology of both the process and the word for "glass" itself unambiguously identifies both the birthplace of the art of glassmaking and delineates the path through which the art spread through the ancient world.

The first application of glass was for the imitation of precious stones among which lapis lazuli was a particularly valuable and admired gemstone in ancient times. Lapis lazuli played an important role as an item of permanent value and was highly prized as an item in the international trade of those times, much as the diamond is today. Kings could offer no better gift to other kings than objects of lapis lazuli. It was inevitable that, as soon as the technology of making glass was invented, one of its prime applications would be the imitation of this much sought after, rare, valuable, beautiful blue gem. In the third millennium B.C.E. lapis lazuli was imported into Akkadia and Sumer from the mountains of Afghanistan, 1500 miles to the east. It was traded by Akkadian merchants an equal distance to the west, and into upper Egypt.

Professor Shinju Fukai of Tokyo University, an archeologist who campaigned in Iraq-Iran since 1956 and became director of the an expedition into the area in 1976, was struck by the relationship between lapis lazuli and the origin of glassmaking in the third millennium B.C.E. "Why did glass suddenly come into use?" asks Professor Fukai, rhetorically, and then readily supplies the answer: "At present, the most reasonable explanation is connected with lapis lazuli. In the ancient Middle East, particularly in northern Mesopotamia, the blue, purplish blue or greenish blue variety of lapis lazuli became the favorite material for jewelry and other ornaments."[21]

Gemstones born in a furnace were then, as today, considered less valuable than original stones which are mined from the mountains. Akkadian and Sumerian are the earliest languages which differentiate real gemstones from their imitations in glass. The Akkadian word for lapis lazuli was *ugnū*. Professor Oppenheim, defines the differentiation:

> The contrast, "genuine" and "artificial" when referring to colored precious stone is expressed in Akkadian by the terms *kūru* and *sādû* respectively which appear in the genitive after the name of the stone. Thus *ugnū-kūri*, literally "lapis lazuli from the kiln," denotes lapis lazuli colored glass, and *ugnū-sadî* literally "lapis lazuli from the mountain," the genuine stone....These designations begin to appear in the second half of the second millennium in texts from Assyria and the West.[22]

The Akkadian word *sadû* for "mountain" originated from the word for breast, i.e., a woman's breast. It is interesting to note peripherally that the Hebrew word for mountain is *sad*, and is still colloquially in use to designate a woman's breast.[23] The concept of artificial gems, i.e., glass imitations of precious stones, can be traced philologically as the performance of the art passes from one culture to another. The fact that it appeared first in both the Akkadian and in the Sumerian languages fixes the beginning of the art within the area in which both languages were coevalent. The definitive words and concepts were inscribed on the Akkadian tablet almost two millennia before equivalent words appear in the Greek and Roman languages.

The oldest record of the arrival of the concept of artificial gemstones into Egypt appears there not in the Egyptian language but in correspondence to Egypt written during the so-called el-Amarna period, letters from Assyria, Babylonia (Akkadia) and (Hurrian) Mittanni written in an Akkadian dialect (Middle Assyrian). International trade and intercourse of all kinds were conducted in that language, the *lingua franca* of the entire Near-Eastern area. One of the earliest references, for example, appears on a letter from the Babylonian King Burnaburias II (1375-1347), informing the pharaoh that his gift includes ten lumps of *genuine* lapis lazuli. He adds that the pharaoh's wife will also receive 20 carvings in the form of musical instruments, assuring him that they are made of "lapis lazuli from the mountain!"[24]

Names for the major constituents employed in the process of the manufacture of primary glass are also absent from every other ancient language but Sumerian and Akkadian. Quartzite pebbles or sand, the basic material in glass, was defined in Akkadian as *Immanaku*, which fused together with the alkaline flux obtained from the ashes of the *naga* plant produced *zukû* or glass. R. H. Brill of Corning succeeded in synthesizing these elements under conditions equivalent to those obtained in Akkadia. - "The product that resulted was not only a glass, but a glass of unexpectedly high quality," reported Brill.[25]

The transmittal of the concept of the differentiation between artificial and natural gems and the geographical route along which it passes coincide with the movement of tribes like that of Terach and of his son, Abraham, and of their descendants from east to west during the very period designated in the Old Testament. The reasonable conclusion, based on philological, physical and documentary evidence, is that the 3600-year-old Assyrian tablets recording the first known formula related to the manufacture of glass were written by a scribe of the culture of the tribe of Terach and that such people were the first to manufacture and to trade in artifacts of glass. Subsequent evidence attests to a continuing, remarkable, symbiotic relationship between the peoples of that culture and glassmaking, a relationship that continued for several thousands of years. The spread of the art continued to be coevalent to the dates and concomitant to the routes of Semitic migrations, and consequently of the Hebrews.

It eventually became utterly absurd to deny the "West Asian" provenance of most of this material; the arguments reverted from whether the art was practiced at all in those areas in pre-classic times to the question of how far back in time the art was therein practiced and from whence the art had originally come. While the accepted date of the appearance of the art in those areas slowly and steadily receded, the barbed question of pre-Egyptian, West Asian manufacture of glass artifacts remained to be resolved. The Egyptophiles stood steadily and stubbornly unmoved, but more circumspective scholars approached the question with a deference to other possibilities.

Paul Fossing authored a treatise on glassmaking in 1940 which became a historiographical watershed and forced a shift in the perception of the provenance of the glassmaking art. Noting the dearth of examples from both Egyptian and Asian sources, Fossing nevertheless affirmed that glass vessels were indubitably being produced in Mesopotamia at least as far back as 1300 B.C.E. He put forward the possibility that the art had developed independently in Mesopotamia and Egypt.[26]

Finally, in 1968, Donald B. Harden, a most prestigious glass historian, was obliged to obliquely intimate acceptance of the "Asian origin for glass," and take note of the arguments of H. C. Beck, who had proposed the initiation of the art had taken place in Mesopotamia in the mid-third millennium B.C.E. "Most students, if not all," wrote Harden, "would now accept an Asian origin for glass, though we are today no nearer to deciding the exact date of the invention of glass as an independent substance, as distinct from vitreous glaze on a stone or other base."[27]

Harden based his somewhat qualified acceptance on the persistent eruption of revolutionary evidence; he had already overextended himself by stating a few years earlier (1960) that glass vessels had come into use about the late seventeenth century and "were made by the sand-core technique, which was probably a Mesopotamian discovery."[28] Harden's bold statement

14

was made in the flush of a reaction from the commonly accepted point of view; his original, admittedly myopic focus had been engendered by the universally held, narrow perspective of the archeological community and by his experiences in compiling a masterful work on "Romano--Egyptian" glass recovered from Karanis in the Egyptian Fayoum:

"During my two years at Ann Arbor and the next winter season on the excavating staff in Egypt," Harden candidly confessed in 1983 to the twenty-third Annual Seminar on Glass, "I naturally became too Egypto-oriented."[29] In 1967 Harden hesitatingly placed the date of the origin of the production of glass vessels back another 200 years from Fossing's projection of 1300 B.C.E. He cited a long roster of important finds:[30]

> Examples [of glass vessels] that must be, at latest, early 15th century are known from various sites in the Asiatic Near East. Woolley found some fragments at Atchana (Alalakh), dating from level VI (end of the 16th century at latest) onwards;[31] Starr found many important fragments at Nuzu (near Kirkuk) in stratum II (1st half of the 15th century).[32] There are early-to--middle 15th century examples from Assur also, especially from two tomb-groups, nos. 37 and 133,[33] which yielded five reasonably complete pieces, comparable in shape to Nuzu-ware pottery and in one instance to a glass vessel from Maherpras tomb at Thebes in Egypt of roughly the same date (Thutmos III, early-middle 15th century B.C.); and a similar glass of the middle of the second millennium, again of a Nuzu pottery shape, comes from Tell al Rimah.[34]

The examples cited by Harden are by no means a complete inventory of all that were in evidence at the time. The vessel bearing the name of Thutmose III (1490-1436) was being advanced as the main and only substantive claim to the existence of glassmaking in Egypt and continues to be presented as positive proof of glass manufacture in Egypt at so early a date. Although the Sargon vessel was purported by some to have been an import from Egypt, the fact that the Thutmos vessel might have been an import into Egypt was universally overlooked, albeit examples of glass vessels dated earlier than the mid-second millennium were rarer than those of Mesopotamian provenance. In addition, the possibility that even if such items could be labeled "Made in Egypt," the employment of foreign artisans is a likelihood if not a certainty. Such a conclusion derives handily from the boastful inscriptions in which the pharaohs describe their marauding raids into Canaan, list the vast amount of plunder purloined on those incursions and picture the artisans captured, bound and brought to Egypt as slaves.[35]

Dr. Harden was charged by the British Museum to author a catalogue of its collection of Greek and Roman glass. In the catalogue Harden deferentially pushed back the date of the initiation of the art of glassmaking in "western Asia" yet another 100 years, and was consequently constrained to point out that Egypt was not the birthplace of the art after all: "It is now generally accepted that the first manufacture of glass vessels and other objects in any quantity took place in western Asia in the late 16th century and in Egypt in the early 15th century."[36]

POMEGRANATE VASE, CORE-FORMED, 14th-13th CENTURY BCE. The pomegranate was a Mesopotamian fruit which figured in Mesopotamian and Jewish art from an early period. *Photograph courtesy of the Israel Museum.*

The artifacts of glass unearthed from all the excavated Akkadian sites which are dated somewhat earlier than and contemporary with the time of the Terach, father of the Hebrew patriarch Abraham, represent the corpus of the earliest examples of manufactured glass. The finds of the subsequent Hurrian period, as for example at El Rimah (Tell al Rimach) in northern Mesopotamia, at Mari and at 'Agar Quf in central Mesopotamia are dated about 1500 and 1400 B.C.E. respectively. Among these ancient artifacts are items executed in an advanced mosaic technique which must have taken hundreds of years of development, and which have hardly been improved upon since that time. Projecting backward from these dates brings the origin of glassmaking to circa 2000 B.C.E., coincident with the Akkadian period and the earlier finds at Atchana, Eshnunna, Eridu and Ur and elsewhere.

The acceptance of West Asian provenance for the origin of glassmaking by the archeological community at large did not come about through objective reasoning but as a grudging acknowledgment of evidence which could no longer be ignored. Nor was the entire community ready to concede to that proposition even after a huge trove of glass artifacts of particular significance was unearthed at Hurrian *Nuzi*. The excavations were first carried out by Harvard University in conjunction with the American Schools of Oriental Research and the University Museum of Philadelphia. A more prestigious group of American sponsors could hardly be assembled.

Professor Richard F. S. Starr of Harvard headed the team of distinguished archeologists who issued the report on the campaign of 1927-1931. A prodigious quantity of locally manufactured glass artifacts was found; the diversity of colors, designs and applications eloquently demonstrate a technology of unexpected virtuosity and of superb artistry.

Until that time virtually the entire thrust of archeological research had been confined to the Egyptian, Hellenic and Roman theatres, and the "classical" world was assumed by many to be the womb of civilization. Until then erudite scholars were still mindlessly echoing the myth that Egypt was the matrix in which the gestation of the art of glassmaking had occurred. Suddenly the Americans were confronted with a magnificent, manifestly local operation whose products had many of the characteristics of Egyptian ware, and many more. The vast array of colors and forms and techniques displayed a prodigious pyrotechnical proficiency and was executed with consummate artistry. Being contemporary with the oldest examples of Egyptian glass, the indications that even some of what had been considered

Egyptian glass may not have been Egyptian after all emerged from the findings at Nuzi.

Glass objects were found in all types of structures, temples, courts, the palace, administrative buildings as well as in upper-class private dwellings. Eleven thousand glass beads and amulets were recovered, a great quantity of which were found in "temple A," significantly dedicated to the Semitic fertility goddess Ishtar.

> Thousands of beads were scattered over the floor [of the temple], some still retaining remnants of the copper wire on which they were strung. These were mostly in glass, a few in blue frit, and fewer still in various types of stone. The variety and size and form among the glass beads was very great, ranging from elaborate multiform conceptions of four strings of beads of different type cast into one down to the simplest, tiniest spherical bead. Spherical, semi-spherical, cylindrical, elliptical, fluted, ribbed, flat, and rectangular and many other variations and combinations of the shapes were present in large numbers. Many of the glass beads were multi-colored, with one color laid over a foundation of another in the same manner as the Egyptian decorated glass of the same period. The colors used, in the order of their frequency, are blue-green, white, yellow and black.[37]

"Beads were common throughout all of the Nuzi buildings," and had most interesting applications. Some beads were unpierced, and the discovery of an unbaked brick into which a row of elliptical and circular eye-beads were set substantiated the fact that they were used as decorative wall treatment. Beads were evidently strung in ropes along the wall just above eye-level upon glazed wall-nails in another type of architectural decoration. A particular style dubbed "eye-beads" served many purposes. They were usually elliptical, with a raised ridge surrounding a white area with an iris of yellow or black. Some were pierced through the edge with two or four equidistant holes. These multiple perforations imply the fastening of patterns of beads onto cloth. The probability that such beaded fabrics existed tickles one's sartorial imagination, just as one's architectural fancy is stirred by the image of walls strung with brilliant, vari-colored beads.

Unusual shapes turned up; frog-shapes, human heads and peculiar tubes bent at a 100-degree angle; mosaic beads were not uncommon; barrel-shaped green-glass beads decorated with spirals, dots or loops of white or yellow inlaid glass; beads imitating agate stones with a pattern of clear, white and

COMPOSITE EYE-BEADS OF THE 14th to 13th CENTURIES BCE.  Ancient eye-beads are
characteristically Near-Eastern and figured as significant components of trade goods world-wide
for over three millennium.
*Photograph courtesy of The Corning Museum of Glass.*

dark coloring; beads marvered and combed into festoon and zigzag patterns;
the multiplicity of treatments provide indisputable evidence of the virtuosity
of the glassmasters of Nuzi and the antiquity of their art.

> There is a great deal of artistic experimentation with the forming of beautiful
> glass objects, but there is a sureness of execution and skill in the handling of
> glass that defines glassworking as an established craft specialty.  The tour de
> force craftsmanship and variety of processes and objects indicate a well-known
> and exquisitely exploited technology. [38]

In addition to beads there were pendants: in plant-bud forms, female
symbols, cycladic figurines, the body of a couchant lion, three forms of
decorated sun-discs (one with the sun in the center, another with eight
radiating rays, as well as a variation with the dots between each ray), a
variety of zooforms including many fly-beads as well as rams-head, bulls-
head, and many mosaic types.  Richard Starr, in his report on the excavation

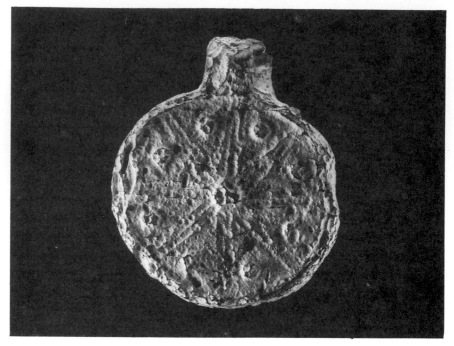

SUN-DISC GLASS PENDANT FROM NUZI, MID 15th OR EARLY 14th CENTURY BCE. The eight rayed motif (some with dots interspersing the rays) was incorporated into Canaanite and Judaic art; it is similar in style to the star motif on the gold medallions recovered from the 14th century BCE ship which foundered off the Turkish coast (See chapter 4).
*Photograph courtesy of The Corning Museum of Glass.*

at *Yorgan Tepa* (the site of ancient Nuzi), notes that glass vessels in evidence in the temples, courts, rooms of the palace and in private dwellings were "of pretentious size and arrangement" and adds that the quantity of decorated glass vessels "is sufficient to show that such objects were by no means a rarity in Nuzi....Its quantity, distribution, and likeness of material to the glass beads and plaques of the temple leave no doubt that it was of local manufacture."

Nonetheless, bowing to the contemporary norm, Starr is prompted to inject that "Although the glass as a whole is undoubtedly of local manufacture, the dissimilarity of the designs to those more typical of Nuzi marks it as foreign in conception. It resembles closely the glass of approximately the same date found in Egypt."[39]

The varied utility, the prolific quantity and the unique applications of the glassware in evidence furnished incontestable proof of local manufacture. There was nothing left but to ascribe the similarity of *some* of the Nuzi glass to glass found elsewhere to be of "foreign" (meaning Egyptian) conception. This projection did not account for the fact that, whereas items and techniques were demonstrated in Nuzi ware which did not appear in Egyptian artifacts, all Egyptian-ware characteristics were included in the Nuzi ware. Had analogous Egyptian glassware been discovered *after* that of Mesopotamia, of course, the juxtaposition of the origin of the style would naturally have been reversed.

Several of the discoveries should have alerted the archeologists to the inconsistent nature of the conclusions drawn in this regard, most significant of which was a large, globular glass head of a copper hairpin found in a strata *antedating that of Hurrian Nuzi by almost a thousand years*. It also antedates the earliest known and acknowledged Egyptian glassware by a similar period of time. "The glass is," noted Dr. Starr, "identical with, and as perfect as, the beads made in Nuzi almost a thousand years later. It is, in fact, in much sounder condition than the majority of the Nuzi glass beads."[40]

Many intricately inlaid glass plaques were included in the vast assortment. Both mace and staff heads in glass were found. An analysis of the material from one of the ceremonial maceheads was conducted by R. J. Gettens of Harvard, who reported that the "material has all the chemical and physical properties of the ancient pigment known as Egyptian Blue or frit, supposed to have been made artificially and used by the Egyptians over a period of many centuries."[41]

A modicum of doubt is thus gingerly inserted: "supposed to have been made and used by the Egyptians."

The ubiquitous presence of idolic figures of the Semitic fertility goddess, Ishtar, in bone, wood and stone as well as glass among the artifacts found at most of the sites substantiated a strong presence of Akkadian Semites, and should have clinched the argument. The prominence and age of the temple to Ishtar among the others, the great number and the particular applications of the glass artifacts found therein indicated a long association of the Ishtar worshippers with glass. The goddess, who was undoubtedly among the idols worshipped by Terach, father of Abraham, never appeared in Egypt in that form.

The range of chemical substances deliberately utilized to produce a

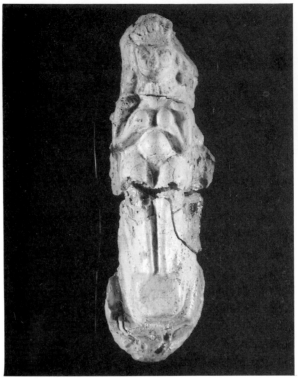

AN ASTARTE (ISHTAR) GLASS PENDANT, 16th CENTURY BCE OR LATER. The Goddess of fertility was worshipped throughout the Semitic world and continued to have a hold on the Jews throughout their biblical history. Statuettes of the goddess were used as a household amulet to foster fecundity in the family as well as for that of their animals and crops. The possessors of these figurines are frequently biblically castigated for paganist practice.
*Photograph courtesy of The Corning Museum of Glass.*

considerable inventory of colors, and the precise proportions in which the chemicals had to be employed to maintain consistency manifest a vitric technology which could only have developed over many centuries, extending the technology back to early Akkadian times. Many of these materials would have had to have been imported from great distances, and are not known to have been used for other purposes. The import of such materials suggests a considerable knowledge of geology and extensive exploration. In addition to the basic soda, lime and silicates, dozens of diverse chemicals such as cuprite, lead and calcium antimonates and the complicated melting and refining processes were necessary to produce the range of colors. The astounding array of chemical substances known to and employed by the Nuzi glassmasters led Pamela Vandiver, of the Massachusetts Institute of Technology, to remark in a modest understatement that "this sophisticated level of chemical technology would not be expected if glassmaking were not a developed craft."[42] Ms. Vandiver concludes that:

> Because of the large numbers of glass objects (over 11,000) found at Nuzi, because of their artistic excellence and the range of manufacturing methods utilized by artisans (including core forming, mold pressing, stamping and grinding), because of the relatively narrow range of composition [indicating the application of a thorough chemical and metallurgical knowledge], because of the variety of ways employed to color glass (some requiring different heat treatments and different oxidation-reduction atmospheres) and because of the variety of other soda-lime-silicate materials which use glass, we conclude that a well-developed glass technology was present in the Near East at Nuzi well before the destruction of the site at about 1400 B.C. The origins of glass must be researched at sites predating the fifteenth-century glass finds at Nuzi.[43]

These impressive facts were nonetheless overlooked. The oversight is even stranger when we read in the report that the Nuzi glass was being examined by the same glass expert, Horace C. Beck, Esq., who had attested to the earlier discovery of glass at Eridu by Hall, manufactured glass dated to beyond 2000 B.C.E. Dr. Beck later affirmed the autochthonous provenance of the Nuzi glass and of glass found at other such sites, but his conclusions were subjected to continued dispute and disbelief. The inculcation of prescriptive Egyptian lore into the fabric of historiography was so deep as to forestall the obvious conclusions that the evidence before them would otherwise have engendered.

The virtuosity of the Mesopotamian masters of glassmaking is dramatically illustrated by artifacts recovered from the palace of Yarim-Lim (son of Hammurabi) near Alalakh at Tel-Atchana. It was again the indomitable Sir Charles Leonard Woolley who recovered glazed and trail-decorated fritware from the earliest level VII of the palace, dated to the time of Hammurabi, its presumed builder, or to about 1800 B.C.E. Wooley states "there can be no doubt" that the Atchana vases were made according to the prescription on the seventeenth-century Assyrian tablet.

Furthermore, intricately wrought polychrome true glass objects were recovered from the very next level, that of Hammurabi's grandson, Niqme-

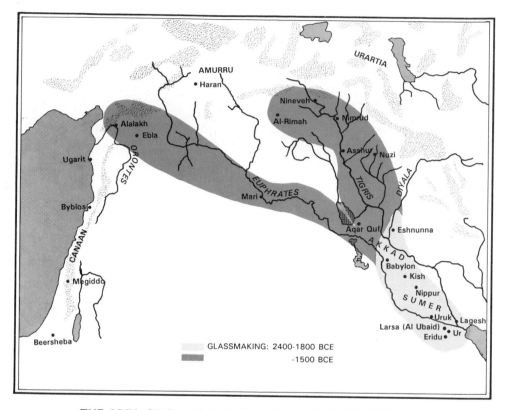

## THE AREA OF GLASSMAKING IN THE MIDDLE BRONZE AGE

The art of glassmaking moved northwestward across Amurru (Aramea) at the crown of the "Fertile Crescent" in the wake of metallurgic pyrotechnology and with the movement of Semitic tribes toward and into Canaan. During this period the first 'core-formed' glass vessels were produced, fashioned by trailing a strand of molten glass around an earthen core and then rolling the still hot assembly over a flat surface (marvering), thus pressing and melding the trails together while they were still hot and malleable. The friable core was scraped from the vessel after cooling. Such vessels thereafter appear in Egyptian tombs, having been plundered out of Asia during pharaonic incursions or obtained as tribute from subservient Asian chieftains.

epukh. From that level forward an astonishing collection of fragments appear; "festoon-ware" with drapes of varicolored trails skillfully marvered into the glass corpus of vessels; millefiore, inlay and other techniques in a wide range of colors which attest to the profundity of the art of the Akkadian (now Babylonian) masters and to the antiquity of the technology. The evolution of the technology and the continuous maturation of artistry demonstrated by the artifacts recovered from successive strata demonstrate a progression which has never been found in any Egyptian environment.[44] The techniques employed by the masters of Alalakh, Nuzi and other such Akkadian and Assyrian glass production centers have never been surpassed, and, except for the invention of glass-blowing, are essentially those employed today by the most accomplished masters of the art.

The dating of glass items found elsewhere in Akkadia and Assyria provide a pattern which clearly depicts the spread northward and eastward and westward of the products and the art from the Akkadian matrix in which they had erupted. At Elamite Tchoga Zanbil (Dur Untash), southeast of Susa, doors with long tubular glass rods inserted diagonally into entry doors,

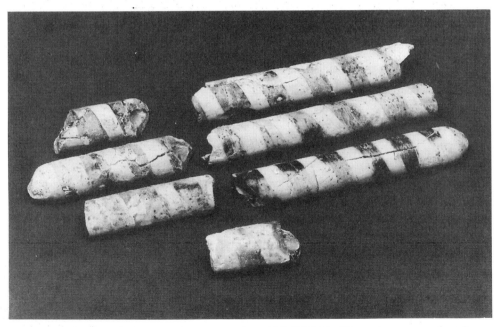

GLASS RODS FROM ELAMITE TCHOGA ZANBIL (SUSA), 1250-1200 BCE. The rods were employed as architectural decoration.
*Photograph courtesy of The Corning Museum of Glass.*

forming an open grill, were dated to the late thirteenth century.[45] Passing up along the arc of the "Fertile Crescent" we take note of two exquisite mosaic vessels found in a cemetery at Marlik, southwest of the Caspian Sea, by E. O. Negahban. Professor Dan Barag dates these items to the fourteenth-thirteenth centuries B.C.E.[46] By this time the art of glassmaking had already crossed over to Canaan.

> Mesopotamian glass objects are, of course, also represented on Syro-Palestinian sites, the area through which Mesopotamian glass and glassmaking technology reached Egypt. Moulded blue glass objects—nude female plaques, plain disc-pendants and spacer beads (often found together)—occur on such sites as Alalakh, Ebla, Hama, Hazor, Megiddo, Beth Shan, Jerusalem, Lachish and Tel Mevorakh.[47]

The art of glassmaking became exclusively the property of certain "Semitic" peoples over the course of several millennia. The pattern of its appearance in and dispersion into the ancient world was unique in the history of technology. The cultural evolution of diverse peoples throughout the world was not chronologically coincident, nor did it evolve at the same rate within each society. Nevertheless, the technological progression within each culture passes through a parallel and predictable succession of disciplines which inexorably pass through progressive stages of sophistication. The use of fire; the arts of basketry, weaving, pottery making; the use of wood, bone and stone tools; the introduction of metallurgy and its evolution through the various "Copper," "Bronze," and "Iron" Ages follow one another so ineluctably that their progression is taken for granted. The measure of every civilization is arbitrarily fixed on the point along the scale of these technologies to which it has attained.

But glassmaking remained a unique art. Long after the clattering industrial age had steamed into scientific maturity, the secrets of the art of glassmaking remained secluded within a privileged group. To comprehend why the manufacture of glass is so unique, so different from all the other arts, it must be first understood that it was not a natural development, that is, it is impossible to accidentally come upon the process. The elements which make up the process of *vitrification* are not coincident in nature, except under conditions that man, until recently, could not duplicate. In order to understand why that was so it is necessary to learn how the liquification of stone is accomplished. Only then can the extraordinary accomplishment of the Mesopotamian glassmakers of the late third millennium B.C.E. be understood and appreciated.

# NOTES

1. Werner Keller, *The Bible as History*, Trans. from the German by William Neil, rev. ed. N.Y., 1981, pp. 31-32.

2. Claudius James Rich, *Memoir of the Ruins of Babylon*, 1815, p. 29. The ability to produce glass is predicated upon advanced metallurgic pyrotechnology. It was at nearby *Jemdet Nasr* that the earliest use of bronze has been proposed. (Ernest Mackay and Stephen Langdon, *Report on Excavations at Jemdet Nasr*, 1931, p. 27.)

3. A. H. Layard, *Nineveh and its remains*, vol. II, 1849, pp. 420-421.

4. A. H. Layard, *Discoveries in the Ruins of Nineveh and Babylon*, 1853, pp. 196-197.

5. Alexander Nesbitt, F. S. A., *A Descriptive Catalogue of the Glass Vessels of All Ages in the South Kensington Museum*, London, Eyre & Spottiswoode, 1878, pp. 12-13.

6. William Froehner *La Verrerie Antique, Description de la Collection Charvet*, 1879, pp. 16-17.

7. F. W. Von Bissing, "Sur l'Histoire du Verre en Egypte" in the *Revue Archeologique*, series 4, XI, 1908, pp. 211-221.

8. Nesbitt, Ibid, p. 9.

9. Nesbitt, Ibid, p. 8. Nesbitt attempts to support his argument by adding, "...we may trace channels of communication by which the art of making it may have been transmitted from Egypt to every part of the globe where it is now or has been practiced."

10. Dan Barag, *Catalogue of Western Glass in the British Museum*, 1986, p. 26.

11. John Punnett Peters, *Nippur, or Explorations and Adventures on the Euphrates*, 1899, p. 134.

12. Robert Koldewey, *Das Wieder Erstehende Babylon*, 1913, Eng. tr. 1914, p. 250.

13. Ernest Mackay & Stephen Langdon, *Report on Excavations at Jemdet Nasr, 1931*, p. 37.

14. Sir Charles Leonard Woolley,

15. Sir Charles Leonard Woolley, *Ur Excavations II*, 1934. p. 366.

16. Hall, *The Civilization of Greece in the Bronze Age*, 1928, pp. 71, 104.

17. Gadd and Thompson, "A Middle-Babylonian Chemical Text," *Iraq*, iii, 1st part, 8/1928, 1936, pp. 87ff.

18. The inscriptions on the cuneiform tablets were originally published by R. Campbell Thompson and then annotated and edited by A. Leo Oppenheim in 1970.

19. Robert J. Charleston, *Glass Furnaces Through the Ages*, p. 10.

20. M. Levey, *Chemistry and Chemical Technology in Ancient Mesopotamia*, 1959, p. 121 f.; A. L. Oppenheim, "The Cuneiform Texts" in *Glass and Glassmaking in Ancient Mesopotamia*, 1970, pp. 1-102, 230-231.

21. Shinju Fukai, *Persian Glass*, Tokyo, 1973, Eng. ed. New York, (Weatherhill/Tankosha) 1977, pp. 15-16. Professor Fukai notes that glass was also used for cylinder seals. Such seals were in the third millennium B.C.E. exclusively an Akkadian product. He attributes the use of glass, however, to "the influence of either Egypt or Mesopotamia."

22. Leo A. Oppenheim, Ibid, p. 10.

23. Per Dr. Pinechas Doron, prof. of Biblical studies, Queens College, N.Y.

24. Leo A. Oppenheim, Ibid.

25. R. H. Brill, "The Chemical Interpretation of the Texts," in L. A. Oppenheim et al., Ibid., p. 113.

26. Paul Fossing, *Glass Vessels Before Glass-blowing*, 1940, pp. 30--41.

27. D. B. Harden, *Ancient Glass I: Pre-Roman*, 1972, p. 46, reprinted from the *Archeological Journal*, vol. CXXV, 1968.

28. Harden, *Syrian Glass from the Earliest Times to the 8th Century A.D.*, "Bulletin des Journees Internationales du Verre, no. 3, 1964, p. 19.

29. Harden, *Study and Research on Ancient Glass: Past and Present*, presented at the Twentythird Annual Seminar on Glass, October 21, 1983, and reprinted in the *Journal of Glass Studies* vol. 26, 1984. Harden's doctoral thesis on glass found by the University of Michigan expedition at Kôm Aushim, (the ancient Karanis) in the Fayoum. It was later enlarged, revised and published in 1936 under the title *Roman Glass from Karanis*.

30. Harden, *Ancient Glass, I, Pre-Roman* a paper given in 1967, reprinted in 1972 under the title *Ancient Glass* p. 46.

31. Woolley, *Alalakh, An Account of the Excavations at Atchana in the Hatay, 1937-49*, 1955. pp. 81 f., 84, 126, 210, 220, 300-302.

32. R. F. S. Starr, *Nuzi, Report on the Excavations at Yorgan Tepa... 1927-1931*, 1939, pp. 455ff./pls. 128-3; Dan Barag, *Mesopotamian Vessels of the Second Millennium B.C., Notes on the Origin of the Core*, 1962, JGS IV, 1962, pp. 12ff.

33. *Die Greber und Grüfte von Assur*, in Wissenschafftliche Veroffenlichungen der Deutschen Orient-Gesellschaft, 65, 1954, pl. 11, f, and 114ff., pl 24, b-d; Barag, 1962 idem, 13 ff.

34. D. Oates, *The Excavations at Tell al Rimah*, 1967, in Iraq XXX (1968), p. 134, pl.XXV, c. and *Studies in the Ancient History of Iraq*, 1968.

35. See Chapter 3, "Egyptian [sic] Glass" for further discussion of the Thutmose III vessels.

36. Donald B. Harden, *Catalog of Greek and Roman Glass in the British Museum*, vol. I, 1981, p. 31.

37. Richard F. S. Starr, Ph. D., *Nuzi, Vol. I*, 1939, p. 92, Harvard University Press.

38. Pamela Vandiver, *Glass Technology at the Mid-Second-Millennium B.C. Hurrian Site of Nuzi* p. 242.

39. Richard Starr, Ibid., p.457.

40. Richard Starr, Ibid., p. 460.

41. Richard Starr, Ibid., p. 457.

42. Pamela Vandiver, Ibid., p.245.

43. Pamela Vandiver, Ibid., p. 246-247.

44. Sir Charles Leonard Wooley, *Alalakh, An Account of the Excavations at Tel-Atchana in the Hatag*, London, 1955, pp. 297-302.

45. Barag, *Catalog of Western Asiatic Glass in the British Museum*, 1985, p. 38.

46. Barag, Ibid., p. 38.

47. Barag, idem, p. 39.

# CHAPTER 2

# THE SECRET ART

## *The Hurrian Connection*

THE ORIGIN OF THE PROCESS BY WHICH SILICEOUS STONE IS TRANSFORMED into glass is referred to in the singular because it appears to have been invented only once in all of human history. The peculiar and particular conditions under which glass is artificially formulated and produced remained a jealously guarded secret through the ages, a secret contained within privileged groups. The custodians of the processes employed in the production of glass were generally a family or other closely knit group who transmitted their closely guarded knowledge from one generation to the next. The seventeenth century B.C.E. tablet, the very tablet which first provides a name for glass and the formula by which it is made, set a pattern of secrecy which endured for 4000 years, well into the twentieth century.

The ancient tablet gave its translators much trouble, for it was deliberately cryptic. R. Campbell Thompson had to deal with the fact that the oldest written record of the art of glassmaking, inscribed in cuneiform Akkadian on an Assyrian tablet, was also rendered in an obtuse cryptogrammic script, deliberately employed to conceal the knowledge from all but the initiated of the glassmakers society. Thompson did not find this literary camouflage unusual; he noted that "it has always been the outrageous custom of certain learned circles to conceal their knowledge from the lay public in a fog of jargon, a pomposity of mannerisms, due, it is hoped, less to personal vanity than to professional protection." Thompson quotes a Kassite tablet of the mid-second millennium:

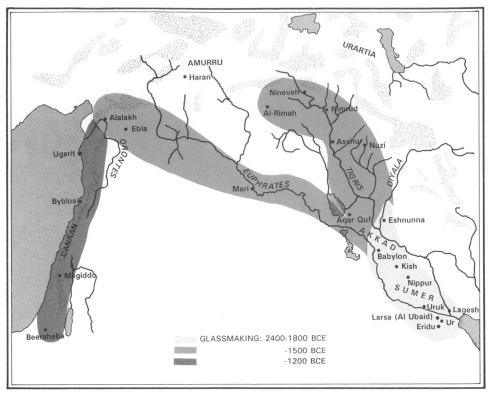

**THE AREA OF GLASSMAKING IN THE LATE BRONZE AGE**

The art of glassmaking arrived at the Canaanite coast in the Late Bronze Age. Bronze and glassware production were introduced into Egypt during this period by artisans from Canaan. The glassware was produced from raw glass imported into Egypt during a relatively peaceful period under the Pharoahs Amenophis III and his heretic son Amenophis IV (who renamed himself "Akhenaten"). Glassware production decreased in quality and quantity during the succeeding aggressive pharaonic period and disappeared from Egypt at the time biblically attributed to the Exodus of the Jews from Egypt.

*mudû mudâ likallim la mudû ul immar*, "let him that knoweth show him that knoweth, (but) he that knoweth not, let him not see."[1] In fact, the technological secrets of every art was jealously protected by guilds of artisans to the present age.[2]

Sir Charles Leonard Woolley's attention was brought to the obtuse writing of the seventeenth century tablet in a report by C. J. Gadd, who collaborated with Thompson on its transcription. The manner in which the chemical formulas are inscribed on the tablet attest to the fact that the glass masters of that culture jealously guarded the "art and mystery" of the process, noted Woolley, who was beguiled by the fact that the writer of the recipe "purposely disguised his meaning by artifices of writing which amount to a form of cryptography intelligible only to members of his Guild, who were doubtless privy to his peculiar cryptograms." Woolley noted in his report on the excavations at Tel-Atchana of the palace of the son and grandson of the lawgiver Hammurabi that the glassware recovered was "made according to the prescription" on the tablet. Woolley emphasized that while neither the Egyptian nor the Syrian glaziers were privy to the secrets of making true glass at that time, the Assyrian tablet, together with the glass artifacts found in the region, attest to the fact that the knowledge was well established in the seventeenth century B.C.E. in the Akkadian culture. In fact, Woolley points out that certain formulas described in the tablet, such as the preparation of the batch by the addition of copper acetate and the inclusion of lead compounds to add brilliance, malleability and ease of abrasion and polishing of the end product, match the material evidence supplied by the late sixteenth century glassware recovered by him from the palace at Tel-Atchana.[3]

The Kassite admonishment against teaching a trade to the uninitiated was anticipated by the Code of Hammurabi, the laws established by the Semitic Babylonian king who ruled from 1728-1686 B.C.E. The right of the maintenance of trade secrets was enforced even against the closest of family ties:

188: If a member of the artisan class took a son as a foster child and has taught him his handicraft, he may never be reclaimed.
189: If he has not taught him his handicraft, that foster child may return to his father's house.[4]

Anita Engle, in her illuminating series entitled "Readings in Glass History," sums up by stating that "the art of glassmaking is not a stage of cultural evolution which all peoples attained to when they reached a certain level of development, as in the case of pottery making or weaving, for example. On the contrary, glassmaking appears to have been the special skill of one group from a specified area, and the industry spread as this group branched out in ever-widening circles."[5]

The history of glassmaking is threaded with lineages which can be traced across borders and over spans of hundreds of years. The process is so eccentric that it remained in the virtual exclusive custody of a closed group of artisans through three millennia. The spread of the knowledge of glassmaking paralleled the movement of the Semitic people from Akkadia through Assyria and Aramea into Canaan, and from Canaan into the rest of the world. When, well into the Christian era, the diverse secrets of the glass industry began to pass to other than Semitic hands, they were fiercely guarded in turn by those that obtained them. As late as the mid-twentieth century only those "in the know" were privileged, or more emphatically, were permitted, to make glass. Venice's passion to secure the secrets of its glass industry impelled it to transfer the industry to Murano, an isolated cluster of islands well removed in the Venetian lagoon. In 1292 the Grand Council of Venice issued a decree prohibiting the firing of furnaces within the confines of the city of Venice, reasoning that the *fornaci* were a fire hazard. It is well understood, however, that the main purpose of the decree was to ensconce the masters well away from prying entrepreneurs, covetous competitors and greedy governments. The Venetian republic and the glassmakers' guild sedulously sought to protect against frequent efforts to purchase, snatch or steal their secrets and to foil attempts to bribe or shanghai the masters of Murano. An ordinance was passed which even proscribed a death sentence to traitorous masters who left the island to work abroad.

The *Signori* of Venice, in fact, did dispatch assassins to murder masters who audaciously departed from their jurisdiction to assume work elsewhere. Even a duke of Venice, when he was as yet an ambassador to France, carried out such an execution on instructions from the republic. When an assassination of a renegade glassmaster was perpetrated, the bells of Murano rang out in chorus to celebrate the execution.

It is little wonder that the secrets of vitric production were divined only once throughout the course of human history. The technology involved, first of all, the harnessing and control of fire, a fundamental force of nature, to a degree which was never surpassed until the industrial revolution was well under way.

Man was thoroughly familiar with glass in its natural forms from the time of the first glimmerings of civilization. Natural glass is a product of nature's most fearsome forces. Lightning striking a particle of quartz can, in an instant, vitrify it into a glassy bead due to the intense heat generated, a heat which attains 3000° Fahrenheit. Meteors, in searing passages through the atmosphere, heat to incandescence, even to the point of evaporation. These alien fragments may contain silicates, which vitrify, and if they survive the passage through earth's gaseous mantle, deposit their glassy remnants upon its surface.

The enormous pressures and intense heat generated within the earth melts rock, and disgorges it through volcanic fissures and craters. Siliceous components of the magma cool into obsidian, pitchstone and other useful glassy substances. Massive geologic pressures and intense heat combine to form flint, the hardest of forms of glass. All forms of glass fracture easily and conchoidally, permitting primitive men to chip them into cutting, penetrating and scraping tools with keen edges and durable points.

Primitive man was, indeed, familiar with the glassy end products of geognostic, tectonic and meteoric genesis. The expedient use of diversiform natural glasses was a crucial element of his progression through successive stages of civilization. Archeologists rate his rise by how masterfully he shaped glassy stones into useful tools and weapons. But the ability to manufacture glass denotes a culture at the level of the Iron Age, the ultimate level of human development until the advent of the industrial society. Man was unable to produce artificial glass until he had learned not merely to make fire but to master it, to attain the temperatures at which siliceous stones can be melted. One culture achieved this remarkable ability before the turn of the second millennium B.C.E.; it was a thousand years ahead of all other of the world's cultures.

Man gained experience with fire as he moved through the metal ages. Gold is easily melted and remarkably malleable; it is also attractive and exceptionally durable. Gold was once freely found in a pure state in the beds of gurgling streams; it was found veined into the layered strata of rocks, exposed by weathering or erosion from where it had been deposited by streams long since dried and gone. Gold was thus readily available until the streams and outcroppings were scavenged clean. Men in the earliest stages of civilization wrought gold into marvelous designs, for early man was as intelligent, and his sensibilities as artistic as those of modern man. He is differentiated from modern man merely by ignorance, for which he cannot be faulted. Thus gold artifacts were manufactured by men of the first era of metalsmithing, the Chalcolithic Age.

In the process of learning to use and control fire, man was enabled to wrest metals from their ores and to produce tools forged of harder metals. Crude copper exuded from certain rocks which lay in close contact with a particularly fierce fire. Man gradually became more proficient with the use of fire, and more adept at fashioning artifacts of such metals as copper and gold, but he was limited to an open system of combustion where most of the energy produced was dissipated into the atmosphere.

The invention of the furnace, a closed system which contained and controlled fire and concentrated the heat, brought man to a higher level of metal technology. Man's pyrotechnology was, however, confined within the strict limits of the type of furnace he had constructed. He was further limited to the temperature attainable by the burning of fossil or organic fuels. The temperatures of the early simple furnaces made possible the acquisition and manipulation of many metals but were insufficient for smelting iron from its ore, and were entirely inadequate for liquefying siliceous stone.

Products of gold, copper, tin, lead, silver, metals which can be smelted out of their ores with simple furnaces, are commonly found from the Chalcolithic Age, the first stage of every civilization in which metals came into common use. This Copper-Stone Age is succeeded by the Bronze Age, in which harder, more durable, more serviceable alloys of these metals were compounded. But the Iron Age required a new, advanced pyrotechnology. It was not until a radically different furnace was invented, a pneumatically drafted furnace which could attain and maintain a heat produced otherwise only by the fiercest forces of nature, a furnace capable of smelting iron from its ore, that the art of glassmaking became possible.

1. *The engineering of a pneumatically drafted furnace is the first requisite for vitrification, for the liquification of siliceous stone.* In 1697, Haudicquer de Blancourt, a practicing glassmaker, recognized the connection between the ability to smelt iron and the discovery of the art of making glass, which he

relates in his book *The Art of Glass*:

> We might fetch the origin of glass from Tubal Cain, the son of Lamech; for being the first chymist that found the way of smelting metals, the uses of iron and brass, whereof he forged the weapons of war, as noted in the first chapter of Genesis. It is not improbable, but he might be the first inventor of glass, because one can scarcely avoid reducing calcined metals into glass, especially when the fire is more than ordinarily violent and the matter remains longer than it ought.

However, even a pneumatically drafted furnace whose furious fire attains sufficient heat for smelting iron is inadequate for melting siliceous stone. Men might strive mightily to bring the fire to its fiercest level by pumping air through its embers by means of a bellows for days on end, and not achieve the desired result. The temperature which man's drafted furnaces could attain was limited by the fossil and organic fuels to which he was restricted. Wood, peat, straw, dung, and other such flammable materials could produce a furnace temperature of little more than 2000° Fahrenheit (1200° Celsius) at best. When man learned to char wood into charcoal he arrived at the ultimate temperatures his fuels allowed, but he still could not manufacture glass in bulk. Melting siliceous stone requires a much higher temperature, in fact, a thousand degrees higher than could be achieved by the use of these organic fuels.

How then was vitrification achieved? *Several more of nature's secrets had to be unlocked before vitrification could be successfully accomplished.* Physically, glass gives no hint of the elements and processes with which it must be formulated. Therein lies the enigma. After the basic requirement of the engineering of a mechanically drafted furnace had been met, three more of nature's mysteries remained to be unravelled. With such a furnace iron could be smelted from its ore and made malleable, but the vitrification of siliceous stone remained impossible. The next requisite, the next of nature's secrets that had to be discovered and applied, was the use of a flux which, mixed with a powdered silicate, would enable the mixture to liquify at achievable temperatures.

The discovery and use of fluxes came about through the appreciation of beauty, one of the essential characteristics which differentiate humans from the rest of the animal kingdom. The use of fire led mankind to manufacture to baking bricks and pots. The products, at first, were bare and plain and incongruous with nature. As nature abhors a vacuum, so does she abhor an artless object. The designs of nature are boundless. Every vacuum is filled with form; if not with substance, then with energy. Nature permits no surface to remain unadorned. A bared surface weathers, and while awaiting embellishment by new life, faces the ever-changing imagery of clouds by day and the sparkling tapestry of stars at night.

It was natural for man, in imitation of nature, to introduce texture, color and detail into objects of his own creation. At first simple stains were used, obtained from the plants and minerals at hand. Gradually he learned to grind minerals to powder, which in suspension in water, fats or oils, could be baked onto the surface of his wares. Certain of these applications marvelously, mysteriously, magically transmuted into a thin, translucent film surfacing the fired wares, often in rich and brilliant colors. This was man's first experience with vitrification. He had discovered that certain caustic compounds, when mixed with particular kinds of crushed stone or sand, produced a fine film more durable and more impermeable than the baked earthen body on which it was applied. These glazes were so thin that they vitrified in the crude kilns of the early potters. The temperature varied greatly, but at some point enough heat was generated to melt the microscopically scant layer painted onto the surface of the ware. The earthen body did not melt; it remained in a granular state. Although it was coherent after firing, it could be reduced more or less to its original state by grinding or pounding.

*The glaze, however, had undergone an irreversible thermal metamorphosis.* Glass is a translucent substance, a supercooled liquid manufactured by fusing siliceous stone with an alkaline metal oxide. Glazes were well known long before the Iron Age. By experimentation with many kinds of minerals potters discovered that the ashes of certain plants enhanced the process of liquefying silicate materials. These first ceramists learned to *lixiviate*, that is, wash or leach the alkaline substances from plant ashes to obtain a purer, more effective form of caustic materials.

2. *Alkaline fluxes reduce the temperature required for vitrification to one attainable with pneumatically drafted furnaces fired with fossil and other organic fuels.* The use of these fluxes resolved the second requisite for bringing vitrification to successful fruition. Soda (sodium carbonate) obtained from the ashes of plants growing in marshy or saline earths, was commonly used; potash (potassium carbonate) obtained from the ashes of hardwood trees (potassium is a Latinized version of pot ash) was equally

common; later natron (mineral soda mined from desert deposits) substituted for soda obtained from plant ashes; lime, obtained from powdered bone or shell and the mineral form of calcium carbonate, lead oxide (litharge) and other alkaline compounds were employed as ingredients useful in bringing vitrification to fruition. Thus the calcined metals to which Blancourt had referred in his seventeenth century treatise met the second condition for the process of vitrification.

All cultures, with one exception, remained arrested at this stage of vitric technology. Two more secrets were concealed within nature's storehouse of mysteries whose revelation and application were required to successfully render glass from silicate stone in bulk. While all cultures arrive naturally at producing glazed pottery in the course of their technological evolution, only one group of artisans somewhere in Akkadia succeeded in resolving the remaining secrets obscuring the process of making sizable objects entirely of glass.

3. *Two firings must be performed.* An efficient furnace suffices for the first firing of the mixture of a granulated silicate with one or more alkaline fluxes. A frit results, a product in which each tiny particle of silicate is coated with a film of glaze but is not vitrified throughout. Occasionally, objects whose volume is minimal, like beads or tiny amulets, did vitrify throughout in early, normally drafted furnaces and led to the false conclusion that the various cultures among which they were found had the capability of producing glass. The great Italian archeologist Schiaperelli, an astute and meticulous scientist, came to this very conclusion on recovering several strings of beads and minuscule amulets from a Fifth Dynasty tomb at Gebelein. Many other scientists were similarly misled by examples of early, minimally sized fritted artifacts which had fortuitously vitrified.

The next secret of the process of vitrification is unveiled by A. Lucas, in his study of the ancient materials and industry:

> The process of glass production involved two distinct stages, the first a comparatively low temperature, probably carried out under 750 degrees, in which the sand and alkali were converted into a frit, the second the conversion of the frit to glass in crucibles in a melting furnace, the upper temperatures probably not exceeding 1100 degrees C. The preliminary fritting was done in saucer shaped pans which were supported in the furnace on a group of cylindrical jars, and the material was then put into clay crucibles and strongly heated in a special furnace until complete fusion and combination had taken

place and the main body of the resulting glass had become homogenous and clear.[6]

Thus the early potters could not achieve true glass production even if all the correct ingredients were present. Objects made of the proper ingredients and fired only once appear quite glasslike on the surface. The resultant material, sometimes referred to as faience, has been responsible for notorious blunders, since it was mistaken for true glass. The furnaces of the potters were suitable for producing frit or faience but inadequate for the successful performance of the next process in which frit liquifies to glass. Having fired a batch of silicate materials into a body of frit, it is necessary to pulverize the mass and refire the powdered material at some 2000° Fahrenheit to convert the frit wholly to glass. But this desired result is unlikely to occur unless still other secrets of nature are applied.

4. *The second firing must be sustained over a long period of time, for many days and nights on end.* Merely attaining a furious temperature of over 2000° Fahrenheit during the second firing will not achieve complete vitrification; the temperature must be stubbornly sustained over a protracted period of time. The metamorphosis of the frit to glass takes place slowly; complete vitrification takes days. Even modern furnaces, in which incessant streams of gas are ejected forcefully from multiple jets directly into the melting chamber to envelop the crucible with white hot, furious flames, are kept persistently firing for days on end to achieve the complete liquification of the crucible's contents.

It is most likely that in ancient times as in modern, several furnaces were employed, one for achieving the fritted material, a second for thorough vitrification and even a third for tempering, that is, a gradual cooling down of the finished product, necessary because the glass would otherwise develop internal fissures caused by the stresses of cooling.

The early melting furnaces had to be steadfastly stoked by hand with the available fuels, and assiduously drafted by persistently pumping one or more bellows which were fixed into the furnace to forcefully feed air through the embers. The furnace had to be constructed of brick thick enough to prevent the heat from penetrating to the outside during the protracted firing period so that the artisan could tolerate standing alongside of it. Modern furnaces are constructed of eight-inch (20 cm.) thick firebrick. The bricks turn a bright, glowing yellow for more than two-thirds of their thickness which fades within the last inch of the exterior. The ancient furnaces would have had to have been made of an equivalent material. Equally important, the crucibles which contain the mixture within the heating chamber must be made of a material which can withstand such fierce conditions.

The fuel employed in the ancient furnaces varied. The diligence with which the bellows were pumped and the variable quality and application of fuel were factors which made it impossible to maintain the unfaltering temperature of modern furnaces. The length of time required to vitrify material in the formative stages of the art of glassmaking was, perforce, considerably longer than that required in the use of modern furnaces for an equivalent bulk of materials.

Would the perfect performance of the above procedures in their proper order achieve vitrification? Not yet!

5. *Cullet must be added to each batch in order for vitrification to invariably come to completion.* It would seem that enough stumbling blocks

CULLET. Shards of broken vessels and lumps of raw glass found at an ancient glassmaking site in the Upper Galilee of Israel, typical of cullet used by primary glass producers through the ages to spur the process of vitrification of silicate materials.
*Photo by the author.*

were placed in the path of a prospective glassmaker of 4000 years ago. Not so! Yet another riddle remained to be unraveled, the solution of which seems ridiculously simple when known, but impossible to rationally resolve if unknown. The mysterious last requisite for vitrification is the introduction of cullet (shards of previously manufactured glass) into the mixture prior to refiring. Glass, which is actually a supercooled liquid, once manufactured, liquifies at a much lower temperature than that required to manufacture it. Cullet activates the process of the liquification of siliceous stone in its fritted stage by remelting first at a lower temperature, spurring the rest of the material into continuing the process.

While achieving vitrification without cullet is possible, it would have been so difficult under the inconstant temperatures of the early furnaces that the glassmakers must have been obliged to invariably employ it to achieve results. Modern manufactories continue to use cullet when initiating the vitrification of a new batch of materials. This peculiar, final requisite presents a version of the classic paradox posed in the riddle: "Which came first, the chicken or the egg?" But, as we can all testify, the process did somehow begin, and continues to the present, each batch stimulated into vitrification by pieces from previous batches. It is an enchanting thought that a molecule or more of the first glass artefact which issued from that first furnace may be included in every piece of manufactured glass today.

Thus glassmaking involves an abstract process in which: the appearance of the ingredients give no hint of the result; the ingredients are not found associated naturally; the right siliceous stone must be employed; an alkaline flux must be added to the pulverized stone; the resultant frit must be refired; a high enough temperature must be attained and maintained for enough time to achieve complete vitrification; and cullet must be introduced to catalyze the process. Unless all these conditions and processes are met and the materials are introduced successively and in the correct proportions, no consistent result can be expected.

The abstract nature of the process engendered continuous inbreeding. The particular and peculiar conditions under which glass is artificially formulated was a jealously guarded family secret transmitted from one generation to the next. Guilds, often little more than extended families, fiercely protected the privileges of its members by making it impossible for outsiders to enter the trades they encompassed, let alone learn the secrets of those trades. The art and science of producing glass and glassware, however, did not evolve out of one culture but resulted from the combined technologies of two diverse peoples.

*The art of glassmaking combines two distinct, independently evolving technologies, the development of pneumatically drafted furnaces and the invention of glazes.*

The two technologies met and married in Akkadia. The Sumerians had discovered the chemical formulas for glazes as far back as 6000 B.C.E.; they were the earliest peoples to have done so. The Sumerians had been glazing pots since 4000 B.C.E., but were incapable of producing glass in bulk because they had never developed pneumatically drafted furnaces. Such furnaces originated in the Ararat mountains in northern Mesopotamia; those mountains were home to two peoples, the Amorites and the Urartians, neighboring inhabitants of the majestic mountains from whose flanks flow the headwaters of the Tigris and Euphrates rivers. They were the master metalsmiths of the latter half of the Third millennium. It is among one or both of these peoples that sophisticated pyro technology originated. The Amorites, known as the Amurru in Sumer, as the Martu in the ancient city of Ebla and biblically as the Amorites, were the Semitic progenitors of the Hebrews. During the fourth and third millennia they descended from the Ararat foothills, spread throughout Mesopotamia, and became the masters of the entire region.

The Amorites have been erroneously regarded as a nomadic people, a reputation acquired merely by quotations from their enemies in which they are dubbed "savages who live in the mountains," who "eat raw meat and don't know a house," etc. Recent research has shown them to be a sedentary people, and records from Ebla of the mid-third millennium B.C.E. confirm an Amorite national existence, 300 years earlier than had been previously proposed. They were an urban people occupying many villages, each with a lugal, or governor, and a complete cast of officials, diplomats, traders and skilled artisans. They were a people famous for their weaving and metallurgy.

Martu was the seat of an autonomous government: there is, in fact, attestation of a "ruler" and at least 12 "elders," which suggests a structure similar to that of Ebla. As far as the economic relations are concerned, administrative texts teach us that Ebla exported fabrics and received in exchange "sheep." The Amorites did not dedicate themselves [solely] to husbandry, a fact we know from these very Eblaitic documents, where they are frequently cited as manufacturers of the precious "Martu daggers," which presupposes a special

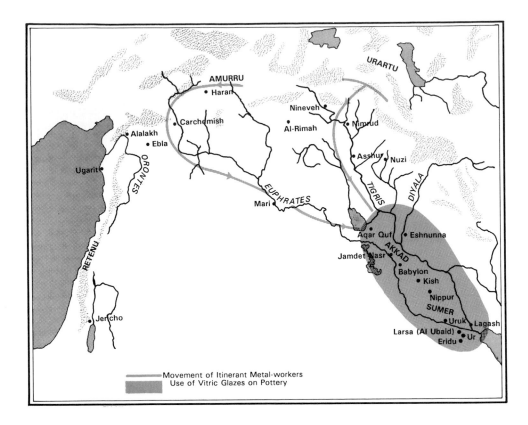

Movement of Itinerant Metal-workers
Use of Vitric Glazes on Pottery

## THE MARRIAGE OF FERRIC AND VITRIC PYROTECHNOLOGIES

The art of glassmaking originated with the combination of two distinct technologies:

(1) The use of pneumatically drafted furnaces of the metal-smelters of the Ararat mountains (the Amorites, the Hurrians or both), itinerant artisans who wandered down along the twin rivers to minister to the needs of the city-states for tools and weapons.

(2) The chemical knowledge of the Sumerian potters, who had developed the formulas for vitric glazes.

technology which convinces us that their knowledge of metallurgy was so profound that they were famous [for them] in the entire area of the fertile crescent.[7]

Amorite daggers were, in fact, so unique that they figured in the inventories of the great city of Ebla in the mid-third millennium B.C.E. under their distinguishing name: Martu daggers. The weapons were manufactured in a number of the Amorite villages. The records of Ebla demonstrate that after the Amorite villages fell under Eblaitic rule the daggers were considered so valuable that they were used as a medium of exchange and for payment of taxes in both bronze and in gold replicas.[8]

The Urartians, of a different cultural genesis, known more commonly as the Hurrians and Biblically as the Horites, also figured in the Hebrew's tribal background. The Hurrians originated from the higher regions around Lake Van; they, like the Amorite artisans, filtered down through the alluvial basin of the twin rivers, absorbing Amorite culture and language in the process. Eventually, during the mid-second millennium, the Urartians displaced Amorite hegemony over the region.

The first smelters of iron, and accordingly the logically presumable inventors of the pneumatically drafted furnace, were among these peoples, and, although the Amorites must be considered, the weight of evidence favors the Hurrians as the primary masters of that pyrotechnology. Itinerant Amorite and Hurrian artisans wandered down along the rivers to ply their trade with the merchants and lords of the great cities of Sumer and Akkadia. The Iron Age, commonly dated as beginning in the Near East at about 1200 B.C.E., was yet a millennium away when some of these metal mongers were already smelting iron.

Archeologists are occasionally surprised to come upon iron artifacts produced by the ancient metalsmiths long before the designated Iron Age. Itinerant smiths who wandered about seeking work at the great centers of civilization were not unusual for those times. Among those peoples purported to have included such artisans were the mysterious Habiru (often purported to be the progenitors of the Hebrews, mainly because of the similarity in spelling) variously described as raiders, outcasts who engaged themselves as mercenaries, or as simple pastoral peoples who occasionally came into conflict with the rooted civilizations. Although not all such tribes were capable of smelting iron, they did render services which included metalworking:

> They wandered from one area to another, sometimes with their own flocks or as skilled craftsmen, smiths, musicians and the like. At other times they hired themselves out for specific functions and periods of times, for example as mercenaries and as private and government slaves.[9]

Akkadians were already familiar with meteoric iron long before the northern smiths introduced the manufactured variety. This is evidenced by the Akkadian word for iron: *An-Bar*, which signifies "stone of heaven."[10] Rare artifacts of manufactured iron appear in Akkadia at about the same time as the equally rare objects of glass. Definitive tests demonstrate that those archeological treasures were unmistakably born in a furnace.

The pattern of distribution of these unusual iron artifacts provides the evidence that they were introduced by the highly advanced northern smiths. Iron objects tend to pop up among the bronze ware exported by these skilled northern craftsmen in the late third millennium B.C.E. to the neighboring regions. A Hittite king of the seventeenth century B.C.E. sat proudly upon an iron throne imported from Urartia. He reigned at the site now known as Acem Huyuk, south of Ankara. The city existed even before the Hittites, when it was known as Barush Handa. Adjoining the city was a *Karum*, an Akkadian trading and artisans' community.

The diverse peoples of Western Asia who came to speak dialects of the Semitic language seem to have originated at the crown of the Fertile Crescent in the area of the biblical Padan-Naharaim. During the fourth and third millennia B.C.E., the Semites spread out from great centers like Ebla and Haran, carrying their culture with them. One branch of these Amorites migrated southwestward toward the Mediterranean, poetically referred to as the Sea-of-the-Setting-Sun; another migrated southeastward into Sumer where they were significantly dubbed the Amurru, or Westerners. By the mid twenty fourth century B.C.E. Semitic-speaking peoples dominated the entire Mesopotamian plain under Sargon I, who reigned from the city of Agade over the first empire the world had known.

> Immigrants flocked into [the Delta] from the north....They brought with them new arts. They were skilled in the working of metal; they introduced the potter's wheel....Under the guidance of the newcomers the south country achieved a prosperity unparalleled hitherto.[11]

The Hurrians began to filter into Akkadia in the wake of the southward movement of their neighbors, the Amoritic, Semitic-speaking peoples soon after the Semites had established hegemony over the area. Although both the Hurrians and the Hebrews originated from the same Ararat Mountains, one from the highlands and the other from the foothills, they were ethnically different breeds and spoke distinct languages. The mixture of the Hurrians with the Semitic-speaking peoples in Akkadia can be discerned from the many distinctive Hurrian personal names found in Babylonian records, particularly those from the region of the river Diyala on tablets dated to around 2100 B.C.E., the time of the Third Dynasty of Ur.[12]

> The Hurrians were a powerful and distinct ethnic group which appears to have originated in the mountains of Armenia, in the region of Lake Van. A large part of the minerals which were worked in the land of the twin rivers came from that area, and the Hurrians must have been among the earliest traders and workers of these products....The Hurrians had intimate contacts with the early Hebrews. The ancient home of the Patriarchs was in the area of Harran, in north-western Mesopotamia....The cultural background of the Patriarchal narratives is closely tied up with the Hurrians and the regions nearby.[13]

In addition to the artefactual evidence provided by the tools and weapons distributed by the itinerant metalworkers on their rounds throughout Mesopotamia and Anatolia, there is significant textual confirmation of the early Akkadian knowledge of manufactured iron. "Iron objects are included among weapons and vessels of gold, electrum and silver" in an inventory text of the Uruk III period, which dates back beyond 3000 B.C.E. "A contemporary lexical fragment also lists iron artifacts."[14]

Objects of glass appear in the area soon after the infiltration of itinerant metalworking artisans from the northern mountains. Some of the oldest manufactured glass items were unearthed by the University of Chicago, for example, at Eshnunna (Tel Asmar), a university town on the Diyala River just east of Babylon. At Eshnunna a code of laws was written soon after 2000 B.C.E. which set the pattern for constitutional government, and for such codes as the 613 strictures handed down to the Hebrews by Moses. Standards of labor and contractual relationships were established at Eshnunna well before the enlarged Code of Hammurabi, which probably derived from it. Scribal schools flourished in Eshnunna and school tablets show that a form of the Pythagorean theory was anticipated and taught. The sexagesimal system developed in Akkadia, perhaps at Eshnunna, and is still in use today, as in the division of a circle into 360 degrees, and hours and minutes into 60 units respectively. Crafts proliferated in the town and glassmaking appears, perhaps for the first time in human history.

Dr. Henri Frankfort directed the excavations at Eshnunna and was amazed to find a cylinder of extremely clear pale green glass with few air bubbles, a type and quality of glass which does not generally appear until 2000 years later:

> Clear glass…was not introduced before Roman times. Our cylinder dates, at the latest, to the Gutium period and belongs more probably to that of the dynasty of Akkad. Of this there can be no doubt whatsoever…It was found definitely beneath walls of a ruined building which had contained tablets of Shulgi.[15]

The find was so extraordinary that doubt was cast upon the date, and we are cautioned to await "further discoveries of equal date and quality."[16] However, Dr. Frankfort's credibility is considerably reinforced by another intriguing discovery: evidence that iron tools were fabricated at the site. Dr. Frankfort expresses his added astonishment over this unanticipated capability, which existed "more than 1500 years before the day when the first iron dagger known was sent, presumably by a Hittite king, as a present to the youthful Tutankhamen of Egypt."[17] The dagger referred to was one with which the famous discoverer of the King Tut's tomb, Howard Carter, was equally beguiled: "the astonishing and unique feature of this beautiful weapon is that the blade is made of iron still bright and resembling steel!" It was a most unusual gift inasmuch as iron was still, more than a millennium later, an exotic material in Egypt.

The pyrotechnology inspired by metal smithing was imported into Akkadia from the Ararat Mountains, but the second requisite for the production of glass, the use of an alkaline flux to reduce the temperature at which silicates could be liquified, was inherent in the ancient Akkadian pottery-making science. Glazing, as we have noted, was already an ancient, seasoned art in Akkadia; the formulas for glazes extend back before the so-called al-Ubaid period, or about 6000 B.C.E. and glazing pots became a common practice about 4000 B.C.E. The marshy delta and the low-lying plains along the Euphrates provided the plants from whose ashes soda could be conveniently lixiviated. It can be readily understood, therefore, that 2000 years later, by the time of Terach, father of Abraham, the potters were adept at formulating glazes of many colors and effects. The furnaces of the itinerant northern smiths furnished the pyrotechnology necessary to produce glass in bulk.

The first application of the art of glassmaking was mainly to the imitation of precious stones and the formulation of cast and cut figurines and objects of adornment. Casting, even the lost-wax process of casting, was already well known from the well-established metallurgic arts. Then a revolutionary method of producing vessels created a new, exportable product, and an industry was born.

The vessels were core-formed. A core, composed of crude earth mixed with organic materials such as straw or dung, was first shaped around the end of a metal rod to the form of the inside of the proposed vessel. Another metal rod was thrust into the molten glass in the crucible within the flaming furnace, and a blob of the glowing liquid was gathered around its tip. The gather was then held above the earthen core and the trail of molten glass descending from it was spirally wound around the core as it was revolved. When the core was completely covered, the ringed mass was rolled (marvered) over a flat stone or metal plate and the coils of molten glass were melded into a homogeneous wall of vessel. The heat of the process would burn out or carbonize the organic substances of the core material during this process and leave the core friable—that is, readily crumbled and scraped out of its glass cover.

Often decorative trails of one or more colors were wound around the finished vessel while it was still hot. These were again marvered into the body of the vessel so that they became integral with it, forming lines of color which ringed the vessel. Another, and a commonly employed variation of this decorative motif was produced by combing the trails down at intervals before the marvering process was done, resulting in festooned design.

The recovery of glass beads, cast amulets and vessels from Egyptian tombs gave rise to the assumption that they were manufactured in Egypt and sustained the argument that perhaps the technology arose, if not earliest, at least independently in the land of the Nile. It is a question which must be addressed before the course of the art and its products to the West can be intelligently pursued.

CORE-FORMED POMEGRANATE VESSEL. An early core-formed glass which may have been retrieved from an Egyptian tomb of the 18th Dynasty but was probably made in Mesopotamia; the fruit was native to Mesopotamia and did not become familiar to the Egyptians until it was introduced during the time of Semitic domination, the so-called "Hyksos" or "Second Intermediate Period".
*Photograph courtesy of the Newark Museum.*

CORE-FORMED KOHL-TUBE (for containing perfume). The herring-bone or festooned design is created by applying trails of differently colored glass to the exterior of a vessel, combing the trails alternately up and down, and then pressing (marvering) the trails into the body of the vessel by rolling it over a flat stone or metal plate while the body and trails are still in a hot, malleable state.

*Photograph courtesy of The Corning Museum of Glass.*

51

# NOTES

1. Langdon, *PBS.x*, no. 4, 342.

2. Thompson, *A Dictionary of Assyrian Chemistry and Geology*, 1936, p. xii.

3. Sir Charles Leonard Woolley, *Alalakh; An Account of the Excavations at Tel-Atchana in the Hatag 1937-1949*, 1955, pp. 297-302.

4. James B. Pritchard, *The Ancient Near East*, vol. I, 1958\73, p. 160.

5. Anita Engles, "Who Were the Early Glassmakers?," *Readings in Glass History No. 1*, 1973, p. 27.

6. A. Lucas, *Ancient Egyptian Materials and Industry*, 1962, p. 191.

7. Giovanni Pettinato, *Ebla, nuovi orrizonti della storia*, 1986, p. 260.

8. Giovanni Pettinato, *The Archives of Ebla*, 1979/81, pp. 171, 173, 198, etc.

9. Harry Orlinsky, *Ancient Israel*, 1960\77, p. 14.

10. Percy S. P. Handcock, *Mesopotamian Archeology*, 1912/69, p. 268.

11. Sir Charles Leonard Woolley

12. H. W. F. Saggs, *The Might that Was Assyria*, 1985, p. 37.

13. Anita Engle, Ibid., 1973, p. 29.

14. P. R. S. Moorey, *Materials and Manufacture in Ancient Mesopotamia*, 1985, p. 100, citing A. A. Vaiman, *Eisen in Sumer*, A. F. O. Beiheft, 19, 33ff; cf. G. Heinrich *Sechster Vorläufiger Öbericht--Uruk Warka*, Berlin.

15. H. Frankfort, *Third Preliminary Report of the Iraq Expedition of the Oriental Institute of the University of Chicago at Tel Asmar*, 1934, p. 56.

16. Barag, Ibid., p. 35.

17. H. Frankfort, Ibid., p. 59.

# CHAPTER 3

# EGYPTIAN [SIC] GLASS

## *The Hyksos Connection*

THE PROCESS OF PRODUCING GLASS FIRST TOOK PLACE IN AKKADIA, A FACT demonstrable by the antiquity of the artifacts found in the region and substantiated by the existence of the requisite technology. Yet the legend that the art originated in Egypt persists, and although a negative fact is more difficult to substantiate, it can be reasonably argued that the Egyptians did not and could not have invented the process, not merely because the most ancient manufactured glass was not found in Egypt, but because ancient Egypt never developed the pyrotechnology requisite for the production of glass.

The evidence that the art, the artisans and the artifacts were foreign to ancient Egypt has far-reaching ramifications. At the core of the issue is the realization that the requisite pyrotechnology remained secluded in a corner of western Asia for two millennia, the same area in which the axled wheel emerged and the Bronze and Iron Ages materialized. Thus the art of glassmaking provides the lens with which we can focus upon that area for a clear view of the evolution of civilization.

So firmly accepted was the legend of ancient Egyptian glassmaking that, until recently, little effort was made to substantiate its verity. The quality of scientific lore regarding the subject can be judged by the circumstance pointed out in a dissertation by Earle R. Caley wherein he notes that until 1957 only 14 ancient Egyptian glass items had been analyzed by Neumann

GAFFERS (GLASSBLOWERS) AT WORK IN A 19TH CENTURY GLASS FACTORY. Wood was needed in vast quantities to fuel the voracious appetites of glasshouse furnaces into the mid-20th century. The huge stacks of firewood seen at the rear of the factory were typical of glasshouses throughout the world. Glassmakers were responsible for decimating entire forests, and the ecological disaster caused by their activity often caused them to be banned from the regions in which they were working. Even in the modern era, in which coal had become an optional fuel, wood continued to be widely employed for glass manufacture.

*A Glass factory "Im Aüle" about 1820. From A. Schreiber,* Nationaltrachten, *1820/27.*

and Gerlmann, two from Thebes and 12 from Tell el-Amarna, and that "none of these specimens can be assigned to a date prior to the XVIIIth Dynasty, and little exact information is as yet available on the composition of earlier Egyptian glass.[1]

We have seen that the process of primary glassmaking involves the consumption of vast quantities of fuel. The ancient melting furnaces had to be steadfastly stoked with wood, and assiduously drafted by persistently pumping air into the embers with one or more bellows. Glassmakers never allow their furnaces to burn down, for it takes a huge expenditure of energy to bring a furnace back into productive use. For that reason glassmakers throughout the ages located themselves in or near forests and were prone to move often as nearby trees were felled and transportation of wood became difficult. Whole forests have been routinely demolished by glassmakers (and, to a lesser extent, by iron smelters) throughout recorded history. The Weald of southern England provides a modern day testimonial to the destruction engendered by such activity. The glassmakers and smiths, having decimated over 80 percent of the vast forests covering most of southeastern England, were banned from continuing the destruction; the industry was forced to move from the woods of the Weald to coal-producing Birmingham and Newcastle.

Where, then, were the forests which would supply the fuel for the Egyptian glassmakers? Wood was a rare commodity in Upper Egypt; even the swampy regions of the delta of Lower Egypt were almost entirely unforested. Wood had to be imported from Upper Canaan, the area now consisting of Lebanon and the Upper and Lower Galilee, where forests flourished in ancient times. Wood was used most circumspectly in Egypt for the construction of the larger boats which plied the Nile, and for the doors or decoration of only the most costly constructions, for important temples and the homes of the wealthiest Egyptians.

It has been naively assumed that the bounteous deposits and availability of siliceous sand and natron (mineral soda) in Egypt were conducive to the production of glass. Consideration was not given to the fact that a wagonful of these easily transportable elements (and of other minerals required for coloring and production) could keep the ancient glassmaker busy for weeks, and, although convenient to have at hand, they were by no means essential to the location of a furnace. In a discussion at the Ninth International Congress on Glass, held in Versailles in 1971, Professor Dan Barag of

Hebrew University addressed the question of the overriding importance of the availability of fuel. "Permit me to talk about a problem which has been raised here by Mme Vassus, that is the problem of fuel and especially of wood which must be used. One commonly makes the error in the field of glass[making]: that is to say that it is necessary to discover glass[making] in sandy regions." Then Professor Barag goes on to point out that the Egyptians of necessity would have had to import wood from Lebanon.[2]

Thus glassmaking could not have become a substantial industry in Upper Egypt; if it was practiced at all, it would have been a restricted activity which only the whim of a pharaoh would inspire and the cost of which only a pharaoh could sustain. It was precisely under such special circumstances that glassware was produced in Egypt during a period which, measured in terms of Egyptian history, passed by in the blink of an eye. It can be stated with assurance that the artisans who worked glass in ancient Egypt were not Egyptians.

The dearth of suitable amounts of fuel makes it even more improbable that the invention of the process of glassmaking could have taken place in Egypt, for such an event presupposes a highly developed pyrotechnology, one which depended on an availability of the very fuel which was absent from ancient Egypt. The Egyptians themselves are witness to that deficiency, for while every tool and every process is depicted on the walls of Egyptian tombs and described on Egyptian papyri, not a single depiction of glass production or even of a drafted furnace capable of the production of glass appears anywhere, in spite of the explicit particulars with which all arts are delineated.

Tomb drawings do provide a precise picture of the limited Egyptian metallurgic capabilities, for the procedures, tools and equipment employed are depicted in meticulous detail. Gold and copper were melted in crucibles suspended over an open fire. The heat of the fire was intensified by blowing air by mouth through tubes. Fans were attached to the end of the tubes; the fire was fanned to sustain the flames, and as the fire nevertheless tended to die down, the fire keepers reverted again to blowing through the tubes. The drawings of this process show the fan as a simple, almost circular line attached to the end of the tube. This led naive scholars to assume that the circle was meant to be a bubble of glass, and the drawings were presented as proof of the existence of glassmaking in Egypt. Scholars who should have known better witlessly ignored the fact that glass in bulk cannot be produced over an open fire. Yet, until recently, reproductions of these scenes were employed almost universally as illustrations of the art in texts on the history of glassmaking. The fact is that even the copper and gold metallurgy depicted in the tombs was a technology imported from Mesopotamia:

> Copper tools are known from both Badarian and Amratian [pre-dynastic] sites, but these implements were generally small and simple (punches, drills and beads) and were hammered from natural copper, rather than smelted and cast from ore. Around 3500 B.C. true smelted and cast copper tools appear for the first time. Like agriculture 2000 years before, metallurgy had developed first in regions like the Mediterranean and Iranian plateau, and spread into Egypt via trade.[3]

Bellows do appear in a few drawings in later Eighteenth Dynasty tombs; they were still, however, employed in conjunction with an open fire. The most advanced use of bellows is depicted in a late Eighteenth Dynasty scene in which the fire fanner stands with each foot laced to a bellows and produces gusts of air by stamping down upon one bellows as he lifts his other foot. It is an intriguing application of a pneumatic technique, but it is still employed to excite a mere open fire, albeit more efficiently than is possible with a fan-tipped tube.

The Mesopotamian climate and soil was far less kind to ancient objects than that of Egypt, infinitely less conducive to preservation; yet examples of the step-by-step development of the glassmaking art have been recovered only from Mesopotamia. No objects evidencing primitive stages of glass manufacture have been found in ancient Egyptian tombs or ruins, as should be expected if an industry had evolved within the culture. The magnificent glass vessels recovered from the tombs of the ancient Egyptian hierarchy universally reflect a fully matriculated, centuries-old technology.

Glassmaking presupposes Iron Age pyrotechnology; but the Iron Age never arrived into ancient Egypt! At the time mosaic and millefiore glass were already being masterfully produced in Mesopotamia, Egypt was still stuck in the Chalcolithic Age, the age of stone and copper. Egypt was boosted into the Bronze Age from the nineteenth through the seventeenth centuries B.C.E. at a time in which the Canaanites and other associated Southwest Asian peoples proliferated in Lower Egypt. The patriarchal chieftains of the autonomous Asian tribes then resident in Lower Egypt ruled all of Egypt for a period of almost two centuries through kings chosen from among them.

The bulk of the information regarding that period of Egyptian history comes down to us from Manetho (323-245 B.C.E.), an Egyptian priest of the Ptolemaic period who has been dubbed the first anti-Semite. In expounding on the history of Egypt, Manetho fabricated a series of dynasties (Thirteenth through Seventeenth) under which hundreds of *Hyk khase* ("foreign kings," commonly transcribed to Hyksos), ruled Egypt. Other Egyptian records show that these hundreds of autonomous tribes were following an age-old tradition in which the Nile delta accommodated the peoples of Canaan not only in times of drought, as is biblically attested in the story of Abraham's sojourn in "Goshen," but became viziers to Egyptian rulers, as is reflected in the story of Joseph.

According to a number of Egyptian inscriptions written at the order of contemporary Egyptian petty princes, six of these "foreign kings" (patriarchal tribal chieftains) were "chosen" by the others to be chief-of-chiefs and ruled all Egypt by common consensus and with the support of most of the Egyptian local barons. These inscriptions were written not only by the supporters of the Canaanite chieftains but were pejorative diatribes inscribed in stone by jealous Theban barons engaged in the overthrow of the rule of foreigners. The information that a chief-of-chiefs was chosen from among these peoples, that they worshipped a single God (Seth) and other facts come down to us through the vainglorious stories of the Thebans concerning their incursions into northern Egypt, their eventual victory over the hated foreigners and the expulsion of the foreign chieftains from Egypt.

Not a shred of Manetho's manuscripts have survived. The main literary source of our knowledge about Manetho is Josephus Flavius, and he leaves no doubt that the "foreign chieftains" were the progenitors of the Jews. The few early Christian priests who had access to Manetho's original writings have similarly employed quotations from Manetho in support of their polemics against the Jews.[4] Manetho is quoted as writing that, after being routed, many of the "foreigners" fled to a Canaanite mountain on top of which they set up a new capital city, Jerusalem.

The Theban conquerors succeeded in obliterating virtually every physical trace of the presence of these people, and except for the boastful recitations of victory, little documentary evidence has survived. The so-called "Hyksos" have been widely treated as a mysterious race who descended out of the desert and mysteriously disappeared back into it. Yet it is almost universally, albeit often grudgingly admitted by recent historians that fundamental changes and substantial progress took place during the period of the rule of the Canaanite chieftains, one of the most critical of Egyptian history. Far from being nomads, the Hyksos were the patriarchal chieftains of highly civilized, technologically advanced, sedentary peoples. They were but the last of many waves of West Asian peoples into Lower Egypt, in each of which Mesopotamian culture and technology was injected into "The Land of the Long River, the river which flows the wrong way, from south to north."

The period of Semitic rule of Egypt is dubbed "The Second Intermediate Period," a phrase which has been used to imply stagnation or retrogression. Kent Weeks noted that the label "Intermediate," is a purely relative term and has no business as a defining word. "In Egyptological parlance [the word] has taken unto itself a pejorative meaning: it denotes decadence, decline, anarchy, bad taste and instability. Now, regardless of how one personally regards the periods in subjective nuance which is not desirable if we are to maintain empirical orientation."[5]

The direction from which Upper Egypt came in contact with Mesopotamian culture and technology is illustrated by a great mural in the tomb of a Theban nomarch, Knumhotpe, at Beni Hassan along the Middle Nile. By the time of the Twelfth Dynasty the passage of commercial traffic from Canaan had become a boon to the nomarchs of Upper Egypt, who collected "customs" from the traders on their way to Nubia. Knumhotpe considered the wealth which accrued to him from the passing traders so important that, in typical Egyptian manner, he attempted to assure the continuance of this lucrative activity after his death by having an eternal traffic of tradesmen painted prominently on a central wall of his tomb. The painting evidently registers an actual event which the baron felt worthy of eternal repetition; it depicts a group of 37 Semites in full size in the act of paying customs duties to the nomarch's officials. A bold hieroglyphic text states that these Asians are supplying him with such important items as stibium, a mineral required for eye makeup. Knumhotpe evidently assumed that the place he would occupy in the hereafter would also lack the mineral, and its continued import needed to be assured. The date given is the fourth year of Senusert II's rule or about 1892 B.C.E. The leader of the caravan of traveling tradesmen is named Abushei, a distinctly biblical Hebrew name; it was, for example, the name of a general under King David. The leader is also referred to as a *hykkhase*, i.e., a "foreign chieftain."

Metal smithing is one of the crafts carried on by members of the group,

A FOOTED VASE, PROBABLY FROM AN EGYPTIAN TOMB OF THE NEW KINGDOM PERIOD (1400-1360 BCE). Glass vessels suddenly appear in Egyptian tombs of the "Warrior Pharoahs" of the 18th dynasty; they were either pillaged from Canaan or Mesopotamia during Egyptian incursions or were obtained as tribute by the Egyptians during the period of Egyptian rule over those portions of West Asia. Such sophisticated ware was produced in Egypt by foreign artisans during a period of relative peace under the pharoahs Amenophis III and his son Akhenaten. Egyptian glassware production declined thereafter and ceased in Egypt at the beginning of the Iron Age (after 1200 BCE), at a time coincident with that in which Israelite settlements appear in Canaan. *Photograph courtesy of the Corning Museum of Glass.*

readily deduced from the presence of an anvil and a bellows loaded on the backs of the donkeys. Here we have the clearly depicted evidence of tools and a trade with which Egypt was familiar only through such itinerant artisans. The laminated bows, the 12-string harp and the lyre being carried by the Semites are also instructive, for Egyptians at that time had no knowledge of such bows and types of musical instruments. The intricately woven and colored clothes worn by the Hebrews attest to the use of an upright loom, equally unknown in Egypt at the time.

ABUSHEI IN EGYPT. A group of Semitic artisan/traders stopping at a customs post set up along the middle Nile by the Theban ruler of the region, Knumhotpe, as depicted on the wall of his tomb about 1892 BCE. The tools and instruments carried by the Semites attest to a knowledge of metallurgy, methods of weaving, musical instruments and weaponry as yet unknown in Egypt. The hieroglyphic script designates the leader of the group as a *Hyk Khase* ("foreign chieftain") who bears the Hebraic name *Abushei*, the same as one of King David's two great generals.

GLASS ARTIFACTS FROM YEB. Objects recovered by archeologists on *Yeb* (Elephantine Island) from a strata in which Canaanite pottery and other items of the Second Intermediate Period were found. The glass items such as the trailed glass ring, the eye-bead pendant, the plain and festooned perfume vials were undoubtedly imports from Canaan or Mesopotamia, as glassware-making technology was as yet absent from Egypt.
*Photograph by the author, reproduced by courtesy of the Elephantine Island Museum.*

Such traders established a colony on Yeb, now called Elephantine Island, located in the Nile at the foot of the first cascade at the border of Nubia. The settlement on Yeb existed as far back as the purported time of Joseph, coinciding with the so-called Second Intermediate Period. The Semitic origin of the settlers is manifested by the easily identified Canaanite pottery unearthed at the site. Similar earthenware appears nowhere in Egypt except at such sites as el Yehudiya (Jew-town), a Semitic settlement in the delta, and is similar to earthenware of the period found at Ugarit and elsewhere in Canaan. Glass beads, rings and perfume vials that undoubtedly originated from the East were also recovered from Yeb. This is the one of the earliest appearances of glass artifacts in Egypt.[6]

The Hyksos, or chieftains from the area of Canaan, erected few gigantic monuments, self-glorifying statuary and self-serving temples such as those which so often drained Egypt of its resources of labor and material, for there were no godly kings among them. The modest worship of a unitary god required no stone image to represent him on earth in competition with other jealous gods. Some archeologists, disappointed by the dearth of gargantuan tombs and narcissistic statuary, dismally declare that during this period, art declined. Museums petulantly concur, for lack of imposing mausoleums, mummies, mastabas and exotic statuary of beastly idols to display.

The Canaanite chieftains managed to rule Egypt in consort for several hundred years, and during their tenure Egypt leaped forward into a new era, advancing enormously in every field of knowledge and endeavor. Wise men came and settled into the delta area, and taught astronomy, and medicine, and mathematics. The great mathematical Rhind papyrus, now in the British Museum, was produced during this period.[7] Thus, although the chieftains sculpted no great statues of themselves, and few small ones, nor fashioned idols of fabulous gods, the arts they infused into the fabric of the culture of Egypt were of a subtler nature, were more durable than the stone of which the idols were carved, and benefited all Egyptians.

The Egyptians sailed the Nile in feluccas, simple boats which were handled adeptly. These boats, however, could not be easily managed on the high seas, for they had no keels. The Aamus, as the Egyptians termed the Semites, added a keel to the bottom of boats, a revolutionary device which stabilized them, made them more maneuverable, safer and seaworthy. Trade with the islands of the Mediterranean blossomed and flourished, and Egypt became a more important factor in the economy of the region. The basic standard weight used in Egypt, as well as other standards, were replaced by the Mesopotamian standards.[8] The Aramaic language and writing eventually replaced Akkadian as the *lingua franca* of the Semitic peoples and became the language of international trade in Egypt as well. Until that time it was the Akkadian word for "glass" and its products which was employed in international correspondence between Egypt and West Asia, for no Egyptian hieroglyphic representing true glass or its products was ever formulated. No indication that such a word existed in the ancient Egyptian language appears anywhere. The closest the Egyptian language came to the concept of glass was "glaze," such as was used in the production of pottery.

The most important impact upon Egyptian economy and life by the Canaanite chieftains was the engineering of an effective control of water resources. Legends, both Hebraic and Arabic, have it that it was, indeed, Joseph who was responsible for this great and everlasting contribution to Egypt. A canal was dug which drew the waters of the Nile into El Fayoum, a basin cradled in a vast depression whose level lay below that of the Nile. It was an ambitious undertaking, for the canal was driven through the desert parallel to the Nile, creating a twin to the Nile for half its Egyptian length; its feeder canals doubled the arable land of Egypt, until then almost entirely relegated to the delta. It is said that Joseph named the great new reservoir which formed in the Fayoum, "Lake Moeris," after the king for whom he was the viceroy. Today, after more than 3000 years, the canal still functions vigorously, and irrigates more territory than does the Aswan Dam. And it does so benignly (unlike the dam, which increases the salinity of the soil as it irrigates, a condition which portends ecological disaster). The canal has always been, and is today, called in Egyptian Arabic: the Bahr Yousef, which translates simply to The Sea of Joseph. It is so designated on the maps of Mizraim, the land which we call Egypt.

Wheels and wheeled vehicles, and the horses and oxen to draw them, were unknown in Egypt until the time of the Canaanite rule. Wheeled chariots, hitched to teams of Asian horses, were introduced for hunting and for war, and the potters of Egypt began to throw earthenware upon swiftly whirling wheels with newly won ease.

Both husbandry and agronomy were lifted toward Mesopotamian levels by the Canaanites who populated the delta region during the Second Intermediate Period. One of the benefits of the earlier trade with Nubia was the introduction into Egypt of the cattle native to Nubia. Another such great beast was brought to Egypt during the progressive period of Semitic rule: the hump-backed cattle, the zebu or Brahman bull from India, which had been bred to be well adapted to the climate and conditions of the area. The barnyard fowl also originated in India, and had already been well known in Akkadia from about 2500 B.C.E. The cackling hens amazed the farmers of Egypt by their productivity, clucking with self-satisfaction as, almost daily, they plunked down another egg. So astonishing was the proliferate performance of these fertile fowl that Thutmose III inscribed onto stone his perplexity about, and his amazement at, the fecundivity of this "foreign bird which gives birth every day"! New fruits were cultivated by the Semites in Egypt—pomegranates, figs, olives, new grains and vegetables. Even the cornflower, a common flower of Canaan, became a favorite of the pharaohs and the tomb painters employed them lavishly.

Tools were refined and perfected. The Semites taught the people of Egypt how to set the helve, or handle, into a socket through the head of axes and sledges, instead of tying the head crudely outside of it. The simple bows the Egyptians used, no more than a strong stem bent back into a single curve, were replaced by superior Semitic bows which were constructed of laminations of wood and bone cunningly and consecutively layered and bent into a composite curve. The shape of scimitars, swords and daggers were modified to make them more effective, and the composition of the metal was improved, to make them sharper and harder.

> With the increase in Asiatic influence during the Middle Kingdom, bronze comes into general use...a whole range of novel weapons was introduced from Asia, such as the horse-drawn chariot, scale armor, the composite bow and new designs of daggers, swords and scimitars....A war helmet, probably made of leather sewn with gold metal discs, was added to the Pharaoh's regalia and is known to Egyptologists as the *Khepresh*, the blue, or war crown. [A word similar to the Hebrew].[9]

More important than these weapons of destruction was the introduction of certain abiding inventions of peace: new spinning devices and the upright loom, long known in the lands to the north, revolutionized the Egyptian weaving craft. New fibers, and new fast dyes made fabrics more durable and colorful and added another dimension to the quality of life. The gentler arts were also improved; a variety of new musical instruments, such as the long-necked lute, the lyre, the oboe, the tambourine and the harp were introduced. With the new music came new forms of dance, and its graceful images became forever inscribed into the graffiti of the nobles and the princes and the pharaohs from that time forward. The Egyptian nobility even placed the newly introduced Semitic games into their tombs, perhaps in the belief that with such games they could amuse themselves eternally. The astragal, a form of dice, made from the tarsal joint of some hoofed animals (incorrectly called knucklebones), were employed in such games as twenty squares, similar to the Indian parcheesi; and in senet, a more ancient game.

The Semites acquainted the Egyptians with many marvelous materials, not the least of which were metals. Precious silver was carried by caravan from the Ararat Mountains of the Hurrian land of Mitanni and Hittite land of Anatolia. Silver was rarer and therefore more valuable than gold in Egypt. Copper had long been brought into Egypt from Alashiya, the island of Cyprus, where it was abundant and cheaper than the copper wrested from the Sinai and from small deposits elsewhere in the surrounding deserts. The quality of copper was improved by the addition of arsenic, and other metals which the Semitic people had long since employed. Lapis lazuli, the gem most desired by royalty, was borne on the backs of asses into Upper Egypt from the far-off mountains of Badakhshan, 3000 miles away in northeastern Afghanistan, along with tin, a metal the Egyptians had never known. The Egyptians were taught to alloy copper with this magic metal, resulting in a new, harder and more durable material which thrust Egypt into the Bronze Age, a new stage of civilization.

Iron was unknown in Egypt at the time of the so-called Intermediate Period, the time of the reign of the Canaanite kings; it never assumed its revolutionary place in the metallurgy of ancient Egypt, for the *Hyk Khase*, the Semitic chieftans, were expelled before the furnaces required to smelt and form iron into tools and weapons were introduced into Egypt. Even more sophisticated furnaces were required for the production of true glass: the beads and artifacts of glass which were imported into Egypt—rare, expensive, exquisite items which only royalty could afford. So treasured was this jewelry that several extra sets were included in the paraphernalia of their tombs. Perhaps they were afraid that the gods would become jealous of their finery and ask for a share, or steal them! After all, were not Egyptian gods as greedy as men, and as subject to bribery?

After the Canaanite chieftains were driven from Egypt and the Semitic peoples expelled or enslaved, progress came to a halt. Certain Theban barons, making good use of the chariots drawn by Asian horses and wheeled wagons drawn by the Asian zebu oxen, plying bronze weapons introduced from Asia, raided and pillaged the areas from which they were introduced. The chieftains of Canaan and Mesopotamia were subjected to the rule of the victorious princes of Upper Egypt, the so-called "Warrior Pharaohs," and were obliged to render tribute to them. It was during this period that the famous glass vessels bearing the name of Thutmose III (1490-1436) were made. Their existence has been advanced as a substantive claim of the existence of glassmaking in Egypt, and continues to be presented as positive proof of Egyptian manufacture at this early date. If such items could be properly labeled "Made in Egypt," the employment of foreign artisans is a likelihood, even a certainty. The circumstances of the arrival of either the glassware or the artisans to produce it can be drawn handily from the boastful, self-aggrandizing inscriptions in which the various succeeding pharaohs themselves describe their marauding raids on Canaan, and list the vast amount of plunder purloined on these excursions as well as the numbers and kinds of artisans captured, bound, and brought to Egypt as slaves. A record of the booty brought back from Canaan and the places from which it was plundered was emblazoned on the temple walls at Karnak.[10]

Thutmose III and his Egyptian army, by his own blustering account, were prime examples of Egyptian predation, a propensity which sometimes slowed the very conduct of their conquest. The siege of Megiddo, for example, was delayed as the defenders in their hasty scramble for safety within the fortress citadel left behind "chariots of gold and silver" and other goods. The pharaoh's chronicler laments: "Would that the army of His Majesty had not set their hearts upon looting the chattels of those enemies, for they would have captured Megiddo at that moment."[11] The Egyptians under Thutmose III reached the Euphrates, the farthest any Egyptian military force ever penetrated into Mesopotamia. The temple of Karnak blazons forth scenes of his 14 separate campaigns, and depicts the subjugation of 350 localities, each represented by a prisoner with his arms bound behind his back. Thutmose installed princes of his own choosing and then took the precaution of carrying off their brothers and/or children to Egypt as hostages. The most blatant braggadocio emblazoned upon the walls of Karnak concerns the plunder taken in the various campaigns. Sir Alan Gardiner notes, sardonically: "The Karnak records are more interested in the booty or tribute obtained than in the conduct of the military operations....We read of gifts sent by the kings of Ashur [Assyria], of Sangar [Babylonia, the Biblical Shinar]."[12]

Harden asks:

What is more likely than that these conquests opened the way for a young and vigorous Asiatic industry to send workers into Egypt to start a glass-vessel industry there before the 15th century was very far advanced? It looks, indeed, as if those earliest workers in Egypt were anxious to honour the Pharaoh as the founder of their industry; for there is no evidence that any one of the three [known vessels carrying the cartouche of Thutmose III] was Thutmose's personal property.[13]

A ready answer to the rhetorical question posed is that it takes no stretch of the imagination to deduce that, glass vessels being at that time among the most precious of gifts, such ware would reasonably be included in the gifts or tribute forwarded to the avaricious Egyptian conqueror, upon which his name would likely be inscribed, or that the ownership of an expensive vessel bearing the pharaoh's name would be a matter of great pride. Some historians hypothesize that Semitic glassmakers may have been brought in along with the loot garnered during Thutmose's raids:

> Glassmaking may have been introduced to Egypt with the expansion of her Empire during the Eighteenth Dynasty, possibly under Thutmose III, who extended his boundaries into Syria [sic] in the East. We shall probably never know if they were prisoners of war or if they returned with the armies to cultivate a wealthy and promising market. There is also the question of imported artisans or locally trained craftsmen under foreign supervision. Although the glass vessel shapes are Egyptian, the quality of the glass and the skill in manufacture suggest a long tradition of working this difficult material.[14]

Actually, there is not a shred of evidence that glass workers were at work in Egypt at the time of Thutmose III. Thutmose did provide evidence, however, that glass items were included in the booty brought back from his forays into Canaan. Included in his inscribed inventory of plundered goods at Karnak are "green stone, every costly stone of the country, and many stones of sparkle.'" The Egyptians had no specific word for glass; they differentiated between "costly stones" and "stones of sparkle" by employing a hieroglyph which has a fire determinative. Thus "stones of sparkle," the closest English can come to the Egyptian term, refers to the fact that these stones were born in the fires of a furnace.[15] The first appearance of the exquisite cosmetic jars in the tombs of Egyptian royalty occur at this time.[16]

It is not until a good part of a century later, after a respite from the effects of the incursions of the rampaging pharaohs of the early Eighteenth Dynasty, during a tranquil period under the rule of Amenophis III (1405-1367), that the manufacture of glassware can first be confirmed as taking place in Egypt. Trade with Canaan replaced predation; workshops and trading posts were reestablished along the Nile by Canaanite artisans and merchants. Glassware-making facilities suddenly appear at Malkata in Upper Egypt, one of which was located within the palace of the late-Eighteenth Dynasty pharaoh during this relatively peaceful period.

We use the term "glassware-making" in this context advisedly, for these artisans probably used cullet, that is, they remelted raw glass produced in and imported from the East and did not produce glass from primary materials. Glass, once produced, melts easily and quickly at a considerably lower temperature than is required for the initial vitrification of siliceous stone. There is a vast difference between the technology of glassmaking and glassware-making. The former assumes an Iron Age pyrotechnical sophistication and a chemical knowledge of which the glassware producer had no need and, indeed, was precluded from learning. The fuel required to melt already manufactured glass is but a small fraction of the amount required to produce it in the first instance. The pyrotechnical problems inherent in the process of glass production are reduced in glassware production to a degree to which artisans at a Bronze Age level can adapt with facility.

We must therefore differentiate between "glassmaking," i.e., the manufacture of glass as a raw material, and "glassware-making," the manufacture of glassware from that material. While the producers of glass (the raw material), were universally capable of producing glassware, the reverse was by no means the case. The sale of raw glass does not compromise the secrets of its manufacture, and thus the glass producer has a valuable product which establishes a stable and secure market for him. The buyers of the raw product, try as they might, are so unlikely to reproduce the process of its manufacture that, in fact, there is no evidence that such an event has ever occurred.

We cannot exclude the possibility, however, expense being hardly a deterrent for a determined pharaoh, that the cost of importing the immense quantity of wood required was borne by Amenophis III to satisfy his hunger for the exquisite products being produced by the master glassmakers of the time within the walls of his extensive palace at Malkata and at two other locations nearby in the South Village, where the workshops and residences of the artisans who worked on the palace were located. The Metropolitan Museum of Art in New York displays an impressive quantity of glassware and shards collected at Malkata which exhibit all of the sophisticated techniques and many, but not all, of the styles of the ware recovered from Nuzi and elsewhere in Mesopotamia. No trace of a furnace was found, but the fact that glass was being worked at Malkata is quite clear, for not only large quantities of fragments of glass vessels, amulets and an assortment of

COMPOSITE NECKLACE OF NON-RELATED OBJECTS.  An amulet, eye-beads and earplugs of the late 18th Dynasty ranging from 1400-1350 BCE.  The production of such items was introduced into Egypt during the relatively peaceful period under the reign of Amenophis III and continued under his son, the heretic Akhenaten.  The renewal of Egyptian belligerency after the demise of Akhenaten brought about an immediate diminution and shortly a disappearance of the art from Egypt.
*Photograph courtesy of The Corning Museum of Glass.*

other artifacts were found distributed throughout the site, but furnace slag, crucible fragments, distinctive droplets which are snipped off from trails in the process of manufacture as well as rods and other indicative elements of manufacture were collected in areas which were clearly workshops.

After the death of Amenophis III, power passed to his son, who changed gods and therefore his name from Amenophis IV to Akhenaten (thus Amen to Aten) and proceeded to build a new city dedicated to his adored Sun God at the site now known as El Amarna. The glassware-making artisans followed the heretic son into this newly established government and cult center. The art of glassmaking flourished and under the benign reign of the young king produced glassware which equalled the beauty and sophistication of the best of Mesopotamian ware.

It was at El Amarna that its excavator, the renowned W. M. Flinders Petrie, uncovered furnaces and scoria of glass[ware]-making.[17] A study of the "refractories" (as Petrie termed the traces of furnaces) and the vitrified material associated with them proved that the upper limit of temperatures attained in those facilities was 1100° Centigrade, hardly sufficient to vitrify siliceous stone.[18] Again, by assuming that the glassmakers of El Amarna were working from raw materials, a mystery was presented. Robert Charleston, in reviewing the matter at the beginning of a study of *Glass Furnaces Through the Ages*, noted that in the open-hearth system employed at El-Amarna "No really high temperatures can have been attained, and the glass was probably worked in a pasty state." The term "glass paste" has been employed often in literature concerning ancient glass, but no one has yet intelligibly defined what the term means. Charleston, realizing the anomalous character of the term, in order to rationalize his statement, hastens to add "The glassy materials were probably subjected to a preliminary fritting process before firing."

True enough! But again the consideration that no sign of the fritting process appears at El Amarna, or, for that matter, in ancient Egypt, suggests that the primary, fritting phase of glassmaking was being performed elsewhere, and the only other areas in which the art of glassmaking could be assigned were Canaan and Mesopotamia. Charleston followed up by noting that the seventh century cuneiform tablets found in the royal library of Assurbanipal, texts which manifestly date from a much earlier period, describe the three types of furnaces necessary for the production of glass from raw materials and that the key one of them is "The first intimation of a more complex type of 'furnace' probably reverberatory in character."

Analyses performed on the glassware of Malkata and El- Amarna provide direct and even more definitive evidence that the fabric of glass employed at these sites was manufactured outside of Egypt. Natron, mineral soda mined from desert deposits, was the alkaline flux available in Egypt for use in the process of vitrification. Canaanite or Mesopotamian soda was derived from the ashes of plants native to the regions which normally contained a fair amount of potash, an alkali which was absent from natron. Analysis performed on Egyptian glass artifacts as far back as 1877 should have alerted scientists to the fact that an inordinate percentage of potassium oxide, potash, was showing up. An analysis of two Egyptian beads by Clemm and Jehn listed 5.45 and 12.15 percentages of potash, respectively, among the ingredients.[19] Earle A. Caley, astounded by these figures, suspects the accuracy of the analysis: "The proportion of potash is reported to exceed the proportion of soda, especially in the second glass, which is so unusual for Egyptian glass that there is good reason to suspect the correctness of the figures."[20] The analyses of the following century, however, should have satisfied Caley that another explanation of the mysterious presence of potash should have been sought, for most of the entire corpus of analyses by different laboratories in different countries show an inordinate amount of potash if Egyptian provenance were assumed.[21] A. Lucas had already posed the question in a masterful work back in 1962:

> The amount of Potash present in some specimens, though small, is nevertheless more than could possibly be derived from natron or natural soda....While the traces of sulphate and chloride might suggest that natural soda was the alkali used, the invariable presence of the small proportions of potash and phosphate is against this, since neither has been found in analyses of Egyptian natron.[22]

Another mysterious ingredient common to the assortment of Egyptian glassware retrieved from the tombs and to the shards collected at Malkata and El-Amarna was cobalt, an element so rare in Egypt as to make its ubiquitous appearance unexplainable except by assuming that the glass from which these items were made was imported into Egypt. A spectroscopic analysis of 60 specimens of ancient Egyptian glass by Farnsworth and Ritchie in 1938 had turned up cobalt in 35 of the specimens.[23] "The finding of cobalt in Egyptian glass, especially at so early a date," points out A. Lucas, "is of considerable importance, since cobalt compounds do not occur in

Egypt." Lucas adds that the presence of cobalt "would seem to indicate that the Egyptian glassmakers of that time were in contact with glass makers elsewhere, who were using this material."[24]

The tie between the glasswork being done at the two sites, Malkata and El-Amarna, was suggested not only by the common presence of cobalt but by the equivalent composition of all elements in the glassware from the two sites. The two groups are "indistinguishable from one another in a chemical sense," reported Dr. B. A. Rising, working under the direction of Dr. Robert A. Brill of the Corning Museum of Glass.[25]

Akhenaten's tenure was of short duration. A new set of aggressively minded kings brought about both the destruction of El-Amarna and the virtual eradication of the art of glassmaking from Egypt. The warrior pharaohs of the Nineteenth Dynasty renewed massive incursions into and the plundering of their Asian neighbors. Glassmaking disappeared from Upper Egypt, never to return. There are a few sites at which it is claimed that glassmaking continued for a short period at Menshiyeh near Abydos, at Lisht, Itjetawy, and at a few other scattered sites in Lower Egypt. The shards found at Menshiyeh "bear a close resemblance" to those of Lisht, notes C. A. Keller of the Metropolitan Museum of Art in New York, "but some doubt exists in my mind as to the existence of a glass factory there."[26]

"The glass shop that had been set up in the village houses at Lisht had no strong chronological association," continues Keller. "Scholars have used various chronological 'linchpins' for the Lisht glass industry." Keller then lists a variety of diversely dated associated objects found in the area from which a much confused dating of the glass shards was done. "It should be stressed," Kelley continues, "that the scattered distribution of the glass find, coupled with the manner in which it was cleared from the site makes it difficult to apply with any confidence any of the dates suggested by the above material to the glass itself."

The glassmaking at Lisht and Itjetawy may well have been introduced during the Intermediate Period during the reign of the Semitic kings and not after the time of El-Amarna. The history of the site goes back to the time of Amenemhat I (or Amenemes I), the time in which trade and relations with the peoples of Canaan burgeoned and an influx of Semites took place, c. 1900 B.C.E. The temple at the site continued at least through the reign of Amenemhet IV and the clay sealings of several following kings were found at the site. Upon the abandonment of the site after the Intermediate Period, tomb robbers established a village on the site of the cemetery complex and the glass shards indicating glassmaking activity were found in the ruins of the village. The chronological confusion was engendered by the manner in which the site was excavated by the Metropolitan Museum's Egyptian expeditions, which started in 1906 and went on intermittently into the 1930s.

At first, in 1907, the excavators dated the glass workshop as belonging to the Roman Period![27] Then, in 1908, the shop was down-dated to the Twenty-second Dynasty.[28] Some of the village structures in which the glass shards were found were subsequently dated as early as the Middle Kingdom and the Second Intermediate Period, the very period of Semitic rule.[29] A thousand years later the village was left to the desert sand. Whether the shards stem from the earlier period is a moot question and this author would go even further than did Keller, and suggest that indeed, glass(ware)making at Lisht was the earliest such installation in Egypt and that it took place during the time of the rule of the Semitic kings, the much-maligned Hyksos. The potash content of the glass at Lisht averages somewhat higher than glass recovered from Malkata and El-Amarna, a fact which makes the provenance of the basic materials more convincingly Canaan and not Egypt.[30] The fact that the glass may stem from an earlier period is also indicated by the fact that the work is cruder and indicates a less-developed technology rather than a deteriorated one, the assumption generally drawn. In any event, the techniques inherent in the production of all the glassware which can be attributed to manufacture in Egypt are ones which took half a millennium to develop.

Elizabeth Riefstahl, in writing about the "Ancient Glass and Glazes in the Brooklyn Museum," was one of those who were mystified by the precipitous appearance of sophisticated glassware in Egypt: "It is curious that the Egyptians, once they discovered glazes and the frit that is so close kin to glass, took so long in learning to make glass itself. It was not until 2500 years after the first glazes and the first frit beads were produced that glass vessels were manufactured in Egypt. They suddenly appear in great perfection and beauty, shortly after the beginning of Dynasty XVIII."[31] The possibility that the vessels of "great perfection and beauty" exhibited not merely a chemical knowledge of glazes but also the accumulated skills of many generations of experimentation and refinement with molten glass was considered by Ms. Riefstahl. "It seems very likely, accordingly, that the sudden eruption of vessels at the beginning of Egypt's expansion toward the

RAW GLASS FOR REMELTING.  Raw glass can be melted easily and quickly, and requires no knowledge of the pyrotechnology, procedures and chemical materials involved in its production. Broken glass and raw glass (cullet) were exported from the Levant over a period of 3000 years and have been recovered from many cargos of ships sunk in the Mediterranean off the Israeli coast.

(A) Modern glass lumps produced in Murano, Venice.

(B) Glass lumps recovered from a vessel wrecked in the first century CE off the Israeli coast.

*Photographs by the author.*

East may have been due at least in part to inspiration from Asia, where the techniques of glassmaking had apparently been perfected." It also seems likely, a consideration Ms. Riefstahl did not mention, that not only were the artisans imported but so was the glass; the Asian artisans working at Malkata were merely remelting glass manufactured in Canaan. The fact that both the fuel and the technology were absent from Egypt and the probability that the first "perfected vessels" found in Egyptian tombs were looted out of Canaan and not made in Egypt were not taken into account in most of the explanations of the mystery of the sudden appearance of such exquisite ware.

The enslavement and eventual exodus of Semitic craftsmen under the pharaohs of the Eighteenth and Nineteenth Dynasties did not only affect the quality of glass work but the very existence of the art in Egypt. The art disappeared from Egypt almost as fast as it had appeared, not to return for another thousand years, not until artisans from Judah settled in Ptolemaic Alexandria together with their art.[32] It is, perhaps, for that reason that the ancient Egyptians never had a word which specifically meant glass. The Ninth International Congress on Glass, held in Versailles from September 27th to October 2nd 1971, employed an Egyptian hieroglyph as a symbol for the congress, printing it boldly on all its literature. A philological study by Birgit Noite, however, had shown that the hieroglyph did not mean "glass," but "glaze," the only form in which vitric material was known to Egyptian artisans.[33] Dan Barag pointed out at the congress with scarcely concealed irony that: "the early Egyptians did not have a separate word for glass but after the second millennium B.C. used for this purpose the term for 'glaze' or terms which referred to imitations of semi-precious stones....This hieroglyph, which is the symbol of this congress, may have also been applied to glass from the XVIIIth Dynasty."[34]

Glass production in Canaan during the period of Semitic rule in Egypt, meanwhile, had become an industry which supplied valuable cargo for seagoing entrepreneurs whose vessels were plying the Mediterranean. Scores of massive ingots of glass were included in the cargo of one such ship which sailed westward along the coast of Turkey at the turn of the fourteenth century B.C.E. The cargo was never delivered; the ill-fated vessel foundered off the Turkish coast near the present town of Kas and lay deep under the dark waters until it was discovered 3300 years later by a Turkish sponge diver; the ingots which were brought to light astounded the scientific world.

# NOTES

1. Earle R. Caley, *Analysis of Ancient Glasses 1790-1957*, 1962, p. 67.

2. Dan Barag, *Bulletin of the 9th Congress on Glass*, Section B II, 1971, p. 195.

3. Michael A. Hoffman, *Egypt Before the Pharaohs*, 1980, p. 207.

4. Josephus, *Against Apion*; Christian priests: Sectus Julius Africanus, *Chronicle*, 221 C.E.; Eusephius, *Chronicon*, 326 C.E.; George Syncellus, ("George the Monk"), in a history of the world from Adam to Diacletian, about 800 B.C.E.

5. Kent Weeks, Ibid., p. 17.

6. The glass items were unearthed from the Second Intermediate Period or an early New Kingdom stratum and are on view in the Museum on Elephantine Island. Found together with glass items such as a ring, beads and a perfume bottle was a figure of Astarte, the Semitic goddess of fertility.

7. Sir Alan Gardner, *Egypt of the Pharaohs*, 1961/79, p. 138.

8. A. S. Hemmy, *Journal of Egyptian Archeology*, XXIII (1937), p. 56. See also Charles Singer et. al., eds., *A History of Technology*, vol. 1, (Weights and Measures), pp. 776-7, as, for example: "The Egyptian short cubit of 6 palms and 24 digits (17.68 or 449 mm. was also the early Jewish cubit at 17.60 (447 mm.).

9. Aldred, Ibid., pp. 142-143.

10. J. H. Breasted, *Ancient Records of Egypt*, Vol. 2, 1906-7.

11. Gardiner, Ibid., p. 192.

12. Gardiner, Ibid., p. 193.

13. Harden, Ibid., p. 48.

14. *Egypt's Golden Age*, Catalog of the exhibition of "The Art of Living in the New Kingdom 1558-1085 B.C.," 1982.

15. R. J. Forbes, *Studies in Ancient Technology*, vol. 5, pp. 121, 2; M. L. Trowbridge, *Philological Studies in Ancient Glass*, 1928, p. 19; Breasted, Ibid., paragraph 473.

16. P. Fossing, *Glass Vessels Before Glass Blowing*, 1940, p. 6; Breasted, Ibid., Paragraph 547.

17. W. M. Flinders Petrie, *Tell-el-Amarna*, 1894, p. 25 ff.

18. W. E. S. Turner, "Studies in Ancient Glass and Glass-making Procedures. Part I. Crucibles and Melting Temperatures Employed in Ancient Egypt about 1370 B. C.," *Transactions of the Society of Glass Technology*, 38, 1954, pp. 436-444.

19. C. R. Lepsius, *Les metaux dans les inscriptions egyptiennes*, 1877, pp. 26-27.

20. Earle A. Caley, Ibid., Table XV, p. 20 .

21. Caley, Ibid. The average proportion of potash in all Egyptian glass of the Eighteenth to Twenty-second Dynasties inclusive analyzed to 1957 was 2.17 percent (table LXXXIV) and of the Ptolemaic and Roman periods was 2.71 percent (Table LXXXV). Glass from Elephantine Island of the second-first centuries B.C.E., in which only 0.03 percent potash was found on the average reflects the use of natron at that late time, as it does in the glass from Alexandria of the period between first century B.C.E. to the first century C.E., in which the average potash content was determined to be 0.01 percent (Table LXXXV). The dramatic difference between the two periods suggest that glassware made in Egypt up to the second century B.C.E. was produced from glass manufactured elsewhere.

22. Lucas, Ibid., pp. 186-187.

23. M. Farnsworth and P, D. Ritchie, *Technical Studies*, VI, 1938, pp. 155-173.

24. Lucas, Ibid., p. 189.

25. C. A. Keller, "Problems in Dating Glass Industries of the Egyptian Kingdom: Examples from Malkata and Lisht," Metropolitan Museum of Art, New York, p. 22, quoting R. H. Brill, "Preliminary Notes on the Analysis of Some Egyptian Glasses from Malkata and Lisht," submitted to the Egyptian Department of the Metropolitan Museum of Art, March 26, 1982.

26. Keller, Ibid., p. 20.

27. *Bulletin of the Metropolitan Museum of Art II*, 1907, pp, 62-63.

28. *Bulletin of the Museum of Modern Art*, 1908, p. 184.

29. *Bulletin of the Metropolitan Museum of Art*, IX, 1914, p. 210.

30. Brill, Ibid., 1982, as quoted by Keller.

31. Elizabeth Riefstahl, *Ancient Glass and Glazes in the Brooklyn Museum*, 1968.

32. D. B. Harden, *Ancient Glass*, 1972, p. 53; Fossing, *Glass Vessels Before Glass-Blowing*, 1940, pp. 7, 12, 47; Ray W. Smith *Glass from the Ancient World, The Ray Winfield Collection*, 1957, p. 17.

33. Birgit Nolte, *Die Glasgefasse im Alten Agypten*, 1968, pp. 6-10.

34. Barag, Ibid., p. 186.

# CHAPTER 4

# INGOTS OF GLASS

## *The Canaanite Connection*

A 65-FOOT-LONG MERCHANT VESSEL, WHICH SANK OFF THE SOUTHWEST COAST of Turkey at the turn of the fourteenth century B.C.E. with all of its considerable cargo stowed securely on board, is one of the most spectacular archeological finds of recent times. The cargo of the ship, much of it intact and reasonably well preserved, provides an unprecedented insight into the period. Included in that cargo were seven-inch-diameter ingots of raw glass, the earliest ever found, which were clearly on the way to a destination where they would be remelted and transformed into precious jewels, amulets, furniture inlays, goblets and other vessels. The shipwreck lies 140 feet and more below the surface of the sea along one of the sea lanes traversed by the Myceneans and Canaanites.

The ill-fated vessel foundered off Ulu Burun, the third of a series of lonely intrusions of the rugged Taurus Mountains into the sea south of the picturesque seaside town of Kas. No shore exists, for the walls of the jagged promontory plunge directly into the sea. There, posed against the massive cliff, a white vessel rests at anchor: the research vessel of the Institute of Nautical Archeology (INA), *Virazon*, is a fairly sizable vessel, yet it appears puny, overpowered by the sheer wall of the mountain which provides a backdrop to the scene. It is anchored 50 meters off shore directly above the ancient vessel which lay at the bottom untouched for 3300 years.

The archeologist's encampment is implanted at various levels on protrusions of the rocky precipice. Ladders spring from one jerry-built, screened enclosure to another fixed into the cliff above it; the research room

DIVERS OF THE INSTITUTE OF NAUTICAL ARCHEOLOGY.  The two "wet-suit archeologists" are recovering amphorae full of glass beads from the wreck of a late 14th century ship off Ulu Burun, Turkey.  Beneath them a cascade of copper and tin ingots descends down the slope of the ocean bottom 150 feet below the surface of the sea.  One of the scores of 7 inch diameter, 25 pound glass ingots recovered from the wreck can be seen lying exposed at the right center. *Photograph courtesy of the Institute of Nautical Archeology.*

ULU BURUN ENCAMPMENT. Typical sleeping quarters for two at the archeological site at Ulu Burun, near Kas, Turkey.
*Photograph by the author.*

perches on a concrete slab implanted into the lower reaches of the precipice; two ladders higher up on the face of the cliff, a cement platform is positioned on a projection which offers the only possible place on which a room large enough to serve as a gathering and dining room could be rigged; the small sleeping quarters, precariously lodged here and there even higher up on the rocky ledges, vividly recall *National Geographic* photographs in which seabirds are nested into crevices of cliffs, tending their young above a rocky footing of surging, white-surfed seas. Two outhouses sit precariously atop rocks and project out over the sea at both extremities of the camp. The outhouse selected for use depends on whether the tide is running toward or away from the diving area.

The archeologist under whose direction this project and many other undersea excavations are conducted, Dr. George Bass, is one who has been devoted to research on ancient sunken vessels for over 25 years and who founded the INA for that purpose in 1973. This "wet-suit archeologist" revolutionized the technology of undersea recovery, applying approved archeological surveying and recovery techniques in order to properly document sites and to accurately record and identify artifacts retrieved from them. Dr. Bass encouraged sponge divers to report to him on evidence of ancient wrecks. His team meets with them, teaches them what to look for and has developed a relationship which produced positive results. Such a sponger reported strange "biscuits with ears" resting on the sea-bottom; the diver had come upon these mystifying objects less than an hour away by motorboat from Kas, a picturesque village sitting on the southwestern tip of Turkey. Dr. Bass investigated, and determined that it was the earliest complete ship and cargo ever found.

Bass gathered a lively, enthusiastic group around him, composed mostly of students from Texas A & M University, and proceeded to institute the investigation of the wreck and the recovery of its cargo with modern equipment under rigid scientific guidelines. Dr. Bass is ably assisted by Cemal Pulak, who serves at Bass' right hand, administering the project with unassuming competence with the able assistance of his wife, Sema, whose accurate renderings of the artifacts dredged up from the deep provide a clear record for scholars to study. A representative of the Turkish government is stationed with the group, a youthful commissioner whose duty it is to assure that no artifacts recovered from the vessel disappear from Turkey. A doctor who specializes in underwater medicine, a photographer, a cook and a cook's assistant round out the company. Everyone but the cook and his assistant dive. Even the commissioner, doctor and photographer participate in the routine repeated twice a day in which consecutive teams of three or four divers descend to the bottom until everyone had done his or her assignment. No more than 20 minutes at the bottom in the morning dive, and 16 minutes in the afternoon dive is allowed, inasmuch as the buildup of nitrogen in the blood at such a depth could prove dangerous. The underwater site is mapped in great detail and each object exposed is photographed *in situ* for adding visual details to the site plan.

Recovered artifacts are immediately immersed in salt water containers to

CEMAL PULAK ON HIS WAY DOWN TO THE 14TH CENTURY BCE WRECK. Twice daily a team of divers descend from the INA research vessel, the *Virazon,* to the ancient ship lying at a depth of 150 feet under the sea. A maximum of 20 minutes is allowed for each dive at that depth to prevent an excess of nitrogen from being absorbed into the blood, a condition which may result in painful and potentially debilitating "bends".
*Photograph by the author.*

avoid deterioration before the lengthy process of preservation begins. The artifacts are handled in a room set up one ladder's climb above the tiny dock. Shelves on the rear wall are crowded with plastic containers of various sizes in which the sea-logged objects were immersed. The furnishings consist mainly of a work table, drafting board and a few chairs. After being photographed, sketched from all angles and recorded in a log, the artifacts are eventually transported to a museum further up the Turkish coast at Bodrum especially created to house the material recovered from the sea by the INA.

The cargo of the ancient sunken vessel has proved to be sensational. The ancient ship was laded with thousands of pounds of copper and tin ingots in classic four-handled "oxhide" form typical of the Late Bronze Age, and a host of revealing artifacts, personal and commercial. Hafted tools: axes and hoes were evidence of a civilization which had already reached a significant industrial level. They were remarkable in that the cast hole in the metal heads provided for a helve (wood handle) to pass through, a system which was, as yet, virtually unknown outside of Canaan and Mesopotamia; it had only recently been introduced into Egypt during the period of the Canaanite kings.

A magnificent gold cup, other gold objects and many exciting artifacts of cultural and historical interest were brought up from the depths. Ivory objects fabricated of the teeth and tusks of hippopotamuses and elephants were recovered; they turned out to be particularly significant, for it is known from Egyptian texts that elephants were still being hunted in the Canaanite hinterlands at that time, and skeletal remains of hippopotamuses in the region provide the evidence that such beasts were still wallowing in marshy environments such as existed at the estuaries of rivers along the Canaanite coast. They were smaller varieties of those great beasts, to be sure, but such species nevertheless, whose ivory can be differentiated analytically from that grown by African or Indian beasts.

The tin probably came from the far-off mountains of Afghanistan. The Levantine coast is the point at which the confluence of caravan trails from those areas occurred and from which the shipment was made. Copper was then picked up in Cyprus (which means "copper"), perhaps in exchange for some of the tin or glass. The ship probably sailed a circular route around the Mediterranean, and the composition of the cargo provides important clues to the origin of the vessel, its course and its provenance.

One substance in the cargo in particular ties Canaan to Egypt and provides a clue to the destination of the glass ingots as well. It was, in fact, the second most voluminous commodity carried in the cargo and was contained in over 100 Canaanite amphoras. It was a resin obtained from the *pistacia terebinthus* tree, and both its origin and destination were revealed to Professor Bass in a slim book published in French in Cairo. The professor had fortuitously found the rare book while rummaging around second-hand books being offered for sale in College Station, Texas, where the Institute for Nautical Archeology happens to be located.

The little book I found was written by an Egyptologist Victor Loret to prove his theory that a certain ancient word, written *sonter* in hieroglyphs, meant terebinthine resin. This interpretation allowed him to translate Egyptian texts describing tons of the stuff being imported from the Syro-Palestinian coast, the home of the Canaanites, for use as incense in Egyptian rituals during the 14th century B.C....An Egyptian painting mentioned by Loret shows a Canaanite jar like those on our wreck.[1]

The provenience and destination of the resin suggest those of the glass ingots on board the Ulu Burun vessel; it was thus that the glass must have arrived at Malkata, Amarna and elsewhere in Egypt for the short period of time in which glassware was being produced in Egypt. The rule of Amenophis III ended in the year 1367, Akhenaten in 1350. Glassware may still have been produced in Egypt after that time, albeit in a more limited and cruder manner. The production of glassware in Egypt probably ended with the reign of Merenptah in the year 1214. The Ulu Burun vessel sailed sometime during the middle of these limits of time in which glassware was produced in Egypt. The conclusion to be drawn is, therefore, that since the art was on the decline in or had disappeared from Egypt at the time, new markets existed or were being developed for the glass and that destination of the glass ingots lay elsewhere. It was just prior to this period that glass beads and pendants did begin to appear in Mycenaea and other eastern Mediterranean and Aegean locations.

The evidence for the Canaanite provenance of the glass cargo is further reinforced by the recovery of four gold medallions, the largest of which is a hefty 11 centimeters (4.5") in diameter, which were recovered to date (1988) from the wreck. They are decorated in repoussé with a four-pointed star, a motif found in many Canaanite excavations and commonly depicted by the Egyptian artists on the necks of captured Canaanites.[2] Professor Bass stated earlier on finding the first of these pectorals that it "is surely of Canaanite inspiration" mentioning a number of examples, including a reference "to earlier gold pectorals found in tombs at Byblos, a site which may in fact, have influenced the techniques of goldwork at Tell el Ajjul."[3] The late 15th or early 14th century sun-disc pendant unearthed at Nuzi (see figure on page 20) is clearly a prototype of the medallions recovered from the Ulu Burun wreck.

The implications of the extraordinary recovery of a late fourteenth or early thirteenth century B.C.E. cargo has not yet been fully digested; there can be no question however, that the Canaanites who produced, accumulated and shipped these goods were far from being uncultured, but stemmed from an ancient, well-ordered civilization. Perhaps the most significant recovery from the wreck was a *diptych*, a writing tablet composed of two hollowed and hinged wooden leaves. Wax pressed into the depressions on the inner sides of these wooden covers provided the surface on which the merchant did his calculations or wrote his notes. The diptych found on the wreck is older by many centuries than any other such writing device ever found.

The news that the cargo also included an amphora full of glass beads, and that more than a score of cobalt blue glass ingots had been recovered immediately drew attention to the fact that the glassmaking industry not only existed in Canaan at this early date, but was so highly developed that artisans were not only producing but exporting 25 pound glass ingots seven inches in diameter and several inches thick. This fact should not have come as a surprise to archeologists; they should have been prepared for such a circumstance by one of the instructive finds at El Amarna, tablets in which communication with Mesopotamia and Canaan was recorded. Reference to the weights of imported raw glass in those tablets, written in the Akkadian cuneiform script, provide a direct link to the Ulu Burun ingots. They also provide an intriguing puzzle, inasmuch as we do not know the multiples of the units employed in the El Amarna correspondence, and a comparison with the weights of those recovered from the Ulu Burun wreck is not possible.[4] In general, however, it appears that the weights of the raw glasses referred to in the El Amarna tablets may not only be similar to that of the Ulu Burun glass ingots but that the two groups were also largely of similar chemical composition.

An analysis of the glass ingots was made by R. H. Brill of the Corning Museum of Glass, and, referring to the blue glass found in Egyptian and Mycenean contexts, he reported that "The Ulu Burun ingots are chemically identical to Egyptian cored vessels and to Mycenaean glass amulets."[5] The first group of ingots raised from the depths were a deep blue, which Brill attributed to cobalt as the main coloring agent, an element, as was noted previously, absent from Egypt. Six more ingots recovered in 1985 were "either green with black and white variegation, or, as in certain large ingot fragments, light brown or amber."[6] The ingots thus provide the most credible evidence that glassware manufactured in Egypt in the late eighteenth Dynasty was fabricated from glass produced in Canaan.

The engineering of furnaces capable of producing such bulks of glass

ONE OF THE SCORES OF GLASS INGOTS IN THE CARGO OF THE 14TH CENTURY BCE VESSEL. The production of such massive bulks of glass, averaging around 25 pounds each, attests to the advanced Iron Age pyrotechnology of their Near Eastern producers at a time when the officially designated Iron Age had yet to dawn in the Israelite hills of Canaan. The beautiful, translucent blue color of the glass glints through the encrusted surface of the 3300 year old ingot.
*Photograph courtesy of the Institute of Nautical Archeology.*

bespeak a technical sophistication and development of industry of the time beyond the prognostication of most historians. The existence of such a cargo is also a further indication of the secrecy being maintained about the manufacture of glass and consequently its enhanced value as a commodity. The fact is that once glass is manufactured it can be readily remelted at a reasonable temperature easily attainable in furnaces such as those of potters and metalsmiths anywhere, and that producing glassware from already manufactured glass requires no knowledge.of the secret, mysterious requisites of the process of vitrification. Glass ingots, therefore, became a valuable product for sale, suitable for transformation at their destination into glassware of all kinds, while the secrets of the manufacture of the raw glass remained with its producers.

THE CANAANITE WRECK AT CAPE GELIDONYA. Archeologists of the Institute of Nautical Archeology (INA) recovering objects from the cargo of a Canaanite ship sunk off Cape Gelidonya, Turkey, about 1200 BCE.
*Photograph courtesy of the Institute of Nautical Archeology.*

Glass in ingot form, unlike goblets or bowls, can be shipped without hazard, and was laded on the Canaanite ship along with ingots of smelted copper and tin as well as an amphora loaded with glass beads, which are similarly safe and convenient for export. Perhaps a master glass(ware)-maker accompanied the shipment, on his way to establish himself at some potentially favorable location. The possibility poses as intriguing a question as does that of the suggested presence of one or more tinkers on board another vessel which sank about 1200 B.C.E. off the Turkish coast near Cape Gelidonya. "The one-ton cargo of copper ingots and scrap bronze from Cyprus was found with metalworking tools that suggest a tinker (smith) on board."[7] It was just such itinerant artisans who were pictured half a millennium earlier in the tomb of Knumhotpe, the Egyptian nomarch buried at Beni Hassan.

A large collection of Canaanite weights on board the Cape Gelidonya vessel point to a high level of commercial competence as did cylinder seals, one of which evidently had been carried as a pendant, for it was decorated at each end by a gold cap with loops. A number of scarabs were recovered, items ordinarily thought of as Egyptian amulets but which were in fact introduced into Egypt early on by the Semites. Bronze razors were collected from the wreck, evidence of an ancient propensity for clean-shaven visages which belies the impression that ancient men generally sported beards. The type of ship's lamp, stone mortars and other objects used on board the vessel indicate that the crew was composed of Canaanite seamen.

The Canaanites established seaside settlements throughout the Mediterranean, the main European and African sites where significant objects of glass of the period of Canaanite expansion have been found. Among these objects are distinctive, peculiarly Semitic items which first appeared back in the fifteenth century B.C.E. at Nuzi. Almost 500 examples of headbeads, similar in workmanship and style to ones found in ancient Akkadian sites, show up among glass artifacts recovered from virtually every Canaanite colony. They continue to show up around the Mediterranean until well into the Hellenic period. These brilliantly colored beads are most commonly rendered in the form of a curly-headed, black-bearded Semite gazing goggle-eyed out into the world, and are so singular that they unmistakably mark the cultural origin of the artifacts associated with them. The head-beads take other forms, demon heads, ram's heads, wine grapes, birds, little bells and even phalli, but they are so characteristic as to be easily recognized as stemming from the same

91

HEAD-BEAD, MID 5TH-4TH CENTURY BCE. A glass *head-bead*, perhaps worn as a pendant, typical of those which appeared around the Mediterranean from the 9th century BCE from whose ruins hundreds of these characteristic items have been recovered. Prototypes of the head-beads were found at 15th century BCE Nuzi and elsewhere in ancient Mesopotamia as well as inland along various trade routes.
*Photograph courtesy of The Corning Museum of Glass.*

Mesopotamian culture; they continue over many centuries to be manufactured in the same tradition. The largest collections of these head-beads, well over a hundred examples, are in the Bardo and Carthage museums.[8]

A few sites in which glass was being worked from the thirteenth century B.C.E. forward have been identified throughout the Mediterranean, most of which offer few clues as to the people who operated the furnaces. One such was found at Frattesina, in northeastern Italy, south of Venice near the town of Spina, dated to the eleventh century B.C.E. or later. Analyses of a few fragments of crucible with glass slag attached and other scoria indicate that the temperatures attained were less than 1000° Centigrade. The chemical composition of the glass shows that the alkali used is unlike that of Egyptian natron, a fact which puzzled the investigators since they assumed that Egyptian glass was made of Egyptian raw materials and that Egypt was a likely source for the raw material employed at Frattesina. The mystery of the provenance of the cullet used at Frattesina is easily resolved, of course, by assigning it the same provenance as that of the ingots on board the Ulu Burun vessel.

There is a body of evidence which fixes the region in which primary glassmaking took place to the Canaanite coastal regions, and even to the precise spot in which such an activity may have taken place. The womb of glassmaking was undoubtedly Akkadia, where the gestation of the art developed it to such a degree that it can be safely said that, except for the process of blowing, little has been added to the art since that ancient time. The art has grown more complex since those ancient times, and modern furnaces provide steadier and fiercer fires, but all the elements that comprise contemporary glassmaking artistry were contained in Akkadian technology. The art flowed westward through Mesopotamia, passing its infancy in the care of artisans who plied the glassmaking trade in Hurrian Mitanni, as vitric artifacts found in the Hurrian centers of Mari and Nuzi amply testify; from thence it finally filtered onto the strip of Levantine coast above the present city of Haifa. We are unlikely to ever pinpoint the precise place in which the art first erupted in the Land-of-the-Two-Rivers, but after it reached the Mediterranean, its history becomes fixed in time and place. The art arrived at the Window-to-the-West, the Mediterranean shore, with all its faculties fully formed and the most ancient traditions point to its growing to maturity near a small, otherwise rather inconsequential river, anciently known as the Belus.

By the time the art reached the Levantine coast, the technology of producing not merely beads, amulets and other small castings, but methods of forming vessels had already reached an advanced stage. The first glassmakers may have been the lapidarists, for "molten stone," the marvelous new material, was produced mostly for the replication of rare and colorful gemstones. Perhaps it was the metalsmiths who produced glassware as a by-product of their craft, or perhaps the smiths supplied raw vitric products to the lapidarists whose talents were applied to converting the crude material into brilliant gems. Perhaps it was the potters who adapted the pyrotechnology of the smiths to their own purpose, inasmuch as they had long known the formula for producing glazes, which were the same as those for producing glass in bulk. We shall likely never know just who the earliest glassmakers were because glassmaking evolved from an amalgamation of technologies and did not become an identifiable industry until many hundreds of years passed by. We have learned that by the seventeenth century B.C.E., however, glassmaking had become a trade confined to people who jealously guarded it as their own and passed its secrets on to their descendants. And we have learned that the art passed on around the arc of the Fertile Crescent and rooted itself at the coast of the great sea regarded by the Mesopotamian peoples as the "Sea-of-the-Setting-Sun."[9]

If Akkadia was the womb in which the art of glassmaking gestated and from which it was born and Mesopotamia was the home in which it passed its infancy, then the Levantine coast was the school in which, evolving over the next 1000 years, the art grew to full maturity. No spot on earth has a better or a more lasting claim to importance in the history of glassmaking than does the Levantine coast and its hinterlands. The most ancient traditions refer to the strip of coast from Ashkelon to Sidon and especially to that particular part through which the Belus River flows, a tiny, seemingly insignificant strip of western Asia. The art was practiced at the coast and spread into the forested Galilean and Lebanese hills where the art matured and was practiced for over 3000 years. The revolutionary process of glassblowing, the last great advance in the technology of the art, was invented in the Galilee about the first century B.C.E. Both the products and the masters of the glassmaking art rippled out from that area in ever-widening circles throughout the world; some were exported in the course of commerce, and others were plucked from the area as a consequence of conquest. The first invaders to carry off glassware from Canaan were the Egyptians. Exquisitely wrought glass vessels were included in the loot carried off by the rampaging armies of the Warrior Pharaohs; they found a resting place in the tombs of the Egyptian hierarchy and ended up in museums where they are ironically labeled Egyptian glass. The Assyrians and then the Babylonians over-ran the area and transplanted tens of thousands of Hebrew artisans and merchants into a Mesopotamian diaspora, and the glassmaking industry revitalized in the area in which it was born; the Greeks and the Romans followed in their turn, playing out their roles according to the universal script which conquerors of all ages follow.

It is from Roman literature that we first learn of the importance to the science and art of glassmaking of that particular section of the Levantine coast into which the Belus River flows. The Belus is a brackish stream which forms from springs which spurt from beneath the ring of the Carmel

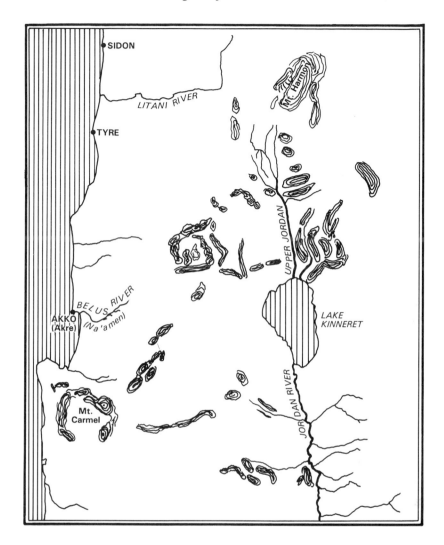

## THE MEDITERRANEAN COASTAL REGION AT WHICH
## THE ART OF GLASSMAKING ARRIVED FROM MESOPOTAMIA

The coastal area around the Belus River was reputed by Pliny the Elder and other historians to have witnessed the origin of glassmaking. These fabulous accounts reflected the fact that the sands of the Belus estuary are rich in silicate, as are the sands of the entire coast; nearby swampy areas provided the plants from whose ashes soda was obtained; the hinterland forests of the upper region abounded with oak trees which provided the hardwood needed for the intense fires of the glassmaker's furnaces; the forests of the lower coastal region provided the soft wood used by the glassware-makers; thus all the essential elements for glass production were prevalent in the region. The region became the center of glassmaking in the Late Bronze Age and remained such for the next three millennia.

95

range and squirms lazily through five miles of swampy terrain; it then threads no less leisurely through a series of sand dunes along the shore. It is not much of a river; in fact, the term river is misleading. It is a convoluted mucky stream, most of which flows through a swamp; a stream which loses itself in the swamp so that in many places it cannot be distinguished from the surrounding morass. It is eight miles long, but only if it is measured generously along all its convolutions.

An Israeli kibbutz drained the malarial marshes in the late 1940s, when Israel was but newly reborn, and Zionist pioneers created a thriving communal farm on the rich, organic soil deposited over many millennia by the meandering river. The river empties gracefully into a conch-shaped bay which arcs around from the modern city of Haifa to the city of Acre. Standing on the beach where the river slips tranquilly into the bay, one sees the battlements of ancient "Akko" boldly embracing the bay on the north, while a view of Haifa at the bay's southern extremity is largely blocked by the complexities of a refinery, its pipes twisting and turning, its towers spitting steam and flaring fire.

It was natural for the Canaanites to equate the sluggish river twisting through the swamp which lay between the Carmel range and the sea with the god of the annual renewal of life. It was surrounded by lush foliage from which a continual flurry of flocks of wildfowl arose; it harbored all sorts of milting fish in its shallows as well as wallowing hippopotamuses; there was a continuous bustle of beasts who descended from the dry hills to slake their thirst in its brackish but quenching waters. Elephants came by to drink and splash in the stream and return to the forests spread over the hills behind the ridge of the Carmel Mountains. The teeming, pulsing life proliferating around the mucky Belus bespoke the presence of Baal, the Semitic god of vegetation, creation and fertility, after whom it was aptly named.

Waterfowl still peck along the shallow shores of the river searching for a fat worm, or stand, one legged, watching for an unwary fish. Not many birds now appear, it is true, but the variety of birds that still scrounge for food in the river's shallows and in the residue of the swamp make manifest what a haven for birds and other wildlife the river and swamp must have been before civilization encroached upon them. Today a well-trafficked and trucked main road sweeps through the swamp and bridges the river near its mouth; a train track parallels the road and crosses the river even closer to the shore, almost at the point where the river casually, quietly weaves into the sea.

The Carmel range looms in the background, almost enclosing the low-lying valley through which the Belus winds. The sands, highly suitable for making glass because of their siliceous purity, were mined for millennia and shipped throughout the world. The river is now named the Na'amen, meaning the "Gracious One" after a Canaanite deity to whom the appellation applied; but its previous name, Belus, is the Greco-Roman rendition of Baal, under whose protection the valley existed. Baal was the deity most adored by the Canaanites. He was particularly revered in the city whose ancient name was Sur, the city presently known as Tyre. Baal was worshiped somewhat differently in every part of the Semitic world. He was responsible for fertility in general, but of the earth and the herds and flocks in particular. He was regarded variously as the son or the grandson of the supreme being El and his wife Asherah. The name of this offspring of El was actually Hadad, but he was almost universally referred to by his title: Baal, or the Master.

Baal was worshiped by the earliest Hebrews. The name comes down to us through the Bible and is locked into the names of many places and persons, as in that of the general Hannibal, (favored by Baal). Baal translates from both Aramaic and Hebrew into "master" and reappears in modern epithets such as that used for the founder of the Lubavitch Hasidic movement, Rabbi Israel ben Eliezer, who is referred to as the Baal Shem Tov (Master of the Good Name). The use of Baal, albeit in its strictly secular sense, in reference to the revered Rabbi Eliezer is particularly curious when note is taken of the admonishments rendered by the Hebraic deity over the propensity of his chosen children to revert to Baal. We note, for example, Hosea's passionate exposition of the reproof of his unappreciative harlot wife, transmitted to him directly by God (El), who complained (2:10): "that I gave her the corn, and the wine, and the oil, and multiplied her silver and gold, which they prepared for Baal," and then laid down conditions for the continuance of his beneficence:

2:18: [thou] shalt say unto me no more Baali
2:19: For I will take away the names out of her mouth, and they shall no longer be remembered by their name.

God's emphasis on the disturbing syncretism evoked by the incorporation of

Baal into Hebraic nomenclature was prompted by its common use as an alternative for El. G. Ernest Wright notes that "We hear of Saul and David naming their children such names as Ishbaal, meaning either "man of Baal" or "Baal exists," and Beeliada, meaning "May Baal know." One of David's warriors bore the name Beeliah, meaning "Yahweh is Baal." This does not mean that the parents of these children worshipped the Canaanite Baal, but that the title was given Yahweh."[10]

The responsibility for human and animal fertility rested with Baal's wife, the Goddess Anath, who also appears as Astarte and in numerous other variations such as the Biblical Ashtorath or Ashtar and as Ishtar in Babylonia. She represented the quintessential symbol of sexual love and was revered no less than were her counterparts, Isis in Egypt and Aphrodite among the Greeks. The worship of Astarte was central to Canaanite religion and its main thrust. Their devotion to Astarte was expressed by acts of the most passionate eroticism of which her devotees were capable, singly, in pairs, or en masse. Temple prostitution, both male and female, was carried on in her name. Spring festivities, engaged in to ensure abundant crops, centered around Astarte, the personification of fecundity.

Astarte was idolized by all the Semitic peoples, for, in addition to providing the pleasures of passion, Astarte guaranteed familial continuity and security in old age. The Hebrews eventually rejected her as they did all other gods, even the Master of the Universe, Baal, on the basis of the singularity and indivisibility of divinity. The God of the Hebrews remained El, to whom they reverted as a universal, undepictable power, symbolized by the tetragrammaton YHWH, (commonly pronounced *Yahweh*).

The myriads of Egyptian, Assyrian, Hittite and other gods encountered by the Hebrews were readily discarded by the Hebrews, but the rejection of both Baal and Astarte proved traumatic because it directly concerned the divine power of creation and consequently fertility, an attribute especially important to the pastoral peoples among them. The adoration of Baal and Astarte was difficult to tear from the passions of the descendants of Abraham in spite of the severe strictures imposed on the Hebrew community, as the Old Testament amply testifies. The attraction of Baal and Astarte was not confined to an abstract concept of creativity; the worship of Astarte provided her adorers with earthly sensual experience. Since the worship of Astarte ran counter to the moral precepts as well as to the religious standards established among the Hebrews, the sexual rites employed in the adoration of Astarte became considered as not only heresy but an abomination. Yet Hebrew mores did not deny sexuality; in fact, the enjoyment of sex was encouraged, but it was viewed as intended for the purposes of procreation and its practice restricted to those "joined in the sight of God." Hebrew mores regarded sexual love as a necessary and healthy element in the relationship between those so joined, and people were enjoined "to be fruitful and multiply."

It proved difficult to tear Astarte from the thoughts and lives of the followers of Yahweh. Hebrew families were prone to furtively retain a figure of Astarte in the hope that she would favor the family with fertility. This propensity for paganism provides us with examples of the association of the ancient Jews with glass, for figures of Astarte are recovered not only from the ruins of Canaanite and Semitic settlements in general but in those specifically populated by the later Hebrews as well. It is one of the few artifacts which mark the culture of its makers or possessors as being possibly Hebrew, for, until the Christian era, the Hebrews in general employed no other identifying amulets or objects which distinguished them from the people among whom they lived.

Questions were asked of the famous collector and author of treatises on glass, Ray Winfield Smith, at an International Congress on Glass held in 1959 after he had presented a paper on ancient glass in which glass figures of Astarte were illustrated and discussed. "I should like to know where these figures we have seen [on lecture slides] were found and what are the approximate dates?" was a typical question posed to Smith.

"We do not know," answered Smith, "But the roughly half-dozen, perhaps of these figures have been found in such places as Palestine and I believe in Syria and Mesopotamia....Now those of you who have seen Mycenaean glass ornaments may have been struck by the fact that they are always covered with a very characteristic whitish layer of decay. These Astarte figures, which have been found on the continent of Asia are characteristically covered with what looks to be just exactly the same layer of decay....[That suggests] that both the Mycenaean ornaments and the Astarte figures might be made out of the same composition of glass, perhaps manufactured at the same common center and shipped out to outlying districts at some considerable distances where they were certainly remelted in small ovens....They seem to be concentrated around about the 6th century B.C. I know [of] about 15 of them but there is some reason to think that the technique went back, considerably further back, perhaps as early as the 15th century B.C."[11]

# THE GLASSMAKERS

Mr. Smith had no suspicion at the time that a few years later the discovery of the thirteenth century vessel at Ulu Burun would lend substance to his conjecture as to the origin of the Mycenaean glass, and that the characteristically Semitic Astarte fertility figures would indeed provide one of the links between the glass artifacts found around the Mediterranean and the Asian producers.

The sandy beaches through which the Belus eases into the sea appear to have played a most significant role in the history of glassmaking; not only was it along this section of the Levantine coast that the art of glassmaking did first become established, but glassmaking flourished in this area for 3000 years. It was in this area that the technology of glassmaking achieved an intricacy and beauty that has never been surpassed; it was from this area that Semitic artisans spread out over three continents, carrying the secrets of glassmaking with them. It is a remarkable fact of history that the art of glassmaking arose independently only once in one area on earth and among one group of people. It was born in the area of the confluence of the Tigris and Euphrates Rivers, developed along the Mediterranean coast at or near the Belus Rivers and it was from this coast that the art and the artisans were exported to the rest of the world.

For many centuries glassware was exported from the Belus-Galilean region, largely through the port of Sidon; then the glassmasters wended their way into the world from the area. It can be stated with virtually complete accuracy that every glassmaking establishment in existence can trace its origin to this area, and to the people who inhabited it. Ancient sources make it clear that the Belus sands were the established standard for glassmaking. Theophastrus, of the third century B.C.E., informs us about the already ancient reputation of the sands of the Belus beach as an essential for the making of objects of glass. Strabo reports on the transport of massive amounts of sand dug from the undulating dunes of the Belus estuary to centers where glassmaking were eventually established under the Romans.[12]

The murky water of the Belus was reputed to have beneficial medicinal properties; it was considered to be holy and healing. Perhaps it gained this reputation because its water tastes so foul. When Heracles, of Greek mythology, entreated the Delphic Oracle for a cure for the wounds inflicted on him by the Hydra, he was directed toward the East where a river sprouting medicinal hydra-headed plants existed. Indeed, Heracles journeyed east, found those very plants on the banks of the Belus River, and was cured (so the fable goes).

> To commemorate this occasion Heracles founded a city on the spot and called it "*AK*," a cure. This is how the Greeks explained the foundation of Akko, which they called Acci, (Ace) before the name was changed to Ptolemais....This legend must have been current in active form for many centuries. All the elements--the river God Belus, Heracles, and a strangely shaped plant of a lily type, appear on Roman coins as late as the 3rd and 4th centuries A.D.[13]

The city of Ak, or Akko, or Ptolemais, is the present city of Acre in Israel. So important is the area to glassmaking history, and so far back into antiquity does its history go, that speculation long held that the art originated on the banks of that muddy river and the dunes of bright sand through which it flows. The most quoted reference to this history is the account of Pliny the Elder, the Roman encyclopedist who wrote in 30 A.D. about an event that presumably took place 2000 years earlier:

> That part of Syria which is known as Phoenicia and borders on Judea contains a swamp called Candebia on the lower slopes of Mt. Carmel. This is believed to be the source of the river Belus, which, after traversing a distance of five miles, flows into the sea near the colony of Ptolemais. Its current is sluggish and its waters are unwholesome to drink, although they are regarded as holy for ritual purposes. The river is muddy and flows in a deep channel revealing its sands only when the tide ebbs....The beach stretches for not more than a half a mile, and yet for many centuries the production of glass depended on this area alone.

Then Pliny repeats a rather fanciful story, relating it, so it would seem from the tone of his writing, with tongue in cheek:

> There is a story that once a ship belonging to some traders in natural soda put in here and that they scattered along the shore to prepare a meal. Since, however, no stones suitable for supporting their cauldrons were forthcoming, they rested them on clumps of soda from their cargo. When these became heated and were completely mingled with the sand on the beach, a strange translucent liquid flowed forth in streams; and this, it is said, was the origin of glass.[14]

While the story is fabulous, inasmuch as a campfire cannot produce the intense heat needed for the production of glass, it does focus on the fact that in Pliny's time the area already had so long-standing a reputation of being an ancient and unique center of glass production that the inception of the art was assumed to have taken place among the dunes of the Belus beach. The true Akkadian origin of the art had disappeared into the mists of time at the time when Pliny the Elder related the fabulous account.

For more than two millennia this area was a major, and, for much of the period, the only exporter of glass products to the world until it became the exporter of its artisans, who carried the art with them. The area played a significant role in human history long before the glassmaking era. The earliest domesticated grain ever found was recovered from caves carved into the Carmel escarpment overlooking the Belus River, where the grain had lain for 10,000 years. Five millennia later the Giblites appeared, the first people of this area of whom we have written records. These people of unknown origin were already sending trading expeditions into Egypt about 3000 B.C.E. Their main center was at Byblos, from whose ruins much information concerning the origins of Hebrew culture was culled. The Semitic and associated peoples who emigrated into the region during the course of the third millennium B.C.E. absorbed or displaced the native peoples. The new settlers identified themselves with the Akkadian appellation *Kinahu*, or *Kinanu* a term we come across in the El Amarna letters of the fourteenth century B.C.E. and the name by which they identified themselves throughout their existence as a coherent people.

The Kinanu, or Canaanites, were the people to whom the epithet "Phoenician" was later applied by the Greeks as a consequence of an activity engaged in by the some of Canaanites who were pursuing a profitable trade in purple dye. This highly prized, royal color was being extracted from a certain mollusk, a murex, found off the shores of Canaan. The Canaanites boiled the mollusk and refined the color from the resultant liquid. In the process of producing the dye, the hands and clothes of these seaside Canaanites inevitably became colored. The word *Phoenikes*, which means "purple" in Greek, was applied by the Greeks to the dye-makers and the nickname *Phoenicians* i.e., the "Purple People," was coined. The Greeks came to designate not only the mollusk-boiling dye makers as the "Purple People," but applied the epithet to all the sea faring Canaanites. The Canaanites, seafaring or not, never recognized the term "Phoenician" as a reference to themselves, even when under Greek and Roman rule.

Pagan Greek and Latin authors never use the name Canaanite in any form. But the "Phoenicians," even in the west, retained it. In the new testament St. Mark, writing for Gentile readers, speaks of a Syro-phoenician woman. St. Matthew, writing for the Jews, calls her a woman of Canaan. Even St. Augustine in the early fifth century

A.D. says that if you ask the country people in Africa who they are they will reply in the Punic tongue "Chanani."[15]

Why, then, do scholars, historians, museums and archeologists persist in employing a misleading misnomer "Phoenician" when a perfectly good, understandable and historically correct term "Canaanite" is available? This malapropic propensity for obfuscation is particularly apparent when the label "Phoenician" is inappropriately applied to objects made in the area more than a millennium before the Greek era. To compound the confusion engendered by such frivolous nomenclature, items produced inland in the Galilean area of Israel as well in the Judean hills, areas which were never a part of so-called Phoenicia, are also persistently and erroneously labeled "Phoenician." We should point out here in this regard that "Lebanon" was in ancient times a mountain, and not a state as is inferred in reading ancient texts and interpolating them to mean the territory of "Phoenicia." The name of the mountain is derived from the Hebrew word *Laban*, which means "white"; this refers to the fact that the mountain is covered for a good part of the year by snow, and also because the stone and soil was of a light coloration. The White Mountain was known in Latin as *Mons Libanus*. In every one of the 65 mentions of Lebanon in the Bible it is the mountain and no other area which is referred to. Marcus Retter delineates the area: "The western part of the mountain was known as Lebanon, the eastern part as anti-Lebanon, In between there was a valley known as the 'Valley of the Lebanon' (Isaiah XI,17). In the non-Jewish literature it was known as 'Coele-Syria.'"[16]

The Canaanites became a nation at the turn of the second millennium B.C.E. The sea faring Canaanites, that is, those based in coastal cities such as Tyre and Sidon, maintained a continuous, close relationship with the neighboring Hebrew tribes, an alliance which endured in peace through most of the history of these two peoples. Flavius Josephus identifies the Phoenicians as "those who live by the seaside," and testifies to the traditional friendship that existed between the two nations and recounts the Biblical reference to that relationship: "Hiram, the king of Tyre, was the friend of Solomon our king, and had such friendship transmitted down to him from his forefathers."[17]

The Hebrews, whose ancient tribal Semitic dialects were Akkadian and Aramaic, adapted upon arrival in Canaan to the dialect of the Canaanites, Biblically acknowledged as "the tongue of Canaan." There was a constant interchange of artisans, products and services between the two peoples, a sort of "common market" relationship. The theological distinction between the Canaanites and the Hebrews was elaborated slowly and became idiosyncratic by the end of the second millennium; but commercial intercourse between the peoples continued unabated despite the cultural differentiation. The trades which proliferated in the conjunctive area of the two peoples included glassmaking, which art appeared at the Levantine coast at a time coincident with that attributed to the arrival of the Jewish progenitors. From that time forward the art was one practiced by the Jews, as is amply testified by a number of Roman historians, the earliest extant record of the association of the art with a people.

Tacitus was a Roman historian (55-117 C.E.) whose anti-Semitic stance was so severe and his recounting of Jewish customs, culture and religion so colored by prejudice that his translator, Kenneth Wellesley, was impelled to pronounce apologetically in his introduction to the work that "The account of the Jews is a fascinating farrago of truth and lies." We cannot expect, therefore, that any gratuitous credit would be given by Tacitus to the Jews beyond that which cannot be denied. Tacitus places the Belus area and glassmaking squarely within the province of the Jews:

> One of the rivers flowing into the Jewish Sea is the Belius, at whose mouth are sands which are collected and fused with natron to form glass. The beach concerned is small and yet inexhaustible whatever the quantities removed.[18]

Tacitus is, at least in this matter, in full accord with the Old Testament: "Zebulun shall dwell at the haven of the sea; and he shall be a haven of ships; and his border shall be unto Sidon" (Gen. 49:13). This is one of the Biblical references to the neighborly conjunction of the Hebrews with the Canaanites in this region, in which the Belus River area is assigned to the tribe of Zebulun and the contiguous and hinterland areas is assigned to the tribes of Zebulun, Asher, Naphthali and Dan.

In performing a benediction over the Belus River area, Moses predicted that "They shall profit from the abundance of the sea and from the treasures hidden in the sand."[19] The commentary of Tar. Jonathan on this passage expands on the relationship of the Canaanites and Jews to the Mosaic reference to the industries of the area: "Joy shall come, for they partake of the fishing and of the purple for the dying of their cloth, and of the sand for the making of mirrors and vessels of glass."[20] Another Midrashic explication of this passage relates that Zebulun complained to the Holy One, "Lord of the Universe, to my brethren you gave beautiful land, and to me you gave the sea. To my brethren you gave fields and vineyards, and to me you gave sand." To which the Holy One replied, "Yes, but did I not give you the snail? Did I not give you glass?"[21] Thus the tribe of Zebulun is not only credited in the Midrash with the production of glass but also with the operation of the purple dye industry, an occupation based upon boiling the royal color from the murex snails harvested from the area, a trade generally assigned to the "Purple People," that is, the so-called Phoenicians.

The tribes of Asher and Zebulun settled into an area which extended into the territory of the Canaanites as far as Tyre. In Joshua 19:27-29 the territory of the tribe of Asher is described as incorporating the Belus River estuary, for it is said that it "reacheth to Carmel westward" and extends "toward the north side...even unto great Sidon" and to "the strong city Tyre." It was from the busy port of Sidon that glassware was shipped in ancient times, and we are told by Benjamin of Tudela that the glassmaking industry of Tyre was still functioning in medieval times as an ancient, exclusively Jewish industry.

Flavius Josephus, in his "Description of Galilee, Samaria and Judea," places Carmel within Jewish Galilee until Roman times: "Now Phoenicia...[is] bounded towards the sunsetting (west) with the borders of the territory belonging to the Ptolemais, and by Carmel; which mountain had formerly belonged to the Galileans, but now belongs to the Tyrians."[22] Josephus proceeds to describe the valley between Ptolemais (Acre) and Carmel (Haifa) and the unique siliceous attributes of the sands found on the banks of the Belus:

> [Ptolemais] is a seaside town of Galilee, built on the edge of a great plain and shut in by mountains. To the east seven miles away is the Galilaean range; to the south is Carmel, fifteen miles distant; to the north is the highest range, called "The Ladder of Tyre" by the natives: the distance in this case is fifteen miles. About a quarter of a mile from the town flows the Beleus, a very tiny stream on whose banks is the tomb of Memnon. Near this is an area fifty yards wide which is of great interest; it is a round hollow which yields crystalline sand. A large number of ships put in and clear this out; but the place fills in again thanks to the winds, which as if on purpose blow into it common sand from the outside. This is at once converted by the mine into crystal. Still more wonderful, I think, is the fact that the crystal which overflows from the basin reverts to ordinary sand. A most wonderful spot.

Leaving the questionable geologic analysis of Josephus aside, we can affirm that the valley between Haifa and Tyre (Ptolemais or Sur) stretches for less than 25 miles along the sea and extends inland for a few miles to the arc of the Carmel range which presses the low-lying land against the sea. R. Campbell Thompson conjectures, somewhat circumspectly, that the other ancient name of the Belus River presently employed on Israeli maps, Na'amen, may have derived from the Sumerian *IM.MA.NA.*, which translates to "sand." Thompson reasons that the Sumerians may have purchased the sand from this very beach and quotes a Sumerian text in which such an association appears evident: "'The hero came to the sand....' To go a step further onto the domain of comparative philology (here again with great wariness and hesitation) we might note the similarity in sound between the Assyrian *immanaku, manaku,* and the Greek *ammokania,* a calcareous sand."[23]

A reasonable presumption to be drawn from Biblical and other ancient references is that Hebrew traders from such tribes as those of Zebulun, Naphthali Asher and Dan were associated with the seafaring Canaanites of Sidon and Tyre and that artisans from one or both of these tribes, the Galileans of whom Josephus wrote, were the glassmakers who mined the sand of the Belus beach and fired the furnaces in the Galilean hills which form the hinterland of the ports of Acre, Sidon and Tyre. That activity can be readily inferred from the passage in which Moses importunes the tribe of Zebulun to render thanks to the Lord for having blessed them with "the abundance of the seas, and of the treasures hid in the sand."

Whether these Jewish progenitors, the Canaanites among whom they settled or, as it seems likely from the record, both peoples, provided the glassmakers of that time is difficult to determine, but it was the Jews who, by virtue of their stubborn religious and temporal intransigence, were uprooted and dispersed, and were the ones who eventually implanted the art of glassmaking throughout the then-known world.

Josephus further relates that the Carmel range "adjoins Gaba, which is called the City of Horsemen,' because it was the city in which retired Jewish cavalrymen settled."[24] The kibbutzim surrounding the ruins of Gaba, and, in fact, throughout this formerly forested area of both Upper and Lower Galilee, are plowing up the scoria of glassmaking furnaces dating far back into antiquity. A great variety of ancient glass objects was also unearthed from the tells of the great ancient cities of Galilee, Samaria and Judea; the oldest of these artifacts provide easily recognizable evidence of the Akkadian origin of the subjects and techniques involved. They include items obviously related to the temple offerings at the Ishtar temple at Nuzi and to other Akkadian sites, objects such as the sun-disc pendant, and figurines of the exotic Goddess Ishtar (Astarte) herself. The appearance of such items in the middle of the second millennium links the glassmaking industry of the Levantine coast to the Semites.

The period of invasions by the Warrior Pharaohs brought about a decline and eventually the end of glassmaking in Egypt but it did not affect the stability of the art in Canaan. A decline of the art in Canaan did, however, follow the incursions of the so-called Sea-Peoples, a period in which the economy of the entire region suffered a severe setback. The settlement of the Israelites in the hills of Canaan reversed this trend and signaled the dawn of a new age, the Age of Iron, which laid the foundation for the revitalization of the ancient art.

# NOTES

1. Professor George F. Bass, "Civilization Under the Sea," *Modern Maturity*, April-May 1989, p. 60.

2. Cemal Pulak, "Excavations in Turkey: 1988 Campaign," *INA Newsletter*, vol. 15; no. 4, December 1988, p. 15.

3. George F. Bass, "A Bronze Age Shipwreck at Ulu Burun: 1984 Campaign," *AJA*, 90 (1986), p. 287.

4. George Bass, Ibid., 1986, p. 282, referring to "Na'aman, Economic Aspects of the Egyptian Occupation of Canaan," *IEJ*, 31, 1981, p. 175. Dr. Bass points out that "the weights of the 'raw glass' in the El Amarna tablets are given as 30 (EA 323:16), 50 (EA 327:10) and 100 (EA 148:8), but we do not know of which ancient units these were multiples. Actual weights of Ulu Burun glass ingots salvaged to date are 2607, 2343, 2182, 2173, 2095, 2003, 1895, 1873, 1818, 1804, 1796, 1762, 1724, 1627, and 1597 gm." Other references by Bass: J. A. Knudtzon, *Die El-Amarna-Tafeln* (Aalen, 1964, reprint of 1915 edition) 770,776, 484; S. A. B. Mercer, *The Tell el-Amarna Tablets*, Toronto, 1939).

5. George F. Bass, Ibid., 1986, p. 282. Bass notes that this was a report of 3 December 1985, and that "Brill does not assume that the Ulu Burun ingots are from the Syro-Palestinian coast. On 2 January 1985 he informed me that 'the chemical composition of the glasses made in Egypt during the 18th Dynasty is well known....The glasses from 'Mesopotamia and Iran,' or perhaps western Asia in general, are of a different chemical type."

6. Cemal Pulak, "The Bronze Age Shipwreck at Ulu Burun, Turkey: 1985 Campaign." *American Journal of Archeology*, January 1988, p. 14.

7. Description of objects on display at the Bodrum museum.

8. M. Seefried, "Les Pendentifs en Verre Faconnes sur Noyau du Musee National du Bardo et du Musee National de Carthage," *Karthago*, XVII, 1973-74, pp. 37-66.

9. Contemporary European orientation, however, inverts the direction of the "sunset" i.e., West, to the direction of the sunrise, the "Levant" (literally: rising), i.e., "East" and it is from the western perspective that we view the area. The word "orientation" literally: "looking toward the East" curiously indicates the direction from which knowledge is derived.

10. G. Ernest Wright, *Biblical Archeology*, 1957\79, p. 109.

11. Ray Winfield Smith, "Mediterranean Glass from the Beginnings to the First Century B. C.," *Bulletin of the First International Congress on Glass* 1959, pp. 37-38.

12. Strabo, *Geog.*, XVI, ii, 25.

13. Anita Engles, "The Elder Pliny and the River," *Readings in Glass History*, no. 3, 1974, p. 3, citing L. Kadmon, *The Coins of Akko-Ptolemais*, Jerusalem, 1961.

14. Pliny, *Natural History*, p. 190.

15. Harden, Ibid., p. 22.

16. Marcus Retter, in a letter to the *New York Times*, Feb. 2, 1984.

17. Flavius Josephus, *Against Apion*, pp. 161, 167.

18. Tacitus, *The Histories*, book 5:5, p. 8.

19. Deuteronomy 33:19. This book was probably written in the seventh century B.C.E. and reflects the ancient traditions of the time.

20. See also L. Ginsberg, *Legends of the Jews*, vol. 3, 459.

21. Anita Engles, "3,000 Years of Glassmaking," *Readings in Glass History*, I, 1973, pp. 6,7.

22. Josephus, *The Wars of the Jews*, Ch. III, p. 225.

23. C. Campbell Thompson, *On the Chemistry of the Ancient Assyrians*, 1925, p. 14.

24. Josephus, *Wars*, ch. III, p. 225.

A HEAD-BEAD OR PENDANT, MID 5TH-4TH CENTURY BCE. Eye-beads and headbeads of characteristic types trace back to Mesopotamian origins and became an integral part of Mediteranean trade. Head-beads were consistently of a Semitic type, similar to that of sculptures dating back to the 3rd millennium BCE Akkadia.

*Photograph courtesy of The Corning Museum of Glass.*

# CHAPTER 5

# THE IRON AGE

## *The Israelite Connection*

THE CROSSROADS OF CANAAN BECAME AN AREA OF CONTENTION BETWEEN THE surrounding powers with the erosion of the hegemony of the Egyptian overlords in the area. Struggles with the Hittites and the Amorites, the incursions of the Sea-Peoples and others all contributed to unstable conditions and to a hiatus in technological development; stagnation continued until the reemergence of local control spurred the dramatic birth of a new, progressive era. The new seminal era unfolded in the latter half of thirteenth century B.C.E., the very period attributed Biblically and archeologically to the settlement of the Israelite refugees onto the hills of Canaan. Two outstanding events were instrumental in transforming the character of civilization: one was the efflorescence of alphabetic writing, which first appeared during the reign of the Semitic kings over Egypt, the much-maligned Hyksos, forecasting a revolutionary surge in communication and in the transference of knowledge. The second event was the proliferation of advanced pyro-technology and metallurgy which ushered in the Iron Age. We quote from the writings of William G. Dever, a brilliant archeologist who, far from following Biblical lore, renounced even the use of the term "Biblical archeology" as being scientifically unjustifiable.[1] Dever, adhering to strict archeological evidence, identifies the advent of the Iron Age with that of the establishment of "hundreds of small unwalled" Israelite villages of the late thirteenth-twelfth centuries:

The economy of these Iron I villages was largely self-sufficient, based mainly

111

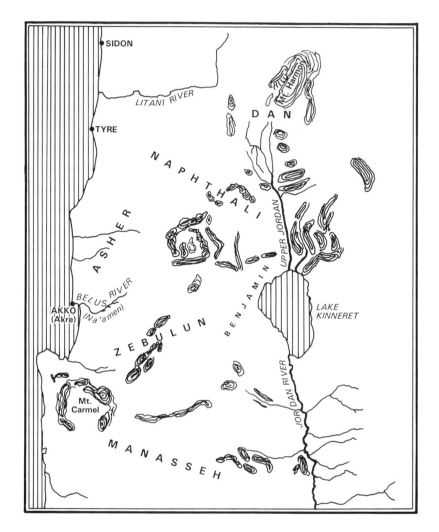

## SETTLEMENT OF ISRAELITE TRIBES IN NORTHERN CANAAN

The Belus area was Biblically assigned to the tribes of Asher and Zebulun; there they were to "profit from the abundance of the sea and from treasures derived from the sand." Purple dye was produced from regional mollusks ("the abundance of the sea") and the Belus beach sands were considered so essential for glass production that they were mined and shipped for the purpose to Roman Italy after glassmaking was introduced at the beginning of the Common Era. The Naphthali tribe spread through the heavily forested hinterland and the Danites later moved into its heights. Benjaminite smiths, the Rechabites, roamed the heavy forests. The region was convenient to the ports from which Canaanite ("Phoenician") vessels departed on commercial voyages around the Mediterranean.

on small-scale but intensive terrace-farming, with some admixture of livestock herding and primitive "cottage industry"....I believe we may safely conclude that these new Iron I sites represent the first *archeological* evidence we have had of one phase of the Israelite settlement in Palestine. I believe these are the very early Israelite villages described typically in the Book of Judges.[2]

The view that the Israelites evolved in some measure from the body of lower-class Canaanite society and not entirely from immigrants from Egypt is a postulate rejected only by fundamentalists. The existence of Canaanite ferric technology is, however, compellingly confirmed in the Book of Judges even to the satisfaction of the fundamentalists. The Canaanite army had no less than 900 such iron chariots at their disposal, they were nevertheless ignominiously defeated with the Lord's assistance and the counsel of the prophetess Deborah who "judged Israel at that time."[3] The Old Testament also attests unmistakably to the fact that the Israelites had smiths in their midst. In Isaiah 44:12 the smith is among the workmen castigated for forging graven images of iron with hammers and tongs "with the strength of his arms."

Both ironsmithing and glassmaking were known and had been practiced for over 1000 years prior to the Israelite settlement into the hills of Canaan; it was the proliferation of that technology which characterized a new age and not its invention. The Jews and their progenitors were always at the core of the civilizations among whom ironmaking and its corollary, glassmaking - pyrotechnology, existed. There exist, nevertheless, mavericks who persist in denying that any Israelite entity existed at all during the time of Judges. "Such scholars have to find some other explanation for the emergence of a network of new settlements in the hill country of Palestine [sic] during Iron Age I," points out the Israeli archeologist, Amihai Mazar, and adds in emphasis that: "During the preceding Late Bronze Age, when the Canaanite culture was at its peak, such settlements were unknown."[4]

What has all this to do with the art of glassmaking? Inherent to ferric technology is the primary requisite for the production of glass, the pneumatically drafted furnace. It cannot be expected that those among the Israelites who wery privy to the knowledge of the other requisites of the vitric arts would be greatly concerned with the production of glass objects at this formative period of Israelite society. The market for such products was among the very wealthy and powerful and life in the Israelite communities was of necessity simple during the formative period of Israelite society. One can expect no more from a newly evolving culture in the process of liberation and recovery from either the trauma of Egyptian domination, from feudal oppression, or from both, whichever variations of the models of Israelite development one chooses to accept.

Nevertheless the metallurgical, and by inference the technological, acumen of the occupants of the proliferating Israelite villages of Canaan attained the highest level which civilization had reached anywhere on earth at that time. This statement clearly contradicts the commonly held conception that the Israelites were or stemmed from nomadic Bedouins who rode into Canaan on the backs of camels with a few scraggly goats following after them. This misconception is maintained by pseudo-historians, who employ it out of ignorance or as a demeaning and obscurantist image, irrespective of the fact that such a representation has long since been shown to be false. Biblical representations, archeological recoveries, ethnological research, and documentary evidence do not support the image so blithely repeated, widely disseminated and commonly believed. This misconception must be dealt with in order to comprehend how it was that such a people became privy to the pyrotechnical and chemical secrets of the art and science of making glass; how it was that they became the ones to carry that difficult discipline into the Diaspora.

The Jews stemmed from a civilization which had first domesticated wild grains; a civilization which had first made use of the wheel; a civilization which had first passed from the age of copper and stone into the age of bronze and from that to the age of iron. Where, then, does the persistent characterization of the patriarchal Hebrews as desert-dwelling Bedouins spring from? The concept cannot be educed from Biblical lore; it is contravened at the outset of Genesis, and contradicted at every successive stage of the unfolding account.

"Abel was a keeper of sheep, but Cain was a tiller of the ground." Husbandry and agronomy are thus registered as the primary occupations of the first of the Hebraic progenitors. Cain, the farmer, was not content with a simple agricultural society. Indeed, "he builded a city and called the name of the city, after the name of his son, Enoch." We are forthwith introduced to Jubal, who "was the father of all such as handle the harp and organ" and to Tubal-Cain, who "was an instructor of every artificer in brass and iron." The pyrotechnical capability of the progenitors of the Jews is thus established at the very outset of the Old Testament. The deep-rooted tradition of

Hebrew pyrotechnology may very well have been passed on into the classical age with the transliteration of Tubal-Cain into *Vulcan.* No other root for the name of the god of fire is known.[5]

We then meet Nimrud, "a mighty hunter before the Lord," who constructed a complex of cities and created a kingdom. "And the beginning of his kingdom was Babel and Erech and Akkad and Calneh, in the land of Shinar. The Biblical text zeros in on Shem, whose name is the eponym of the coined term "Semites." Shem's sons settled in Shinar and "said to one another, 'Go to, let us make brick, and burn them thoroughly.' And they had brick for stone, and slime had they for mortar. And they said, 'Go to, let us build a city and a tower, whose top may reach into heaven.'"

Thus, according to the Old Testament, the descendants of Shem, the so-called Semites, not only built sturdy structures of mortar and brick in Ur, not only did they erect an entire city which became the capital of Shinar (Sumer), not only did they construct a skyscraping ziggurat, but it is thereafter recorded that they remained resident in that metropolis for nine whole generations. It is in the city of Ur that we encounter the father of Abraham, Terach, patriarch of the tribe. It is in this urban context that the Hebrews appear upon the proscenium of Biblical history.

Nor are the Jews depicted as having been farmers in Egypt; they were, indeed, the builders of cities: "And they built for pharaoh treasure cities, Pithom and Raamses." They were among the stone masons, bricklayers, smiths, carpenters, weavers, lapidarists and all the other skilled artisans who had erected the structures, sculpted the statues and produced the appurtenances which collectively constituted the ambience of the noble courts; they were among the musicians, dancers and scribes who generated the cultural environment enjoyed in those courts.

Archeologists are at loggerheads in the reading of the relics of this period. The fact that a new cultural entity, the Israelites, came into being and to dominate a large portion of Canaan during the twelfth century B.C.E. is undisputed and is assumed in all the various models of Israelite settlement now extant, but the conquest of various cities of Canaan by the Israelites is judged by some archeologists to be inconsistent with the Biblical chronology of that conquest; nor did every city cited as having been "destroyed" by the Israelites appear to have undergone devastation at that time. Promulgators of "archeological centrism" were quick to question the accuracy of the Biblical account, a judgment often based on the unwarranted assumption that raw archeological information available at any time is both pervasive and infallible. This opinionated position, incisively termed by Baruch Halpern as "negative fundamentalism."[6] is promulgated by those who, a priori, reject conclusions based on faith, but whose own conclusions have been toppled time and time again by unforeseen discoveries.

Three main schools of interpretation of the archeological data accumulated from the various sites said to have been destroyed by the immigrant Israelites are now current; each broaches another "model" of how the Israelite entity came into existence.[7] The "conquest model," upheld by William Albright and followed to a great extent by Yigael Yadin and others, parallels the Old Testament by assuming that the Israelites settled into Canaan by conquest more or less as given in the Old Testament.

The alternate "infiltration" model proposes that the Israelites, in the main, settled peacefully in unoccupied areas. Professor Yohanan Aharoni, another of Israel's distinguished archeologists, proposes this model, which is expounded in terms of an infiltration of the land by pastoral (some still employ the term "nomadic") and other peoples who migrated into Canaan to become a sedentary people. According to Professor Aharoni, the process of settlement and expansion took place over a period of some 200 years, "and in its wake a mighty population revolution was brought about, unparalleled in the history of the country....The occupational center of gravity passed from the valleys to the hill country, which was henceforth the center of Israelite life down to the end of the monarchy."[8]

The third theory, dubbed the "peasant's revolt" model, is a variation of the second; it postulates the revolt of peasants against feudal Canaanite overlords. The social and religious revolution which ensued attracted and was associated with the arrival of some immigrants and resulted in the institution of a new sociological entity. "The shift from Canaan to Israel was primarily...a shift from hierarchic urban government to tribal self-management, with a corresponding transformation in religious forms, from many gods supporting the hierarchic state to one God bringing tribal peoples to birth and defending their new social system," explains Norman Gottwald, and adds, "The basic division was not between agriculture and nomadism but between centralized, stratified and elitist cities, on the one hand, and the non-statist, egalitarian countryside on the other."[9]

Each model is consistent with a portion of the known archeological record; each has its fervent protagonists and there are, in addition, archeologists who combine compatible elements of each of the three models to produce variations of the themes. Yigael Yadin emphasizes that, while he does not look upon the Old Testament as being without error, "archeology has increased my belief that basically the historical parts of the Bible are true...I think archeology has actually given me, if you ask me subjectively, a greater respect for the Bible."[10]  Yadin wrote that he approaches a dig with a spade in one hand and a Bible in the other, an attitude reflecting that of Albright, Petrie and other such early diggers of ancient rubble.  Yadin's excavations at Hazor produced the evidence which justified his confidence; Hazor's ashes provided clear testimony to the accuracy of the Biblical record concerning the fate which Hazor suffered.  Yadin's viewpoint is shared by many of those who--whatever model of Israelite settlement they prefer to follow, and while rejecting an overly fundamentalist, literal interpretation of Biblical lore--nevertheless recognize the value of the Old Testament as a historical record.  The inconsistencies are often found to lie more in interpretation of the Old Testament than from evidence derived from the remains of civilizations, or rather, from evidence not found in those remains, i.e., negative proofs.

The existence of the Israelites as a viable cultural entity in the twelfth century B.C.E. can no longer reasonably be questioned; in addition to an overwhelming quantity and assortment of artifactual evidence, Israel's existence is positively attested to scripturally outside of the Old Testament by such relics as a stela erected by the pharaoh Merneptah in Egypt about 1208 B.C.E. in the fifth year of his reign.[11]  The inscription on the stela boasts of the pharaoh's military prowess in typical self-aggrandizing pharaonic terms.  In the coda of the inscription the pharaoh recounts, with conspicuous pharaonic hyperbole, how he ruined Libya, pacified the Hittites, captured Ashkelon, conquered Gezer, despoiled all of Canaan, laid waste Israel, desolated the Israelites of their offspring and turned "Kharu (Canaan) into a widow" for Egypt.  Merneptah's prognostication regarding Israelite continuity manifestly proved to be wishful thinking, but his scriptural expostulations led some fundamentalists to assume that Merneptah was, per force, the pharaoh of the Exodus.  The excitement engendered by the subsequent discovery of his mummified body on the west bank of the Nile near Deir el-Bahri was tempered by the disconcerting fact that he could not therefore have been drowned in the Red Sea!  The existence of the children of Israel as a cohesive entity in the thirteenth century B.C.E. was, however, rendered incontrovertible by the existence of his contemporary stela, and the credibility of the Old Testament was enhanced.

Whether one wishes to take the Biblical account at its literal word or not, overwhelming archeological data makes it abundantly clear that by the end of the twelfth century B.C.E. hundreds of well-established Israelite villages existed; a conclusion to which the proponents of the various models of Israelite settlement are inevitably and conjunctively drawn. It is not necessary to choose between the various interpretations of how the Israelite communities of Canaan came into existence for the purposes of the present thesis; it is sufficient to note that all agree that, however it came about, the turn of the twelfth century B.C.E. witnessed the birth in Canaan of a new era of human development, the Iron Age, and that the Israelites appeared on the scene coincident with this revolutionary development. Whatever deviant paths are taken to arrive at the period of identifiable Israelite settlement in Canaan, they all converge into agreement about the coincidence of the Iron Age with that event.

The villages surrounding Ai, the second city said to have been taken forcibly by the Israelites in their conquest of Canaan and the heart of Israelite settlement, provide convincing evidence of the agronomic and industrial sophistication of the Israelites. While no evidence has yet been turned up which would verify the military aspect of that event (a negative proof employed by the critics of the Biblical rendition), the surrounding hills are proliferate with evidence of a multiplicity of Israelite villages established during that very period. Typical of Israelite dwellings of the time and region is a house occupied by the family of Ahilud in the ancient neighboring village of Khirbut Raddana. A storage jar handle turns up in the excavation of this house on which Ahilud's own name is inscribed in old Hebrew script.[12] The handle socket of an iron mattock was also found in Ahilud's house, both of which objects thus attest to the existence in the same house of the twin aspects of Iron Age sophistication, iron smithing and alphabetic literacy.

A variety of other tanged and hafted bronze tools and weapons and a well-worn grinding stone found at Raddana and Ai and at other such centers of Israelite habitation attest silently but convincingly to a well-developed and widespread cottage industry in which villagers imported metal ingots and wrought them into agricultural and other tools. The self-sufficiency demonstrated by the local production of such objects suggests that they were unavailable to the hilltop communities from the surrounding peoples, and that the Israelites, who arrived with the required knowledge, were constrained to produce metal, and most unusual for the times, iron tools for themselves. The incidence of Israelite iron tools through the twelfth century is not substantial, to be sure, but it is widespread. An iron plow blade was found at Gibeah of Saul (Tell el-Ful); two iron sickles of the tenth century B.C.E. were unearthed at Beer-Sheba; a sickle was one of the two iron artifacts recovered from Tel Masos dated between the thirteenth and the tenth centuries B.C.E. At Megiddo a blacksmith's workshop from the Solomonic period was identified together with a considerable hoard of iron artifacts; hoes; plowshares; goads; sickles; spearhead; shovels; chisels; knives; rings; nails and materials identified as iron ore, slag and ash[13] an iron-working facility which bespoke a tradition of iron working and marks the onset of a widespread use of iron implements.[14] The evidence of the development of iron making as an industry in the Israelite areas of Canaan is reinforced by the fact that after 1200 B.C.E. the finds of iron artifacts increase dramatically and exceed the number of iron artifacts from all other areas.[15] At Taanach, at a time contemporary with the Megiddo blacksmithing facility, an intensive investigation of a group of iron artifacts "with a *terminus ante quem* of ca. 925 B.C....was studied metallurgically." It was determined that, by the end of that period, iron-making technology in the area included the process of the carburization of iron into steel, the final elaboration of iron-manufacturing technology and the climax of the Iron Age. "[The evidence] suggests that steel was being consciously produced by the tenth century B.C."[16]

Familiarity with ferric pyrotechnology is reflected in a passage of the Old Testament in which Egypt is metaphorically alluded to recurrently as a [fierce and fiery] furnace of iron from which the Israelites were rescued.[17] An intimate Biblical knowledge of metallurgy is discernible in a reference to Canaan as "a land whose stones are iron, and out of whose hills thou mayest dig copper." Copper is extracted by underground mining whereas iron is smelted from surface stones.

A survey of settlements in Judea and Samaria during Iron Age I--the period when Ahilud lived--reveals that the hill country was literally covered by small villages like those at Ai and Raddana. Of 102 sites identified, some 90 were newly founded....Characteristically, the villages were unfortified and occupied by apparently peace-loving people. In fact, one reason they relocated in an inhospitable environment that had not previously supported anyone was to escape the better-equipped inhabitants of the more fertile lowlands.[18]

This modern appraisal of the hundreds of Israelite settlements as being essentially unfortified, peaceful communities in which the Israelites, by and large, mixed and associated with the peoples of the region, is fully in accord with the Old Testament. Israelite settlement resolved into a mutually advantageous and often respectful relationship with Canaanite neighbors in which an exchange of expertise was bound to take place. Chapter 1 of Judges summarizes the gregarious aspect of the second stage of Israelite settlement: "And it came to pass, when Israel was strong, that they put the Canaanites to tribute and did not utterly drive them out." To make the history of this developing relationship clear, a multiplicity of examples are cited, in which virtually every one of the Israelite tribes pursued positive and peaceful alternatives which led to a loose amalgamation of the two peoples, a relationship which continued almost uninterrupted from that time forward.

The children of the Kenite, Moses' father-in-law, it is written, left Jericho together with the children of Judah to dwell south of Arad

> ...among the people....The children of Abraham did not drive out the Jebusites that inhabited Jerusalem, but the Jebusites dwell with the children of Benjamin in Jerusalem unto this day....Neither did Manasseh drive out the inhabitants of Beth-Shean and her towns, nor Taanach and her towns, nor the inhabitants of Ibeam and her towns, nor the inhabitants of Megiddo and her towns, but the Canaanites would dwell in that land...Neither did Zebulun drive out the inhabitants of Kitron, nor the inhabitants of Nahalol, but the Canaanites dwelt among them, and became tributaries.

The same process held true for the tribe of Asher with the inhabitants of Akko, Sidon, Ahlab, Achzib, Helbah, Aphik and Rhob, for "the Asherites dwelt among the Canaanites." A permanent and peaceful association also held true for the tribe of Naphthali "which dwelt among the Canaanites" of Beth-shemesh and Beth-abnath, who became "tributaries unto them," and it held for the tribe of Dan, whose association with the Amorites was somewhat more tenuous. "Yet the hand of the house of Joseph prevailed, so that they [the Amorites] became tributaries."(Judges 1:21-35)

Thus, the associations between the Jews and the Canaanites in and around the area of the Belus River, along the coast to Tyre and inland to the forests and mountains referred to by the historians of the Roman era are well warranted to have been peaceful and cooperative. The tribes of Asher, Zebulun, Naphthali and Dan, the four Israelite tribes which were located in the very area in which glassmaking is attested, are the very ones specifically selected as having an ongoing symbiotic relationship with the contiguous Canaanites of the area.

The mixture of the peoples led to trouble for the Israelite Yahweh worshipers, of course, inasmuch as the idol worship (and in particular that of Astarte) of the indigenous Canaanites rubbed off on the Israelites and caused considerable grief. That aspect of Biblical historiography is not germane to our thesis, however, and we shall defer to another much-quoted but erroneous interpretation of a single Biblical phrase taken out of context and employed for the construction of a popular theory which holds that the knowledge of iron manufacture was nonexistent among the Israelites but practiced by the invading Sea-Peoples, the Philistines: "Now there was no smith found throughout all the land of Israel...." It is interesting that those archeologists who are most obdurately opposed to the acceptance of Biblical evidence are the very ones who most avidly quote this passage, ignore the explication which follows and the context within which the phrase is set. The rest of the truncated sentence reads: "for the Philistines said, lest the Hebrews make them swords or spears." Thus the Philistines were well aware of the metalworking capabilities of the Israelites and, being at that time in the conqueror's seat, either removed the smiths or prohibited them from carrying on their trade. The next few paragraphs then explain the circumstances of the prohibition, and the limit of its application:

> But all the Israelites went down to the Philistines, to sharpen every man his share, and his coulter, and his mattock. Yet they had a file for the mattocks, and for the coulters, and for the forks, and for the axes, and to sharpen the goads. So it came to pass in the day of battle, that there was neither sword nor spear found in the hand of any of the people who were with Saul and Jonathan; but with Saul and with Jonathan his son was there found.[19]

Many facts emerge from this compact passage; the Israelites were cited as being already in possession of a large quantity and varied assortment of metal agricultural tools which, we are led to conclude, they had previously manufactured; the Philistine's prohibition against the conduct of metalworking was intended solely to preclude the manufacture and maintenance of military metal gear by a people capable of that manufacture, and not to inhibit the necessary sharpening and upkeep of farming and other tools; while the Philistines attempted to limit the ability of the Israelites to produce weapons by insisting that even the sharpening of pre-existing tools be performed under their eyes, a pointed allusion is inserted which confirms that the Israelites did possess sharpening devices, and evidently continued to utilize them; the Israelite forces joining Saul and Jonathan who were hiding out on Mount Ephraim are excepted from the weaponless people under Philistine control; the Israelites are thereafter recurrently described as being well armed. It is also related that "the Hebrews that were with the Philistines before that time, which went up with them into the camp from the country about, even they turned to be with the Israelites that were with Saul and Jonathan"[20].

Archeological evidence could not be more supportive of a diametrically opposite conclusion to that drawn by those who assign an ironworking capability to the Philistines and deny such a capability to the Israelites. To the embarrassment of the proponents of the tenuous theory constructed on a single Biblical phrase taken out of context, not a shred of evidence can be found which supports the ironworking propensities of any of the Sea-Peoples prior to their appearance on the Levantine coast. In addition, no evidence exists which indicates that the Philistines developed such a capability soon after their incursion into lower Canaan. No evidence of iron manufacture exists in any early Philistine site. The rare iron artifacts found in a Philistine environment were clearly nothing more than imports intended to serve as jewelry or for ceremonial purposes and not for weapons or tools. In Ashdod, the Philistine capital, a site which was extensively excavated, not a single iron implement was found in the early Philistine strata. At near by Tel Qasila, one of the few Philistine sites where a few iron objects were found, none appear until the end of the eleventh century; an iron bracelet then appears, but of the same type recovered from even earlier Israelite sites. Yohanan Ahorani describes the bracelet as a throwback to "a phenomenon noted in Israelite I, when the new metal was rare and costly, serving mainly for jewelry." In the excavation of an earlier temple, however, an iron blade with an ivory handle was found; it was obviously intended for ceremonial use, and was of a type similar to ones imported into Cyprus and the Aegean area. "It is precisely such an exceptional find that testifies how greatly iron was regarded as a precious and rare metal."[21]

The above-cited team of investigators of the iron artifacts from Taanach, in the process of placing the results of their analyses alongside archeological and historical material from all areas of the eastern Mediterranean, did a thorough investigation of the few iron artifacts recovered from Philistine sites. Whereas "the results suggest that by the late 10th century blacksmiths supplying northern Palestine [sic] were able to produce carburized iron (steel)," they note with considerable conviction, "complementary studies of iron artifacts from Philistine sites did not reveal such consistent technical achievements." The four signatories to the report on the Taanach investigations came to the conclusion that: "There is no convincing evidence for iron production from Philistine sites," and wryly add, "and very little for copper production."[22] We must assume that, likewise, these Aegean invaders were completely lacking the capability of making glass.

The Israelite villagers of the pre-Solomonic period did not only exhibit metallurgic competence but architectural and agronomic expertise attested to by the modest but well-designed new types of housing they introduced into the area, and by the well-ordered terracing on which cereals (and eventually vines, nuts, and olives) were grown. A high degree of autonomy of the villagers, an amicable communal inter-relationship, and an advanced technological knowledge is amply demonstrated by the type and proliferation of cisterns serving the community. The cisterns were of a sophisticated type, new to the area and were the product of many centuries of development. An interconnecting complex of three cisterns, for example, was found under two houses of Ai to which access was easily gained through a cistern cap which formed part of the floor of the houses, thus providing the inhabitants an "almost inexhaustible water supply." The other archeological evidence accumulated from these villages similarly indicates a clear pattern of independence, which Callaway, the excavator of Ahilud's house, characterizes as "isolationist and highly individualistic." Callaway then adds in emphasis that this may explain why it was so difficult to establish a monarchy, for: "From the beginning, Israel was self-sufficient, family-centered and characteristically independent."[23]

The city-state society which was a distinguishing feature of the so-called Second Intermediate Period was reconstituted in Canaan by the Israelites. A proliferation of autonomous regional urban centers, each of which controlled a limited hinterland, associated themselves into a confederation similar to that which had existed in the period prior to that of the Warrior Pharaohs. The

Old Testament reflects the anti-royalist predilection of these independent Iron Age Israelite peoples in no uncertain terms, an attitude which carried over into and past the Solomonic period and has remained a cardinal Judaic bias throughout Jewish history. "In those days there was no king in Israel; every man did what was right in his own eyes."[24]

The second great thrust forward into a new stage of civilization which took place at this critical juncture of history was the proliferation of alphabetic writing, the earliest record of which was found at Serabit al-Khadem in the western Sinai. Semitic-speaking slaves were put to work in the remote desert turquoise mines by the Egyptians soon after control by the Semitic chiefs was shattered and Egypt and Canaan was subjugated to the Theban nomarchic rule. There is no doubt that the redactors of the inscriptions were the Semites, and not the Egyptians, for much of the graffiti scrawled over the rock surfaces near the mines was addressed to Semitic deities, among whom the favored ones appear to have been El and his consort Elath (Astarte). The content of the messages certifies the cultural pedigree and marks the status of the inscribers: "Oh, my God" reads a plea from an erudite Semitic slave, "rescue me from the interior of the mine!"[25]

It was the great Sir William M. Flinders Petrie who had first come across fragments dated before 1600 B.C.E. on which these Proto-Sinaitic inscriptions appear.[26] Some 22 characters composed the parallel ancient Hebrew alphabet (properly *aleph-bet*), a group of symbols which heralded a new age of literacy, an *abecedary* which has formed and has remained the familiar basis for all of the Western writing systems to the present time. Such an "abecedary" was found in an Israelite storage pit at Izbet Sartah,[27] dated to about 1200 B.C.E., the beginning of the period of Judges and probably within a generation of the establishment of the presumed Israelite settlements. The text of five lines appears to have been written by two persons; the last line is composed of all 22 letters of the Hebrew aleph-bet and was evidently written by a student practicing to write it.[28] Universal literacy had become feasible. The aleph-bet was born.

Examples of proto-Canaanite alphabetic inscriptions appeared throughout the area of Israelite settlement at Megiddo, Shechem, Beth-shemesh, Lachish, Gezer and elsewhere. Among the peoples who assayed the literatic leap into the future were those who were simultaneously familiar with Akkadian, as cuneiform tablets unearthed in Hazor and elsewhere attest.[29] The Old Testament takes the literacy of the immigrating Israelites for granted. In

Joshua 18:6, for example, Joshua instructed that three men from each tribe be dispatched to "describe the land into seven parts, and bring the descriptions hither to me." It is this propensity for the written word that has distinguished the Jews throughout history. "Israel was extraordinary," proclaims Norman Gottwald, "in being the one socially revolutionary people in the ancient Near East to produce a literature and to survive as a distinctive cultural and religious entity."[30]

The people of the hills, the Israelites, therefore, stemmed from an ancient Mesopotamian culture and carried that culture and technology to new levels of sophistication. Glass artifacts with classic Mesopotamian motifs reappeared in Canaan along with the florescence of the Iron Age. Nude Astarte-type plaques, disc pendants and spacer beads, and other molded blue glass artifacts, frequently found together across the arc of the Fertile Crescent in such sites as Nuzi, Mari, Alalakh, Ebla and Hama, have been recovered from Hazor, Megiddo, Beth Shean, Jerusalem, Lachish and Tel Mevorakh (northern Sharon, Israel).[31] Core-formed vessels dating from the sixteenth to the thirteenth centuries were found at Alalakh, and fragments of a glass beaker of a similar type were retrieved from Megiddo.[32]

Archeological sites on Cyprus, Crete, Rhodes, southern Greece and Anatolia have yielded core-formed vessels and a host of other glass artifacts of the period which were formerly attributed to Egyptian manufacture and which now, clearly, must be re-assigned to Canaan, or at the very least, to have been produced from glass made in Canaan. Anomalous characteristics of these items has led to much dispute over their real origin. "Some of the types of these dark blue glass objects occur at Nuzu [sic] and elsewhere in Mesopotamia, and on Palestinian [sic] sites, but none is found in Egypt."[33] The fact that pomegranates and a uniform group of blue-glass Astarte figures are prominent among the artifacts found stamps the makers as Semitic and the provenance as Canaan or Mesopotamia rather than Egypt, for neither the fertility goddess nor pomegranates were native to Egypt.

The chronology of the appearance of glassmaking in and disappearance from Egypt leads conveniently into all three models of Israelite settlement into Canaan, whether that settlement came about entirely, partly or minimally as a result of an exodus from Egypt of a body of skilled Semitic workmen who had been enslaved in the New Kingdom. It is understandable that the first period of the Israelite settlement in Canaan was hardly conducive to the production of exotic, expensive glass artifacts; they were a luxury product

CORE-FORMED POMEGRANATE VESSEL, 14TH-13TH CENTURY BCE. Such vessels were found in Cyprus and are similar to the more ancient examples from Akkadian Mesopotamia. The appearance of pomegranate vessels, head-beads and eye-beads mark the penetration of Canaanite commerce across the Mediterranean. The use of the pomegranate as Jewish cultural design motif stems back to the Book of Genesis, in which such use is specified and it continued as a element of Jewish artifacts and architecture of the first Temple Period.
*Photograph courtesy of The Corning Museum of Glass.*

reserved for royalty and "persons of special distinction. Since the departing Jews did not belong to this strata of society," wryly notes Frederic Neuberg, "it is hardly likely that they took any glass objects on their wanderings."[34] For the same reason it is hardly likely that the Israelites would immediately turn to the production of glassware for their own use, but rather to the production of the iron and bronze tools and of the agricultural paraphernalia which are precisely the types of objects which have been found.

The cargo of the ship wrecked off Ulu Burun and other evidence, however, indicates that glass cullet was a valuable export product and its manufacture an important industry of the region which carried on into the Roman period. We learn of that activity from Roman sources, the earliest written mention of the industry. The period of Canaanite and Mesopotamian decline which ensued after the imposition of Egyptian rule, the subsequent demise of the Babylonian Kassite Dynasty, the general decline of Assyrian civilization, the invasion of the Sea-Peoples and other factors brought about a diminution of the production of glass throughout the Middle East. But the art never disappeared; the sophisticated pyrotechnology which the Israelite people possessed lent itself to the revitalization of glassware production. As the Iron Age generated momentum in the hills of Canaan and as Israelite society became entrenched and evolved into sovereign nationhood, objects of glass reappear. The new crop of glass artifacts are simpler in decoration and adapted more to utility and to ritual purposes than to lavishness. A jug recovered from Lachish is an example of this new category of glassware. It is decorated with a palm leaf design, the leaves attractively arranged on either side of a vertical branch. The palm leaf pattern thereafter reoccurs continuously in Israelite art as one of its standard motifs. Glass rods bearing the same type of ornamentation and topped with a representation of a pomegranate were found at Hazor and at Megiddo; these were evidently some sort of ritual scepters.

The utilitarian application of glass during this period is well illustrated by the production of glass cosmetic palettes. These shallow bowls were more commonly made in stone or faience and employed from the eighth through the early sixth centuries B.C.E. in the grinding and mixing of cosmetic pigments as indicated by a pestle found at Hazor in close proximity to such a palette.[35] A number of glass versions of these thick-walled, cast, glass palettes have been obtained from private dealers from areas like Shechem, Samaria and one was found at the excavation of Megiddo in a stratum which also included two faience palettes.[36] The use of these special items seems to have ceased after the Assyrian incursion, although a few scattered examples have turned up farther afield in a later Achaemenid and Hellenistic periods.

The resurgence of the Levantine glassmaking industry, which followed fast upon the heels of the establishment of the states of Israel and Judah, is more noticeable in the production of trade goods. A close association between the sea-faring Canaanites of the Levantine coast and the Israelite monarchy led to a expanded production of glassware and to an increase in its distribution throughout the Mediterranean and the Near East. The beaches along the Levantine coast such as that through which the famed Belus River flowed were the provider of the siliceous sand, the forests of Galilee and Lebanon provided the fuel, and ports like Sidon provided the facilities through which glassware began to reach every land around the Mediterranean.

One of the distinctive items distributed by Canaanite seafarers throughout the Mediterranean were "eye-beads." The "eyes" were formed from concentric rings of vari-colored glass which produced a startling impression of a glaring eye, a technique which was also used in the production of the "head-beads." The technique and style were developed in Semitic Akkadia and refined in Hurrian Mitanni. Eye-beads surfaced briefly in Egypt at El-Amarna. Typical of the genre, notes Professor Dan Barag, is "A unique fragment in white glass from the excavations at El-Amarna in the department of Egyptian antiquities in the British Museum...decorated with a guilloche pattern and eyes in blue, which have parallels in Mesopotamian glass of the same period."[37] The appearance of the ubiquitous eye-beads marked the arrival of glassware in every Canaanite colony and trading post. It was a trade which Moses had reputedly foreseen when he predicted that the tribe of Zebulun would profit from "the abundance of the sea and from the treasures hidden in the sand." The route of the establishment of glassmaking can be clearly discerned by following the appearance of this very particular item. It was developed early in Mesopotamia, appeared for a time in Egypt and then found its way around the Mediteranean on vessels like that which ended up under the sea at Cape Ulu Burun.

The glassmaking propensity of the Israelites lives on in legend. An Arabian folk tale recalls a deception practiced by King Solomon upon the Queen of Sheba; the wily king had a pavement of glass installed in a section

EYE-BEADS, 6TH–3RD CENTURIES BCE. Eye-beads of various types were distributed around the Mediterranean by the sea-faring Canaanites (commonly referred to as the "Phoenicians") and served as important trade goods of the Jews in opening trade with China and India. The core-forming, trailing and tooling techniques employed are consistent with similar items from ancient Mesopotamia.
*Photograph courtesy of The Corning Museum of Glass.*

of his palace which deceived the visiting queen, who believed it to be a pool of water. The legend is clearly mythical, inasmuch as an expanse of flat glass or mirror was beyond the capabilities of the ancient glassmakers, but myths often contain real elements of a tribal memory and therefore must always be considered, albeit taken with a considerable dose of salt. The Talmud does report that: "White glass has ceased since the destruction of our temple,"[38] from which statement we must deduce that such glass was used in the temple.

The creation of the states of Israel and Judah did not create a problem of hegemony between the Israelites and the Canaanites; if anything, the bond between the peoples grew firmer. The long period of peace and growth came to an end when new forces from the East overran the area, destroyed the state of Israel and transported its most skilled craftsmen into the Land-of-the-Two-Rivers. The glassmakers of the Mediteranean coast were among these displaced Israelis, for the art burgeoned in the land in which it was born, and eventually became identified as Achaemenid, Persian and Sassanian glassware.

# NOTES

1. At first Dever argued that the term "Biblical archeology" be abandoned, opting for the regional identification: "Syro-Palestinian archeology" (Herschel Shanks, "Should the term "Biblical archeology be abandoned?" *BAR*, May\June 1981). When the anachronistic application of a term coined by the Romans in the second century of the Christian Era was subjected to criticism, Dever proposed that the term "new Biblical archeology" replace what we must assume to be the "old Biblical archeology." This semantic difference was evidently inspired by the emergence of the term "new archeology" which includes such technologies as neutron activation analysis, magnetronomy, remote sensing, thermoluminescence, paleozoology, paleobotany, ethno-archeology" etc. (Hershel Shanks, "Dever's 'Sermon on the Mound,'" *BAR*, Mar.\Apr. 1987). The followers of the "old" discipline, of course, welcome the application of these modern technologies no less than do the radicals and the question remains of why the exercise in semantics is being performed at all.

2. Shanks, Ibid., quoting from a paper presented by Dever at the AIA convention, January 1989.

3. *Judges* 1:19-4:15: And the Lord was with Judah; and he drave out the inhabitants of the mountain; but he could not drive out the inhabitants of the valley, because they had chariots of iron. And Deborah, a prophetess, the wife of Lapidoth, she judged Israel at that time... [She instructed Israelite general Barak]: I will draw unto thee... the captain of Jabin's [the king of the Canaanites] army, with his chariots and his multitude; and I will deliver him into thy hand...for the Lord shall sell Sisera into the hand of a woman. And Sisera gathered together all his chariots, even nine hundred chariots of iron....And the Lord discomfited Sisera, and all his chariots and all his host...and there was not a man left.

4. Amihai Mazar, "On Early Cult Places and Early Israelites: A Response to Michael Coogan," *BAR*, July/Aug., vol XV, no. 4, 1988, p. 45.

5. According to Isaac Mozeson, author of *The Word*, Shapolsky Publishers, New York, 1989.

6. Baruch Halpern, *The First Historians*, 1988, p. 4.

7. Volkmar Fritz, "Conquest or Settlement," *BAR*, June 1987, vol. 50, no. 4, p. 84: The "conquest" school includes William F. Albright, G. Ernest Wright, John Bright and Paul Lapp; the "peaceful infiltration" school was developed by Albrecht Alt, Martin Noth

and Manfred Weippert; the "peasant revolt school" was initially advanced by George Mendenhall and subsequently promoted by Norman Gottwald and Cornelis de Geus.

8. Yohanan Aharoni, *The Archeology of the Land of Israel*, 1978, (Eng. Ed.), 1982.

9. Norman K. Gottwald, "Were the Early Israelites Pastoral Nomads?" *BAR*, Vol. IV, no. 2, June 1978, p. 6.

10. Hershel Shanks, "BAR Interviews Yigael Yadin," *BAR*, Jan./Feb. 1983, vol. IX, no. 1. The *BAR* pursued the subject with subsequent articles by the proponents of the various models of Israelite settlement.

11. G. W. Ahlstrohm and D. Edelman, "Merenptah's Israel," *JNES*, vol. 44, no. 1, Jan. 1985, p. 59.

12. Y. Aharoni, "Khirbet Raddana and Its Inscriptions." *IEJ*, 21, 1971, pp. 130-135.

13. G. Schumacher, *Tel el-Mutesselim I*, 1968, figs. 192-194, pp. 130-131, plate 42.

14. Yohanan Aharoni, Ibid., p. 156.

15. J. C. Waldbaum, "From Bronze to Iron," *SIMA*, 1978, pp. 17-23.

16. T. Stech-Wheeler, J. D. Muhly, K. R. Maxwell-Hyslop, R. Maddin. "Iron at Taanach and Early Iron Metallurgy in the Eastern Mediterranean," *AJA*, vol. 85, no. 3, July 1981, p. 255.

17. I Kings 8:51; Deuteronomy 4:20; Jeremiah 11:4.

18. Joseph A. Callaway, "A Visit with Ahilud," *BAR*, Sept.\Oct. 1983, vol. IX, no. 5, pp. 44-52.

19. I Samuel 13:19-22.

20. I Samuel XIII: 19-23

21. Aharoni, Ibid., p. 156.

22. Stech-Wheeler et al., Ibid., p. 260.

23. Callaway, Ibid., p. 53.

24. Judges, 21:25.

25. William Foxwell Albright, *The Proto-Sinaitic Inscriptions and Their Decipherment*, 1966.

26. Sir W. M. Flinders Petrie, *Researches in Sinai*, 1906, pp. 129 ff; A.E. Cowley, *The Sinaitic Inscriptions*, reprinted from *The Journal of Eastern Archeology*, vol. XV parts II & IV, 1929, pp. 200-218.

27. Trude Dothan, "In the Days When the Judges Ruled--Research on the Period of the Settlement and the Judges," 1981, p. 35.

28. Aaron Demsky and Moshe Kochavi, "An Alphabet from the Days of the Judges," *BAR*, Sept./Oct. 1978, vol. IV, no. 3, pp. 23-25.

29. B. Landsberger and H. Tadmor, "Fragments of Clay Liver Models," *IEJ*, 1964, no. 14, pp. 201-218.

30. Norman Gottwald, *The Tribes of Yahweh: A Sociology of the Religion of Liberated Israel, 1250-1050 BCE*, 1979, pp. 592-599; Norman Gottwald, review in *BAR*, July/Aug. 1982, Vol. VIII no. 4, p. 60, of John Bright's new revision of *A History of Israel*.

31. D. Barag, *Catalog of Western Asiatic Glass in the British Museum*, vol. I, 1985, p. 39.

32. Barag, idem.

33. Harden, Ibid., p. 49, esp. footnote 16. See also T. E. Havernick, "Beitrage zur Geshichte des antiken Glases. III Mykenishes Glas; IV Gefasse mit der Masken; V. Kleine Beobachtungen technischer Art," *Jahrb. des romisch-germanischen Zentralmuseum Mainz*, VII, 1960, pp. 36-58.

34. Frederic Neuberg, *Ancient Glass*, 1962, p. 51.

35. Dan Barag, "Cosmetic Palettes from the Eighth-Seventh Centuries B.C.," citing: Y. Yadin et. al, *Hazor II*, 1960, p. 61, Pl. CVII:20-21. Barag notes that "The majority of the stone palettes were discovered on sites in the kingdoms of Israel and Judaea [including early ones from] Hazor, Beth Shan, Megiddo, Dothan, Samaria, Shechem, [and later ones on sites in] Bethel, Gibeon, Tell en-Nasbeh, Ramat Rahel, Beth Shemesh, Gezer, Lachish, Tell Beit Mirsim, Kh. Rabud, and Beersheba and other sites along the coast." Some stone palettes similar to those from the land of Israel, were also found east of the Jordan.

36. Barag, Ibid., p. 16.

37. Dan Barag, Ibid., 1985, p. 37.

38. Palestinian Talmud, Ch. IV, p. 59b.

# CHAPTER 6

# THE SECOND DIASPORA

## *The Roman Connection*

IT IS UNLIKELY THAT ANY ANCIENT ROMAN EVER MADE GLASS.  GLASSMAKING technology, although already 2000 years old at the time of the birth of the Roman Empire, was unknown to the Romans until after they had launched their well-ordered campaign to conquer the world.  Once they had become conquerors, Romans could scarcely deign to engage in the rigorous, perverse, sweaty toil which the production of glass and its products entailed, even if they had become privy to the secrets of the trade.  Roman law was designed to maintain a facade of superiority over  subject peoples; the law precluded the Roman upper classes from engaging in such a lowly activity and dissuaded any Roman citizen from so doing, for to do so was to stoop to the level of a slave, or, at best, to the demeaning social status of a foreign laborer.

Conquering peoples disdain to engage in manual labor; artisanship is scarcely a goal to which conquerors aspire.  Arts and crafts are regarded by a self-styled master race as odious occupations relegated to inferior peoples.  The product is admired; the practice is scorned.  Among the privileges accruing to conquerors is the power to oblige the vanquished, whether as slaves, serfs or freemen to perform all manual labor.  The Romans were no different in this regard than were the Greeks, whose culture they had absorbed, especially when it came to abjuring participation in as difficult a discipline as making glass and glassware.  "To the Greeks glass was something new; to the Romans something unknown," unequivocally states the

A RAMS-HEAD PENDANT, 6TH-5TH CENTURY BCE. The pendant is possibly from Carthage, from which site hundreds of head-beads have been recovered. Head-beads and pendants were largely but not always anthropomorphic in form. The subjects varied but the technique is easily recognized.
*Photograph courtesy of The Corning Museum of Glass.*

English glass historian W. A. Thorpe, and adds in emphasis, "The Romans, that is, the Latin-Italian people were not glassmakers and not glass-minded."[1]

Blue-blooded Plato relegated artisans to the lowest social strata of his ideal society. Plato's mentor, Socrates, the erstwhile stonemason, loved to lounge around sculptor's workshops; but as Greeks became conquerors they also became dilettantes. Thereafter, while appreciating and lauding works of art, they relegated not respect but contempt for the artisan. Aristotle, no less than Plato, propagated an arrogant attitude toward artisanship; he inculcated his pupil Alexander with the proposition that "the finest type of city will not make an artisan a citizen."[2]

The conquering Greeks, in their turn, followed the autocratic example which the Egyptians, Assyrians, Babylonians and Persians had set before them in assuming a regal, supercilious stance toward manual labor. The Greeks convinced themselves that they were of superior, even divine blood and employed slaves, freedmen or foreigners to carry on occupations considered mean or mundane and fit only for slaves and "barbarians." The antipathy toward physical labor permeated Hellenic culture; the attitude was reflected in the way Greeks viewed the gods; Ares, the god of war, was among the revered, gloriously handsome divinities. Ares, Apollo, Hermes and all the other radiantly beautiful creatures of the Greek pantheon contrasted sharply with Hephaestus, the crippled god of the forge, who was disdainfully depicted as a brutally ugly being hobbling lamely about Mount Olympus. Homer underlines the contempt with which the other gods regarded both the physical deformities and the base occupation of the empyrean smith by attesting that Hephaestus served the various gracious gods as a source of "unquenchable laughter."[3]

Mass murder, destigmatized under an obscuring pseudonym, "war," was thus glorified under the aegis of Ares while laborious creativity was demeaned as being, at best, comic. Xenophon transcribed this attitude into an equation of Greek comportment; he insisted that pride in the performance of noble military functions must be juxtaposed against contempt for the inherently ignoble occupations of artisans. "Greek citizens," Xenophon proclaimed to his fellow citizens with pointed emphasis, "are prohibited from practicing crafts where Greeks are in military control.[4]

The Romans, in any event, were entirely ignorant of the process of making glass at the time their armies thrust into the Near East. Despite the Roman label ubiquitously applied to glass of the subsequent period in archeological collections and museums everywhere, even the glassmakers of the later Roman period were unlikely to have been Romans. The best that can be claimed for the ancient Romans is that glass and glassware was produced in the Roman provinces during the period of Roman rule; it was produced in Rome itself by foreigners during the last half of Rome's existence as an imperial power.

For the first five 500 years of Roman existence, the only contact Rome had with glassware was through imports from the Near East. Later, glassware was manufactured in the domains under Roman rule by artisans from the Near East. Jews were a large proportion of the skilled artisans who were distributed throughout the Roman diaspora behind the Roman legions. Their identity is difficult to distinguish due to the confusion engendered by their inclusion in the generalized category of "Orientals" or in the less generalized but still inclusive category of Phoenicians or Syrians or Palestinians in Roman as well as historiographical literature. These abstruse references to oriental artisans reinforced the propensity of many historians

AN *Amphoriskos*, 2ND-1ST CENTURY BCE. The provenience of the vessel is given as "Eastern Mediterranean". Festooned glass vessels were being produced in *Eretz Israel* and Mesopotamia for more than a millennium before the Greeks and Romans had even acquired a word for glass. The word *vitrum* appears in Latin for the first time in the year 54 BCE.
*Photograph courtesy of the Corning Museum of Glass.*

to ignore altogether the Jewish introduction to the West of technological innovation as slaves and freemen.

No thoroughgoing attempt has ever been made to collect and study all the available evidence--literary or archeological-- relating to the status and the part played by the Jews in ancient glassmaking. One finds extremes of scholarly opinion; by some a major role is assigned to Jewish glassmakers in antiquity, while others have ignored their share altogether.[5]

Consumption, not creativity, was the concern of Roman gentlemen. Their objective was luxurious ostentation and the reinforcement of their assumed right to have the world support their privileged position. Although the distinction between plebians and patricians dimmed with the development of the republic, lower-class Romans nevertheless strove for noble similitude as Romans, if not as noblemen. A Roman household was considered unworthy of the name without its retinue of slaves.

The number of slaves employed in each household varied from perhaps a squad of eight among the *petit bourgeois* to as many as 20,000 in the *familia Caesaris*. Libanius, head of a philosophical school in Antioch, complained that teachers were so ill-paid that they could afford no more than three or four slaves apiece. Slaves were not relegated to mere menial tasks, nor additionally to crafts, but performed as trusted stewards, musicians, geometricians, grammarians, managers of farms and estates, masters of ships and even as money-lending bankers.[6]

Plebeian Roman sentiments regarding hand-work reflected those of their noble peers, and are comparable to those of modern Americans towards ditch diggers or stoop farm labor, occupations consigned to immigrants from starving nations or to illegal immigrants from Mexico. Cicero wrote a didactic treatise in 44 B.C.E., directing its teachings to his 21-year-old son; in it he apposes Roman precepts to those of the Greeks:

Now in regard to trade and other means of livelihood, which ones are to be considered becoming to a gentleman and which ones are vulgar, we have been taught, in general, as follows....Vulgar are the means of livelihood of all hired workmen whom we pay for mere manual labor, not for artistic skill; for in their case the very wages they receive is a pledge of their slavery....These privileges Xenophon, a pupil of Socrates, has set forth most happily in his book entitled *Oeconomicus*. When I was about your present age, I translated it from Greek to Latin.[7]

Cicero emphasized his repugnance elsewhere toward Roman engagement in manual labor by restating in unequivocal terms that "all craftsmen are engaged in a lowly art; for no workshop can have anything appropriate to a free man."[8]

The standing of a Roman citizen was no less sullied by engaging in common trade than by engaging in manual labor. Only land management and agriculture were recognized as legitimate occupations of a Roman, so long as slaves or serfs sweated at the work to be done. A proper Roman was obliged to abjure participation in participation in production and engage in commercial market activity only on a large scale and never on a retail level. The agronomic exception to this prohibition still exists as a cultural carry-over to modern times; we still do not speak of gentlemen merchants, gentlemen artisans, gentlemen manufacturers or even of gentlemen capitalists. Only gentlemen farmers are accorded a niche in genteel society.

The closest a Roman landowner could legitimately approach the lowly activity of a merchant was to grant usufructuary rights to brickmakers or potters to clay deposits found on his estates and to contract for the purchase and sale of the products made of that clay. Even this activity was frowned upon and the question was raised as to whether the clay was a product of the soil, in which case the sale of products made from it was arguably an acceptable Roman enterprise, or whether its sale constituted a distinct commercial enterprise unrelated to farming, in which case such sale had to be renounced as being incompatible with Roman status.

The Theodosian Code, for example, addresses this very question and brings it into focus; the code was intended to exempt estate management from taxation, but when Constantine introduced the *collatio Lustralis*, a tax on *negotiatores*, "Even the Roman bureaucrats and lawyers were uncertain about its status; witness the disagreement among the jurists (Digest 8.3; 33.7; 25.1) as to whether clay beds were counted among the *instrumenta* of the estate."[9]

Glass artifacts began to appear as a stable part of Roman trade after the invention of glassblowing in the first century B.C.E. Among the earliest references to the import of products of glass in the corpus of Roman literature is contained in a speech by the selfsame Cicero, given in defence of Rabirus Postumus, the son of a "very important tax farmer." Postumus

A BLOWN GLASS JUG OF THE EARLY PERIOD OF THE ROMAN OCCUPATION OF JUDAH.  The square vessel was recovered from a site near the Israeli kibbutz Mishmar-ha-Emek.  It is a common type of storage and packing bottle of the early Roman empire.  The durable heavy walls and the square shape makes for ease and security in shipping liquids.
*Photograph by the author, courtesy of the Mishmar-ha-Emek Kibbutz Museum.*

had been imprisoned for crimes committed during his stint as royal treasurer of Alexandria. "It is true that the goods invoiced were only cheap showy articles of paper, linen and glass;" slyly inserted Cicero in Postumus's defense, thereby informing us of the existence of that trade.  Cicero then added, "Many ships were packed with these...."[10]

The vainglorious Roman conquerors relished flaunting their prowess and their plundered wealth.  After Roman forces under Pompey took Jerusalem on the Holy Jewish Atonement Day in 63 B.C.E. the Jewish king Aristobolus and his family were paraded ignominiously through Rome in a triumphal procession, along with a host of other captive Jews.  Jews had already been part of the scene on the Italian peninsula from time immemorial. An early documentary reference to Jewish presence in Rome derives, ironically, from "their banishment [in 151 B.C.E.] out of Rome and Italy," which took place at a time "in which an embassy from the Jewish prince Simon was honorably received by the Roman Senate and dismissed with assurances of friendship."[11] The exclusion was based upon the corrupting influence of Roman morals by Jewish religious propaganda.

The most impressive monuments of Rome were thereafter erected by the Jewish slaves brought from "captive Judah" (as an inscription emblazoned on a newly minted Roman coin boastfully memorialized the defeat and enslavement of the Jewish population); at least three of the great structures constructed by the many thousands of Jewish slaves were dedicated to the memory of the defeat of the nation from which the slaves were taken. Two of these impressive monuments still stand, renowned the world over and visited by millions of admiring tourists. The majestic Arch of Titus was erected as a permanent memorial to the triumph of the three Flavians over the Jews; "the gigantic structure of the amphitheater [referred to world wide as "The Coliseum," as if there was only one] was built by the forced labor of the Jewish war captives in a phenomenally short time."[12] The third structure known to have been built by Jewish slaves was later destroyed by fire; it had been laconically dubbed "the Temple of Peace" by the Romans, and housed the sacred vessels looted from the Jerusalem temple.

Roman narcissism, being thus served by these acts of braggadocio, was further titillated by an exhibition devoted to a boastful display of riches their swords and spears had won. In the year 61 B.C.E. the great general Pompey and some of his officers, gloating over their triumphs, vaunted their newly won wealth by staging in the temple of Jupitus Capiloninus in Rome an exhibition of vessels carved from colorful semiprecious stones. These startlingly beautiful vessels were among the treasures obtained during the Roman campaigns in the Near East. The impressive exhibition was a smashing success and whetted the appetites of the Roman rulers for exotic ware.

The market for such luxury items received a great impetus from the exhibition held in Rome. The hankering of Roman plutocrats after the particularly impressive artifacts displayed ostentatiously in the temple of Jupitus stimulated the glassmakers of Sidon, Galilee and Alexandria to expand the production of glass imitations of semiprecious stoneware. The eastern artisans had also been producing vessels intricately wrought of sections of glass canes, *murrhine*, which not only matched but surpassed natural stone in brilliance and color and added fascinating integral design to the fabric of the vessels.

A MOSAIC MURRHINE OR MILLEFIORE BOWL OF THE LATE 2ND OR EARLY 1ST CENTURY BCE.
Valuable murrhine glassware was first introduced into Roman Italy in the late 1st century BCE.
"Murrhine was an oriental dealers word," noted the English glass historian, W.A. Thorpe.
*Photograph courtesy of The Corning Museum of Glass.*

"Murrhine vessels have come to us from the East," announced the elder Pliny. There were marbled effects duplicating the most riotously colored agate; there were glass vessels which included hues and effects rarely found in nature; there were vessels formed of a mosaic of varicolored glass tesserae; there were also the most precious and impressive *millefiore* vessels, also a mosaic in execution, but composed of sections of multilayered canes, each section of which already encompassed an intricate, miniaturized, colorful pattern.

The needs of the market were met; not only were the glass vessels every bit as striking as the stone varieties, they were generally less expensive (except for the *millefiore* varieties). The well-to-do middle classes were also able to afford them and to boast of their possession. The ownership of the expensive varieties of glass vessels became a flag of affluence, the ultimate ratification of Roman superiority. Pliny states with awe that in the time of Nero two small glass cups were valued at 6000 sesteres.[13] Pliny also relates, if we are to believe the story, that when the Roman consul Titus Petronius realized that Nero would have him killed, he smashed a murrhine ladle which had cost him 300,000 sesterces. But Nero, touting his status as an emperor, surpassed all others by purchasing a single bowl for the healthy sum of 1,000,000 sesterces. Pliny comments on the remarkable durability of this exotic, foreign material, glass, by describing how an ex-consul "drank from a *murrhine* cup. He was so fond of it that he could gnaw its rim; and yet the damage he so caused only enhanced its value...and there is no other price of murrhine even today that has a higher value set upon it."[14]

Another kind of carved glass, developed purely as an expensive tour-de-force, was the *vasa diatreta*: cups, bowls and vessels made with glass thick enough to permit the carving of several lightly connected layers. The outer layer was sculptured into geometric patterns or into floral, faunal or anthropomorphic forms; the center portion was almost entirely cut away, leaving almost invisible posts by which the outer design remained attached to the third innermost layer, which formed an integral, inner vessel. The Roman term for the glass cutters who performed this infinitely patient and skillful work was *diatretarii*, a word which was adapted from the Greek and which, in turn, was derived originally from the Hebrew word for cutting or chiseling. The familiarity of the Hebrew sages with Diatreta ("cut glass") vessels and with the consummate skill required for their production is reflected in the Midrash, in which the delicacy of execution and intrinsic

A DIATRETON OR "CAGE CUP," c. 300 CE. Such meticulously carved vessels were sometimes employed as a lighting fixture. The Latin word "Diatreton" derives from an ancient Hebrew word for "chiselling" or "cutting" and relates to the extremely difficult and time-consuming work involved in the production of such a tour-de-force of glassware manufacture.
*Photograph courtesy of The Corning Museum of Glass.*

value of such value of such vessels are used to illustrate the two most precious aspects of adhering to God's commandments, that is, not merely to obey the commandments but to act upon them:

> It can be compared to a king who instructed his servants: "Guard those two cut-glass vessels [*diatreti*] for me; and take the greatest care of them." As he was entering the palace, a young calf standing nearby gored the servant, with the result that one of the vessels broke. The servant appeared before the king trembling, and when asked: "Why are you trembling?" he replied: "Because a calf gored me and made me break one of these two vessels." The king thereupon said to him: "That being so, you must be all the more careful with

145

the second one." This is also what God said: "At Sinai you prepared two cups--"*We will do*," and "*obey*"; by making the golden calf, you have shattered one--"we will do"; be very careful with the second one--*we will obey*.[15]

The Midrash is rich with other references to Diatreta. It is significant that in Esther Rabbah the word appears in an Aramaic adjectival form: "Diatiri" i.e., "carved glass [vessel]". The operation is thus indicated in a form which is absent from Latin and from all other languages.[16] *Murrhine* was also "an Oriental dealer's word."[17] Thus the Hebrew terms for certain glassmaking operations became incorporated into Greek and Latin and have been transcribed therefrom into all other languages as a universal generic description of those varieties of glassware.

Where, then, was the early Roman period glass made and by whom? It was none other than the Roman emperor Diocletian who bore witness to the Jewish character of the glassmaking industry of Eretz Israel, the land of Israel. In the year 301 C.E., Diocletian issued an edict which fixed the prices of products being exported throughout the Roman Empire. Professor Kenin Erim of New York University, excavating at Aphrodisias in 1970-1972, recovered over 150 additional fragments of the record of tariffs fixed by Diocletian in his edict.[18] The list specifies the prices of glassware from only two areas of the Roman Empire, one being Judea, from which area the glassware is specifically referred to as *vitri Ijudaici* (Jewish glass), and the other being Alexandria, from which area the glass is designated as *vitri Alexandrini* (Alexandrian glass).[19]

The name Judah (Latin: Judaea) was officially expunged by Hadrian in 135 C.E. in a vindictive reaction to the stubborn resistance of the Jews in the Bar Kokhba war; the area was thereupon incorporated into the newly constituted Provincia Syro-Palestina. It is obvious from the Diocletian edict, however, that the term "Jewish glass" was so ingrained into the vernacular of the times that it had become a generic term for the glassware from that region and that the term had continued in use for centuries thereafter even after the Jewish glassmakers had established themselves elsewhere in the Roman diaspora. The Diocletian edict is witness to the identity of the original practitioners of the art, it having been issued some two centuries after Judah was no longer officially in existence as such.

Another fragment of the Diocletian *Edict on Prices* was found in the ancient Anatolian city of Synnada. Many Anatolian cities harbored substantial Jewish communities, and, curiously, it is in those very cities that the production of glassware appears to have taken place. Thus at Sardis, the site of one of the largest synagogues of all time, glass cullet in some quantity and evidence of at least glassware-making was recovered. Epigraphic evidence of significant Jewish presence has turned up in Apameia (modern Dinar), located in the Phrygian highlands of Pamphylia. Apameia was an important Roman administrative center at the hub of the principal trade routes of that easternmost province. The presence of Jewish communities has been epigraphically confirmed in the area at Acmoneia and at Synnada, and it is from those cities that glassware of the period has been recovered.

The Afyon Museum of the region contains a collection of Roman period glassware which was catalogued by C. S. Lightfoot under the aegis of the British Institute of Archeology at Ankara. Lightfoot noted that some of the eastern-type glassware appears to have been of local production, and, since the authochthonous peoples of the region were ignorant of the vitric arts, "it might be supposed that the Jewish communities played a particular role in the creation of a local industry."[20]

The Jewish presence at Acmonia is attested by a *menorah*, a seven-branched candlestick, carved into a marble column which may be presumed to have been torn from a local synagogue of the period. An engraved flask, "the most interesting of the glasses from outside the boundaries of Afyon Province," was found at Dinar, similar to other examples found at Apameia and elsewhere. A late Roman engraved bowl was also found at Dinar, again similar to others found as far afield as the northwest Roman provinces and Nubia.[21] The bowl is deemed so remarkable that it was featured as one of the most outstanding examples of the vitric arts of the Roman Period at an exhibition organized jointly by the Corning, British and Römisch Museums entitled *Glass of the Caesars*. "Acmoneia," Lightfoot reminds us, "lay in the Apamene *conventus* and, like Apameia, had a significant number of Jewish inhabitants.

The glassware classified in the Diocletian edict as Alexandrian glass was fixed at a higher price level than that classified therein as Jewish glass, reflecting the fact that the Alexandrian industry was devoted to the production of elaborate, exotic and expensive glassware directed at the upper-class market, while the glassware made by Jews in Judah was of a more common type, and was that glassware commonly turning up in substantial quantities throughout the Roman Empire. Only those two proveniences of glassware

A "GOLD-BAND" BOX, FIRST HALF OF THE 1ST CENTURY CE. The lidded box was among the glass artifacts imported into Roman Italy from the Near-East in the first half of the 1st century CE. After the exhibition of imported precious stoneware at the temple of Jupiter in Rome, Near-Eastern glassmakers replicated exotic stoneware in glass, and many of their products surpassed the stoneware in value and beauty. The fabric of the pictured vessel imitates precious stone by a combination of striations of translucent dark blue, green and purple glass with opaque white and colorless glass bands encasing gold foil.
*Photograph courtesy of The Corning Museum of Glass.*

were recognized by Diocletian. Significantly, Sidon and Phoenicia do not figure in the art of glassmaking in the edict, indicating that, although the ports of Sidon and Tyre are recorded as being the major ports from which glassware was being shipped, the main manufacture of Jewish glass was being carried on in the hinterlands, an industry now in evidence from the scoria of ancient furnaces emerging from kibbutz farmland throughout the upper and lower Galilee.

The art of glassmaking spread from the Galilee and Judah to Alexandria soon after that Ptolemaic city was founded. The Romans became the city's rulers during the period in which glassmaking matured from an industry restricted to the supplying of exotic objects for the rich and powerful to an industry capable of satisfying a wide market. The Jews, constituting about 40 percent of the Alexandrian population, were at the forefront of the skilled crafts of that bustling city, and were preeminently the glassblowers. Hadrian Augustus, in a vituperative critique of the Alexandrian Jews, paid them some backhanded compliments, crediting them with carrying on the skilled crafts of the city and placing the revolutionary process of glassblowing pointedly among them:

FROM HADRIAN AUGUSTUS TO SERVIANUS THE CONSUL, Greeting: [The Jews in Alexandria are] prosperous, rich and fruitful, and in it no one is idle. Some are blowers of glass, others makers of paper, all are at least weavers of linen or seem to belong to one craft or another; the lame have their occupations, the wounded have theirs, the blind have theirs, and not even those whose hands are crippled are idle.

Thus, both the glassmakers of Judah and of Alexandria, the major producers and exporters of glass and glassware of the Roman Imperial period have been identified by Roman emperors as being Jews. It was not long before these eastern glassmakers were established in Rome and adjacent to the Roman encampments throughout the empire, the better to serve the expanding market. The process was probably initiated during the reign of Augustus (27 B.C.E. to 14 C.E.) after he had added Egypt to the Roman Empire and demanded glassware as part of his tribute. The supply failed to satisfy him, so he ordered that Alexandrian artisans be brought to Rome to establish the art. There is no extant record of how this order was carried out, but glassmaking appeared in Rome at about this time, coincident also with the manumission of thousands of Jewish slaves who had been previously hauled into Rome as captives of war. "For having been brought to Italy as captives," Philo relates, "they were freed by their owners and not forced to violate any of their ancestral customs." Slaves and freemen began to constitute a large proportion of the population of Rome as Roman conquests expanded into the East. Cosmopolitan Rome began to assume a decidedly Eastern flavor.

It should also be noted that the sheer numbers of the Jews dispersed throughout the Roman Empire bespeak an importance in the life of those times far beyond that generally accredited to them. The Jewish population has been assessed to have reached 7,000,000 within the Roman Empire, judged by various Roman censuses and by various other estimates arrived at diversely in each region of the empire; there were up to another 1,000,000 Jews dwelling in areas under the hegemony of other rulers. The Jews certainly constituted between 10 to 15 percent of the entire population of the Roman Empire at its greatest extent. These Jews were not located in the hinterlands, but at the ports and production centers, at the heart of the Western civilized world where they constituted a much more sizable proportion of the population.

The Jewish priestly class, whose activities receive almost all of historiographical attention, constituted but a tiny proportion of the overall Jewish population. The Jewish artisans, slave and freemen, whose Eastern expertise created a variety of industries along the Roman routes, are hardly noticed in literature; they are hidden among the so-called Orientals or Syrians. One historian estimates that by the first half of the first century the free Jewish population of Rome was at least 20,000.[22] Other sources estimate as many as 40,000. Josephus reported that when the Jewish embassy made a petition to the Roman emperor to remove Herod's dynasty after the tyrant's death in 3 B.C.E.: "it was escorted on its way to the imperial palace by a crowd of 8,000 Jews." The Jewish population continued to grow rapidly for the next century as a result of continued manumission and immigration.

It was from this stratum that the Roman proletariat and its petty bourgeoisie for the most part was recruited. It was from this stratum that the Roman Jews predominantly belonged...these humble immigrants settled by the Tiber and especially in the Trastevere, or right bank. There the boats which brought goods from Ostia docked; there lived harbor and transport workers, boatmen, shopkeepers, numerous artisans; there were sailors' taverns and all trades and industries which could not be admitted into the city.[23]

Thirteen congregations dating from the time of the early Roman Empire have already been identified, chiefly from Greek inscriptions found on the tombstones. How far back in time these congregations existed, and how many more there were is still to be determined. The congregation of the Severians, for example, was clearly established during the time of the Severi, and would therefore date back to about 200 B.C.E.[24]

It was in the Trastevere quarter that the first glassmaking furnaces must have been constructed in Rome, among other sweaty, sooty and odoriferous industries as metalsmithing, unguent manufacturing and the tanning of leather, all of which were mainly, if not exclusively, in the hands of Jews. The area in the foreground of the Porta Portese (port gate) in the Trastevere was known as the *Jew's Field* until the seventeenth century, "just as the bridge over the Tiber was called, in the Middle Ages, the *Jew's Bridge*. In the Trastevere stood the oldest synagogue. If one wanted to reach the gardens of Caesar outside of the city, one had to pass the Jewish quarter."[25]

Trastevere (Transtiberis), i.e., the other side of the River Tiber, or in modern terms "the other side of the tracks," was in the southeastern part of Rome, a dreary slum area with crooked streets and dingy workshops. Pope Benedictus VIII gave a charter in the year 1019 to the bishopric of Portus, whose jurisdiction extended over the island of the Tiber and Trastevere, in which he designated the area *fundum integrum, qui vocatur Judaeorum*, "the whole district, named after the Jews."[26] While the Jews were not confined to a special quarter until the institution of the ghetto in 1556, the majority had always inhabited and labored in Trastevere;[27] in that year all the Jews of Rome were forcefully confined to a portion of that quarter by the cruel Paul IV Caraffa, a pontiff hated by the Christians hardly less than by the Jews, who referred to him as the reincarnation of the Biblical Haman. The bridge Quattro Capi, otherwise known as the Pons Judaeorum, led to what became the Via del Pianto, the "Street of Lamentation," which became the heart of the *vicus Judaeorum*, later referred to as the ghetto.[28] Thus the district was continuously a center of Jewish life as well as the craft center of Rome for a millennium and a half. The industries of the area varied as the Jews were thereafter proscribed from engaging in their traditional occupations; the arts which were allowed to linger as Jewish

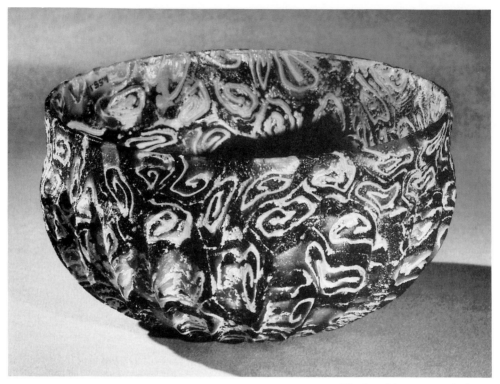

A MOSAIC RIBBED BOWL, LATE 1ST CENTURY BCE-1ST CENTURY CE. The bowl is composed of canes of opaque white in translucent amethyst and colorless glasses. The exotic glass murrhine, diatreta and mosaic vessels imported to Roman Italy from the Levant were popular among Roman plutocrats as expensive status-fixing possessions.
*Photograph courtesy of The Corning Museum of Glass.*

vocations endured in that squalid environment. It was not until 1885, under King Victor Immanuel, that the first steps toward the abolishment of the ghettos were taken.

The Trastevere district lay along the Appian and Latin Roads, the bridgeheads for communication "with the great harbors of Puteoli and Brunisium, with Capua and Naples, with the seaside resorts and country estates at Baiae and its environs."[29] Glassmakers from Alexandria founded glassmaking facilities on the coast between Cumae and Liternum in 14 C.E. and at the Porta Cassena in Rome. Pliny mentions that glassmakers from the region he referred to as Syria established themselves in Campania, an area south of Rome near the Volturnus River;[30] the sand from the river supplied the silicate required for glass manufacture and the nearby fashionable cities and resorts of Pompeii, Herculaneum, Capua, Neopolis, Cumae and Salerno supplied a ready market. In C.E. 79 the ashes erupted from fiery Vesuvius and preserved many examples of the work of the artisans of the region as well as of imported glassware.

The existence of another recently discovered ancient synagogue which served the considerable Jewish proletariat community at the port of Ostia suggests that the Jewish work-force was an important factor in the importing and industrial activities of the area. The synagogue, built on a strategic and valuable site near the seashore in the first century, "was made more handsome in the second century, and further modified in the late Empire."[31] The building's identification was made explicit by Jewish symbols, including a candelabrum carved onto its capitals. A funerary inscription of an archisynagogus found later attests to the existence of an unsuspectedly sizable Jewish community at Ostia. The name of the community leader, Plotius Fortunatus, was distinctly Roman, and were it not for the designation of his position as head of the synagogue his Jewish identity would never have been recognized. "The name helps to explain why the Jews of Ostia were so elusive," writes Meiggs in a revelationary apology for overlooking the existence of the Ostian Jewish constituency, "I overlooked the fact that it was common Jewish practice to adopt Roman names."[32]

The Eastern provenience of many of Roman workers and guild members are often evident from their reference to the place they came from and occasionally from their descendance; thus the inscription "Asclepiades, son of Simon from Cnidus" informs us that the man bearing the Roman name was not only a Jew but where he was from. While freed slaves usually took their first two names from their owner and retained their slave name as a cognomen, "their sons and grandsons could adopt more respectable names."[33] Thus most of the many millions of Jews of the Roman period, having passed through hundreds of years of Hellenic and Roman dominance, cannot be identified by their names, a factor which is generally overlooked and which is rarely considered in historiographical literature.

The importance of Jews at the ports is further reinforced by the numbers of Jews known to have been buried at the other Roman harbor-cities of Puteoli and Portus. Most of the trade with Alexandria and the East into the Roman area took place through the ports of Puteoli. The burials "indicate callings which have to do with commerce and navigation."[34] In

Puteoli still another synagogue existed "in the first century of the Christian Era (Acts 28:13 and 14), and a street of glassmakers, which also contained a quarter for incense makers."[35] Among the glassware ostensibly made at Puteoli is "a very fine bottle now at the Pilkington Museum which was wheel engraved to illustrate a scene in the town of Puteoli near Naples."[36] At least three flasks have been found with representations of buildings along the Puteoli coastline, a design which was probably commonly employed, judging by the wide distribution of these distinctive vessels. One was found in Piombini, another in the catacombs of Rome and a third in Portugal.[37]

The Jewish catacombs of Rome afford another glimpse into the association of the Jews with the art of glassmaking. Five catacomb complexes have been uncovered, with hundreds of tombs that carry a wide variety of artistic renderings. Although the oldest of these complexes of underground tombs were discovered by Bosio in 1602, the anti-Semitic climate of the times served to bury the knowledge for 300 years. They remained almost forgotten until the middle of the nineteenth century; they were again rediscovered in 1904, but scientific exploration of them commenced considerably later; during these long periods they were left to the ravages of treasure hunters and despoilers.

The artistic renderings in the various media employed in the catacombs contain pagan as well as Jewish symbols, a significant testimony to the diverse composition and tastes of the Jewish population during a period of several hundred years. In addition to depictions of scenes from the Old Testament and such standard symbols as the menorah, lulab, etrog, grape clusters and vines, Torah arcs, the portals of the Jerusalem temple, the shofar and trumpets, there are representations of genii and divinities such as Pegasus, Victory and Fortune which eloquently testify to the fact that contemporary Jewish culture was far from being monolithic, let alone universally strictly orthodox. The lions which flank the arc of the Torah, the eagles, the peacock and other birds and animals, as well as human, even nude figures are well represented in Jewish catacomb art. Jewish art existed as a prototype for "Christian borrowing, reinterpretation and adoption."[38]

Many of these symbols and figures appear on molded glassware of the period and are commonly, too often mistakenly ascribed culturally to Greek, Roman or Paleo-Christian art. Common among the artistic artifacts of the catacombs are examples of so-called gold-glass. Gold-glass is not glass of a gold color but composed of a design in gold foil which is laminated between two layers of glass. The bottoms of gold-glass vessels containing such designs, after being broken carefully away from the sides of the vessels, were imbedded into the walls of various tombs. Some of these round laminated discs bear inscriptions in Latin and Greek as well as renderings of various of the above-mentioned motifs. A favorite Hebrew inscription, rendered in Greek and sometimes in Latin letters, is composed of the words *pie zeses* (drink and live). A number of designs appear in catacomb art in which fish on a platter, "obviously the Sabbath meal" are depicted.[39] This theme in Jewish art predates and bears no relationship to the use of fish (*ichthys*) as a symbol of Christ among the early Christians, so chosen because the letters of the word form an acrostic of the phrase "Jesus Christ, son of God, Saviour." The depiction of fish in gold-glass vessels, as well as renderings of fish in other media (such as in mosaic floors) is often mistakenly attributed to Christian art.[40]

It is possible but unlikely that some early Christians, many of whom were recruited from among the Jews, can be counted among the early glassmakers. The Christians continued many of the conventional cultural practices of the Jews, notable among which was the funerary custom of inhumation; the Jewish catacombs served as a model for Christian entombment.[41] The early Christians also continued the practice of imbedding gold-glass fragments into the walls of their tombs with, however, Christian symbols. Since the Christian catacombs were well advertised, the use of gold-glass implants has become referred to as a Christian art. The Christian versions of gold-glass do not appear until the third century, however, well after the precedent had been set by the Jews.

The possibility of pagan Romans engaging in the highly circumscribed, even secret art of making glass is even more implausible. The glassmakers of Roman Italy, no less than their cousins in Palestine and Alexandria, produced what the market demanded and turned out glassware with pagan and Christian symbols, and with popular phrases. Among these latter are the well-known "drink and live" and the so-called "gladiators' cups," awarded to a victor as a treasured prize. "We cannot determine with certainty whether this ware was produced by Jewish artists, but there is some probability that such was the case," states Vogelstein gingerly and reasons that "from antiquity to the end of the Middle Ages the manufacture of glassware was a craft especially followed by the Jews, and in it they attained

A GOLD-GLASS BOWL FRAGMENT. Gold-glass vessel bottom of a type imbedded into the walls of Jewish tombs. The use of such vessel fragments in Jewish entombment anticipated the similar practice by the Christians; the Latin words "Pie Zesis," appeared in Jewish contexts and were also employed on vessels produced for the Romans.
*Photograph courtesy of the Israel Museum, Jerusalem.*

156

A GOLD-GLASS FRAGMENT OF THE 4TH CENTURY CE WITH CHRISTIAN MOTIF. The depiction of a shepherd and flock replaced the Jewish themes for use in Christian burials. The Jewish practice of imbedding such gold-glass bottoms of bowls into the walls of tombs and of the use of the phrase "Pie Zesis" was continued by the Christians.
*Photograph courtesy of The Corning Museum of Glass.*

a high degree of skill."[42]

The best that can be said for the role of the Romans in the dispersal of the art of glassmaking throughout the Roman world was expressed by Phoebe Phillips in her *Encyclopedia of Glass*: "The Romans did more for the glassblower than just provide roads and ships; they created stable trade routes, appreciated and paid for the best artistry, provided the luxury market with what it wanted and the ordinary market with what it needed."[43] This astute observation sums up *in toto* the extent of the participation of the Romans in the art of glassmaking. Axel von Harden adds that "Although Syria-Palestine remained the cradle of 'modern' glassmaking and Alexandria continued to produce fine luxury ware, Naples, Rome, northern Italy, southeastern France, Cologne and other cities along the Rhine could also claim an efficient industry established mainly by Jewish glassmakers emigrated from Palestine in the 1st century."[44] Pliny includes Spain in the areas in which glass workshops were set up.

Second in importance only to the harbors serving Rome on the western coast of Italy, and one of the greatest and busiest ports of the entire Roman Empire, was Aquileia, a city seldom mentioned in history in general, and entirely absent from Jewish atlases. Not even the *Encyclopedia Judaica* takes note of the fact that a community of Jews, numbering in the thousands, dwelt and worked in Aquileia. Aquileia was located at the crown of the Adriatic Sea, halfway between the modern cities of Trieste and Venice. A thousand years before Venice became the glassmaking capital of the world, Eastern glassmakers were practicing their art in the area. The area was probably more important to glass history than was Rome in ancient, no less than in modern, times.

The intriguing mystery surrounding the initiation of the art in Italy and later in Venice has ancient ramifications, for the upper Adriatic littoral may have been the first area of the European continent to which the technology of primary glassmaking arrived from the Levant. The river valleys that traverse the distinctive Dolomite section of the Alps to the Adriatic sweep up to the passes into what the Romans called Pannonia and Noricum, and through them into all of central Europe. The Romans conquered and controlled the area in order to trade with what they termed the barbarian inhabitants of central Europe and to prevent them from invading Italy by reinforcing the mountain barriers with a military presence.

Legends about the Veneti always set them apart from the surrounding

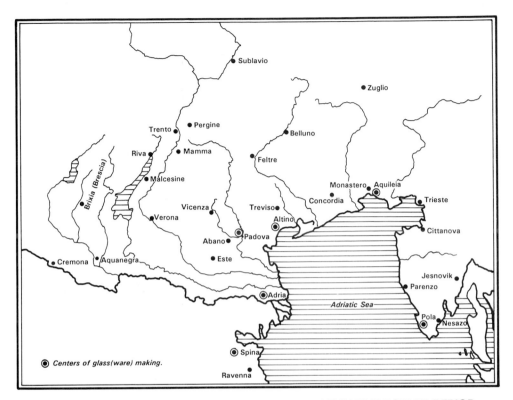

Sublavio

Zuglio

Pergine

Trento

Belluno

Riva

Mamma

Feltre

Brixia (Brescia)

Malcesine

Monastero    Aquileia

Concordia    Trieste

Vicenza

Treviso

Verona

Altino

Cittanova

Abano    Padova

Este

Jesnovik

Cremona    Aquanegra

Parenzo

Adria

*Adriatic Sea*

Pola

Nesazo

◉ *Centers of glass(ware) making.*

Spina

Ravenna

## GLASSWARE PRODUCTION IN NORTHEAST ITALY IN THE ROMAN PERIOD

The northern Adriatic Sea provided access to the trade routes into central Europe. The Romans constructed roads from Rome to Aquileia, which became the hub for such trade and a major port through which contact with the East was maintained. Jews were prominent among the eastern artisans and tradesmen who flocked into the region. Glassware was first imported and then produced at Aquileia, Adria, Altino and the Istrian peninsula, and later around Padova and Spina; primary glassmaking was eventually introduced into the area and began to spread across northern Italy, only to disappear with the invasion of the Huns.

peoples and from the Celtic tribes over the Alps.  Polybius (200-118 B.C.E.), the Greek historian and a mentor and friend of great Roman General Scipio, mentions the incursions of the Celts into the valley of the River Po, but notes that: "The part of the plain which borders on the Adriatic had always belonged to another very ancient tribe, that is the Veneti; in their customs and their dress they scarcely differed from the "Celts, but they spoke a different language and the tragic poets have many fabulous tales to tell about them."[45]

Livy (59 B.C.E.-17 C.E.), the Roman scholar who wrote a monumental *History of Rome* comprising no less than 142 books, tells an entirely different tale.  According to Livy, Antonas, one of the Trojans, who had worked consistently for peace and the restoration of Helen and was therefore allowed to go unmolested, joined forces with the Anatolian tribe, the Eneti, and penetrated into the head of the Adriatic, where they expelled the resident Eugani tribe.  "The spot where they landed is called Troy," continues Livy, "and the neighboring country the Trojan district.  The combined peoples became known as the Venetians."[46]

Tacitus (56-115 C.E.?), whose distinguished career led to his becoming governor (*legaetus Praetorious*) of Britain in addition to writing most quoted histories, presents yet another version of the origin of the Venetians.  "I don't know whether to classify the Venedi with the Germans or the Samaritans."  Tacitus admits and explains

> The Venedi have adopted many Samaritan habits; for their plundering forays take them all over the wooded and mountainous highlands that lie between the Peucini and the Fenni.  Nevertheless they are to be classified as Germans [that is, as Celts], for they have settled homes, carry shields and are fond of traveling--and traveling fast--on foot, differing in all these respects from the Samaritans, who live in wagons or on horseback."[47]

So much for the Roman renditions of history!  Aerial surveys show the existence of a port city underlying the Roman city of Aquileia, an ancient city of which nothing is known.  Who were the pre-Roman settlers who constructed this port and other such ports along the northern littoral of the Adriatic?  The indigenous tribes were not seafaring peoples.  The logical candidates for the establishment of a port facility are either the seafaring Greeks or Canaanites (the so-called Phoenicians).  No evidence of Greek culture has been found in the area but some pre-Roman distinctly Levantine glass artifacts have been found, not only at Aquileia but also in the graves of peoples across the Alps. The reasonable course of arrival for such objects would have been either through the Adriatic or across southern Russia into the Danube basin.

During the Roman period the art of glassmaking appeared at Aquileia and other centers at the head of the Adriatic: Altino, Spina and Adria on the western flank and around to the east at Pola and the Istrian peninsula. The art began to spread through the Po Valley and up into central Europe when its advance was terminated by the invasion of the barbarians who swept over the Dolomites and effectively brought the advance of civilization to a halt in the area.

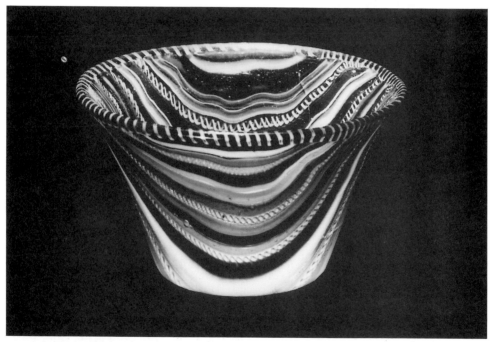

A RIBBON GLASS BOWL, LATE 1ST CENTURY BCE. The ribbon bowl represents another type of exotic glassware which was produced by artisans who had been introduced into Alexandria from *Eretz Israel* during the Ptolemaic period, and was thereafter exported to the West. A Jewish community numbering in the thousands resided in Aquileia. The signatures of two slave (or former slaves), one of whom was a woman, were molded into glassware made in Aquileia and are among the first names of glassware producers known. A comprehensive collection of exotic as well as common-place glassware has been recovered from Aquileia and other sites around the northern Adriatic littoral.
*Photograph courtesy of The Corning Museum of Glass.*

Aquileia was especially important as a gateway to imports from the East, both of goods and artisans. The bustling city assumed increasing significance as the legions established themselves along the routes laid down along the river valleys that traversed the Alpine Dolomites, wound over lofty passes through Pannonia and Noricum into central Europe and reached out to the Baltic coast. The port of Aquileia served as the funnel through which Eastern products as well as the products of central Europe were fed into the Roman European provinces and into Rome itself.

It may be that the upper Adriatic littoral was the first area of the European continent to which the art of primary glassmaking, that is, the production of glass and glassware from raw materials rather than from cullet, arrived from the Levant, earlier even than the basic industry arrived at Rome itself; at least, the first evidence extant of that activity has been recovered from its ruins. Glass products were a conspicuous part of the cargos which were unloaded along the five kilometers of canals which led in from the Adriatic to service the city; glassmakers soon followed the artifacts. There is no doubt that these artisans came from the East; the technology employed and the physical characteristics of the locally produced goods which have been recovered from the area are identical to those which were made in and imported from the Galilee and Alexandria.

The Jewish community of Aquileia, which existed from the earliest period of the Roman occupation of the Aquileian area, may have become one of the largest outside of Judah, exceeded only by the community at Rome itself and at Alexandria. "There can be no doubt," writes Yves-Marie Duval, interpolating from the voluminous writings and correspondence of St. Jerome and others, "that one can abstract the existence of thousands of Jews in Aquileia and in the region."[48] Other scholars have noted the many references to the substantial Jewish influence on Christian affairs in Aquileia and nearby towns.[49] A Jewish population of many thousands is also manifested by numerous Hellenicized inscriptions of Eastern immigrants.[50] Many other inscriptions indicate that the great Roman port, indeed, harbored a significant Jewish population from the earliest incidence of Roman influence, long before the Christians made themselves felt in the area.[51] The existence of a great synagogue is attested by a funerary inscription of the third to early fourth century dedicated to the daughter of the head of the elders of the synagogue.[52] We learn further about the existence of a great Aquileian synagogue from indisputable evidence. Responsibility for the destruction of an obviously important synagogue by fire in the fourth century by Christian arsonists was denied by Ambrogio in a letter addressed to Theodoric in December of the year 388, in which the event was characterized as "an act of providence."[53]

A good portion of the inscriptions on the tombs of the area identify the deceased by vocation; some specify that the deceased was either a slave or a freedman. The textile industry is well represented among these inscriptions and the complexity and sophistication of the industry is delineated by the fine distinctions of the categories of arts involved in the industry, both in materials (wool, linen or silk) and in quality. Both the manufacture of textiles and the dyeing of fabrics were arts which were then and continued to be notable occupations of the Jews throughout Europe into the modern age. Similarly, the metalworking trade, another vocation in which Eastern artisans were dominant under the Romans, was separated into lead-, iron-, gold- or silver-smithing. Lead was used largely for conduits; one slave left a leaden tube to be used as his headstone, which he inscribed: *Aq(uileiae) Iuvinalus f(acit)*, which translates to "Iuvinalus of Aquileia made this."

The introduction of glassmaking into the area is evidenced by the discovery of the scoria of glassmaking furnaces and has been verified by a few intriguing signatures of Aquileian artisans molded into the glass. Two glass vessels with inscriptions were found in Linz, an Austrian city on the Danube which lies along the Roman route across the Dolomites. The vessels bear the inscription *Sentia Secunda facit Aquileiae vitra,* which contains a name which piques our curiosity because the feminine form of the phrase marks it as being the name of a woman. She was also a slave or the descendant of a slave, as was another such glassmaker who proudly molded his name into his vessels: *C. Salvius Gratus*. Salvius was a name commonly taken by slaves and remained the name of their descendants, many of whom eventually became gentlemen of stature.[54]

A third name found on glassware recovered in Aquileia is that of Ennion, the most famous of Roman period glassmakers, whose workshop was based in Judah before the name was officially changed to Syro-Palestine by the Romans. Harden advanced the hypothesis that Ennion had established a branch workshop at Aquileia, but it soon became evident that Ennion's ware came among the large quantity of glassware imported before glassmaking was introduced. The importing of glassware into Aquileia from the East was continuous throughout its history regardless of the existence of local facilities.

A CUP SIGNED "ENNION MADE IT". The best known of all the glassware-makers of the Roman period is Ennion, whose signature in Greek appears on glassware imported to Roman Italy from *Eretz Israel*. Ennion is a Greek transliteration of the Hebrew name "Anania". Vessels signed by an almost equally famed glassware-maker of the period, "Aristeas of Sidon" have also been recovered from Roman sites in Italy. A family tomb in Beth Shearim, Israel, bears that same inscription, and, although of a somewhat later period, may be of the family of the glassware-maker.
*Photograph courtesy of The Corning Museum of Glass.*

The Jewish community suffered through an early and a particularly virulent persecution in the area of Aquileia. Christianity had been implanted into the region in apostolic times, certainly before the end of the third century; St. Mark traditionally wrote or translated his gospel into Greek in Aquileia after having been sent to the city by St. Peter from Rome. St. Hermagoras, who was born in Aquileia, followed St. Mark into Aquileia and was consecrated the first bishop of Italy over a diocese which only ranks next to Rome in antiquity. By the end of the fourth century Valerian presided in Aquileia over the bishoprics of Venetia, Istria, Noricum, Pannonia, Como, "and as some say, even Augsberg."[55]

The destiny of the Jews awaited the resolution of the initial struggle of the church against the Arians and pagans, both of whom regarded Jesus as human. Chromazio, the episcopal head of the church in Aquileia, after crushing these heretical groups, turned malignant attention to the Jews, who numbered in the thousands. A most malevolent repression ensued and Jewish institutions were demolished. "There cannot be any doubt that in Aquileia...at least until 388, a synagogue existed," unequivocally states Luila Cracco Ruggini, a writer who examined the actions of Chromazio against the Jews.[56] No Jewish structure is known to have survived into the fifth century, and definitive traces of the considerable Jewish presence are relegated to a few scriptural, morphological and indirect references.

At Monastero, a suburb of Aquileia, little more than a few meters removed from the Roman ruins of Aquileia itself, stands a museum. It is a simple but impressive modern structure whose facade boldly proclaims that it is a "PALEO-CHRISTIAN MUSEUM." The museum consists of but one huge room within which is featured remnants of the walls of an ancient building and an extensive mosaic floor. One is immediately struck by the fact that the walls of the building and the floor bear no relationship to each other. The crude ashlar blocks of the bases of the walls plow across the masterfully wrought mosaic patterns in utter disregard of their layout; the walls disdainfully rip through the names of donors which had been carefully integrated into the mosaic fabric of the floor. One need not be an archeologist to recognize that those responsible for the walls were not merely indifferent to but contemptuous of the mosaic floor of a building which stood on that very spot and of which only the tesserae remain.

Old Testament themes are represented in a number of Aquileian glass relics; one plate is decorated with an incised depiction of Daniel in the lion's den.[57]  Another section of a surviving glass vessel features Abraham and Isaac in the foreground and the facade of the Jerusalem temple clearly placed above them in the background exactly as it appears in the context of other Jewish art.[58]  The design molded into the Aquileian glass vessel is, for example, a replica of the depiction of the Temple facade on a silver tetradrachma of Bar Kokhba, struck in 133 C.E. just before the conclusion of the Second Jewish War against Rome.  The same image appears, for another example, on a gold-glass bottom of a vessel from the Jewish catacombs dated the third-fourth century C.E. and now deposited in the Biblioteca Apostolica of the Vatican.  Nor are Italian gold-glass vessel fragments with Jewish themes relegated exclusively to Rome.  A gold-glass vessel bottom is also displayed in the Aquileian museum; it pictures Moses about to strike a huge desert rock to produce a miraculous flow of water.[59]  All of these Aquileian renderings of common Jewish art themes have been hitherto presented as Paleo-Christian art.

OIL LAMP FROM AQUILEIA.  The presence of a Jewish community in Aquileia is attested by the tomb inscriptions and by such objects as the pictured oil lamp with a *menorah* molded into it.

ABRAHAM OFFERING THE SACRIFICE OF ISAAC. In this fragment of a vessel recovered from the ruins of Aquileia, the architectural facade appearing above the figures, typical of many other renditions of the Jerusalem temple, clearly stamps its Hebraic character; the vessel has been, nonetheless, accredited to "Paleo-Christian" art by unobservant scholars.
*Photograph courtesy of the Aquileian Museum.*

A GOLD-GLASS FRAGMENT. The bottom of a bowl similar to those recovered from Jewish catacombs of Rome and elsewhere. Moses is depicted in the act of striking the rock from which water poured to assuage the thirst of the Jews in their Exodus from Egypt.
*Photograph courtesy of the Aquileian Museum.*

Saint Ambrose resided in Aquileia, as did Saint Jerome. It was very likely St. Jerome's Aquileian experience which led him to complain bitterly and resentfully that the Semitic artisans, mosaicists and sculptors were everywhere, that not only was retail trade in their hands but that they controlled the export of industrial products such as those made of glass, silk and leather. The saint cited glassmaking as one of the trades "by which the Semites captured the Roman world."[60]

The invasion under Attila the Hun was no less destructive of the suffering community of Jews than it was of the Christians who suppressed them; the devastation of the area affected both Jewish presence and glassmaking and obliterated whatever traces of Jewish presence were left under the Christians; the city was destroyed in 452, and in the year 552 the citizens who returned were again driven away and the area was ravished. Commerce and artisanship, including the art of glassmaking, virtually disappeared. The glassmaking art did mysteriously surface here and there in the area during the following five centuries. Glass mosaic tiles were evidently being locally produced; the island of Torcello, to which some of the refugees from the mainland escaped the depredations of the invading barbarians, contains evidence of a group of furnaces which were in operation during part of this period.

Glassware from the East found its way into every western region into which the Roman legions encamped and settled. North Africa, Spain, Noricum, Pannonia, the four Gauls, the two Germanies and Britain each experienced a similar progression of events. The conclusion of military action was followed by a parceling out of the territory to the Roman soldiers who had completed their duty; the indigenous population, slaves and serfs, were put to tilling the soil and serving their masters, the newly enfranchised Roman landowners as well as the officials drawn from the local hierarchy-- whose allegiance to Rome was purchased with a bribe of Roman citizenship and a continuation of their privileged social position. The ensuing affluence of the new nobility thus established stimulated an increase in the quantity of imported goods. Army gear, villa furnishings and the emoluments of luxurious accessories, clothes and furnishings of suitable status were in great demand by the members of the reconstituted establishment. The cost of importing was soon alleviated by the import of slaves for the stimulation of local production, by encouraging the immigration of artisans whose sophisticated skills were novel to the backward hinterlands of Europe and by inviting entrepreneurs whose contacts and worldly wise bartering were indispensable for the purpose.

The production of certain products, however, was not only beyond the capabilities of the indigenous population but also beyond those of the slaves brought in from most areas, even those from areas with more advanced cultures. The manufacture of glass and glassware is an outstanding example of such an industry; the knowledge of the process was contained within certain Near Eastern Semitic groups and did not filter through to other cultures. Semitic glassmakers were among those encouraged to immigrate into newly established Roman territory, and they did. The Eastern artisans set up their enterprises in strategic market areas and supplied their wares to the burgeoning class of Roman and non-Roman overlords. The history of Jewish penetration into the areas opened for settlement by the Roman legions begins with the use of slaves and continues with an influx of free artisans.

> According to a chronicle the most ancient Jews in the Rhine district are said to have been the descendants of the legionnaires who took part in the destruction of the Temple. From the vast horde of Jewish prisoners, the Vangioni had chosen the most beautiful women, had brought them back to their stations on the shores of the Rhine and the Main, and had compelled them to minister to the satisfaction of their desires. The children thus begotten of Jewish and Germanic parents were brought up by their mothers in the Jewish faith, their fathers not troubling about them. It is these children who are said to have been the founders of the first Jewish communities between Worms and Mayence. It is certain that a Jewish congregation existed in the Roman colony, the city of Cologne, long before Christianity had been raised to power by Constantine.[61]

The second influx of Jews into the Roman-occupied territories of Europe took place with the spread of the network of roads. Jewish craftsmen "went through Marseilles into Gaul, and crossed the Alps into the Rhineland."[62] Communities of Near Eastern artisans and merchants sprang up along the routes, reaching as far as Cologne. The ruins of two early synagogues in that city situated on the banks of the Rhine River at the limit of the Roman Empire attest to the importance of the Jewish presence. Frederic Neuberg points out that "The oldest settlement in Germany was in Trier (a ghetto) and the first glasshouses of the Rhineland were founded there. After Trier, the oldest ghettos are in Cologne and Andernach, and it

A MOLD-BLOWN, BARREL-SHAPED BEAKER, 1ST CENTURY BCE. The beaker was found in *Eretz Israel* ("Syria"). This style of beaker began to appear in Europe behind the Roman legions as they drove through Gaul as far as Cologne. At first imported from the Near-East, such beakers and other glassware were later produced locally as Near-Eastern artisans and merchants established communities near the Roman encampments.
*Photograph courtesy of the Yale University Art Gallery.*

170

is significant that the oldest-established glasshouses in Germany are likewise those in Cologne and Andernach."[63] Glassmaking was an art practiced in that Roman outpost soon after the Jews settled into it; glassmaking, in fact, appears throughout Gaul coincident with the establishment of Jewish communities. One of the objects retrieved from the ruins of ancient Cologne was a gold-glass plaque ornamented with a depiction of a menorah, the Jewish seven-branched candelabra; the plaque is now a part of the collection of the Cologne Museum.[64] The design of the menorah was similar to another such gold leaf rendition of a menorah sandwiched into a gold-glass medallion in the Roman catacombs of the Galleria San Georgio, complete with a funerary inscription which ends with the Hebrew word *shalom* (peace). Other equivalent gold-glass plaques are in various collections, and some also depict the facade of the Jerusalem temple.[65]

It was not long before Jewish artisans were to be found in every important site of Roman Gaul and Germany.

> The Jewish merchants whose business pursuits brought them from Alexandria or Asia Minor to Rome and Italy, the Jewish warriors whom the emperors Vespasian and Titus, the conquerors of Judea, had dispersed as prisoners throughout the Roman provinces, found their way, voluntarily or involuntarily into Gaul and Iberia....The Gallic Jews, whose first settlement was in the district of Arles, enjoyed the full rights of Roman citizenship, whether they arrived as merchants or fugitives, with the peddlers pack or in the garb of slaves....In the Frankish kingdom founded by Clovis, the Jews dwelt in Auvergne (Arvena), in Carcassonne, Arles, Orleans, and as far north as Paris and Belgium. Numbers of them resided in the old Greek port of Marseilles, and Beziers (Biterrae) and so many of them dwelt in the province of Narbonne that a mountain near that city of that name was called *Mons Judaicus*....The Jews of Frankish and Burgandian kingdoms carried on agriculture, trade and commerce without restraint; they navigated the seas and rivers in their own ships. They also practiced medicine, and the advice of the Jewish physicians was sought even by the clergy, who probably did not care to rely entirely on the miraculous healing powers of the saints and of relics. They were also skilled in the use of weapons of war, and took an active part in the battles between Clovis and Theodoric's generals before Arles (508).[66]

W. A. Thorpe, the English glass historian, reports that the semitic artisans who had settled along the route of the Roman legions, "had their quarters in the great industrial cities, with the family tradition of their successors at Altare, Murano and in Normandy, they combined a willingness to migrate, a fervent sense of parenthood, a racial solidarity, a genius for selling, semitic qualities that no other glassmakers ever possessed." Thorpe continues to relate that by the late Roman period in

> Nice, Marseille, Orleans, Bourges, Treves, and above all, Paris, industrial capital was controlled by the Semites....Their activities were not confined to the black-coat business of bankers, ship-owners, money-lenders, and wholesale produce merchants. They were the leaders in the professions of law and medicine and in the arts of jeweler, goldsmith and silversmith.[67]

The equally prestigious German glass historian, Axel von Saldern, agrees, noting that while Syria-Palestine remained the cradle of the newly created industrial glassmaking due to the invention of glassblowing and while Alexandria continued to produce luxury ware, "Naples, Rome, northern Italy, south eastern France, Cologne and other cities along the Rhine could also claim an efficient industry established mainly by Jewish glassmakers emigrated from Palestine in the first century."[68]

Von Saldern points out the unmistakable similarity of certain glass products of Palestine such as the ribbed-bowl with those retrieved from Egypt, Rome or Avignon and that others found throughout the Roman Empire, the "so-called Sidonian mold-blown ware," "snake-thread bottles," and "'saddle'-flasks" were "apparently made exclusively in Palestine."

As long as the art of glassmaking remained in Jewish hands, it grew in artistry and application. Thorpe points out that the decline of the art of glassmaking and that of the numerous other disciplines introduced into Gaul by the Semites, was brought about by

> the growth of anti-Semitism in the Merovingian Gaul during the 5th and 6th centuries. This movement had been made familiar in its religious aspect as a conflict of the Christian church with the Jews, but the real issue was racial and commercial. The Germans who invaded Gaul discovered that the capital of the country was largely in the hands of the orientals, in some trades their superiors as craftsmen, and invariably their superiors as men of business....The glass industry suffered with the other rackets of the Semites [and] high class models disappear when anti-Semitic propaganda was most intense.[69]

GLASS *RHYTA*. The dates of these two drinking vessels span six or more centuries. They are glass replications of European drinking cups made of animal horns. The rhyton on the left, reputedly found on Mt. Carmel, dates to the 1st century CE and is of a type produced in *Eretz Israel* for export to the hard-drinking European market soon after the Romans established themselves in the Holy Land. The Rhyton on the right is said to have been produced after the 5th century CE in Sassanian Persia, where the art of glassmaking burgeoned as a result of the influx of Jews escaping Roman persecution after the Bar Khochba revolt was put down (see chapter 9).
*Photograph courtesy of the Newark Museum.*

Manual labor did not achieve respectability until well into the Christian period. The church did not relish dependence on Eastern artisans who stubbornly refused to relinquish their religion or who practiced it surreptitiously when circumstances forced them to assume a Christian facade. The secrets of the arts practiced by the Eastern artisans, especially the secrets of the art of glassmaking, remained confined to the Semites who practiced them. The dependence of the Roman establishment on that privileged group for glassware, both locally made and imported, led to St. Jerome's bitter complaint about the hold Semitic artisans had on the Roman world through the exercise of their unique skills, among which the art of glassmaking was conspicuously confined to the Semitic "Orientals".[70] This humiliating dependency engendered a humble attitude toward labor; the church pragmatically promulgated a program of replacing the stiff-necked Eastern artisans. The guilds were formed, put under the protection of specialized Christian saints, and members were required to be or to become Christians. Monasticism was fostered and a regimen of manual labor introduced, a process which served as an additional means of placing the arts under church control.

> The effect of the western view was to restore respectability not only to the artisan but to manual labor, to remove the disrepute under which it had suffered during all of ancient times. And this monasticism played a significant role. From the beginning, the monks had been mindful of the Hebrew tradition that work was in accordance with God's commandment.[71]

The Jews were driven from most manual trades; whatever Jewish artisans remained in the guilds ostensibly converted to Christianity. Conversion was, however, unevenly enforced because no substitutes existed for certain skilled artisans. Jewish glassmakers were given specific exemption from conversion as a condition for continuing in their occupation.

> In Cologne... where the guilds succeeded in ultimately barring Jews from almost all of industrial occupations, they still allowed them to become glaziers, probably because no other qualified personnel was available. This exception was reminiscent of the Greek glassblowers in seventh-century France who claimed to produce glass as well as the Jews did.[72]

Glassmaking was a unique exception to the otherwise strictly enforced edicts which issued forth with insistent regularity from a church which had become powerful enough to impose its strictures upon society and to bend the nobility to its purpose. The Dark Ages which descended upon Europe was accompanied by recurrent repressions of the Jews; time and time again Jews were expelled from various areas, only to be recalled when the economies of the regions suffered adversely by their absence. Some of the glassmakers eventually converted; others sought greener pastures to the east and south, and never returned.

Meanwhile, in Eretz Israel, the Land of Israel, in Alexandria and in the Fayoum of Egypt, the industry flourished.

The art of glassmaking was given great impetus by the invention of glassblowing, since the process made the products affordable. The Jewish

FILIBERTO, PATRON SAINT OF THE GLASSMAKERS OF ALTARE (NORTHWESTERN ITALY).
Glassmakers are dimly seen at the fiery "glory holes" of the furnace at the lower left of the timeworn painting. S. Filiberto was one of the numerous saints assigned to oversee the trades and guilds. Glassmakers in the area of Cologne were excepted from the otherwise strictly enforced requirements for conversion.
*Photograph by the author; the painting hangs in the parochial church of the glassmakers of Altare, Italy.*

sages who compiled the Midrash all worked at trades, and their familiarity with the process of glassmaking is reflected in Midrashic references, extensions of the Talmudic reference in Job in which wisdom is described as being more valuable than gold or sapphire or glass, the most costly of earthly materials.[73] The Palestinian Talmud describes the fusion of glass by rolling (the production of agate glass by marvering differently colored molten glass together), as well as the layering of glass and cutting through the layers (the production of cameo and diatreta glassware).[74] In Genesis 2:7 it is written that God formed man out of the dust of the earth, and he blew into his nostrils the breath of life. The elements of the process of this ultimate act

A "LOTUS BUD BEAKER", 1ST CENTURY CE. The beaker was produced in *Eretz Israel* for export to the Central European market. "Lotus bud" beakers were typical of a type of drinking vessel adapted to the foibles of hard drinkers. The style replicates metal prototypes and was designed to assist the inebriated to hold on to slippery vessels. One of two similar beakers in the Yale University Collection was recovered from Caesarea in Israel.
*Photograph courtesy of the Yale University Art Gallery.*

of creation are likened in the Midrash to that of blowing glass, in which the breath of man becomes the soul of the vessel he creates just as the breath of God becomes the soul of man.[75]

A glass vessel, it is written, begins with the breath (*neshimah*) of the glassblower, which flows as a wind (*ruach*) through the glassblowing pipe, and finally comes to rest (*nafash*) as an ethereal element within the vessel. Man's soul (*neshamah*) stems from the same root, *neshimah*, and refers to that element of the soul that is bound to the body and "rests" there. *Ruach*, which means a wind, is the part of the soul that binds the *neshamah* and *Nefesh*.

Throughout the upper and lower Galilee, and all along the Judean shores, men were blowing soul into hot glass.

# NOTES

1. W. A. Thorpe, *English Glass*, 1949, p. 2.

2. Aristotle, *Politics*, 3.3.2

3. Homer, *Iliad*, 1.599.

4. Xenophon, *Oeconomicus*, 4.3.

5. Dan Barag, *Ancient Glass in Modern Research*, 1972, p. 123.

6. Philo, Judaeus, *Quod imnis Probus Libus Sit*, p. 157.

7. Cicero, *On Duties*, I, xii, II, xxiv. 87, xxv.

8. Cicero, Ibid., 1:150-151.

9. M. I. Finley, *The Ancient Economy*, 1985.

10. Cicero, *Pro Rabirio Postumo*, an oration given in 54 BCE.

11. Hermann Vogelstein, *The Jews of Rome*, 1940, pp. 9, 10.

12. Vogelstein, Ibid., p. 65.

13. Pliny, *Natural History*, Book XXXVI, p. 379.

14. Pliny, idem.

15. *Midrash Rabbath*, translated by Rabbi S. M. Lehrman, Soncino Press, London and New York, p. 330.

16. References to diatreta are also found in: Genesis Rabbah, section 9; Ruth Rabbah, section 19; Exodus Rabbah, end of section 27; Esther Rabbah to I,7. See Smith, *Dictionary of Greek and Roman Antiquities*, Third American Edition, New York, 1858; *A Dictionary of the Targunum, The Talmud Bible and Yurushalmi, and the Midrashic Literature*, Vol. I, Pardes Publishing Co., Jerusalem, 1950.

17. Thorpe, Ibid., p. 3.

18. Dan Barag, "Recent Epigraphic Discoveries Related to the History of Glassmaking in the Roman Period," *Annales du 10th Congress*, Madrid-Segovie, 1985, pp. 113-116. Barag refers to: Erim & Reynolds, 1973, with notes by K. D. White and D. Charlesworth.

19. Barag, Ibid., p. 114, quotes the disappointment of Dorothy Charlesworth in discovering that only Judea and Alexandria are specified as exporters of glassware: "This is extremely vague and covers only a surprisingly limited range....It allows for only two sources, Alexandria and Judaea, which implies that other East Mediterranean glassmaking

centers were not exporting products not sufficiently distinguished from Alexandrian or Judaean to require separate tariffing and presumably that the major centers of the West, Italy and Cologne area were not trading with the East Mediterranean."

20. C.S. Lightfoot, *A Catalog of Glass vessels in Afyon Museum,* British Institute of Archeology at Ankara, Monograph No. 10, BAR International Series 530, 1989, pp. 15,16.

21. Donald B. Harden, *Glass of the Caesars* (a catalog of the exhibition so named), Olivetti, Milan, 1987, pp. 203,4.

22. Vogelstein, Ibid., p. 17.

23. Vogelstein, Ibid., pp. 17, 18.

24. Leo W. Schwarz, *Great Ages and Ideas of the Jewish People*, p. 118; Vogelstein, Ibid., p. 27.

25. Vogelstein, Ibid., p. 25.

26. David Philipson, *Old European Jewries*, 1895, p. 122; D. Cassel, "Juden," *Allgemeine Encyclopedia*, XXVII, editors: Ersch und Gruber, p. 148.

27. A. Berliner, *Geschichte der Juden in Rome*, vol. I, 1893, p. 105; Philipson, idem.

28. Philipson, idem.

29. Vogelstein, Ibid., p. 77

30. Pliny, Ibid., XXXVI, p. 194.

31. Russell Meiggs, *Roman Ostia*, 1960\77, p. 587.

32. Meiggs, Ibid., p. 587.

33. Meiggs, Ibid., pp. 4, 214.

34. Vogelstein, Ibid., p. 43.

35. J. P. Brown, *Lebanon and Phoenicia*, I: "Beirut," p. 111.

36. Ian Burgoyne, "The Evolution of Glassmaking Techniques," *Journal of the Pilkington Glass Museum*, June 1980, vol. 80, no.1.

37. Frederic Neuberg, *Ancient Glass*, 1962, p. 77.

38. Erwin R. Goodenough, *Jewish Symbols in the Graeco-Roman Period*, 1953, vol. 12, ch. 2, p. 22.

39. Vogelstein, Ibid., p. 39.

40. For a full discussion of the use of fish, bread and wine as Jewish, pre-Christian symbols and of including fish et. al regularly and even ritually as part of the Sabbath meals, see Erwin R. Goodenough, "The Symbolic Value of the Fish in Judaism," *Jewish Symbols in the Graeco-Roman Period*, vol. 5, 1953.

41. Vogelstein, Ibid., p. 34.

42. Vogelstein, Ibid., p. 39.

43. Phoebe Phillips, *The Encyclopedia of Glass*, 1981, p. 34.

44. Axel von Saldern, *Glas von der antike bis zum jugendstil*, 1980, p. 19.

45. Polybius, *The Rise of the Roman Empire*, Book 2:17.

46. Livy, *The Early History of Rome*, Book 1.

47. Tacitus, *Germania*, 46.

48. Yves-Marie Duval, "Aquilee et la Palestine entre 370 et 420," *AA*, p. 263: "Il ne fait pas de doute qu'on ne peut faire abstraction des milieux juifs d"Aquilee et de la region."

49. Luila Gracco-Ruggini, "Ebrei e Orientali in Aquileia," *AA*, pp. 352-382.

50. B. Forlati Tamaro, "Iscrizioni greche di Siriani a Concordia," *AA*, pp. 383-392.

51. Giovanni Brusin, "Orientali in Aquileia romana," *AN*, XXIV & XXV, 1953-1954, pp. 56-70.

52. Luila Cracco Ruggini, "Il vescovo Cromazio e gli ebrei di Aquileia," *AA*, VIII, 1975, p. 363.

53. Ruggini, idem.

54. M. D. Calvi, *I Vetri Romani*, 1969, p. 11.

55. Hamilton Jackson, *The Shores of the Adriatic: The Italian Side*, 1906, p. 24.

56. Ruggini, idem.

57. Rosa Barovier Mentasti, "La coppa incisa con 'Daniele nella fossa dei leoni' al museo Nazionale Concordiese," *AN*, Anno XIV, pp. 157-172.

58. Luisa Bertacchi, "Due vetri paleocristiani di Aquileia," *AN*, Anno XXXVIII, 1967, pp. 142-150.

59. M. C. Calvi, "Il miracolo della fonte nel vetro dorato del museo di Aquileia," *AN*, Anno XXX, 1959, pp. 38-48.

60. St. Jerome, *Comm. in Exekiel*, xxvii, in *Pat. Lat.* 25, 313, "Orbe, Romano Occupato."

61. Heinrich Graetz, *History of the Jews*, vol. III, 1967, p. 41.

62. Frederic Neuberg, *Ancient Glass*, 1962 p. 56, quoting Daremberg and Saglio, *Dictionaires des Antiques Grecxques et Romanins*, vol. III, p. 939.

63. Neuberg, Ibid., p. 56.

64. Neuberg, Ibid., p. 70, quoting from: M. Schwab, and A. Reifenberg, *Estratto dalla Rivista di Archeologica Cristiana*, 1939, XV, 3,4.

65.  Neuberg, Ibid., p. 70, referring to descriptions of such gold-glass plaques in *Archives de l'Orient Latin*, vol. 1884, Chapter VII, pp. 439-465; Leopoldt Angelos, *Das Judische Goldglas*, Berlin, 1928; see also Erwin R. Goodenough, *Jewish Symbols in the Greco-Roman Period*, vol. II, illustrations 962-975. Item 975 is presumably from Cologne.

66.  Graetz, Ibid., p. 35.

67.  Thorpe, *English Glass*, 1935, pp. 7, 8, 11, 75, 76.

68.  Axel von Saldern, *Glas von der Antike bis zum Jugendstil*, 1980, p. 19.

69.  Thorpe, Ibid., p. 77.

70.  St. Jerome, Ibid.

71.  Casson, Lionel, *Ancient Trade and Society*, 1984, p. 147.

72.  Salo W. Baron, Arcadius Kahan and other contributors, ed. Nachum Gross, *Economic History of the Jews*, 1975, p. 40.

73.  Job, XXVIII, 1-17.

74.  *Palestinian Talmud*, ch. IV, p. 59b.

75.  Exodus 23:12, 31:17 and: Moshe Chaim Luzzatto, *Derech haShem* (The Way of God), 1983, part 2, pp. 347-8, referring to the Midrash *Bereishis Rabbah* 14:9, *Devarium Rabbah* 2:9 and *Shaar haGilgulim* I.

A PLATE OF THE MID-FIRST CENTURY BCE FOUND NEAR EN-GEDI. This cast and magnificently carved glass plate is one of a set of three plates found by the archeologist Yigael Yadin carefully wrapped in palm fiber and perfectly preserved in a cave near En Gedi in Israel. They were hidden in the cave about 40 BCE and were therefore produced before that time. The clarity of the crystal and the perfection of the workmanship attest to the highly advanced chemical knowledge and technological proficiency of its producers. The platter is now on exhibit in the Israel Museum's Shrine of the Rock. A blown glass flask was found together with the plate, proof that the practice of that revolutionary technology was already being performed in *Eretz Israel* at that time.
*Photograph courtesy of the Israel Museum, Jerusalem.*

182

# CHAPTER 7

# THE GLASSBLOWERS

## *The* Eretz Israel *Connection*

"TO THE GREEKS GLASS WAS SOMETHING NEW; TO THE ROMANS SOMETHING unknown," unequivocally stated the English glass historian, W. A. Thorpe, and added in emphasis, "The Romans, that is, the Latin-Italian people were not glassmakers and not glass-minded."[1] The ancient Greeks were barely familiar with glass objects and entirely ignorant of the technology by which glass was produced. The process of glassmaking was unknown to the Greeks until after Alexander the Great invaded Asia on his miraculous march of conquest. The mechanics of the art remained a mystery to the Greeks long after they had become the rulers of the area in which the art was being practiced. There is no reference whatsoever to the manufacture of glass in ancient Greece; the very first such reference to a glassmaker in Greece appears in the Christian Era; a sepulchral inscription then provides us with the name Euphrasios, a Jewish glassmaker who died in Athens.[2]

"We look in vain," complains Mary Luella Trowbridge, the author of the monumental work, *Philological Studies in Ancient Glass*, after combing diligently though Greek and Latin literature for a reference to glassmaking. Trowbridge's search led to her conclusion that: "As a foreign product, its nature was not sufficiently understood [by the Greeks] to prevent it from becoming confused with other substances."[3] The few references to glass objects in ancient Greek literature were invariably made in a foreign context. Theophastrus was the first Greek to refer to glass, and, not having a specific word for it, he used the Greek word *kyanos*, a term for glaze or paste (similar to that used for the production of faience). Theophastrus exhibited his lack of knowledge of the substance by proclaiming that "there are three

183

kinds of 'kyanos': the Egyptian, the Scythian, and third, the Cyprian."[4] Herodotus later made a differentiation between kyanos and glass by correctly defining the latter *lithos chyte* (molten stone). That label remained in use (sometimes shortened to *lithos*) even after a word for glass was coined: *hyalos*, which eventually came to identify glass as a palpable substance different from all others. The origin of the term "hyalos" is a mystery. Greek lexicographers and etymologists say it may derive from *hyelin* "to rain," since glass tends to be bright and shiny like wet objects.[5] One might equally postulate the derivation from the Hebrew חול (pronounced khal or khol) meaning a crystalline sand, since the Greeks were likely to have eventually learned that glass was being manufactured from sand, such as the sand of the Belus River estuary.[6]

MOSAIC CANE SECTIONS. A section of a mosaic cane and a bead made from such a cane, dated to between the 1st century BCE to the mid 1st century CE. The technology of producing mosaic canes and the highly prized products made from mosaic canes existed in the Levant for more than a millennium before the Greeks and Romans acquired a name for the material from which they were made.
*Photograph courtesy of The Corning Museum of Glass.*

The Romans were no less ignorant about glassmaking until they met with the industry on their Eastern adventures. Trowbridge was equally frustrated in her search through early Latin literature for a word which literally means glass as a distinct substance. "In early Latin literature," Trowbridge renews her complaint, "one may search in vain for any mention of glass, although there is no doubt that the Romans were perfectly familiar with the material itself."[7] Although the early Romans had experienced contact with glass through imported ware and thus had become familiar with the product, they were utterly ignorant of its genesis. Latin remained devoid of a word for glass until the Romans made do with a transliteration of the Greek term "hyalos" into *hyalus*. About that same time the Latin word *vitrum* appears for the first time in a speech by Cicero (54 B.C.E.),[8] and in Lucretius' *De Rerum*.[9]

Thus 2000 years passed after glass was first produced before any European was able to refer to glass in his own language by a specific name. The best that can be claimed for the ancient Romans is that glass was produced in the eastern Roman provinces during the period of Roman rule; glass was imported into and eventually produced in the western provinces and in Rome itself by foreigners during the latter half of Rome's existence as a sovereign power.

Where, then, was the Roman period glass actually made and by whom? Every type of glassware found entombed with its Roman possessors or recovered from the ruins of Roman period structures has also been found in *Eretz Israel*, the Land of Israel, in an earlier time frame. The advanced technique of glassblowing was already being invented somewhere in Galilee during the time the Romans were first encountering the process of glass-making in their military adventures around the Mediterranean. The revolutionary process was perfected in the first century B.C.E.; it reduced the cost of production, multiplied productive capacity, made cheaper forms of glassware available to the middle classes and spurred the export of glassware. It so happened that the expansion of Rome into the East took place during this very period and the western Roman provinces provided a substantial market for these new vessels. It was merely the coincidence of these events which led to the identification of blown glass with Roman hegemony. Glass containers for perfume and oil and for the ashes of the deceased, and, eventually, glassware from which to eat and drink became a staple product within middle- and upper-class Roman period households, while the exotic glassware-made in *mosaic, millefiore, diatreta* and *murrhine* techniques titillated the tastes of the very rich. Ownership of the finest examples of the latter costly ware became a matter of pride and status, while the plain blown ware served more practical purposes.

The standardly applied term "Roman Glass" is, therefore, misleading, for it camouflages the true provenience of the product and attributes a technology to a people who never practiced it. "Jewish glass, Roman period" would be a more appropriate and far more accurate label for virtually all the glassware produced during the historical period in which the Romans conquered much of the Western world. Jewish artisans of Eretz Israel, Alexandria and the Fustat produced virtually all of this ware, and Mid-Eastern artisans, Jews for the most part, were the ones who carried their craft into the Roman diaspora.

The earliest blown glass vessels were recovered from Eretz Israel; they were the products of a robust, ongoing industry. One of these early pieces, a flask, was found, for example, together with a magnificently cast and carved bowl by the distinguished Israeli archeologist Nahman Avigad in a

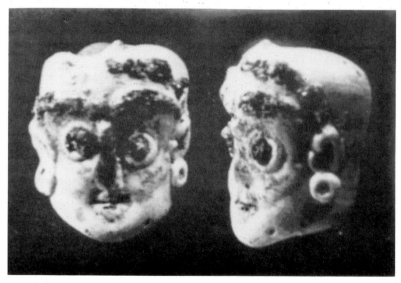

HEAD-BEADS FROM EN-GEDI. Two goggle-eyed head-beads recovered from near En-Gedi, similar to many being distributed around the Mediterranean and elsewhere except for the fact that most others are male and sport a black beard whereas these, found among a group of head-beads depicting black-bearded males, are depicted as earringed females. The eyes of the head-beads employ the same production technique as do the "eye-beads," which had an even wider distribution. Early examples of blown glass were also found at En-Gedi.
*Photograph courtesy of the Israel Museum.*

pre-Herodian Jewish cemetery at Ein-Gedi in Israel.  The site was destroyed by 40/37 B.C.E., and the bottle must, therefore, pre-date that time.[10]  The ubiquitous head-beads, similar to those surfacing from Canaanite colonies around the Mediteranean, most of which are dated to an earlier period, also showed up in the ruins of Ein-Gedi.  The manner in which these startling but highly decorative items were employed is well demonstrated by a complete necklace found in Tharros in Sardinia, in which a headbead served as a centerpiece.  The Ein-Gedi examples consisted of representations of both bearded male and earringed female heads.[11]

The Jews evidently treasured their glassware and took it with them when they hid out in the desert.  In 1955 two complete glass bowls and several hundred fragments of a variety of glass vessels of a later period were recovered from the so-called Cave of Horror, a cave in the Judean desert.  The shapes and material are characteristic of Judean manufacture.  "On historical and archeological considerations," writes Professor Dan Barag, "we have to attribute this material to the period of the Bar-Khochba, i.e., about the first third of the second century A.D."[12]

Older blown vessels have since been unearthed from dated sites, even from the heart of Old Jerusalem, where cast bowls, glass rods, hollow tubes, some blown bottles and other blown glass were found underneath a pavement which was laid down no later than 50/40 B.C.E.[13]  These vessels were evidently blown from the already formed glass tubes, and not from molten glass in a furnace crucible.  This secondary process is to be expected in an urban environment, but which, at the same time, amply demonstrates that the technique of blowing glass vessels had become a familiar one to the Jewish artisans at this early date.  Such blown glassware, found throughout Eretz Israel, provides the evidence that, at the very time glassmakers were first being installed in Rome, glassblowing, a technology accruing from 2000 years of intimate experience with the art, was already being practiced widely in Eretz Israel.  A great quantity and assortment of glassware shards was recovered from the ruins of shops which lined the street at the base of the Temple Mount.  The similarity of much of this ware to that of the furnace refuse found within Old Jerusalem indicates that much of the glassware being sold in these shops was produced in Old Jerusalem itself.

It is difficult to determine how far back glassware production was being performed in the city of Jerusalem, for much of the raw glass and other material indicative of such manufacture comes from undated sources.  The

LUMPS OF RAW GLASS, SHARDS OF BROKEN VESSELS (CULLET), AND GLASS RODS FROM HERODIAN JERUSALEM. Refuse from a glassware-making facility in the heart of the Jewish quarter of ancient Jerusalem dating to the mid-1st century BCE. Included in the cullet were quantities of shards of blown glass and partly blown glassware. The archeologist in charge, Professor Nahman Avigad, consulted with Dr. Gladys Weinberg and Professor Dan Barag, well-known experts on ancient glass, who confirmed that "no evidence of this sort has been found at any other site in the world." The Jerusalem glassware was undoubtedly fabricated from raw glass produced elsewhere in *Eretz Israel* for remelting in urban areas like Jerusalem by a glassware-maker; in modern times a glassware-maker in Hebron melts soda-pop bottles for the purpose. *Photographs reprinted by courtesy of Thomas Nelson Publishers, Nashville, Camden and New York, publishers of* Discovering Jerusalem, *by Nahman Avigad.*

# The Glassblowers

TUBES FOR BLOWING INTO VESSELS. The earliest known examples of the art of glass-blowing were included in the hoard of glass refuse from Herodian Jerusalem. Vessels were blown from preformed tubular glass, a process still being performed by modern glassware-makers who are now termed "flame-workers" to differentiate them from those who work directly from molten glass in crucibles fired in furnaces.

RODS FOR REWORKING INTO ARTIFACTS. Among the thousands of glass shards in the refuse recovered from Jerusalem were great quantities of rods of glass, many of which bore the impression of the pincers which held them while they were being drawn. Some of the rods were twisted while being drawn.

*Photographs reprinted by courtesy of Thomas Nelson Publishers, Nashville, Camden and New York, publishers of* Discovering Jerusalem, *by Nahman Avigad.*

Pool of Bethesda, for example, a reservoir constructed to contain water for the temple lying inside the East (Lions) gate to the city, was filled with material containing lumps of raw glass and the slag and scoria of glass furnaces. The "White Fathers" who excavated the site from 1959-1962, preserved only a portion of the material they retrieved; it was the diligence of Anita Engles, a writer on glass history who had long held that such production was indeed indigenous to Jerusalem, which brought the remainder of this material to public attention. The fragments of vessels recovered from the detritus "ranged from the late Hellenistic period (prior to glassblowing) up to late Islamic," reported Ms. Engles. Excavations outside the Damascus Gate from 1964-1966 by the British School of Archeology in Jerusalem under Dr. J. B. Hennessy produced another wide assortment of material, some of which came from stratified and dated levels and confirmed that glassware production endured over a long period of time nearby that site.[14]

Such indicative material has been showing up throughout the excavations in and around Jerusalem. Material recovered from the Jewish Quarter of the Old City of Jerusalem prove that it was a center of glassware production from at least the first centuries B.C.E., and remained so for a long time thereafter, a fact which has been thoroughly authenticated by substantial recoveries of definitive material in the process of the reconstitution of that quarter by the State of Israel over the last two decades. Fragments of so-called Islamic glass, that is, of glassware produced in the Jewish Quarter of Jerusalem during the Islamic period (661-1250 C.E.) are particularly proliferate. That such large quantities of this material were found in association with "wasters, unfinished pieces, and other refuse connected with the manufacture of glass[ware] such as actual lumps of raw glass, of the same color as the finished fragments--is quite surprising," writes Rachel Hasson of the L. A. Mayer Memorial Institute for Islamic Art in Jerusalem, adding that "this tenacity in glass[ware] production continued, despite such catastrophic disturbances as the Khwarezmian destruction of the city in 1244."[15]

It should not be surprising, therefore, that it is recorded that, soon after the advent of Islamic rule over Jerusalem, the Ommayad caliph Abd el-Malik (685-705 C.E.) employed a group of Jewish glassmakers (or, more likely, glassware-makers) for the production of glass lamps for the great Dome of the Rock in Jerusalem.[16] The duties of the 300 slaves (mameluks) were clearly specified, as were the duties of certain Christian and Jewish servants who were exempted from the poll tax. Ten Christian families were delegated to make and clean the mosque mats and to sweep out the conduits. Ten Jewish families were delegated to sweep the mosque after visitations and to keep the ablution places clean. The numbers of these Jewish janitory families rose in number to 20 in a later period. Ten other Jewish families were assigned to produce "glass vessels, glass rods, glass lantern bowls and glass plates for the lamps," wrote Jama ad Din Ahmad, the fourteenth century Jerusalemite chronicler of these events. "And it was designated that also from these men no poll tax was to be taken, nor from those who made the wicks for the lamps; and this exemption continued in force for all time for them and for their children, who inherited the office after them, from the days of Abd el-Malik forevermore."[17] Ten heads of families comprise a *minyan*, the number of adult males required by Jews to conduct certain religious rites, and would represent at least 50 persons.

The Jews of Jerusalem turned out a class of glassware of purple, blue and red glass colors decorated in a distinctive trailed technique (purple trailed ware) in the Jewish Quarter of Jerusalem well into the Mamlik period (1250-1717 C.E.). This glassware has been found far afield at Fustat in Egypt, at Samarra in Iraq, at Hama in Syria, and elsewhere[18] and is conventionally classified in glassmaking literature as Islamic glassware. Purple trailed ware was but one among a variety of products of a robust national glass industry, raw glass, cullet and finished glassware found strewn along the routes leading out in all directions from Eretz Israel. In the Negev at Mo'a, for example, the contents of a fortress and caravansary were preserved by a fire which put an end to its usefulness as a way station along the main mercantile route from Gaza to Nabatean Petra. The route was in use from the third century B.C.E., long before the Romans came into control. The caravansary was burned down in the Roman period, during the early third century C.E. The rich finds consist of simple everyday vessels such as cooking pots, juglets, lamps and tools used by the fortress guards on the one hand, and the more valuable objects that were part of the merchants wares on the other hand. Decorated Nabatean earthenware and Jewish blown glassware were the bulk of the exchange goods in evidence, a considerable sampling of which is now on display in the Museum of the Desert in Beer-sheba.

Throughout modern Israel *kibbutzniks*, Israeli communal farmers, are plowing up quantities of glass shards and the scoria of furnaces. The early writers on glass history took note of the existence of the widespread evidence of a substantial ancient glass industry throughout Eretz Israel. Anton Kisa, an early scholar of glass history, was impressed with the relationship of the Jews to the art of glassmaking,[19] and Frederic Neuberg followed in his footsteps. His book, *Ancient Glass*, is replete with references to the symbiotic relationship between the Jews and the art.[20] Both writers often employ the terms "Palestinian" and "Syrian" anachronistically but apologetically, but while the latter writer bows to the use of Syrian as indicating provenience, he notes that the "Jewish influence on Syrian glass is demonstrable." As far as the use of "Roman" or "Roman Empire" in the identification of eastern glassware of this period, however, Neuberg is unequivocal: "This term is geographically quite false and misleading." The bias of the archeological field at the time these writers penned their treatises was still colored by the Egyptian mystique, so they may be forgiven for assuming that the Egyptians as such were involved in the art. The anachronistic use of the Greek name "Phoenicians" for the Canaanites also permeates their work and adds to the confusion regarding the identification of the practitioners of the art.

Both writers attempt to honestly interpolate the facts as they know them from the limited and distorted state of archeological knowledge of their times in the light of their own gut feelings. Thus Neuberg, noting that the Jewish population of Alexandria is "said to have numbered several hundreds of thousands," adds that "it is most unlikely that the Jews, who had played so prominent a part in the intellectual, cultural and economic development of Alexandria, would have been mere passive spectators of the development of the Alexandrian glass industry." Neuberg then quotes Kisa, who suggested that "the Jews learned the art of glass painting from the Egyptians and the Phoenicians and practiced it in their native land, as well as in their settlements in Syria and Italy." The fact that artisans from Canaan were the artisans of both ancient Egypt and Phoenicia had not yet occurred to these well-meaning writers.

Neuberg, sojourning in Israel, was brought face to face with the ubiquitous appearance of glassmaking evidence throughout Eretz Israel, material being overlooked by archeologists. These worthy excavators were devoted to digging into tells, urban centers which had laid down evidence, strata by strata, of historical periods of their existence. At that time archeologists were prone to focus on the stratified remains of urban communities, cult centers, military or administrative headquarters. Little attention was paid to the countryside beyond the citadels. It is, however, precisely in out-of-the-way, formerly forested environments that the fast-disappearing remnants of unique and unmistakable evidence of ancient primary glassmaking can be found throughout the Holy Land, lying exposed to the elements and to the ravages of man.

Such areas offer no promise of museum-worthy statues, idols and golden treasure and were heretofore neglected; yet only remote areas can provide information regarding the esoteric art of producing glass from its raw materials. The evidence of primary glassmaking lays in the periphery and hinterlands of civilization because the huge quantity of fuel needed to fire the furnaces drove the glassmakers into the forests. As the artisans decimated the trees within a radius of a few hundred meters, they abandoned their furnaces and constructed new ones in virgin territory. The archeologists, perforce, did not encounter glassmaking facilities within the confines of their urban excavations, but merely the finished products, and the mystery of where the fabric of such products was made remained unsolved.

Primary glassmaking did take place, however, throughout the areas where dense forests once flourished in Eretz Israel. Kibbutzim now spread their farms throughout the countryside, paved roads now crisscross the land, and new communities are springing up like mushrooms. The fragile evidence is fast disappearing under the condominiums arising in formerly expansive open areas and as a consequence of the deep plowing practices of the modern farmer. Now that archeologists are turning their attention to more comprehensive studies of ancient environments to obtain a better understanding of village and hinterland life, the evidence of glassmaking, which lies not buried deep within the stratified detritus of successive civilizations but on or near the surface of open land, has largely been obliterated.

In 1962 much of that evidence was still extant and Frederic Neuberg strove to bring attention to it.

> In Palestine the slag heaps of former glasshouses still exist. Fragments and rejects from former manufacture have been found nearby. Among these are endless numbers of glass fragments consisting mostly of blown glass produced in a period of several centuries right up to the beginning of the Modern Era.[21]

Neuberg notes the existence of evidence of glass manufacture at Beth Shearim, and at "Sussita, (Hyppos) on Lake Tiberias" and of early blown glass elsewhere, and brings attention to "the construction of the Jerusalem-

Jaffa railway line [which] brought to light a great number of glasses and glass fragments. Further north along the line, the street of tombs at Hab-Beth Jubrin, and Askalon in the south, were very rich in finds." Neuberg's observations were ignored, and the deep plowing presently being practiced in Israel continues to disgorge and disperse the residue of ancient glass-making operations from countless sites throughout the upper and lower Galilee and along Israel's sandy shores.

Following in Neuberg's footsteps, the author made a survey of the kibbutzim and came upon the masses of indicative material which are being exhumed from the subsoil of the communal Israeli farms, the kibbutzim. Responsible members of fourteen of these communal farms immediately recognized samples of furnace scoria shown to them and confirmed that such material was regularly being plowed up and discarded. Many kibbutzim maintain small museums which are managed by dedicated members of the kibbutz. Some of these amateur archeologists took the trouble to preserve bits of the material recovered from a multimillennial interment. However, they tended to conserve only finished ware or fragments of finished ware, for they did not recognize the scoria of furnaces or did not understand its significance. Unfortunately, most of the material which was preserved cannot be dated accurately because it is not found in a datable context and therefore data obtained therefrom is dismissed by archeologists as unconvincing evidence. The associated materials which were occasionally kept as curiosities, however, are sufficient to provide proof that glassmaking was widely practiced in Eretz Israel in very early periods and that glassblowing was invented in the region, an event which may, indeed, have taken place even before the first century B.C.E.

At the kibbutz Hagoshrim, located in the upper Galilee, I met Nimrud, one of the remarkable amateur archeologists whose spare time is devoted to a passionate interest in the past. Nimrud was serving his stint for the kibbutz as the bartender in the kibbutz guest hotel. In his free time, Nimrud avidly pursued his archeological hobby until it became illegal for an unauthorized party to excavate at an ancient site. Nimrud's second name, Zakkimovich, had been reduced to Zakkai (an acronym of *Zera Kodesh Israel*, and otherwise meaning "not guilty"!) from Zakkimovich on the occasion of the settlement in Israel of his family, whose odyssey had included passage through Poland, Germany, Spain and Holland. Nimrud was born near the Mount of Hazor and it was there, in his younger days, that his interest in archeology was fired up. He insisted, vaunting his youthful archeological prowess, that he

NIMRUD ZAKKAI. Nimrud is one of the many amateur kibbutz archeologists whose passionate pursuit of their "hobby" in their spare time led to the salvage and preservation of ancient artifacts found in and around the kibbutzim. The glass beads were recovered from tombs near Hagoshrim by Numrud. Kibbutz museums in which ancient artifacts are exhibited are proliferate, but the activity of enthusiasts like Nimrud has been curtailed by the Israel Department of Antiquities in order to control the methods of excavation and thereby to secure the archeological value of the artifacts found.
*Photograph by the author.*

had known of Hazor's identity from studying the Bible and literature long before scientific excavation came to confirm Hazor's existence at the mount.

Nimrud's father was killed in battle against the Arabs in 1952, at a time when Nimrud was also soldiering in the Israelite army. Nimrud came to Hagoshrim in 1955, married and now boasts of six children. He studied agricultural engineering, completed his university studies in two years, and applied his knowledge to developing new varieties of corn and cotton.

"I also worked at building freezer-house machines. I designed machines which could freeze 45,000 tons of meat, eggs or fruit yearly." Nimrud was now well into his discourse. He motioned to another kibbutznik to take over the bar and sat down with me, placing a pair of drinks on the table before us. "After having produced 1270 freezers over a period of 12 years I got tired of talking to machines! I inveigled the kibbutz management to let me work at the bar, where I could talk to people."

Upon learning of my interest in his endeavors, Nimrud invited my wife and myself to meet him in his home after he had completed his shift at the bar. His modest residence stood amid a brilliant display of flowers. "It's another hobby of mine," said Nimrud as he greeted us at the door, observing our astonishment at the array of exotic blossoms, "I developed some of these flowering plants." After serving us coffee he led us to a ramshackle building in which his collection was housed. In the vestibule stood a glass-doored cabinet whose three shelves were crowded with glass vessels and artifacts of all shapes, periods and techniques. He proudly pulled out three drawers of the chest on which the cabinet stood to expose thousands of glass fragments, representing an even vaster variety of glassware. He pointed proudly to some misshapen lumps of glass and to fragments of what appeared to be a crucible with a frothy glass adherent to the inside surface. They were clearly scoria of a glassmaker's furnace.

Nimrud stated that some of the finished ware was associated with Hellenistic artifacts and was recovered from a cave in which he had found over 150 oil-lamps, several hundred beads, earrings and other decorative objects. An Alexandrian coin seemed to clinch the argument. "I started investigating sites in Hagoshrim in 1956, only a year after my arrival, and have been digging ever since. Perhaps you have heard of Tel Anafa? I figured out where that site should be located by studying Josephus Flavius. It turned out to be exactly where Joe had placed it, right over there between kibbutz Shamir and Kefar Szold." Nimrud went to the door, waving his hand toward

VESSELS AND ARTIFACTS FROM HELLENISTIC AND PRE-HELLENISTIC TOMBS NEAR KIBBUTZ HAGOSHRIM. The assortment of glassware and fragments found in the area cover a chronological range from the pre-Hellenistic into the Islamic periods, attesting to the persistence of glassmaking in the Upper Galilee.
*Photograph by the Author.*

the north.

"The mound covers about 350 square meters and is about ten meters high. Yet it took over ten years before anyone paid attention to my findings." He glanced at me, impishly, and flipped the Alexandrian coin. Tel Anafa, located just south of the head-waters of the Jordan River near Dan, was subsequently excavated from 1968 to 1970 under a grant by the Smithsonian Institution by the Museum of Art and Archeology of the University of Missouri. The mound is about 160 meters long and 110 meters wide, but only three well-defined Hellenistic period (Seleucid) strata were investigated within an area of 344 square meters, obviously the area referred to by

FURNACE SCORIA. Evidence of primary glassmaking being plowed up around Kibbutz Hagoshrim in the Upper Galilee. The various stages of glass manufacture are represented in the photograph: frit (a product of the first stage of glass manufacture); partially vitrified material attached to a furnace or crucible fragment; a lump of completely vitrified material; and a vessel fragment, evidently cullet.
*Photograph by the Author.*

Nimrud. The Seleucid settlement was implanted on the site no later than the early second century B.C.E. and flourished until the first century B.C.E., when it probably fell to the forces of Alexander Janneus and was incorporated into the Hasmonaean Kingdom before his death in 76 B.C.E.

Floors were covered with mosaics made of exceptionally small stone and glass tesserae. No second-century B.C. parallels for such rich appointments have as yet been found in Israel. Equally unparalleled is the abundance of molded glass vessels found everywhere on the site in levels beginning about 150 B.C. Fragments of about seven hundred and fifty glass bowls and cups...have been found thus far. Thus, the number in use during the seventy-five years of the settlement's history, both on the acropolis and in the lower town, must have run to many tens of thousands.[22]

In a paper presented at the Eighth International Congress of Glass, David Grose reconsidered previous assumptions regarding the pre-Roman glassware and concluded that the excavations at Tel Anafa "have not only filled a lacuna regarding the types of glass current during that time but they have shed light on one of the most prominent manufacturing centers of the Hellenistic age."[23]

The acropolis and upper town were constructed under the Seleucids and were undoubtedly inhabited by the Greek overlords, bureaucrats and their servants. Such towns are not considered Jewish in archeological parlance;

BLOWN GLASS VESSELS FROM TOMBS NEAR KIBBUTZ HAGOSHRIM. Amateur archeologists of various Kibbutzim insist that some blown glassware is found associated with pottery of the Hellenistic period, which would set the date of the invention of glassblowing earlier than has been heretofore projected.
*Photograph by the Author.*

but it is manifestly silly to suppose that any member of the noble hierarchy was a maker of the glassware found in the rich Greek (and later Roman) mansions exposed by archeologists atop these tells. The artisans lived more modestly elsewhere and worked in the forests extending out from the Seleucid city. "The only explanation for their abundance at Tel Anafa must be that they were made nearby," surmised Saul Weinberg, the excavator in charge.[24]

"Here are some of the shards I recovered from around Anafa." Nimrud pointed to a large boxful of glass vessel fragments. Many shapes and colors were included; but most startling were the sections of what were unmistakably blown glass vessels. If Nimrud had indeed collected this material from a Hellenistic strata as he insisted, then here was evidence of glassblowing which antedated all previous projections for the initiation of the process.

Saul Weinberg was unequivocal in insisting that all of the "tens of thousands" of glass vessels used by the Seleucid overlords were cast and not blown. Yet Nimrud was not alone in claiming that examples of pre-Roman blown glassware were indeed recovered, not only from the area of Tel Anafa but from many sites throughout *Eretz Israel*. The technology was undoubtedly in existence about the time the Romans established hegemony over the area, a process which took place after their conquest of Jerusalem in 63 B.C.E., and it is not unreasonable to assume that it had already been practised for some time before that date.

Glass shards recovered from urban centers represent but one aspect of the industry, and do not necessarily attest to the production of glass. The less glamorous scoria of furnaces, found strewn about the open countryside, is far more important, for the unattractive, even ugly product of the first stage of glass manufacture, frit, supplies the definitive evidence of the actual production of glass. Such furnace residue was interspersed among the glass fragments Nimrud had collected from the region around Tel Anafa. The earth which had been excavated to create pisciculture (hydroponic fish-farming) pools nearby Hagoshrim was replete with such material. Furnace slag together with glassware fragments had also been plowed up at a number of sites on the Hagoshrim kibbutz farmland itself. Included in the mind-boggling collection, in addition to furnace slag and scoria, were imperfectly blown vessels. These distorted objects are certain indicators of local manufacture, for they are clearly unsalable items produced at the site and set aside as cullet for remelting. Nimrud insisted that some of the blown

GLASS BRACELETS FROM TOMBS NEAR KIBBUTZ HAGOSHRIM.  The glass bracelets and beads recovered from tombs in the Upper Galilee are similar in style and composition to those found across Europe in Roman and Byzantine contexts.
*Photograph by the Author.*

glassware was unquestionably found in a Hellenistic period context, which would place their production well before the time generally acknowledged to have been that of the first appearance of the revolutionary glassblowing technology.

Nimrud had also collected ancient vitric materials from locations outside of the kibbutz Hagoshrim.  Some of the trailed and marvered core-formed glass vessels were pre-Hellenistic.  Byzantine bracelets and bells in his collection came from near by Hor Shat Tal, where they had been recovered along with other items of various periods.  A grave from a much later period rendered, among a variety of men's and women's jewelry, a blue glass figure of Christ, sporting a halo which was molded into the breast of the figure. The maker had evidently been at a loss as to how to hang the halo over the figure's head. "I have found things even from the Islamic period. Glassmakers were working in this area for many hundreds of years. There are a great many Jewish graves around but the authorities stopped me from investigating them. It is illegal to open Jewish graves. What a pity! How can we learn about Jewish history if we cannot disturb a few old bones? Look at this piece."

Nimrud held up a piece of glass on which was molded the Star of David, above which temple pillars were evident. "This must be from an much later period, or else it could be that the star is coincidental and the pillars represent the temple of the golden calf, as described by Flavius."

"Look at this obsidian." Nimrud held up a shiny brown wedge. "It is from this area, the only place in Eretz Israel where obsidian can be found. Lots of quartz is also around. The Dan River bed is loaded with quartz sand. That's why the glassmakers were working in this area."

A sampling of Nimrud's material was turned over to the Beit Ussishkin Museum at the kibbutz Dan. At that modest but impressive establishment Giora Gisis, the curator, showed me fragments from nearby Qivat Qatiya (Blacksmith's tell). There were also glass drops intended for inserting into the bezels of rings; the gemlike glass ovals were recovered from a Dolman dated back to c. 800 B.C.E. (Iron Age I), which was uncovered at the kibbutz Shamir, located, as was noted above, nearby Tel Anafa. There were several large bellows' nozzles in the museum's collection. "Hundreds of these have been found in this neighborhood," offered Gisis, noting my interest. "We assumed that they pertain to the iron smelting industry, which we know was being practiced here in ancient times." It had not occured to the archeologists that such massive bellows are also employed by glassmakers. The two industries are commonly pursued in the same forested areas since both require massive amounts of fuel. The nozzles were found at and around Tell Dan; some nozzles date back as far as 1500 B.C.E., the beginning of the Late Bronze Age. A substantive selection of large bellow's nozzles from the area is displayed in the Hebrew Union College Museum in Jerusalem. They leave no doubt as to the pyrotechnical proficiency of the artisans working in the area. The striking evidence of an advanced pyrotechnology presented by a large quantity of surviving bellow's nozzles is consistent with the movement of glassmaking around the crown of the fertile crescent and with the documentary and archeological evidence of ancient Amorite and Hurrian activity.

Nearby the kibbutz Dan I came across Amnun Assif, the driver of the kibbutz Ma'an Barukh, who spends his free time assembling and managing the Museum of the Hula Valley, a most impressive prehistorical museum. In the museum's storerooms only a few glass artifacts were left, Amnun having turned over most of his historical period finds to the Dan Museum. I interviewed members of other kibbutzim in the upper Galilee area which did not maintain a museum; one after another acknowledged that similar material was constantly turning up and that the material was occasionally turned over to interested parties in the kibbutzim with museums or to the Israel Department of Antiquities. At the Kibbutz Shamir, for example, Moshe Kagan, an accomplished artist as well as a passionate amateur archeologist, immediately recognized the samples of frit I had brought with me. "I have seen a lot of that kind of material at Banias," he exclaimed excitedly, "but no one has paid much attention to it."

Kagan brought out some of the glass shards collected from Banias (Caesarea-Phillipi) a site near the Golan Heights now in the process of excavation. Among the fragments was a "teardrop," the characteristic, unmistakable clipped end of a glassware-maker's trail. It was clear that the entire region was replete with evidence of an extensive conduct of the art of glassmaking over a long period of time; it was also evident that most of this valuable evidence was being forever lost through ignorance, negligence and apathy.

I was privileged to visit the site of a vast new city being built between Haifa and Sfat, Karmi-el, with Dr. Moty Aviam, the archeologist heading the Israeli Department of Antiquities in that sector of Israel. The development of a new city replete with broad, tree-lined boulevards was taking place around Mount Zagag, which translates from the Arabic to "Mount Glass." The entire mountain and extensive areas of the surrounding countryside are covered with glass shards. In a cursory survey of the area, I identified three additional sites where glassware-making had obviously been conducted on a massive scale. The hills and valleys of the region surrounding Mount Zagag were heavily forested at one time, a perfect locale for the activities of primary glassmakers. Unfortunately, the entire area around Mount Zagag is being developed on a huge scale and time is running out. A salvation excavation was conducted near "The Mountain of Glass" itself, but the pressure of development leaves little doubt that the evidence will fast disappear from all the surroundings which are being bulldozed away.

It should be noted that since broken glass is always reused by the glassmakers as cullet, such fragments, as well as raw glass lumps accidentally left over at an abandoned furnace site, are bound to be small in size and quantity unless left precipitously as a consequence of a disaster. The purpose of a collection of broken glass can often be determined by the presence of trail droppings, sure evidence of the activity of a glassware-maker. These small, sometimes minuscule leftovers are crude in appearance and the uninformed finder naturally assumes them to be of little value. The droppings from a glassware-maker's trails can be less than a centimeter in diameter, and are obviously difficult to distinguish in the furrows left by the plow; they are, however, a recognizable and perfect proof of the performance of the art at a particular site. The fact that this evidence still turns up at so many sites throughout Israel after two millennia of plowing is, perforce, significant.

Beads of the late Canaanite period and some glassmaking evidence of later periods were stored in a warehouse of the museum at kibbutz Hazorea, for example, a facility run by member Ezra Meyerhof. Hidden away on the top shelf of the museum storeroom is a row of cardboard boxes containing a large collection of glass shards, mainly but not restricted to an assortment of Hellenistic and Roman period fragments of glassware. Among them were items with spiral trails which recalled glassware of that type found in Roman Gaul, being similar in both technique and color.

The kibbutzim of the lower Galilee proved to be no less rewarding. At the kibbutz Mishmar ha-Emek, member Micha Lynn had put together a most impressive collection; ancient glassware and shards from a span of hundreds of years were in evidence in the kibbutz museum. Micha led me down into a cool, dank storeroom under the museum of the kibbutz; from the stacks of vessel shards he extracted lumps of raw glass and pieces of vitric materials backed with what was either a frothy residue from the heating process, and others attached to a friable piece of an earthenware crucible, much like those I had seen at the kibbutz Hagoshrim. Clearly, manufacture at the site was attested by these masses of amorphous but manifestative material. Most of it had been gathered near Geva, a site being excavated under Micha's supervision.

"This comes from Geva." Micha grinned, holding up the frothy fragment

Ezra Meyerhof at the Museum of the Kibbutz Hazorea.
*Photograph by the Author.*

and turning it from side to side so that its characteristics could be clearly understood. The glass glinted in the light of the incandescent bulb above it. "The Geva tell is near our kibbutz."

Geva Parashim (Tel Abu-Shusha) was an Israelite city whose known history dates from the Late Canaanite period (the Late Bronze Age) into the time of the Crusaders. The city was overrun during the incursion into Canaan by Thutmose III, a campaign which ended with the capture of the critical fortress-city of Megiddo. The story of that invasion is emblazoned on the walls of the Temple of Karnak in Egypt and Geva is featured among the smaller cities destroyed by the army of Thutmose III. Geva revived and became an important Israelite agricultural and crafts center.

In the Roman period Geva was a borderline, predominantly non-Jewish, city which featured importantly in the struggles of the Jews against the Romans. Josephus Flavius relates that in 60 C.E., after the destruction of

Micha Lynn at the Museum of the Kibbutz Mishmar-Ha-Emek.
*Photograph by the Author.*

Caesarea by the Romans, the Jews again attempted to destroy Geva.[25] In 73
B.C.E. it was burned down by the Hasmonaean King Alexander Yanai; it was
restored by Gabineus by order of Pompey. Thereafter Geva melded into the
overall "Syro-Palestinian" society under Roman and Byzantine domination.
Josephus relates further that the city was called "The City of Horsemen
because those horsemen that were dismissed by Herod the king dwelt therein."[26]

The area around Geva however, harbored a more mixed population. In
the heart of the lower Galilee, just east of Geva and of the coast between
Haifa and Acre where the Belus (now the Na'amen) River melds into the
Mediterranean, for example, lies Kefar Hananiah, which was an indubitably
and thoroughly Jewish community in the Roman period. The excavation of
this historic site was initiated in 1986 under the direction of David Adan--
Bayewitz of Bar-Ilan University. The stimulus for the study came from
rabbinic literature, in which two major sites for pottery-making were cited

GLASS VESSELS FROM GEVA. The vessels are part of a collection of artifacts recovered from the excavation of Geva on exhibition in the museum of the Kibbutz Mishmar-ha-Emek. *Photograph by the Author.*

**Figure 13**

by name; Kefar Hananiah was one, Shikhin the other. Bayewitz reported that it was definitely determined that

> The Jewish settlement of Kefar Hananiah was the principal supplier of kitchen pottery to the Galilee...from about 50 B.C.E. until 430 C.E....Kefar Hananiah ware was the predominant kitchen pottery at pagan and Christian, as well as Jewish settlements....This is the first time that the production of a Jewish Galilean manufacturing center of this period is being systematically studied.[27]

As the investigations under Bayewitz continued it became clear that a major pottery-producing industry was in operation not only at Kefar Hananiah, but at nearby Shikhin, that the communities of potters had gained a good portion of the Galilean market, and that the products reached as far as the Golan Heights. On one occasion Bayewitz showed me a piece of pottery with a

SHARDS OF GLASS FOUND NEAR GEVA. The profusion of shards of glass in the area of ancient Geva evidence the activity of glassware-makers in the area. The presence of some furnace scoria associated with the cullet suggests that primary glassmaking may also have taken place. *Photograph by the Author.*

glassy grey-green material adhering to it. It looked as though vitric material had boiled over the side of the pot and then had cooled and solidified. I happened to have a piece of frit with me which I had culled from the scoria of a glassmaking furnace found at a kibbutz near Kefar Hananiah. It was, at least visually, a perfect match!

It was possible but unlikely that glassmakers would have been permanently established at Kefar Hananiah. Glassmakers, as was mentioned above, unlike potters, were independent itinerant producers who followed forest trails into virgin territory, consuming vast quantities of locally available fuel and moving on. The evidence of the existence and operation of glassmaking is therefore ephemeral and is fast disappearing under the plow.

Workshops of various kinds were exposed on Geva's periphery by the efforts of Micha Lynn and several other members of the kibbutz Mishmar ha-Emek who undertook responsibility for the excavation project. The residential area stood over a low bluff; a structure was exposed which was composed of several rooms, including one with a colored mosaic floor ostensibly used for meetings, a building which may well have served as a synagogue. A row of rooms were hewn into the bluff below the residential area. Olive presses dominate two of the rooms; other such rooms were used for processing flax; a press for the production of linen oil attests to another product of the Geva flax industry; a wine press and large wine storage area served to slake the thirst of the community above the workshops; a burial cave with a mosaic floor adjoining the workrooms was also exposed. Glass fragments and scoria proliferate at the outskirts of the 375- acre area of the ruins of Geva, and are particularly profuse near the workshop area.

"You ought to see Shlomo Kurtz or Shimon Avidon of the kibbutz Ein ha-Shofet," said Micha, smiling impishly. "They have a much broader collection."

That was my next stop. In several cases of the Ein ha-Shofet kibbutz museum, resting inconspicuously among an impressive display of finished glassware, lay a few bits of the scoria and vitrified lumps which represented all three of the stages of glassmaking; fritted material representing the first stage; fragments of a crucible with adherent raw glass accruing from the second stage; tailings from pontil trails attested to the third process being performed, the actual manufacture of glassware. A large and varied assortment of vessel fragments and lumps of raw glass found in association with these three evidences of actual glass manufacture indicate the use of cullet. Positive evidence of the three basic processes thus provided proof that not only glassware was being made on nearby sites, but that raw glass was being produced, evidently for sale to glassware producers at such urban centers as Jerusalem.

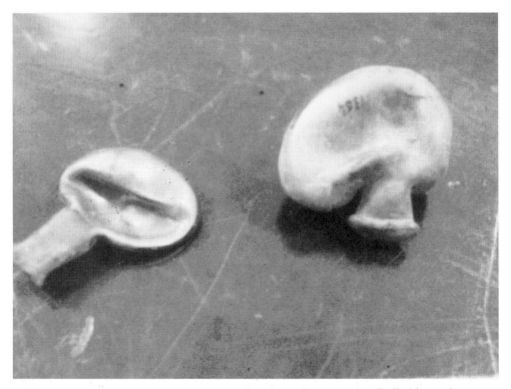

ILL-BLOWN GLASS VESSELS FOUND IN ASSOCIATION WITH GLASS SHARDS. Badly blown glass vessels, if collected at all by museums and not discarded as valueless, are relegated to archival storage, since they are not museum quality specimens. Such items are, however, vital evidence of glass (ware) making, for, being unsaleable, they were used as cullet; whole vessels such as the ones illustrated are extremely rare, but fragments of ill-blown vessels are often found associated with broken glass which was normally gathered and sold to glassmakers for use as cullet.

*Photograph by the Author.*

## The Glassblowers

Ein ha-Shofet was near the kibbutz Mishmar ha-Emek, in an area which had been populated by the Jews during the Roman period; it was close to Kefar Hananiah and to Beth Shearim, one of the main Jewish centers of the Talmudic period. Extensive excavations were conducted at Beth Shearim by the Jewish Palestine Exploration Society under B. Mazar, in 1936-1940, and continued under N. Avigad into 1953. Great Jewish sages studied and wrote in Beth Shearim. It was here that the Mishnah was compiled and that Judah ha-Nasi (Judah the Prince) and other great sages were buried in a complex of catacombs hewn into the slopes surrounding the village. It was the seat of the Sanhedrin after the fall of the Second Temple, and the sages worked at various trades to earn their living, as was the practice in those days. Beth Shearim became a beehive of industry and trade as well as an important center of religious study and pilgrimage. Glassmaking was a major industry of Beth Shearim.

The reverence for human labor and creativity was intrinsic to the teachings of the Mishnaic rabbis. "He who does not teach his son a craft teaches him brigandage," the *Mishnah Kidnur* admonishes parents. "The creator of the universe," it is said as a reminder of the dignity of labor, "labored for six days; may we do less?"

The creator of the universe is recalled in another paragraph which reflects in poetic imagery the closeness of the writer to the process of glassblowing: "If a vessel of glass, made with breath blown by a mortal, can be re-shaped if it is broken," sings the Mishnaic poet, "how much more true is this of a human being made with breath blown by the Holy One, blessed be He; as it is said: 'The Lord God formed man from the dust of the ground and breathed into his nostrils the breath of life.'"[28]

Imagery sometimes took a more mundane turn in Mishnaic parables. "One who loved him called him a 'son of a goldsmith.' One who hated him would call him a 'son of a potter.' One who neither hated or loved him would call him a 'son of a glassmaker'".[29] Whatever are the merits of the classifications thus presented, it is clear from the references that metalwork, pottery and glass manufacture were common crafts of the Land of Israel, and well known to the redactors of the Mishnah.

Glassblowing provided the sages with a lyrical analogy to Jewish survival: "Even as the sand which he puts into the flame a man gets a transparent mass from which he makes a vessel of glass, even so the Jews came forth living from the fire."[30]

Mishnaic and Talmudic literature are replete with references to glass and glassmaking. Neither Hellenic nor early Roman literature reflect the same easy familiarity with which the art is treated and never refer to the art as theirs. Through the detailed discussion of the question of uncleanness of glass as a material used and made under different circumstances, important for the maintenance of the laws of Koshruth, a familiarity of the sages with glass and with glassmaking is revealed:

> In the Jerusalem Talmud, Pesahim 1,6 (and elsewhere) it is mentioned that Yose ben Joezer of Tsrida and Yose ben Johanan of Jerusalem ruled that vessels of glass are unclean. At the time this ruling was issued (about the period of the Maccabean Wars), glass vessels were rare and expensive. The archeological evidence indicates that in this period there first began the large-scale production of glass vessels of the kind used at pagan feasts (symposia etc.); and apparently the two rabbis feared the introduction of new customs tainted by the assimilationist and foreign influences."[31]

The knowledge of the use of cullet in the manufacture of what is termed "utensils of crystal [zakhukhit]" is evident from discussions in which vessels made from broken ware are declared anew susceptive to uncleanness. A reference to "utensils of alum-crystal" in the passage also attests to a familiarity with the use of alkali in the manufacture of glass.[32] The collection of cullet and its distribution to glassmakers working far off in the woods is reflected in a Talmudic regulation which applies specifically to the class of Jewish tradesmen who collected broken glass for delivery to the producers for use as cullet. The collector would gather the broken glass, lade them into sacks which were then slung over the backs of asses and taken off along the rural byways to the producers. The traveling tradesman would obtain finished ware from the producer, which he brought back to urban centers for resale. These journeys were long, occasionally taking an entire week, and the collector was often unable to arrive at his destination before the sundown which initiated the Sabbath. The tradesman was thereupon flung into a dilemma, for all work must cease on the Sabbath, especially work which included lifting or carrying. On the other hand, it is prescribed that an animal must be cared for, even if labor on the Sabbath was involved.

The ruling was made, therefore, in consideration of the animal, that if a tradesman and his laden ass arrived at their destination after sundown on the Sabbath, and the loads consisted of broken glass, the tradesman, even if he was within the confines of his own courtyard, was restricted to untying the knots which held the sacks which must then be allowed to fall to the ground. "It was the same," expounded the rabbi in answer to a question on the matter posed by his disciple, "as if the tradesman were carrying sacks of corn." If, however, the sacks were loaded with finished glassware then the tradesman was allowed to bring soft pillows or mattresses from his home and place them under the falling sacks!

The type of furnaces, and the fact that glassmakers employed several furnaces are also described in the Mishnah. The lime-burning furnace, that is the furnace in which an alkali is produced, the fritmaking furnace and the furnace at which the glassblowers perform their magical operations are all referred to in a single paragraph regarding their use, in which they are simultaneously differentiated from the potter's kiln. "A pit-oven (frit-furnace) that has a pot-rest is susceptive to uncleanness; and that of the glassblowers, if it have a pot-rest, is susceptive to uncleanness. The kiln of the lime-burners, and the furnace of glassmakers, and the oven of potters are susceptive of uncleanness."[33]

A discussion in the Mishnah regarding the responsibility for breakage of glassware taken from a glasshouse on approval or otherwise consigned without payment broaches an interesting legal question.[34] A rabbi is quoted as saying, "In Tyre and Caesarea and their satellite towns, such a situation would not arise, because they are big cities and they are not interested in giving things out on approval. If a man takes a vessel from a glasshouse (*zagag*, a place where glass vessels are made or vended), it is as if he buys it." Thereupon rabbi bar Aboudama of the renowned but small town of Zippori retorted: "Yes, that's all right for big cities like Tyre and Caesarea and their satellite towns," and the scholar then proceeds to suggest that the glassmakers of his (or other outlying areas) should consign merchandise, but at their own responsibility.

The rabbis specified that the *Kos Tiveri*, glass cups manufactured near Tiberius, were uniquely suitable for the examination of the color of liquids, and particularly of wine because the fabric of glass was so thin and clear that it permitted precise classification of the liquid.[35] The fame of the *Kos Tiveri* was international, for it was also accepted as a standard for judging quality and measurement in Babylonia, where its exceptional clarity and delicate fabric is attested to by Rabbi Abbaye, head of the Babylonian academy. The practice of employing the Tiberias cup for a precise determination of the quality of liquids was "transmitted at one of the schools in Babylon by a Palestinian rabbi of the fourth century who acted as a messenger between the two communities. When the question was asked why only a *Kos Tiveri* was to be used for such examination, the head of the Babylonian school, R. Abaye, explained that consistent light weight of Tiberian glass was such as to allow perfect measurement and that "since it is so thin the colour of the wine can be distinguished better than in any other cup."[36]

The uniqueness and exclusivity of the glassmaking art are Talmudically emphasized. Whereas the knowledge of crafts in general were inevitably transmitted to artisans of faiths alien to the Jews, glassmaking is specifically excluded from such dispersion of knowledge: Rabbi Yose, living in the heart of the industry in the Galilee about 300 C.E., is quoted as saying that it is forbidden to teach the trade to an idol worshipper (that is, to a gentile). He thereupon provides specific examples: "There were two families of craftsmen in Geru, one makers of glass, and the other of adornments. The makers of adornments taught their trade to the gentiles, and they were pushed out of their trade. The glassmakers did not teach their trade to the gentiles, and the trade remained in their hands."[37] A fragment of a document identifies Geru as the city of Acre, and thus refers to glassmakers working around the Belus River estuary.[38] The site referred to by Rabbi Yose may very well lie on the grounds of an Israeli factory just north of Haifa, which location appears to fit his description perfectly. The factory turns out highly secret products. Great quantities of glass fragments and furnace scoria lie undisturbed on its grounds; the material lies strewn about an area now closed to investigation, awaiting a future opportunity for study.

The wonder of the glassmaking world, a great nine-ton slab of glass, rests in Beth Shearim, nearby the final resting place of the great sages. The astounding, massive slab was brought to light in an excavation of what is evidently an enlargement of a natural cave. Its 8.8 tons of solid glass makes it the third largest single piece of glass ever produced by man; it is exceeded only slightly by the 200 inch lenses made by Corning Glass, one of which is defective and is now in the Corning Museum and the other of which was successfully installed in the Mount Palomar telescope.[39] The huge block of glass was, until recently, completely ignored! A plaster model of a building had been mounted on it and it was assumed to be merely a base for the exhibit until Professor Dan Barag of the Hebrew University brought attention

AN 8.8 TON GLASS SLAB AT BETH SHEARIM.  The wonder of the glassmaking world, a huge slab of glass weighing 8.8 tons was produced by the glassmakers of the "Holy Community of Beth Shearim," the village in which the great sages wrote a good part of the Mishnah. The Rabbinic redactors of the Mishnah all worked at a trade, and it is likely that some of them were among the glassmasters of Beth Shearim.
*Photograph by the Author.*

to the fact that the slab was not concrete or plaster or stone but a single, massive slab of glass.  "In the course of clearing the cistern the bulldozer encountered a large buried slab.  Since the slab was too large to be moved, it was left where it was, lying flat, and the surrounding debris was leveled even with its base," wrote Robert Brill, Administrator of Research of the Corning Museum, upon recently undertaking a study of the glass.[40]

The fact that the massive glass slab was manufactured *in situ* has never been questioned, for it is unreasonable to postulate that it was produced elsewhere and carried to the site where it now rests.  The production of such a monumental mass of glass presumes a technology which, with all the expertise and knowledge we have gained over the past 2000 years, remains a feat which has never been duplicated with the use of the materials and fuel then available. Nor has anyone yet produced a completely satisfactory explanation of how the Jews of Beth Shearim did in fact produce it. Robert Brill, with the assistance of technicians from the Technion at Haifa, cored the slab and subjected the three-inch diameter, foot-and-a-half-long core to extensive analysis. Brill determined that it was indeed one solid mass and that "to melt a glass of the slab's composition with the same degree of vitrification it was probably necessary to heat something over 11 tons of batch to about 1050˚ Centigrade and hold it for perhaps five to ten days." Brill then audaciously proposed a hypothesis that it may have been manufactured by constructing a huge reverberatory furnace around a limestone-brick enclosure in which the raw materials were contained.[41] While the vitrification of such a massive quantity of silicate and other materials by heating it from the side and above seems hardly credible, it is the only explanation so far proffered. It would take a considerable length of time to bring 50,000 or more pounds of raw minerals up to the required temperature to begin with, a time which Brill did not include in his estimate. The temperature of 1050° Centigrade which Brill determined would have to be maintained consistently for an additional period of a week or more, would necessitate the continuous stoking of the massive, reverbatory type furnace with tons upon tons of wood and would require the manual forcing of a powerful draft of air day and night throughout the period by an unremitting pumping of a series of bellows. It is difficult to visualize complete vitrification taking place throughout the mass under the circumstances hesitantly suggested by Brill, in which the fire would of necessity be mainly above the mixture of materials. In any event, it is clear that the production of the glass slab at Beth Shearim was a *tour-de-force* of the first magnitude.

It may be that Beth Shearim was not the only site at which huge masses of glass were produced. Two large glass floors (as they were first termed) were uncovered at near by Arsuf in 1950 by Drs. P. P. Kahane and Immanuel Ben-Dor, whose description of the glass floors matches that of the monumental slab at Beth Shearim. Unfortunately, they were not preserved intact and only a few glass fragments were saved from the Arsuf excavation. These relics were examined by Brill, who concluded that "there might be a connection between the 'glass floors' at Arsuf and the Beth Shearim slab."[42]

One of a group of tombs hollowed out of the Beth Shearim hills bears an inscription in Greek, announcing that the entire burial chamber "belongs to

Aristeas." An inscription on the side of the vault further identifies the occupant: "This is the tomb of Aristeas the Sidonian." Still a third inscription in big bold letters incised in the plaster covering the arcosolium leaves no doubt as to Aristeas's piety: "May the rest be peaceful of Aristeas the pious of the pious."[43] It so happens that one of the few names of glassmakers which were incorporated into the molds of Roman period glassware was "Aristeas the Sidonian," rendered as such in Greek in precisely the same form as the tomb inscription. Variations of the name are molded on similar glassware in various forms: Ariston, Artas, Aristo Sidoni and Aristo Sido, and we may easily assume that they were all one and the same person. Whether the occupant of the tomb was actually that of the signatory glassware-maker is open to considerable doubt, since the tomb appears to be of a later date. Whether or not such is the case, the fact which emerges is that Aristeas was the name of a family of Sidonian Jews who maintained a tomb at Beth Shearim.

Sidon, Tyre and Antioch were the convenient ports from which glassware made in the Galilean and Lebanese forested areas was shipped across the Mediterranean, and vessels bearing the name of or attributed to Aristeas were found, for example, in Cyprus and the Po Valley of Italy.[44] Aristeas himself evidently worked in Cyprus for a time, since a cup unequivocally produced by the same hand is molded with the alternate phrase: "Aristeas the Cypriote." The fact that the eastern glassware-makers were on the move during this period thus becomes credible.

Sidon has been widely acclaimed as the site at which glassmakers produced glassware, partly because of references to the export of glassware from that port into far reaches of the Roman Empire and mainly because the signature "Aristeas of Sidon" and the indications that Ennion also stemmed from that Canaanite city gave credence to Sidon as their base of operations. There is no evidence whatsoever that either of these renowned glassware-makers produced glass, although nothing precludes their engaging in that primary operation. It has been taken for granted that because Sidon was a Canaanite city and from the Greek forms of the names that the glassmakers were either Greeks or Canaanites (so-called "Phoenicians"). The fact that producing raw glass was much more likely to have taken place in the hardwood-forested hinterlands inhabited by the tribes of Zebulun, Asher, Naphthali and Dan, and that the population of Sidon itself had a sizable Jewish component has been heretofore overlooked by both historians and

BOWL SIGNED "ENNION MADE IT", 1ST CENTURY CE. The work of the most renowned of glassware-makers, many of whose products were shipped from Sidon to Europe. The same dove-tailed rectangle was used by "Aristeas of Sidon" to enclose his signature.
*Photograph courtesy of the Yale University Art Gallery.*

archaeologists.

These oversights need to be addressed, and an abbreviated review of the relevant history of Sidon is therefore in order. Although a positive association of the sea-coast-situated Canaanites and the Israelites goes back to Solomonic times and earlier and although Sidon and its hinterlands fell within the province of the Jewish tribes Zebulun and Asher over considerable periods, we might begin in 677 B.C.E., when the islet of Sidon was laid waste by the Assyrian king Esarhaddon. Surviving elements of the city's population and a good proportion of the population of the Sidonian hinterlands were deported, to join the Israelites dispersed 45 years earlier into the

218

Babylonian diaspora. The Sidonian captives were replaced by Babylonians, mainly from Cuthah, a village lying between the Euphrates and the Tigris east of Babylon in the area to which Jews had been deported previously.[45]

The remnants of the indigenous population of the Sidonian region reasserted themselves as time went on and within a century the island city and its culture had fully revived, the venerable name of Sidon was again applied to the city and the inhabitants of the city and of its mainland environs were thereafter universally referred to as Sidonians. The Judahite priestly hierarchy disdainfully dubbed the YHWH worshippers of the region "Cutheans," thereby casting an aspersion on their legitimacy and their right to assist in the rebuilding of the "House of the Lord" in Jerusalem. The circumstances of the report in Ezra regarding the rebuilding of the temple demonstrates, however, that in 520 B.C.E. not only did monotheistic practice still exist in significant measure in the northern sectors of Eretz Israel but that a transference of fealty to the Israelite Lord had taken place among many of the autochthonous as well as immigrant polytheists.

The YHWH worshippers among the Sidonian and Samarian population pleaded for the opportunity to participate in the rebuilding of the Jerusalem temple: "Let us join you in the building," they beseeched the Jerusalemites, "for like you we seek your God, and we have been sacrificing to him ever since the days of the Eserhaddon king of Assyria, who brought us here." The northerners were scorned as "adversaries of Judah," and their plea went unheeded. No accusations of idolatry are embodied in the recriminations employed to justify the jealous obstructiveness of the Judahite priestly hierarchy. In this instance, the Judahites did not question the adherence of the northerners to the Torah, indirectly acknowledging them as true sons of Abraham and Israel. "...the whole controversy between the two groups of Moses' followers was subordinated to the sole question of which place, Zion or Gerizim (the mountain on which the "House of the Lord" had been built by the Samarians), had been chosen by God for His habitation."[46] The refusal to recognize the right of the erstwhile Israelites to participate in the rebuilding of the Jerusalem temple was based solely on the flimsy legal pretext that Cyrus's order to restore the Temple was addressed exclusively to the Jerusalemite Jews. "The house which we are building for our God," they petulantly proclaimed, "is no concern of yours."[47]

A good portion of the Samarian population, although precluded from participating in the rites at Jerusalem, nevertheless continued fervent obeisance to the God of Israel. It can be noted, for instance, that Sanballat, the governor of Samaria incorporated the Israelite Lord (now the Lord of Jerusalem) into the name of his son; a second generation descendent of Sanballat, likewise a governor of Samaria, also bears a theophoric name and employs a seal which is inscribed in Hebrew in the Old Hebrew script.

In 351 B.C.E. the Canaanites took the opportunity to break free from foreign rule at the time when Artexerxes III was deemed to be too weak after he failed to reconquer Egypt. This act proved to be imprudent, for two years later Artexerxes returned to subdue Egypt. The wrathful conqueror thereafter captured and vengefully destroyed Sidon, then the leading Canaanite city. The Sidonian captives, including a considerable contingent of Jews who had sided with the rebels, were exiled to Babylonia and to Hyrcania (Mazanderan) on the south shore of the Caspian Sea. *It was then that glass(ware)making first appears on the shores of that great sea.*

The Assyrians could not rest long on their laurels for they soon had to face up to the formidable forces descending across the Taurus mountains and along the shore of the Anatolia under the Macedonian adventurer, Alexander. Darius III of Persia attempted to stem the tide at Issus, the historic gateway from Asia Minor to Syria and Egypt, but his forces were thoroughly thrashed. Alexander's cavalry pursued the fleeing Persian and his bedraggled hosts over the passes of Mount Amanus and swept into Damascus while Alexander led the main forces of his army down the coast toward Egypt.

Damascus was the capital of the Persian satrapy of the area and its loss forced Darius to retreat to the east to lick his wounds. A Hobson's choice was presented to the Samarians: resist and suffer immediate assault or accommodate to Alexander and chance retaliation by an angered, resurgent Darius. The Sidonians did not hesitate; having been decimated and humiliated by Antexerxes III, they welcomed Alexander with open arms. Other Canaanite cities such as Byblos, Aradus and Tripolis were equally hospitable; only the Tyrians, traditional rivals of the Sidonians, refused to acquiesce to Macedonian rule. The importance of Tyre as a port city made its capture imperitive. Alexander, having digested most of the Samarian region, launched a siege of the island city; the Tyrians put up a fierce resistance, but surrendered after seven months to suffer merciless retributive punishment.

The final blow to Persian hegemony came with the fall of city of Samaria at the end of the year 333 B.C.E. During the next winter, while Alexander was enjoying a precipitous accession of Egypt to his rule, Samaria revolted, counting on support from Darius, who was preparing for a decisive encounter with Alexander. Had Alexander's forces been delayed in Egypt or had Samaria been able to withstand a new siege; history might indeed have been written differently. Unfortunately for Darius neither circumstance was to occur. Upon Alexander's arrival at the scene in the spring of 331, the loyalists turned over the rebels to Alexander. A group of Persian supporters managed to escape, and took refuge in a desert cave fifteen kilometers north of Jericho, where they were found by their Macedonian pursuers and slaughtered. Some two hundred of their skeletons were found in the cave, together with papyri written in Aramaic, legal documents which attested to their ownership of properties in Samaria. The optimistic refugees had obviously expected to return to Samaria immediately after the defeat of Alexander.

The Samarian Jews, together with those of the entire region of the former state of Israel, were faced with a dilemma. Since they were being denied the basic rights of priesthood and an accessible place of worship by the Jerusalemites, and since Samaria and other cities were being defiled by the Greek practice of Pagan idolatry, they sought to establish their own House of the Lord wherein they could carry on their faith and duties. They asserted their right to build the House of the Lord upon Mount Gerizim, a place sacred from time immemorial, citing the Bible as their authority. "When the Lord your God brings you into the land," Moses had indeed enjoined the Chosen People, "there on Mount Gerizim you shall pronounce the blessing."[48] A new temple was constructed on Mount Gerizim and the political center of the community was established at Schechem, at the foot of the sacred mountain.

*The community referred to itself in Greek as "The Sidonians of Schechem"!*[49]

The designation was assumed advisedly by the YHWH worshippers of Schechem because the Judahites had coopted the term "Israelites." The fact that the YHWH worshippers of Mount Gerizim felt comfortable with the appellation, "Sidonian," attests to the existence of a deep-seated memory of the significant Israelite presence in pre-exilic Sidon, one which could only be explained by an intimate association with the tribes of Naphthali, Dan, Asher and Zebulun and by a persistent continuity of faith through the period of two transplantations and the passage of almost four centuries.

The port of Sidon became widely vaunted as a glassmaking area also through its attribution as the source of glassware made by the most noted of the period's glassware-makers, Ennion, whose Greek inscription translates to "Ennion made me," and appears on glassware found throughout the Roman Empire. A glass jug bearing that inscription was found in the Jewish quarter of the "Upper City of Jerusalem."[50] The jug was found in a niche between two rooms of one of the elaborate houses of Jewish notables who resided in the area. The mansion was probably destroyed in the year 70 C.E. when the entire district was leveled and burned by the Romans. It is one of four such jugs which have been found so far which were evidently blown in the same mold. Several fragments of vessels which can certainly be attributed to Ennion were also retrieved from the Upper City, one of which matches perfectly with a vase signed by Ennion and found in Cyprus.

The first century C.E. products of the Ennion glassworks-- bottles, jugs, vases and cups of impressive workmanship--have shown up even farther afield than those of Aristeas. Ennion glassware is displayed in museums as far apart as the Metropolitan Museum of New York, the Hermitage of Leningrad, the Municipal Museum of Pavia, the Aquileia Museum and the Haaretz Glass Museum of Tel Aviv. The lower portion of the Metropolitan bottle (whose provenience is noted as presumably Jerusalem) is composed of six panels, one of which bears the now famous phrase, "Ennion Made Me," and the other five of which depict decorative motifs related to the Jewish Feast of the Tabernacles: a narrow-necked, single-handled jug, a wide-mouthed two-handled vase, a pair of crossed keys, a cluster of grapes and a double panpipe. The borders and other sections of the vessel contain the type of gadrooning, grapevines and tendrils which are characteristic of Ennion ware.

Ennion's Sidonian identification derives from the signature of that other master "Aristeas of Sidon." Two *skyphos*, or two-handled cup handles stamped with the phrase, "Eirenaios the Sidonian," were found in Catania and Syracuse respectively and add substance to the reputation of Sidon as a glassware-producing center. The two other glassware-makers of the first century period whose names were molded into their ware, Phillippos and Neikon, were likewise assumed to be part of a Sidonian glassmaking industry. The entire group of Roman period glassware bearing the names of their makers are ubiquitously referred to as "Sidonian glassmakers" and their product as "Sidonian glassware" in all literature on the subject. A mystique

222

ENNION JUG, MID-1ST CENTURY CE.  One such jug was found in the Jewish quarter of Jerusalem and is exhibited in the Haaretz museum at Tel Aviv; the illustrated jug, one of four found to date from the same mold and bearing the Ennion signature, is on display at the Corning Museum of Glass.
*Photograph courtesy of The Corning Museum of Glass.*

has been constructed around this designation, so that glassware found in Gaul and on the Black Sea is referred to as "Sidonian-type glassware" in museums and literature.

This narrow interpretation of the provenience of a class of the early Common Era glassware of Eretz Israel ignores the fact that even the glassware manufactured in such urban environments as Antioch, Sidon, Tyre and Jerusalem must have been based on raw glass produced in the hinterlands. Judging by the evidence found in the field, the primary glassmaking industry was widespread throughout Eretz Israel and extended up into the Lebanese forest-land; it was gathered and distributed from many centers of the area and shipped from ports like those mentioned above as well as more southerly ports like Ashkelon and Caesarea. Antioch and Gaza were also the termini of routes leading to China and India, and therefore important centers where merchandise was gathered for shipment eastward as well as westward. There is strong evidence that glassware as well as raw glass was being manufactured at many inland industrial sites. Archeological evidence bears out the proposition that all glassmakers were capable of making glassware, whereas the reverse was not necessarily the case, and therefore it is no surprise that glassware was being turned out at the same sites where the raw material was also being produced. Most curious is the identification of some of the glassware found and almost certainly manufactured at Beth Shearim, clearly a major glassmaking center, as being of a Sidonian type!

Clues to the identity of the few known glassmakers of the early Common Era period can be culled from the names themselves. "Ennion" is a Greek rendition of "Hananiah" or "Anania," as in the thoroughly Jewish town of Kefar Hananiah mentioned previously. Ananiah is the name of a settlement just southeast of Jerusalem, a town mentioned in Ezra and Nehemiah, in the ruins of which a Judean seal impression was found. An *Anniano* was one of many Jews buried in the Roman catacombs of Monteverde, as the inscription on his tomb indicates: "Here lies Anniano, young Acante of eight years and two months, son of Giuliano, elder of the Synagogue of the Campesii."[51] The Graecized form of the name, as rendered by the renowned glassmaker, is rare, but it appears in numerous related Hebraic forms. Another such variation, "Annianos," is, significantly, the name of a family tomb in the catacombs of Beth Shearim.

A third name molded into glassware of the period is "Jason," a name commonly employed by Jews of the Hellenic period. A Jason is buried in

A                                                                    B

A

**A SO-CALLED "SIDONIAN" BOTTLE, 1ST CENTURY CE.** Molded into the bottle are Judaic motifs which reappear on bottles made later in Jerusalem with Christian as well as Judaic symbols. (See illustration of "Bottle with Jewish Symbols", Chapter 11).

B

**MOLD-BLOWN DOUBLE-HEAD FLASK, 2ND-3RD CENTURY CE.** Bottles blown to forms similar to the early "Sidonian" types but molded with anthropomorphic forms became popular on the Roman market.
*Photographs courtesy of the Yale University Art Gallery.*

ENNION CUP, MID-1ST CENTURY CE. Several cups from the same mold bearing the signature "Ennion made it" have survived. More than twenty signed jugs, amphoriskoi, cups and bowls have been found to date, as well as numerous fragments which were formed in Ennion's molds or which have Ennion's characteristics.
*Photograph courtesy of the Newark Museum.*

catacomb 13 in which Aristeas, the pious Sidonian, found his final resting place. That circumstance allows us to posit the possibility of a relationship between the three families, Ennion (Annianos), Aristeas and Jason, a characteristic relationship between glassmaking families which extends into the modern period. Some Jewish Jasons are famous, as, for example, the historian "Jason of Cyrene," who wrote a five-volume history incorporating the story of the revolt of Judah Maccabee; while the original was lost, an abridgement survives, the apocryphal Second Book of Maccabees, whose anonymous author credits Jason of Cyrene as his source. The first Jewish ambassador to Rome was Jason ben Eleazor, sent as the personal envoy of Judah Maccabee in 161 B.C.E. to plead the case of the Jews. The high priest presiding those events was also named Jason; it was he who proceeded to reform Judaism and was deposed for attempting to substitute the gymnasium for the Temple as the focus of Jewish life.

Variations of the name "Jason" are Jesus, Joseph, Joshua or Yossi.[52] Josephus informs us that many persons named Jesus preferred to use the form "Jason." Jesus is itself a Hebrew name, as is evident by the most famous Hebrew bearer of that name. If any more evidence of that fact is required, we might simply add that a Jesus of Yahmour was likewise buried in a Beth Shearim catacomb. Yahmour is situated east of Sidon and an exceptional collection of Sidonian-type blown vessels were recovered from tombs in the area. The catacombs of Beth Shearim also contain the crypt of Yossi, who is designated as the head of the Synagogue of the Sidonians. The specific designation indicates that there was a large enough community of Sidonian Jews resident in and around Beth Shearim to maintain their own synagogue. The reference to a synagogue in the singular points to a synagogue catering to local Jewish-Sidonian resident families rather than to the many synagogues which must have served the sizable Jewish population of Sidon. Thus multiple relationships appear of families of Jews buried in the hallowed crypts of a major glassmaking center of the lower Galilee, Beth Shearim, to Sidon and its hinterlands. The coincidence of their names with the names of families engaged in glassware-making make an association of members of those families with the art credible.

Sidon is referred to as "the Holy and /(city of) refuge" on a molded, opaque yellow glass disc of 77/78 C.E.,[53] and it is reasonable to assume that a large colony of Jews existed in and around that city during the very period of the so-called Sidonian glassmakers. Antioch was another such center, and is designated as a source of glassware on the bottom of a characteristically square bottle of the same period. The jug is of unknown provenience, having passed from one private collection to another. The inscription molded into its base, however, quite clearly proclaims it to be a product of "Paulinos of Antioch."[54] The Paul of Christian fame, it is hardly necessary to mention, was a Jew before he became a Christian, and the name, a Roman-pagan or Roman-Jewish name of the first century only became popular among Christians from the third century onwards.

The identification of glassware made in Eretz Israel cannot, however, be narrowed to Sidon, as the excavations in Jerusalem and Beth Shearim have revealed and as a tour of the museums maintained by the Israeli kibbutzim makes amply clear. Many of the museums of the kibbutzim in the upper and lower Galilee contain evidence of glassmaking materials dating from the pre-Hellenistic well into the Islamic period, evidence which was obtained on their premises. The materials are usually unattractive and so little attention is paid to them and they are rarely exposed. The wonder is that such earthy-looking materials were preserved at all by persons who generally did not appreciate their significance. The few glossy samples which were set aside were being treated as curiosities.

Evidence of glassmaking around Caesarea can be found in the museum of the kibbutz named after that famous Roman port, and the area surrounding the immense Crusader constructions are replete with shards and scoria. The fragile cover of rural land provides the proof of the widespread glassmaking activity over a period of several millennia. Unfortunately, the creation of a kibbutz and of its motel and golf course relocated or replaced much of the original topsoil, rendering a further study of large portions of the area difficult. The examination of earth moved from one area of the golf course to another in the process of its construction reveals a variety of materials similar to that recovered from the earth dug out further north in the creation of the fish-ponds. The farmlands of the kibbutz surrounding the Caesarea ruins glitter with shards of glass, and await diligent investigation.

At Jalame, north of Caesarea and just south of the Carmel range, a significant glassware-making facility was studied by Professor Gladys Weinberg some 20 years ago. "Millions of glass chips" were recovered from "several floors of compacted splinters of glass." Cullet at two distinct factory waste areas include "knock-offs" and "cut-offs" from blown vessels, droplets and deformed vessels. This material and other abundant evidence of glassware-making leave no doubt as to the existence of significant fourth century production of glassware at the site.[55]

Until recently archeologists were prone to focus upon tells, the stratified remains of urban communities, cult centers, military or administrative head-quarters. Little attention was paid to the countryside beyond the citadels. It is in out-of-the-way, formerly forested environments that the fast-disappearing remnants of unique and unmistakable evidence of ancient glassmaking can be found, and was found by the author in surveys limited to material lying exposed to the elements and to the ravages of man. Such areas offer no promise of museum-worthy statues, idols and treasure and were therefore neglected; yet only such areas can provide information regarding the esoteric art of glassmaking.

Another factor leading to the lack of interest in the evidence of glassmaking lying about Israel is that, although archeologists are to some degree academically knowledgeable about the process by which vitrification takes place, the knowledge does not seem to extend to recognition of the evidence of primary glassmaking activity. The problem is therefore aggravated by the fact that not only is such evidence most unlikely to be found where archeologists are prone to practice their discipline, but that even when it is encountered, the evidentiary materials pass as anomalous, irrelevant material by the archeologists themselves. The author learned these disconcerting facts while conducting surveys of possible glassmaking sites in Israel. None of the score of archeologists in the field to whom evidence of glassmaking found by the author was shown recognized the material; many shamefacedly admitted that they had indeed come across such material but had paid no attention to it.

The first requisite for understanding glass manufacturing evidence is to differentiate between *glassmaking*, i.e., the manufacture of glass as a raw material, and *glassware-making*, the manufacture of glassware from that material. While the producers of glass (the raw material), were universally capable of producing glassware, the reverse was by no means the case. Many glassware-makers had no idea as to how glass was made. The distinguishing scoria of glassmaking is absent from those sites where artifacts of glass were manufactured solely from supplied raw material.

Glassware and glassware fragments consume the attention of archeologists and make attractive museum displays but the drab, homely scoria of glassmaking has been routinely overlooked. A trove of glassware shards at a given site may be evidence of cullet, and therefore of glassware-making, but cullet is not necessarily evidence of glassmaking, although it is also an essential ingredient of the process of making the raw material. There is a vast difference between the technology of glassmaking and glassware-making. The former assumes a pyrotechnological sophistication and a chemical knowledge of which the glassware producer had no need, and, in fact, was commonly prevented from obtaining.

Cullet, in the form of raw glass lumps, ingots or shattered glassware, was anciently shipped far and wide for remelting and reprocessing by artisans who remained ignorant of its composition and incapable of producing the material for themselves. Both aspects of that procedure are amply demonstrated by the scores of massive ingots of glass included in the cargo of the 3300-year-old Canaanite ship which foundered off Ulu Burun, and by the scores of tons of cullet on board the vessel which sank over two millennia later at Serce Limani, both of which wrecks are presently being excavated by the Institute of Nautical Archeology under Prof. George Bass. The recipients of the former cargo, whether Anatolian, African or European, were as yet 1000 years away from the capability of producing glass. The traffic in raw glass from the Levant continued for several millennia, mute testimony to the containment of the secrets of glass manufacture within the privileged group of artisans. The twelfth century C.E. vessel sunk off the Turkish coast at Serce Limani was found carrying 65 tons of cullet westward; the ship was plying the same course as that of the Canaanite vessel of 2400 years earlier and may have been destined for Venice, where the glassware-making industry was under way but where glassmaking had not yet been introduced. Raw glass lumps were found to be included in the cargo of vessels which foundered off the Israeli coast, the same type of raw glass cullet which is found on land all along the Israeli coast from Ashkelon into Lebanon. Such material was reviewed by the author with Dr. Ehud Galili, head of excavations off the Israeli coast from his headquarters at Newe-Yam, near Dor. Large lumps of completely vitrified material, some weighing as much as ten pounds, were in evidence; they had been recovered from ancient wrecks all along the Israeli coast from Ashkelon to the borders of Lebanon, the limits of Dr. Galili's excavations. They are precisely the type of raw glass which can be expected to have been exported for manufacturing glassware by artisans who had no idea as to how the raw material was produced. The regular recurrence of this raw glass in the cargo of vessels destined for a trip around the Mediterranean and the distribution of such wrecks along the entire Eretz Israel littoral strongly suggests that the production of such material was an important industry in that ancient land.

The fundamentals of ancient glassmaking must be understood in order to be able to distinguish characteristic evidence of the art and to be sensitive to the areas in which we are likely to encounter it. Account must first be taken of the fact that vitrification was not achieved in a single operation; we have learned that the first firing of the basic components produces frit and not glass. To complete the process of vitrification it is necessary to pulverize the frit and refire it at 1100° centigrade or more, that is, at the ultimate range of temperature achievable in a drafted furnace fueled with organic material, and cullet must be added to catalyze and facilitate the process of vitrification. It is likely that several furnaces were employed by the ancient glassmakers, one for producing the frit, a second melting furnace for final vitrification and even a third (or a compartment of one of the other furnaces) for tempering. The extreme conditions under which these processes had of necessity take place caused crucibles and furnaces to fracture, spilling out partially vitrified material. The discarded fragments of the crucibles as well as of an abandoned furnace would normally be coated with such waste.

Where, then, were glassmakers likely to be working and therefore where should archeologists now expect to find glassmaking sites? What constitutes the unique evidence of a glassmaking facility? We have learned that glassmaking requires vast quantities of fuel. While the availability of silicate and alkaline materials was important, the far more critical need of the ancient glassmaker was fuel. It was convenient for the ancient glassmakers to be near beaches where siliceous sand was available or near streams from whose beds quartz pebbles could be collected or near a mountain from which quartz could be mined; it was also convenient to be close to lush, swampy areas where grew plants from whose ashes soda could be rendered; it was more than convenient, however, it was vital for the glassmaker to have a substantial supply of fuel continuously and readily available. One cartful of easily transported mined quartz or siliceous sand and of an alkali could keep a furnace occupied for weeks; but the massive amount of dry wood (the main fuel available) required in the process presents a problem of supply. The furnaces of glassmakers are not allowed to burn down even when production is interrupted, for it takes days of firing to bring a furnace back into productive use. For that reason glassmakers throughout the ages located themselves in or near forests and were prone to move often as nearby trees were felled and transportation of wood became difficult. A furnace could be quickly and economically erected and then abandoned for a new one reconstructed at a location closer to the trees. Vast forests have been routinely demolished by glassmakers (and, to a lesser extent, by iron-smelters) throughout recorded history. Witness, for example, the decimation of the forests of the Weald of southern England and of the Friulli of northeastern Italy by such activity. There is every reason to assume that a similar ecological devastation took place in ancient times as a result of the production of glass.

It is evident, therefore, that we cannot expect to find a glassmaking site in an urban environment. While glassware-makers may have busied themselves within an industrial adjunct to an urban community, or even within the community itself, glassmakers could not long sustain their industry in such circumstances. Today in Hebron, for example, an adept glassware-maker transforms soda-pop bottles into crude but respectable hand-blown glassware. The manufacture of glass is, however, difficult in modern Israel because the cost of fuel in that energy-poor country renders such an industry uneconomical. In the survey made by the author in 1987 it was found that the evidence of ancient glassmaking is ubiquitous where forests once flourished in upper Israel, areas now being deep-plowed by kibbutzniks and cultivated by Arab farmers. Two years later, determined to further the investigations, I returned to scrounge around the Israeli countryside. A student at Bar-Ilan University, Moshe Cohen, had heard of the investigation through his professor, David Adan-Bayewitz, was interested in pursuing the subject for his master's thesis and joined the search. Moshe was a lithe, enthusiastic lad who had already done a considerable amount of field work in preparation for my arrival, at which time we were ready to set out on our venture. Our efforts were rewarded beyond our expectations.

Heading north from Herzeliyah, about halfway to Netanya, a sign pointing to "Bene Zyon" led onto a dirt road leading west. About 100 meters along the rutted road an even cruder earthen road separated an orange grove from an onion field. A lone cypress stood majestically overlooking the field of rather dry and bedraggled-looking onion stalks. Some 100 meters further, almost invisible through the trees of a copse was a farmhouse; the frames of two greenhouses stood at right angles to the house, skeletons without a cover under a hot June sun.

The onion field and the adjoining orange grove were saturated with the scoria of a glass and glassware-making industry over an area of at least four dunams. We strode onto the onion field, trying as carefully as we could to avoid trampling on the onions. We immediately picked up a small blue-trailed rim of a glass. Within the space of an hour a complete assortment of the characteristic scoria of a glassmaking installation revealed themselves. Included were examples of every stage of glass and glassware-manufacture, fritted materia, cullet, trail droppings and partially vitrified materials clinging to fragments of a furnace.

A farmer, whose grounds spread out between Bene Zyon and the sea no more than a kilometer to the west, mentioned that he had observed numerous glass fragments around some ancient ruined structures while playing in the area as a child. Following his directions, we climbed through the rambling

232

hillocks to where a branch of the Poleg River, now completely dry, cuts through the area. The weathered stones of numerous ancient structures poke through the overgrowth and at the base of one hillock an arched construction leads down to a cave-like hollow. A corner of a structure just above the arch is topped with a mosaic ledge. In spite of the dense grasses which cover the area we were able to pick up material similar to that we had gathered at Bene Zyon some two kilometers away.

Proceeding northward, we passed by Umm el-Fahm, an Arab charcoal-producing village in a valley of the hilly area about 18 kilometers southwest of Megiddo. Judging by the name, which means "Mother of Charcoal" the industry must have a long tradition in the area and suggests that this was indeed a forested area suitable for glassmaking. We stopped off to visit my old friend Micha Lynn at Mishmar ha-Emek. After serving us cool drinks, Micha took out a box of shards, and among the pieces of vessels we found a half-dozen "teardrops," the characteristic drops of glass which a glassware-maker clips off and discards before beginning to trail around a vessel. At the museum Micha pointed to a group of small blown perfume bottles referred to in glassmaking literature as "tear bottles" because of their characteristic shape. "These are Hellenistic," he stated with emphasis on the Hellenistic. His statement picked up a discussion we had had two years earlier.

I repeated the earlier argument. "Archeologists insist that blown glassware cannot be dated so early. Glassblowing is not supposed to have started until the Roman period."

"Yes, that is what the archeologists say." Micha jabbed his fingers at various samples of pottery in the case. "But look at these oil lamps. Classically Hellenistic. And so is this earthenware. It was all found together. Nothing of the Roman period came out of this tomb." As we went from case to case Micha insisted that various of the other collections of blown glassware were associated with Hellenistic ware in the tombs from which they were recovered.

"Look at this one!" Micha exclaimed. In a case among a variety of other glass artifacts was a particularly large and well-executed jug, some 20 centimeters high, with a massive handle looping down to a fingered, well-ordered attachment to the vessel side. The sophistication of the execution and the generous dimensions of the vessel bespoke a considerable period of technological development which, according to accepted standards, would have placed its date to no earlier than the end of the first century of C.E.

"I would date what was found together with this vessel to 200 B.C.E. Certainly no later than 100 B.C.E. I don't care what anyone says. This piece is definitely from the Hellenistic period." The insistence of these amateur archeologists that blown glass was found in a Hellenistic context has been routinely ignored, partly because much of it was not excavated under strict controls and also because the outlying tombs from which some of the glassware were recovered were frequently reused. Thus the Hellenistic period ware may be in a tomb in which glassware was added with a later burial. The consistency with which all of the kibbutz amateur archeologists insist upon the earlier dating for some of the blown ware has, so far, not ruffled the staid archeological community.

Nimrud Zakkai, of the kibbutz Hagoshrim, had also been adamant about the Hellenistic dating of some of the blown glassware he had unearthed. On returning to discuss this matter with him he cited a large family tomb he had excavated which had been in use from Hellenistic times over a period of several hundred years. "When family tombs became crowded, room for a new cadaver was made by pushing the bones of one of the previous tenants of the tomb to one side, together with the artifacts with which the deceased was buried--rings, pottery and so forth. The last body buried in the tomb from which this ware was recovered was in a box which had been pushed into such a group of bones. The box had broken the leg bone, which remained at right angles around the box. That broken leg, together with the lie of the other bones and the deposit of a pattern of nails left from the decayed coffin, clearly delineated where the box had stood. An intact blown bottle was nested under the skeleton's armpit and a broken cup which was not blown but made of precisely the same type of glass was held in the other hand of the deceased."

"All the artifacts associated with that group of bones were Hellenistic," Nimrod continued, emphasizing his point with a stabbing finger. "We found Hellenistic tools and faience. All of them were Hellenistic. Absolutely yes. I took pictures and when I finished the work I made a complete album of pictures for the government. All the albums of my finds were given to Jerusalem together with the finds. A friend from the kibbutz Dan, Dr. David Amir, an archeologist licensed by the government, helped me record everything."

We experienced the same insistence at the kibbutz Ein ha Shofet, where perimeter of the establishment, hanging from the walls, sitting on the windowsills and flanking the doors to the offices, potted plants bursting with sprays of blooming flowers lent color and life to the arrays of clattering robots. Shimon was at work adjusting the operation of a huge machine which was privileged with a room of its own.

"I will be with you in five minutes," Avidon waved to us in greeting. We adjoined to a huge, high-ceilinged shed area attached to the side of the factory to wait away from the tumult of the machinery. Hundreds of birds were nesting above the trusses holding the wavy metal roof, and their singing, chirping and chattering rivalled the din issuing from the factory's interior. Avidon soon joined us and led us along flowered walks to the kibbutz museum.

Avidon was adamant that various of the blown glass artifacts were of the Hellenistic period, regardless of the denial voiced by visiting archeologists such as the illustrious Prof. Ahorani, each haughtily averring that such dating was impossible. The three testifiers, Lynn, Avaron and Nimrud, were witnesses of some credibility, but were not the only kibbutz "collectors" who made a similar claim to blown glass antiquity.

I had previously submitted samples of a few of the glass fragments from Mishmar ha-Emek and Ein ha-Shofet to the *Stazione Sperimentale del Vetro* of Murano for analysis, including a sample of fritted material from the Ein ha-Shofet museum collection, a "teardrop" of a glassware-makers trail and a few glass vessel shards. The analyses showed a consistent silicate-sodium-lime content with some potassium traces, a composition characteristic of most of Roman period glassware. "On the basis of the above analyses and the information you sent me," reported Dr. Marco Verita, research director of the facility, "I think that the vitreous materials found are interesting and demonstrate the existence of glass manufactures in the sites where they have been excavated."

On learning of these results, Shimon Avidon informed us that the lumps of glass attached to earthy fired materials exposed in the museum's cases, one of which was included in the analyses, were not actually from the kibbutz grounds but were recovered from the nearby kibbutz Elyaqim, about ten kilometers northwest of Ein ha Shofet. He drew a map and directed us to look at the north side of a privately owned field on highway 70 near Elyaqim.

We located the spot easily, parked the car near a bus stop and trampled

BLOWN-GLASS VESSELS FROM TOMBS IN ISRAEL. The vessels date to the first few centuries of the Common Era. Fragments of the vessels in the form of a date were included in the cullet recovered in the Upper Galilee near the Kibbutz Hagoshrim; such vessels, modelled after a distinctly near-eastern fruit, are found throughout the Roman Empire. Many, for example, are included in the collection at Aquileia. The mold-blown "Sidonian" type bottle bears in relief the single and double-handled vases symbolic of vessels employed at the Jewish Succoth rites. *Photograph courtesy of the Israel Museum.*

down through the brambles of a rather deep ditch separating us from a plowed field of steel-gray-colored earth. Cohen rushed ahead, and no sooner had he reached a cleared field when he called out, excitedly, "Look at this!"

I struggled through the soft, powdery grey earth which seeped over my shoe tops and worked its way toward my toes. Cohen was holding up a walnut-sized jewel-like lump of glass, which upon examination proved to be encrusted on one side with the fired earthen material which had by this time become quite familiar to us. This particular field had not been intensively farmed, and was replete with fist-sized rocks which lay unculled from the soil. The area had the barren aspect of a moonscape, except that a sparse, bristly stubble poked its way up here and there through the rock-infested surface. Hope arose, therefore, that the more virgin condition of the surface layer would be more apt to conserve whatever evidence existed of ancient human activity at the site. The prayerful conjecture was immediately substantiated.

Pottery shards were profuse throughout the surface, including a great number of broken handles, roughly oval in section and about three centimeters across the wider diameter. Cubes of mosaic floor tiles identical in color and workmanship with those we had observed at Bene Zyon were also to be found. Within 20 minutes an assortment of fractured glass lumps and shards of glass vessels was collected which ranged over the complete gamut of glassmaking evidence. Fritted materials in every stage of vitrification, an assortment of glass cullet of vessel fragments, and carbonized crucible and furnace fragments with partially vitrified material clinging to them completed an unmistakable picture of primary glass production.

At Giv'at 'Oz, a kibbutz mainly populated by Hungarian Jews about two kilometers south of Megiddo, we went to the museum in charge of "Kitchy." The name is a diminutive form of Katan, or its endearing form, Katanchik, meaning a diminutive man. Kitchy's given name was Isra Aron; he comes from Hungary, is 61 years old and is the father of three children. We apologized to Kitchy for coming at the inconvenient hour of 2:00 P.M. Kibbutzniks get up at 4:30 A.M., perform their assigned duties all morning and then, after dinner, take their rest, which often includes a nap. Kitchy was understanding about our arrival at an inopportune hour and willingly gave up his rest in order to accommodate us.

At the museum an astounding collection of several thousand examples of sophisticated mosaic, millifiore and cane work are stored with shards and scoria in an alcove of the museum of the kibbutz Giv'at 'Oz. Smaller containers hold parts of bracelets and other items in a wide range of intricate techniques and combinations of colors. The material clearly dates over an extended period of time, from the Hellenistic into the Islamic period. Many clearly distorted or badly made items were among the shards, just as one would expect to find in a collection of cullet, and to clinch the question of local manufacture, two pieces of fritted material had also been fortuitously collected.

Kitchy gingerly told us that we were the first ones to have ever inquired further about the glassware and fragments found in the area, samples of which were prominently featured in the museum display. The statement sounded incredible, as the existence of the museum is well known. Upon being pressed for a reason for such oversight, Kitchy sardonically added: "Many have visited the museum, including renowned archeologists who admired our collection, but you are the first ones interested in the source of the glassware and the first ones to look into our back room collection of broken glass."

All of the items on display in the museum were recovered from or near the kibbutz. The amazing array of material was found in a marshy area just south of Megiddo which the original kibbutzniks of this and other kibbutzim in the area had cleared; malaria was, in fact, one of the common ailments of the original settlers. We visited the site and discovered that the Israeli army had subsequently bulldozed out the area in order to install a restricted military area. A barbed fence encloses more or less a hectare of the former Giv'at 'Oz property. Little hope remains of recovering substantial further evidence from the area; the entire side of the slope was removed and dumped elsewhere. Another fenced-off area to the south still appears untouched and further investigation may render results. Imposing Tel Megiddo rises majestically just north of the area, and many fine examples of glassware were recovered from its ruins.

Heading toward Jalame, we stopped about two kilometers north of Isfiya. A small herd of scraggly goats made way for us as we scrambled through the brush up the hillside sloping up from the road. The wooded rise was gouged out to make place for a ramshackle dwelling wherein lived an Arab family. Three women and a host of children came out to find out what these strangers were doing on their property. After listening with obvious incredulity to our explanation that we were searching for bits of glass, they welcomed us with twinkling eyes and watched our strange behavior with barely suppressed giggling laughter. Some tiny pieces of ancient glass glittered at the edge of the clearing, which we ignored until Cohen's sharp eyes landed on first one, and then another clump of opaque, partially vitrified, white and blue glass encrusted into a dirty and frothy fritted matrix. Turning them over we saw that smudges of a black-charred earthy material adhered to their backs. Thus, while glassware-making on a large scale had been found and investigated earlier at nearby Jalame, primary glassmaking was in evidence at this site. It may very well have been one of the forested sites at which the raw material for the facility at Jalame was produced. The slopes rising up from the clearing on which the Arab houses stood, were, in fact, thickly wooded.

The highway led from Jalame past Beth Shearim to the foot of the Carmel range and we maneuvered our way up rutted and rocky dirt roads to Dalyat el Karmel, a site which Professor Shimon Dar, an archeologist at Bar-Ilan University, had mentioned to his student and my companian, Moshe Cohen. We came across an unattended, smoking pile of blackened earth where charcoal was being produced on the hilltop. An area about five meters across was dug out to a depth of a half meter within which a two-meter-high mound of blackish carbon-filled earth arose like a miniature fuming volcano. The base of the mound was ringed with rocks, some of which were fragments of architectural columns. Great masses of brambles were piled up around the depressed area to block the wind, which we felt gusting up regularly.

A sizable green lump of glass lay gleaming near where the charcoal was being produced but little else was in evidence. We were intrigued by the numerous charred circles found scattered thickly about over an extensive area, evidence that charcoal making was a long-standing industry in the region. The charcoal producers obviously moved about in the forests much as did the glass- and iron-makers.

We next visited the dig at Zippori (Sipphoris). Shards of glassware were in evidence all along the road which passed through the dig. Standing imposingly over the site is an old building, on three sides of which five different sections are being excavated by students from Duke and Hebrew Universities, largely Americans on a five-week campaign. Dr. Jim Strange, one of the three archeologists in charge of the site (Dennis Groh and Tom Longstaff being the other two) had found an accumulation of charcoal, glass trail droppings and other glass shards in an ashlar enclosed area which he believed might have been a furnace. Outside of the structure many shards of glass were scattered around.

"When I found the little droplets I said 'Aha!' Nobody believed me," said Dr. Strange. "It wasn't until we got into the actual charcoal and dirt and ash and so forth that the use became evident. The crucible must have been taken out after the last time it was charged up and used but the furnace was never cleaned out after that. We found a half-dozen droplets and about a dozen pieces of partially melted and distorted glass." Adjoining the installation was an earthen balk, immediately beyond which a mikvah, a Jewish ritual bath, was uncovered. The mikvah was just inside the building, whereas the presumed glassware-making installation was in the courtyard on the opposite side of the wall of the mikvah. Strange said the building "seemed to date to the first half of the fourth century."

Looping back toward Herzeliya, we stopped at the Ma'a Barot kibbutz to confer with Professor Shimon Dar, Cohen's archeology professor, who resided in the kibbutz. Professor Dar had launched a project of surveying archeological sites on the Carmel range which had so far not been excavated. We discussed the abysmal ignorance of archeologists regarding the process of glassmaking and the embarrassed statements by many of the archeologists after being shown samples of frit and other furnace scoria that they had not paid any attention to such material.

"What you are looking for? Show me!"

We unwrapped an assortment of fritted materials, trailings and distorted glassware which we had gathered. Prof. Dar looked at them, and mused, "I know what nice glass is, Roman or otherwise, but I would not have picked up such material, and believe me, I have good eyes. I did find an interesting distorted bottle such as you mention, but had not given any thought to its purpose. It is now in Bar-Ilan University"

The next day we went to locate one of the sites Professor Dar was surveying, Khirbet Kirach, on top of the Carmel Mountain range, and found him and members of a surveying team already there in a jeep, to which we transferred; we never would have made it to the site in our car. The dwelling area was on top of the hill, adjoining a special working quarter containing oil presses, wine presses and much evidence of other crafts being performed at the site.

"Perhaps you can find evidence of ancient glassmaking hereabouts; we haven't found such evidence yet." Dr. Dar stated. He gave us 20 minutes to survey the area. Assuming that the glassmakers would not be working close to habitation we ranged some 200 meters down the slope from the dwelling sites and scrounged around for evidence. We came across three areas in which a considerable number of glass shards and furnace scoria were in evidence. Both areas were littered with cubes of mosaic flooring tesserae, items we had found associated with shards and scoria wherever we had gone.

We next headed for the coast, and stopped off at kibbutz Nach Sholim, where we met Isra Hirshberg and Kurt Raveh, who gave us the key to the museum and told us to make ourselves at home. The kibbutz was funded by Baron Rothschild for the purpose of making bottles for wine which was to be produced at Zichon Yakov, a nearby *moshav* (village cooperative). The enterprise was unsuccessful. The museum displays samples of the ill-fated glass factory, but mainly items recovered from the sea, of which a vast variety of all ages and times are exhibited.

The cursory two-week survey turned up 21 previously unrecognized sites where glassware-making was being performed, 9 of which contained certain evidence of primary glassmaking. They were dispersed throughout Israel, from the heavily populated Tel-Aviv area to the borders of Lebanon.

What conclusions can be drawn from this evidence? Cullet was common to these sites. A large but anomalous assortment of broken glass suggests several possibilities. It may merely represent garbage; it may have been accumulated for sale to a producer of glass or glassware; it may be evidence of either the production of glass, of glassware or of both. When, however, a collection of broken glass also includes ill-formed elements of glassware and perhaps even a complete but distorted item, an actual production site is indicated, since such items would not have been sold but are likely to exist only at a production site. Large chunks or small lumps of clear glass are also, of course, evidence either of glassmaking or of glassware-making, especially when such clumps are attached to furnace fragments.

Another definitive relic of glassware-making derives from trailing, a process characteristic of glassware-making. Glassware-makers trailed the *metal* (as the molten vitric material is referred to in the trade) from their *pontils* (the metal rods on the end of which the "metal" is gathered) spirally around a core to produce "core-formed" vessels. Trailing was also employed to apply decorative trim to vessels, to form handles and other such applications. The glassware-maker had to clip off the beaded end of a trail before

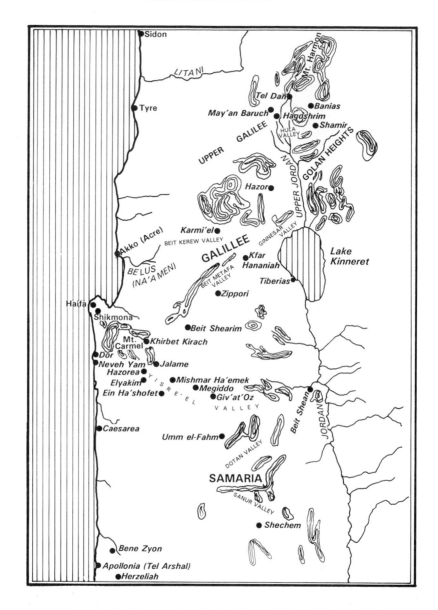

**ANCIENT GLASS(WARE) PRODUCTION SITES IN ISRAEL
INVESTIGATED BY THE AUTHOR**

The production of vitric products proliferated throughout *Eretz Israel* in formerly forested areas of Samaria and the Galilee and along the shore. Evidence of primary glassware production in nine of the sites investigated by the author is disappearing under modern deep-plowing practices or is being bulldozed away for urban development.

242

he began to apply the trail in order to start a clean line. These tiny teardrop or kidney-shaped tips, often measuring merely a fraction of a centimeter in diameter, are easily missed in an accumulation of cullet or ignored; they are, however positive evidence of glassware-making.

Since bellows were essential to provide the draft necessary to attain and maintain the temperature necessary for vitrification we may expect that if quantities of bellow's nozzles are found in an area, that glassmaking, iron-smelting (which also employed drafted furnaces) or both were being performed in that area. Smelters and glassmakers often operated in the same forested area, especially when iron ore was also to be found close by. Thus the northwestern Apennines around the glassmaking community of Altare, the thickly forested Weald of England , the Lorraine and other such areas hosted both arts contemporaneously. Hundreds of ancient earthenware bellow's nozzles were found in the upper Galilee. It has been assumed that they were employed by iron-smelters; they may equally be evidence of glassmaking.

The material which is unique to glassmaking is frit. Frit provides positive proof of the conduct of primary glassmaking, for frit is distinct from all other natural and manufactured products and has but one reason for being produced, which is to make glass. When fritted material is found, separate from or included with cullet, then the conclusion must be drawn that the production of glass from raw materials was being performed. Regrettably, frit is being passed by unnoticed and unheralded.

What then does frit look like? In its virgin and unattached state it is rare, since its purpose for existence was not as an end product but only as a transient stage of glassmaking. The glassmaker was not concerned with the shape or appearance of his product as was the faience-producing potter. It is not an attractive material, in fact, we may safely say that it is generally an ugly, clumpy material whose sole claim to grace is a glassy surface. Its color may range from deep, dirty brown to nebulous variations of the intended final color. It may be completely opaque or attain a measure of translucence depending on how far along it had been brought toward vitrification. It is different in look and composition from natural stone, but somewhat similar to partially vitrified obsidian, its natural equivalent.

Frit is most likely to be found attached to fragments of the crucible in which it was being produced or to fragments of the furnace within which the crucible was being fired, since it was not unusual for the crucible to break and for the frit to spill into the furnace. Furnace fragments coated with fritted material are ubiquitous areas where glassmaking was being performed due to the abandonment of furnaces by glassmakers in their frequent moves. Occasionally a large portion of unattached fritted material is encountered; it most likely resulted from a spill which became contaminated with extraneous material and was therefore discarded. It is precisely these types of evidence which have been regarded as irrelevant materials, the circumstance acknowledged to the author by a number of archeologists in the field upon being shown typical samples of frit and of frit-coated furnace fragments.

A typical characteristic which helps visual identification of frit-glazed furnace fragments is the charring of the material beneath a glassy-looking coating of frit. The depth of this blackish layer may range from almost nothing to a centimeter or more in thickness, depending on composition of the furnace material (especially the amount of organic matter within it) and the thickness of the flow of frit over the surface.

The most startling revelation of the survey conducted by the author was that the evidence of primary glassmaking, strewn about on sites which had already undergone archeological investigation, had been routinely ignored. No one archeologist can be faulted, for the oversight seems universal. We shall focus in passing on one prime example of the myopic condition of the archeological community regarding the art of glassmaking: the evidence permeating ancient Apollonia, south of Caesarea.

Apollonia faces the sea. Huge sections of Crusader-built walls lie helter-skelter along the sea's edge where they had tumbled from the top of a steep escarpment overlooking the beach. A barbed wire fence encloses a restricted seaward section of the escarpment plateau. Fifty meters inland from that outer fence stretch parallel, taller fences, some two meters apart, each crowned with ominous, razor-edged barbed wire. The twin fences circle an extensive area in the center of which stand a group of buildings constructed by the British to police the shoreline and now serve as an Israeli military compound. Fritted material in all stages of vitrification, almost all of it attached to fired earthen materials, are clearly visible and are distributed in abundance for several hundred meters along the rim of the escarpment. On several occasions during the few hours spent in surveying the area, an army jeep patrolling the other side of the twin fences passed by and requested an explanation of our presence. Satisfied with our response, one of the patrolling Israeli soldiers stated enthusiastically that there were "loads of glassy materials" lying around on his side. He stepped out of the jeep, picked up four pieces lying at his feet and heaved them over the fences at us. They proved to be excellent examples of four successive stages of vitrification: a lump of opaque frit, two furnace fragments with flows of partially vitrified frit over their blackened surfaces and a large lump of jewel-like, clear blue glass.

Down along the beach, adjoining an area where bathers wallow in the Mediterranean, glittering glass tid bits can be culled by the thousands from the sand just above the water-line. The worn edges of this bead-like glass gravel were well rounded, bespeaking many centuries of wave action and of sand abrasion. About a hundred meters further along the beach a wire fence blocked the path, placed there to protect people from falling sections of the Crusader walls which had once rimmed the escarpment. The caution against trespass was occasioned by the fact that one of these huge blocks had fallen from the top of the escarpment onto a fisherman and crushed him. A portion of the fence was cut and folded back in disdain of the designated danger and a well-trodden path through the opening testified to the fact that the fence proved no handicap to fishermen who now perch comfortably atop the huge fallen sections of Crusader walls which had rolled conveniently into the Mediterranean surf.

A variety of vitric materials is imbedded in the embankment, among which was a block of clear, brilliantly blue glass whose fractured face measured a hefty 22 x 5 centimeters. Just a few meters away a most intriguing cluster of frit and imperfectly vitrified glass protrudes from the earthen wall. It appears to be an mass of vitric material dumped from a crucible measuring about 18 centimeters in diameter at the narrow bottom and tapering up to some 30 centimeters in height.

Most startling, however, is the fact that incorporated into the fallen Crusader walls are large hunks of material in various stages of vitrification, from opaque frit to clear blue glass. Among the numerous items thus employed as building material is a massive layer of frit measuring some three meters long and two-thirds of a meter at its widest. It obviously penetrates deep into the wall of the fallen structure within which it forms a sort of strata.

Virtually no shards of completed vessels are in evidence anywhere on the site, although, by dint of diligent searching a few vessel fragments can be found. The dearth of remnants of glassware and, by contrast, the vast variety, abundance and spread of primary glassmaking scoria indicate that the site, although, by dint of diligent searching a few vessel fragments can be found. The dearth of remnants of glassware and, by contrast, the vast variety, abundance and spread of primary glassmaking scoria indicate that the industry at this site was devoted to the production of glass as a raw material. It was an industry so vast in scale and of such lengthy duration that the Crusaders availed themselves of its discards as significant building material. Relics of the industry can be found scattered far and wide away from the beach area. A few kilometers away, for example, alongside a path into the park in the town of Herzeliya Petuach, lies a block about 80 x 35 x 25 centimeters, thickly encrusted with partially and fully vitrified material from which passing visitors have been manifestly chipping souvenirs.

The blocks of clear blue and greenish-blue glass imbedded here and there in the Crusader walls, in the detritus of the wall of the escarpment and atop its rim, look remarkably like those being recovered from Roman vessels which sank off-shore along the Israeli coast and now being stored in the nautical museum of on the grounds of the kibbutz Nach Sholim (near Dor). Clearly analysis and study is called for; clearly much will be learned by a proper investigation of the evidence.

Excavations in the area in 1950 revealed glassmaker's furnaces and glassmaking scoria in great abundance, a discovery which came as a surprise to the excavators, since the area had never been considered as a source for glass. Nor was Apollonia unique in the area in this regard. Two other extensive facilities were recognized at Khirbet Jus and Khirbet Sabia, and substantial evidence of glassmaking activity turned up at a dozen other sites around Apollonia, at the previously mentioned Bene Zyon, several others at and around the near-by town of Herzelia (including its cemetery), and at Khirbet Um el-Uleika, Miska, Tavsor, Khirbet el-Khadra, Kefar-Saba, Nebi Yemin, Khirbet Bernikia. Other sites, such as Antipatris, have evidently been associated with the industry and further investigation will undoubtedly produce more evidence of the industry. The glassmaking industry continued at a high level through the Byzantine and well into the Arab period. How far back in time such production extends, and how much wider it spread remains to be determined.

It is to be hoped that a new awareness of the glassmaking process and evidence will be engendered so that the unconscionable oversight of the past will be quickly rectified. If it is not, then the deep-plowing kibbutzniks, the developers of new communities in "virgin" areas, et. al, will soon eradicate

The continuing discard of the evidence of the art as irrelevant material is even more inexcusable. It was, after all, a unique art, one which required the ultimate in pyrotechnology, an achievement which was not surpassed until well into the industrial age. It is an art which anciently achieved an artistic virtuosity which has never been surpassed. It is time the art and the people who performed it were recognized.

The products of the glassmakers of Eretz Israel, and even the glassmakers themselves, found their way into the Far Eastern heart of China well before the Romans arrived in the Near East. The Chinese possessed an advanced pyrotechnology and a profound knowledge of glazes, but they had never solved the remaining, baffling secrets of vitrification.

# NOTES

1. W. A. Thorpe, *English Glass*, 1949, p. 2.

2. Mary Luella Trowbridge, *Philological Studies in Ancient Glass*, 1930, pp. 114, 133, citing: E. Gersprach, *L'Arte de la verrerie*, 1885. Gersprach proposes that since Euphrasius is not Greek he must be a Christian or a Jew; inasmuch as we have learned since Gersprach's 1885 treatise that it is most unlikely that any Christians in Byzantium practiced the art, we are left with a near certainty that the deceased was a Jewish glassmaker.

3. Trowbridge, Ibid., p. 134.

4. Theophastrus, S.IV: III.

5. Trowbridge, Ibid., p. 22.

6. Suggested by Isaac Mozeson, author of *The Word*, Shapolsky Publishers, New York, 1989.

7. Trowbridge, Ibid., p. 59.

8. Cicero, *Pro Rabiro Postumo*, 14, 40.

9. Lucretius, *De Rerum*, 4, 145 ff.

10. N. Avigad, *IEJ*, 12, 1962, p. 183; B. Mazar, *IEJ*, 14, 1964, p. 128.

11. B. Mazar and I. Dunayevsky, "En-Gedi: The First and Second Seasons of Excavations 1961-1962," *Atiqot V*, English series, 1966.

12. Dan Barag, "Glass Vessels from the Cave of Horror," *IEJ*, vol. 12, nos. 3-4, 1962. p. 208.

13. N. Avigad, "Excavations in the Jewish Quarter of the Old City of Jerusalem," *IEJ*, 22, 1977, pp. 198-200; N. Avigad, *The Upper City of Jerusalem*, 1980, pp. 188-190 (in Hebrew).

14. Anita Engles, "Glassmaking in Ancient Jerusalem," *Readings in Glass History No. 18*, 1984, pp. 9-15.

15. Rachel Hasson, "Islamic Glass from Excavations in Jerusalem," *JGS*, 25, 1983, p. 110.

16. *Encyclopedia Judaica*, Jerusalem, 1972, vol. 7, p. 611.

17. Jama ad Dom Ahmad, *Muthir al Gharam*, 1351. The Arabic text provided by Guy le Strange in: "The Noble Sanctuary at Jerusalem," *J. Royal Asiatic Society*, 1887, was retranslated for Ms. Anita Engles by Avraham Yinon of the Jerusalem

Hebrew University. The new translation renders the items to be produced as "lamps, bowls or beakers, and spittoons." Anita Engles, "The Glassmakers," *Readings in Glass History No. 18*, 1984, p. 75.

18. Hasson, Ibid., p. 112.

19. Anton Kisa, *Das Glas in Altertum*, 3 vols. Leipzig, 1908.

20. Frederic Neuberg, *Antikes Glas*, Darmstadt, 1949, translated from the German by Michael Bullock and Alisa Jaffa (*Ancient Glass*, 1962).

21. Neuberg, Ibid., pp. 6,7.

22. Saul Weinberg, "Tel Anafa," *Encyclopedia of Archeological Excavations in the Holy Land*, vol. I, 1975, p. 68.

23. David Frederick Grose, "The Hellenistic Glass Industry Reconsidered," *Annals of the 8th International Congress on Glass*, 17-25 September 1979.

24. Weinberg, Ibid., p. 86.

25. Josephus Flavius, *The Wars of the Jews*, Book II, ch. 18: "Now the people of Caesarea had slain the Jews that were among them on the very day and hour [when the soldiers were slain]...insomuch that in one hour's time above twenty thousand Jews were killed, and all Caesarea was emptied of its Jewish inhabitants....Upon which stroke that the Jews received at Caesarea, the whole nation was greatly enraged; so they divided themselves into several parties, and laid waste [a number of cities, among which was] Geva."

26. Josephus Flavius, *The Wars of the Jews*, vol. 3, Ch. 3.1.

27. David Adan-Bayewitz, from a report submitted to the Hebrew History Federation Ltd. dated March 12, 1988.

28. *Midrash Psalms* 2.11.

29. *Midrash*, Nos. 11:17:

30. *Deuteronomy Rabba*, ch. 2.

31. Dan Barag, *Ancient Jewish Glass in Modern Research*, 1972, p. 125.

32. *Mishnah*, vol. VI, order Taharoth, Kelim 2:1 and Kelim 30:1.

33. *Kelim 8:9*. Joachim Jeremias, *Jerusalem zur zeit Jesu*, translated from the German by F. H. and C. H. Cave, 1969, pp. 1-3. Jeremias notes that the pit-oven was "Made by lining the walls of a pit with clay or cement and strong enough to serve when removed from the pit." Jeremias infers that a pit-oven refers to *a refining furnace*. Other interpreters guess that a pit-oven might refer to *a smith's fireplace*. To those knowledgeable about glassmaking, however (the otherwise erudite translators were clearly unfamiliar with the process), it is clear that the description and the context in which it appears apply perfectly to the two furnaces required for glassmaking.

34. Brand, *Glass Vessels in Talmudic Literature*, 1978. p. 109.

35. *Palestinian Talmud*, Nidda II. 6, 21a and 50b.

36. Engles, Ibid., p. 42.

37. *Talmud*, Avodah Zarah II, 1 40c.

38. Engles, Ibid., p. 41; L. Ginzberg, *Serdai Talmud Yurushalmi*, Hebrew, 1936, p. 272.

39. Robert Brill and John F. Wosinski, "A Huge Slab of Glass in the Ancient Necropolis of Beth She'arim," a paper submitted to Section B of the VIIth International Congress of Glass, Brussels, 1965, pp. 2, 3.

40. Robert H. Brill, "A Great Glass Slab from Ancient Galilee," *Archeology*, vol. 20, no. 2, April 1967, p. 89.

41. Brill, Ibid., 1965, p. 99.

42. Brill, Ibid., p. 92.

43. N. Avigad, *Beth Shearim; Archeological Excavations from 1953-1958*, Hebrew, 1971, p. 31, pl. 13.

44. M. C. Calvi, "The Roman Glass of Northern Italy," *Bulletin of the Haaretz Museum*, 8, 1966, p. 61.

45. II Kings XVII:24.

46. Elias J. Bickerman, *The Jews in the Greek Age*, Harvard University Press, Cambridge and London, 1988, p. 12.

47. Ezra XVII:3

48. Deuteronomy XI:29.

49. Bickerman, Ibid., p. 13.

50. Yael Israeli, "Ennion in Jerusalem," *JGS*, no. 25, 1983, p. 65.

51. Dott G. Bluestein, "Storia degli Ebrei in Roma." P. Maglione and C. Strini, p. 23

52. R. Dussaud, *Un Nom Nouveau de verrier Sidonien*, 1920, p. 232.

53. Dan Barag, "Recent Important Epigraphic Discoveries Related to the History of Glassmaking in the Roman Empire," *Annals of the 10th International Congress on Glass*, 1985, pp. 111-112.

54. Barag, Ibid., pp. 109-110.

55. Sidney Merril Goldstein, *A Preliminary Study of the Glass Manufactured at Jalame in Israel*, 1970, pp. 11-13.

# CHAPTER 8

# THE LINEN, GLASS, SPICE AND SILK ROUTE

## *The Chinese Connection*

AN EMPEROR OF CHINA, INTRIGUED BY THE SPARKLING, IMITATION JADES AND colorful eye-beads which had been brought into China for centuries by Western traders, upon learning that the exotic artifacts were man-made in a furnace, requested that this strange material be produced within his realm. A glassmaking facility was obligingly built and operated by some foreigners to the great delight of the Chinese court. Thus, it was said, was glassmaking introduced into China.

There are numerous Chinese literary works concerning this event, among which the most commonly quoted version is a historical work of the fifth century, the *Pei-shih*,[1] in which it is related that, during the reign of Emperor T'ai Wu (424-452 C.E.), traders from the West came to his capital and stated that they could produce precious stones of any color for the emperor by melting together certain minerals. They were given leave to obtain the minerals from the nearby hills. They did so and were successful in producing glassware even superior to that which had previously arrived from the West.

The story is not without merit, reported the scholar Herada Yoshito in his study, *Ancient Glass in the History of Cultural Exchange*. The tradition has it that certain Western traders boasted that they could produce *liu-li*, "glass," in five colors, that is, that they could duplicate five different precious stones by fusing together locally available minerals, and that, challenged to do so, they proceeded to perform the process so perfectly that the resulting gems were indeed of greater beauty and brilliance than was the imported variety.

EYE-BEADS, 6TH TO 3RD CENTURIES BCE. The provenience of these widely distributed types of beads are presumed to be *Eretz Israel* or Persia. The deportation of Jewish artisans from Israel and Judah coincided with a resurgence of the art of glassmaking in the Persian diaspora, and the beads made in the two regions are indistinguishable in technique. Eye-beads and head-beads were an important ingredient of trade throughout the Mediterranean during the first millennium BCE and eye-beads in particular became as important an element in the development of trade with the Far East as it had been around the Mediterranean.
*Photograph courtesy of The Corning Museum of Glass.*

The scenario given by Yoshito is the persistent core of most of the traditional renderings of the story, many of which become fabulous from that point on. It is related, for example, that the emperor was so fascinated with the result obtained by the foreign artisans that he issued an edict ordering that a palace be constructed of the strange new material. Such a palace was indeed built, large enough to accommodate more than 100 people. The overwhelming brilliance of the translucent structure struck those who viewed it as a miraculous creation.

There are a number of subsequent romances in Chinese literature in which Chinese emperors employed glass, which Yoshito presumes were inspired by the fifth century tale. One such was written a century later; the Emperor Wu of the Han Dynasty, it is said, built a shrine with white glass doors, so that heavenly spirits might pass through easily along with the light which shone through the ethereal material. Another romantic tale, *Hsi-ch'ing Tsa-chi*, written on a more earthly theme, relates how the emperor Ch'eng, also of the Han Dynasty, so loved his queen that he built a bathhouse with windows of precious green glass. Thus it can be inferred that the palace of T'ai Wu, if not made entirely of glass, may at least have had windows of glass, which would at that time have been miraculous enough to generate the expanded fable.[2]

It now appears, however, that glassmaking was introduced into China even earlier than would appear from the fables, perhaps as far back as the fifth century B.C.E. Artifacts of glass had been trickling through along ancient byways to central China long before that time. Glass beads and amulets were universally appreciated and were prime products for exchange throughout the ages. The use of glass beads as a means of exchange continued well into our modern era; the colonization of the world was accomplished largely by means of barrels of beads brought to appreciative primitive peoples. Columbus, upon first arriving in the New World, obtained the good will of the Carib Indians with colorful beads of glass; Manhattan Island was purportedly purchased with a handful of glass beads; the American West was won by exchanging beads for beaver skins; from the South Sea islands to Alaska, glass beads were dangled before the eyes of peoples for whom they represented costly gems and who were amazed that such precious items could be obtained for a parcel of land which was largely free for the taking, or for the skins of animals who reproduced without end, or for the nuggets of yellow metal which lay loose in the beds of streams. More advanced cultures were equally enamored with glass beads and with glass as acceptable substitutes for precious stones. Just as the Near Eastern avidity for lapis lazuli spurred the production of glass imitations at the onset of the art and thereby implemented the conduct of trade, so the appetite for glass simulations of jade assisted in the development of trade to the Far East.

Although silk was the most important and exotic of Chinese exports, other prime products for Western importation should not be overlooked; cinnamon, cassia (the bark from which a form of cinnamon is ground), jade, camphor and a variety of other Chinese products were greatly in demand. The ancient association of the Jews with this trade is evidenced by the references to these uniquely Oriental products in ancient Jewish literature, an attestation which is reinforced by the etymology of the terms employed. "The earliest mention of cinnamon and cassia occurs in the Book of Exodus: in 30:23 Moses is instructed to take 'principal spices, of pure myrrh five hundred shekels, and of sweet cinnamon [*kinnamon besem*] half so much,' and in 30.24 to take 'of cassia [*kiddah*] five hundred shekels,'" notes Lionel Casson in a masterful work, *Ancient Trade and Society*.

The names of the Oriental spices come down to us through the contact of the Greeks with people who spoke Aramaic, from whose language both words, "cinnamon" and "cassia," derive, and who were the intermediaries of the trade. Herodotus (3.111) mentions that the word derived from the coastal Canaanites, the people referred to by the Greeks as "Phoenicians," and stated that "the word *kinnemon* (written as kinnamon in Proverbs 7.17 and Cant 4.14) entered Greek as *kinnamomon*, a form whose ending possibly arose by the association with the spice *amomon*. The word in Exodus for cassia, *kiddah*," continues Casson, "appears in Greek as *kitto*. Another [Biblical] word is *kesi'ah* (Psalms 45.9) whence the Greek *kasia*."[3] Thus, by interpolating the etymology given by Herodotus we perceive that traders who spoke Aramaic were the ones who transported these spices from Southeast Asia or southern China to the Canaanite coast from whence it was distributed into the Mediterranean.

Until the Han period (202 B.C.E.-220 C.E.) Far-Eastern products reached the West by passing through several hands and by diverse routes. The land routes from China pierced the territories of many tribes and arrived at a point in the region of the Pamir Mountains where merchants from the South and West were encountered. The local "kings" took tribute for permitting peaceful passage, and for providing protected posts for the exchange of goods laded on beasts plodding in from East, West and South. "Somewhere in the Pamirs the Chinese caravanners turned over their merchandise to local traders or Indian middlemen who had come up from the south. The Indians hauled their share back home to forward it to the West by ship, while the others plodded on to Persia."[4]

The first glass artifacts to reach China by such an arduous means of exchange were in the Near Eastern tradition. Among the earliest of these objects found to date in the Far East is a Persian-period blue-glass lion, reposing calmly upon a pierced, rectangular base. It is almost identical in size and design with another couchant lion found in Teheran, and with still a third found in Egypt.

> On being shown these lions, Mr. Sydney Smith of the British Museum
> immediately recognized that they are in the Near Eastern Asiatic style, and he
> especially called attention to the manner by which the ribs are indicated; this
> is especially Asiatic, and occurs as early as the Sumerian period. It is, for
> instance, present in the copper bulls brought back by Sir Leonard Woolley,
> and in sole of the early specimens collected by the late H. R. Hall. Mr. Smith
> regarded our specimens as of the fifth or fourth century B.C., not later.[5]

Beads of a similar color and date to that of the glass lion were retrieved from
sites all along the routes into the heart of China and from graves at Lo Yang,
the capital of China in late Zhou times (prior to 256 B.C.E.). The Right
Reverend William Charles White, who served as a Catholic bishop of Honan
at the time of the discovery, was the driving force behind the excavation of
the Lo Yang tombs.[6] White excavated diligently during his term as Bishop
of Honan, and uncovered a vast collection of grave goods from the royal
tombs at Chin-ts'un, in Honan Province, which were ascribed to a date
between 550 and 380 B.C.E.[7]

A great variety of glass artifacts was recovered. Among them were the
ubiquitous eye-beads of the same technique and design which had been
exported from Canaan throughout the Mediterranean and Near-Eastern world.
These unique beads, manufactured by overlaying a glass core with sections
of rods composed of concentric circles of differently colored glass, produce
a startling impression of staring eyes. Such "eyes" were often characteristically clustered, usually six "eyes" grouped around a center "eye." Characteristic eye-beads have subsequently been recovered from tombs in Hubei,
Shandong and Henan provinces of China. "Composite eye glass beads of this
type were familiar to the Eurasian continent, and have a wide distribution,"
writes Takashi Tanichi of the Okayama Orient Museum, and lists numerous
sites across Southern Russia, the Mediterranean and Europe from which
examples were recovered. "Chinese type is similar to the Iranian or Eastern
Mediterranean type," Tanichi cryptically adds.[8] The eye-beads recovered
from a tomb in the Dailaman district of Iran were accompanied by core-
formed kohl-tubes, of a type similar to others found in Nimrud and Vani
(Georgia) and related to those produced in the Land of Israel were dated to
the sixth B.C.E. "at the earliest."[9] These finds, and many more which have
recently come to light, attest to a substantial traffic which wended its way

GLASS EYE-BEADS FROM PERSIA.  A necklace of the first half of the 1st millennium BCE, said to be from Amlash, Iran.  Characteristic eye-beads were found all along the trade route from Persia to Lo-yang, the capital of China, where they appeared in the royal tombs some time between 550 and 380 BCE.
*Photograph courtesy of The Corning Museum of Glass.*

from the Mediterranean coast into the heart of China just before the "silk route" became a single, unified passageway between East and West.

About the second century B.C.E., items appear of a composition which suggests that an indigenous Chinese glass production came into operation. The result of an analysis conducted by C. G. Seligman and H. C. Beck is particularly intriguing. Barium was determined to be a major element of a good portion of these items, an element which had not shown up in Near East glassware. Lead oxide, which was employed in the manufacture of Near Eastern glass, appeared in the Chinese samples in unusual proportions.[10] Thus the fact that local manufacture of glass took place in China at this time became virtually a certainty. A few of the beads with Chinese characteristics must have found their way back to the Mediterranean, for Seligman found that "beads made with the peculiarities of the Chinese specimens have also been found at Caesarea."[11]

Although the Chinese were unfamiliar with the process of producing glass until that time, they had nevertheless had long since attained the pyrotechnical ability to produce glass. That fact is attested to by the appearance of an advanced form of ferric metallurgy around 500 B.C.E. A surprising aspect of the advent of this technology is that the Chinese seemed to have immediately launched into the production of cast iron without passing through preliminary stages of working "wrought" iron. In order to make wrought iron it is sufficient to bring the ore to the melting point of 1083° Celsius. The *bloom* that results is a spongy mass which requires repeated heating and hammering to pound away the slag and to integrate the iron globules into a unified, homogenous mass. Subsequent reheating, hammering and quenching forms, hardens and shapes the iron into useful and durable implements.

Cast iron, however, requires a temperature of more than 1400° Celsius, at which point the slag is drawn off, and the molten metal can be poured into molds like bronze.[12] The production of cast iron in the fifth century B.C.E. proved that pyrotechnology of the Chinese unequivocally included the capability of performing the first of the requisite processes for making glass, that is, they were knowledgeable in the use of pneumatically drafted furnaces. The excellence of ancient Chinese bronze work demonstrates a tradition of 1000 years of the mastery of casting; the equally long tradition and excellence of Chinese porcelain ware prove that a knowledge of glazes was certainly not lacking in the Chinese alchemical catalog. It only remained for the introduction of the last of the secrets, of the process of reheating a pulverized frit to accomplish homogenous vitrification, and of the use of cullet to consistently bring about that result, for the Chinese to be able to produce true vitric artifacts. The questions which remain to be answered are. Exactly when did this knowledge arrive? How was it disseminated?

The fact that trade between the Near East and the Far East antedated the Common Era by many centuries is amply evidenced by glass beads which have been found in central Asia, China, Arabia, India, Burma and Indonesia, where they were clearly an important element of exchange. During pre-Han times the traffic to and from the Far East passed through the hands of mid-Asian, Indian and North African intermediaries. The sea routes led back from the Far East through the Red Sea to join the flow of spices from Yemen through Nabatean hands at Petra. Some merchandise was even unloaded on the Egyptian coast, to be transported across the desert to the central Nile and then transshipped downstream to the Mediterranean. The land routes led through wild, inhospitable territories in which both human and natural obstacles made traffic difficult and costly. The complicated, expensive and risky process impelled both the Chinese and the Western nations to seek a more direct means of exchange.

Silk was the most important Chinese ingredient of that trade and objects of glass obtained in the West were one of the most convenient and valuable goods to be used as a means of exchange in India and Afghanistan. Silk was not unknown in the West; silk produced from wild Asia Minor silkworms was known and used among the Near Eastern civilizations of Hellenic times. However, sericulture was peculiarly, uniquely and anciently a Chinese industry and the quality of Chinese silk made from the cocoons of cultivated silkworms was so superior that it displaced the use of locally produced silk when it became available.

The process of raising silkworms, reeling off filaments hundreds of yards long from their cocoons and weaving them into beautiful, remarkably strong and stable fabrics dates back to the very beginning of Chinese civilization. A silk fabric found in Zhejiang Province dates back to the astoundingly early date of 2700 B.C.E., a time when, according to accepted archeological chronology, China was still in the process of emerging from its Neolithic period.[13] The invention of the drawloom revolutionized Chinese silk manufacture and the industry attained exceptional sophistication by the time of the Han period. The drawloom made possible the weaving of complex embroidered patterns with as many as 400 to 600 threads per linear inch and enabled the embroiderers to work free-hand to produce any shape desired. The ingenuity of the Chinese embroiderers was allowed full artistic range and they took full advantage of that capability by executing the most intricate designs in shimmering silk. Marvelous faunal and floral designs and stylized versions of mythical creatures such as the *feng-huang* bird and the dragon adorned the garments of the upper-class Chinese; they clad themselves in silken masterpieces while alive and were buried luxuriously in them after death. It is little wonder that Western aristocrats avidly sought the sumptuous silken fabrics being flaunted by their counterparts of the East.

The Han rulers were eager to achieve a more advantageous trading position and sought to establish a stable and secure land route to the West. China's land access to the Western merchandise and markets led along scattered caravan trails through areas controlled by tribes who were often hostile and predatory. The Turkic-speaking *Hsiung Nu* pastoral people, (the so-called *Huns* who invaded Europe several centuries later), were a particularly persistent threat to the Chinese; the Great Wall was built to withstand Hsiung Nu incursions from the north. In order to protect his western flank the Emperor Wu (141-87 B.C.E.) sent his general, Zhang Qien, to secure a passage to the West.

The lessons learned from warring with mounted Mongol tribes induced the emperor to introduce cavalry into his own armies. The most fabled horses of the time came from Persia. They were reputed to be "blood-sweating" steeds from Ferghana (Turkestan), raised on the luxuriating alfalfa of the area. General Zhang Qien brought both horses (albeit they did not sweat blood) and a whole range of plants, including grape vines and alfalfa seeds, back to China. In the year 97 C.E., "after reducing the last contumacious prince, Pan Chao crossed the T'ien Shan mountains, and with an army of 70,000 men advanced unopposed to the shores of the Caspian Sea....More than fifty kings' acknowledged Chinese overlordship and sent their heirs as hostages to Lo-yang."[14]

Lo yang, it will be remembered, was the area from which Bishop White unearthed glass artifacts of the pre-Han period. The overland route connecting East and West was secured. Trade burgeoned. A new era began. In the West, however, no one power succeeded in controlling the land routes from the Mediterranean to the Pamirs for an extended period of time. The Elamites, Assyrians, Babylonians, Persians, Greeks, Bactrians, Medes,

Scythians, Parthians, Romans and Sassanians successively implanted themselves along sections of the main arteries of the commercial stream coursing through Mesopotamia and connecting to the umbilical Chinese artery. The one factor which made a continuous flow of commerce possible through the Near East and along the newly constituted and secured throughway across the Asian continent was the role of the Jewish traders and artisans. Throughout the time of the hegemony of one or the other power over lesser or greater portions of the critical Mesopotamian hub of the trade routes, these merchants, bonded by a common language and culture, dealt freely with one another across otherwise hostile borders. Jews dealt with each other in trust from the territories of contending powers even during periods of violent military confrontation.

The progenitors of the Jews had been at the heart of Eastern trade and of the glassmaking industry long before the time of Abraham. Most of the area east of the Zagros Mountains was still in a preliterate state until well into the second millennium B.C.E. at which time contact with Akkadia propelled the kingdom of Elam to a higher level of culture. In its principal city, Susa, numerous cylinder seals were found, some of them manufactured of a beautiful blue glass of Mesopotamian manufacture. At Tchoga Zanbil, some 40 kilometers south of Susa, King Untashgal (reigning c. 1265-1245 B.C.E.) erected a great cult complex centered around a ziggurat. In the hall of worship adjoining the ziggurat Dr. Roman Girschman, excavating with the French archeological expedition, unearthed other such blue glass seals.[15]

Why did glass suddenly come into use for cylinder seals at this time? At present, the most reasonable explanation is connected with lapis lazuli....[16]It is believed that this lapis lazuli came from the Badakhashan region of northeastern Afghanistan, clearly indicating that there was trade at that time [3500 B.C.E.] between Badakhashan and Mesopotamia, 2400 kilometers apart.[17]

Characteristic Mesopotamian glassware ended up in the northern Iranian highlands, shortly after its appearance in the Elamite region, in the area which lay astride the extension of the trade routes through those highlands toward China. Dr. Ezat O. Negahan, of the University of Teheran, excavating at Marlik in the Gilan Province in 1961 and 1962, came upon two exquisite glass vessels, which were dated to between 1200-1000 B.C.E.[18] It was the beginning of a series of northern Iranian finds testifying to a substantial trade in glassware, a trade which reached the Pamirs, the mountain range impeding the throughway and limiting access to the ancient Chinese Empire.

One of the startlingly beautiful vessels found by Dr. Negahan was a situla-shaped vessel fabricated entirely of a mosaic of lozenges. Each lozenge is composed of sections of multicolored rods ordered into a beautiful geometric arrangement; which, fused together, form a fabric which superbly multiplies the intensity of the effect of the individual sections. The intricate mosaic pattern extends into a button-shaped protrusion at the bottom. The technique and design are both clearly related to similar types found earlier at Nuzi and Assur in northern Mesopotamia and at Alalakh in Arameia. The mosaic technique was employed at least as far back as 1500 B.C.E.; similar vessels of that early date were recovered from Tell el Rimach in northern Mesopotamia and others dated to 1400 B.C.E. were found at Aqar Quf in central Mesopotamia.[19]

A second Marlik vessel was of equal magnificence; it was shaped into the simple form of a beaker, but was fabricated in a dazzling array of horizontal bands, each band composed of pairs of alternating zigzag patterns of differently colored rods; the multi-tiered bands were in turn separated into three registers by sets of horizontal bicolored striations. The use of brilliant red, white, blue and yellow colors in the composition of these masterpieces demonstrates the extraordinary chemical and metallurgical competence of the mid-second-millennium producers.

Many other sites in northern and northwestern Iran have provided evidence of ancient trade in masterfully executed glassware. Fragments of ninth century B.C.E. mosaic glass were recovered at Hasanlu, and from the tombs at Dailaman, in the province of Gilan.[20] These tombs yielded glass beads which are significantly similar in style to the beads recovered from the tombs of Lo Yang in China. No vessel fragments were found at Dailaman; while similar beads were found at both Hasanlu and Marlik, the variety of patterns and colors, and in particular the eye-beads from Dailaman give us a comprehensive and definitive cross-reference to the Chinese equivalents from a period which followed shortly thereafter.

The glassmaking industry faded in Assyria and Iran during a dark time of depredations by competing forces; it was restored in the area as a consequence of the implantation of Israelite artisans, deported in 733-732 B.C.E. from Israel into Assyria by Tiglath-Pileser III. The Assyrian monarch

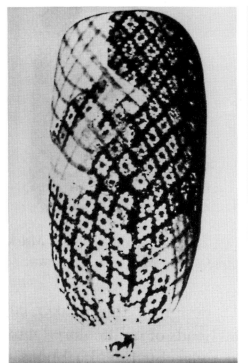

VESSELS FROM GILAN PROVINCE, IRAN. A situla-shaped mosaic vessel (A) and a banded beaker (B) dating to between 1200 and 1000 BCE found at Marlik in northern Iran. A dark period of glassmaking ensued until the end of the 8th century BCE, at which time, coincident with the implantation of Israelite artisans into the region by Tiglath-Pileser III, a renaissance of the art occurred. Gilan province lies across the route to China; many hundreds of the ubiquitous eye-beads have been recovered from sites in the province dating from the 4th-1st centuries BCE. *After Shinji Fukai, Persian Glass, Weatherhill/Tankosha, New York, Tokyo, Kyoto, 1973/77.*

had ascended to the throne in the eighth century before the Common Era and proceeded to transform his faltering dominion into a mighty empire which drew valuable tribute from its vassal states. The treasures obtained by tribute and conquest were carefully listed by the emperor's scribes and consisted of such valuables as "Gold, silver, tin, iron, elephant hides, ivory, multi-colored garments, linen garments, wool [dyed] bluish-purple and reddish-purple, maplewood and boxwood...horses, mules, cattle and sheep, camels she-camels with their young."[21] However, Tiglath-Pileser's most important achievement was not the transfer of treasure but of artisans and his most important innovation was the "perfection of the process of mass deportation and resettlement" in the "form of enforced exchanges of population: selected residents, outstanding craftsmen and soldiers were taken from the newly conquered provinces in the west." These able-bodied and skilled Israelites and their families were resettled in Assyria and Media in exchange for "Aramean and Chaldean tribes from Babylonia [who] were brought as colonists to the western provinces."[22] A fragmentary Assyrian source specifies that 13,150 Israelites were exiled into Assyria at the time. "[Outstanding craftsmen were] resettled either in regions of Assyria that had been depopulated by the ravages of the ninth century, particularly in the district of Gozan, or on the northern and northeastern borders of the Empire."[23]

The region of Gozan was located on the Chabor River, a branch of the Euphrates, and was "one of the most important of the Assyrian provinces [which] had been laid waste both at the end of the tenth century and during the ninth century, in the course of the military campaigns of Ashur-Nasirpal II, and had gradually been restored from the time of Tiglath-Pileser III onwards."[24] The region of Gozan was to become an important post along the soon-to-be-secured silk route.

Tiglath-Pileser annexed Samaria and then the Galilee, at whose center was Megiddo; the Assyrian frontier now stretched through the Jezreel Valley and the valley of Acco to the threshold of Tyre. Assyria was now in control of the very area in which glassmaking had reached its Mediterranean apogee, and the glassmakers from this area were undoubtedly among the artisans transferred to Assyria, for their art was revitalized in the region through which it had passed a thousand years earlier and in which it had persisted almost to the time of Tiglath-Pileser. The removal of the most skilled artisans had the reverse effect upon glassmaking in the Land of Israel where it diminished and almost disappeared. Tiglath-Pileser was succeeded by his son, Shalmaneser, whose short-lived reign gave way to Sargon, who "pretentiously adopted the name of the founder of the Kingdom of Akkad 1700 years earlier."[25] It is Sargon's name which was incorporated into a glass vessel and which, as we learned in Chapter 1, confounded the pundits of early glassmaking history.[26]

The so-called "alabastron of Sargon II" is one of the earliest glass vessels which was not core-formed; it may have been either carved from a single massive block of glass, or cast in a mold and then tooled to its final shape. Its thick, green, transparent walls are engraved with a lion and with cuneiform characters which blazon forth the name of the Assyrian emperor for all posterity to marvel at. It was excavated near Nineveh, in the ancient city of Nimrud, and its location and the form of writing suggest that the impressive vessel was not of Assyrian but more generally of "Mesopotamian" or of "Babylonian" origin.

Some 140 years later the "king of Akkad," the Babylonian Nebuchadnezzar, fully cognizant of the technological and commercial advantages gained from the resettlement of the Israelites by his Assyrian predecessor Tiglath-Pileser, followed the example set by the latter monarch by deporting additional thousands of choice Jewish artisans, soldiers and their families into Babylonia (Jeremiah 52:28). Following the fall of Jerusalem at the turn of the sixth century, 10,000 crack troops and artisans and their families were taken out of Judah by the Babylonian king, Nebuchadnezzar, and again, a great cultural and technical upsurge took place in Babylon at the expense of the Judaean Israelites. We are Biblically informed that among the craftsmen were sailors and singers, carpenters and smiths and other craftsmen who were employed in the massive building projects of Nebuchadnezzar. The cataclysmic experiences the Israelites and Judaeans experienced under the Assyrians and Babylonians were partially resolved on the succession of a benevolent Cyrus to power. Many Jews returned to rebuild the Temple in Jerusalem under the liberating edict of Cyrus. Returning Jewish artisans revived the glassmaking industry in resuscitated Samaria and the Galilee and returned it to its former status as an important industry of the region, turning out a product which was particularly suited for export. Glass objects become an important element of Mediteranean trade goods from the sixth century B.C.E. forward. Eye-beads also begin to appear along all the routes to the Far East.

Most of the transplanted Jews remained in Babylonia, rooted in the land which their ancestor Terach, father of Abraham, had deserted. Under Babylonian suzerainty this technologically developed, literate population stimulated industry and international commerce to new heights of achievement and exchange; Babylon became a bustling hub through which the routes to China and India and Judah and the West radiated. A substantial contingent of the Judaean exiles was settled around the Chebar River, an important irrigation canal close by the important trading center of Nippur (Ezekiel 1:1), and was engaged in agriculture and crafts. Nippur, being situated on the main road between Babylon and Susa, was one of the increasingly important byways of the trade routes to India and China. "The others, chiefly craftsmen and skilled workers, were transferred to Babylon itself and were employed in the building projects of Nebuchadnezzar."[27] The Babylonian Jewish population grew to more than a million in number.

Commerce through Mesopotamia continued to increase during the entire period of the Achaemenian Dynasty (550-330 B.C.E.), due in no small measure to its position as a vital crossroads of international trade. Northern India had come under Achaemenian hegemony at the end of the sixth century, and became the twentieth province of the empire. Achaemenian period glassware has been recovered from Nippur, from precisely the area in which the Jews were most densely settled. The imitation of metal bowls of the period is a most characteristic feature of the Nippur glassware. These singular vessels are shallow, hemispherical bowls, plain on the interior but molded in relief with a rosette of fluted leaves radiating upward from the base and ending in a raised encircling ridge below the rim. Fragments of one such a glass bowl were recovered by J. P. Phillips during excavations conducted at Nippur by the University of Pennsylvania as early as 1889. Several complete bowls and an alabastron were found earlier (in the 1840s) at Nimrud by Austin A. Layard.[28] The distribution of this kind of glass vessel clearly took place over a considerable range, for the same style of the fragments found at Nippur and manufactured somewhere in that area is characteristic of glass bowls found in Gordion, Jerusalem, Ephesus and Persopolis, and of many similar bowls of unknown provenience, two of which are, for example, in the collection of the Corning Museum.[29] The Ephesus bowl was found in the fill of a temple at Artemis which replaced a precedent temple burned in 350 B.C.E., thus fixing the date firmly to the Achaemenian period. The Babylonian-Assyrian territory was suggested as the provenience of the Ephesus bowl by Paul Fossing.[30] Western Persia was suggested by A. von Saldern as the provenience of the Persopolis bowl.[31] "It is thus possible," cautiously concludes Professor Dan Barag from the sparse evidence at hand, "that the bowl from Nippur and its parallels in Corning and Jerusalem also originated from a Mesopotamian shop."[32]

The very first mention of glass in Greek literature goes far to confirm Professor Barag's tentative proposition. Aristophanes, writing in the year 425 B.C.E., reported on the astonishment of Greek ambassadors to the court of the Persian king when they were served drinks in costly bowls made of

ACHAEMENID PHIALE, 450-400 BCE. These ribbed bowls, imitations of metal prototypes, were an important item in trade from Achaemenid Persia to the West just as eye-beads were for trade to the Far East. The Jewish population in Persia burgeoned to reach some million persons by the dawn of the Common Era; it was concentrated in the fertile heartland between the Euphrates and Tigris rivers and in the mercantile and industrial centers along the trade routes which radiated out from that region to the East and West.
*Photograph courtesy of The Corning Museum of Glass.*

this strange, exotic, transparent material, for which no Greek word yet existed.[33] The Aristophanes story is the first mention of glassware in Greek literature.

The value of such glass vessels has not diminished since the Greeks first boasted of drinking from the exotic ware, for an Achaemenid bowl was sold at Sotheby's in London on July 13, 1976, for 62,000 English pounds. Many examples of the metal counterparts of the Achaemenid glass bowls are also extant. A silver phiale of this type appeared recently on the London market; it is complete with a rosette of 18 leaves and medial ridges and is inscribed in Aramaic, including the name Tryphon, its probable original owner.[34]

Aramaic, the household language of the Jews, was, indeed, the official language of the Achaemenid empire, as well as the lingua franca for much of western Asia through this period.[35]

Eye-beads, typical of the type which formed an integral part of Canaanite trade in the Mediterranean as well as along the route through central Asia into China were particularly common in the Achaemenid period. From Persopolis to Dailaman, virtually every archeological site has provided samples of these characteristic trade goods.[36]

While glassmaking continued in central Mesopotamia it diminished or disappeared in the northern Iranian region.[37] These circumstances lead one to conjecture that, given the increased difficulty faced by the Chinese aristocracy to obtain the highly prized glass artifacts from the area of Iran and the newly won freedom of Jewish artisans to depart from Babylonia, some glassmakers (and smiths?) took advantage of the occasion to move eastward and establish themselves at the core of the Chinese empire in order to serve this developing, lucrative market for their ware. These enterprising craftsmen would have brought Western vitric and ferric technology with them; they would have very likely employed conveniently available local barium ores for the purpose of glassmaking; they would have taken advantage of the sophisticated Chinese knowledge of glazes and colors; they would have had no problem in adapting the advanced pyrotechnology the Chinese had already achieved in producing monumentally sized and magnificently detailed bronzeware to ferric and vitric procedures. The sudden appearance of Mesopotamian--type eye-beads and glassware in the graves of wealthy Chinese in and around Lo Yang and the seemingly simultaneous appearance of an iron industry would logically result from an immigration of artisans at that time in the wake of the Babylonian traders.

The rule of the Achaemenids was followed by a short period of rule by the Macedonians, who were displaced by the Parthians. It was during the tenure of this dynasty (249 B.C.E.-226 C.E.) that traffic and trade to China reached unprecedented heights. Persia became a busy intermediary between the Occident and the Orient.[38] Passage to the East was secured by the Chinese; a new commercial era ensued.

The western connections to the newly unified Chinese land-based route led from Antioch and Tyre and out through Harran and along the upper Euphrates or through Tiberias and Beth Shean across the Jordan River through Palmyra and Dura-Europus down along the central Euphrates after

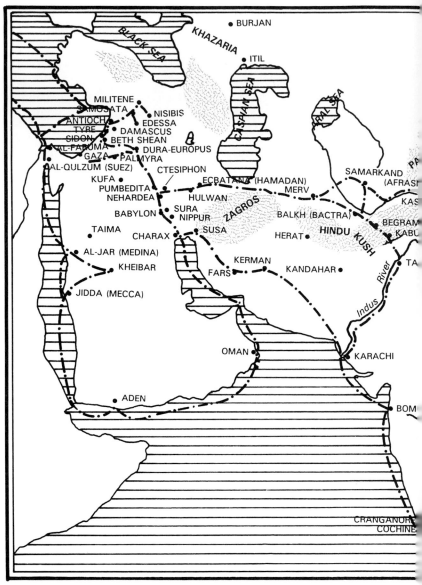

Jewish entrepreneurs, exemplified by the Persian "Rhadanites," established communities along routes connecting the Mediterranean to China and India; they were uniquely able to trade across hostile borders regardless of geopolitical considerations. Jewish artisans produced linen and glass, the principal trade goods for eastern silk and spices. Dyeing fabrics was another Jewish specialty vital to the linen, wool and silk industries and important to both East and West. Jewish merchants traversed Africa into Spain, penetrated Europe as far as Cologne and, after the Khazar conversion to Judaism, routed through Itil and Burjan up the Russian rivers

ANCIENT ASIAN ROUTES ALONG WHICH
EN, GLASS, SPICES AND SILK WERE TRADED

JRUMCHI • HAMI
TURFAN •
LOULAN • ANHSI
TUN-HUANG •
IOTAN MIRAN
• NIYA
AYAS

KANBALIK (BEIJING) •
Yellow River
YU-CHI
NINGXIA
LANCHOW
KAIFENG
LO YANG
CHANG-AN
YANGZHOU
HANGZHOU
NINGBO

Yangtze River

QUANZHOU •

GUANGCHOU •

into Silesia (Poland) and central Europe, completing a commercial web which encompassed the entire hemispheric civilized region. Trustworthy contacts enabled the world-girdling traveler-traders to establish international credit and they became a valuable asset to the countries in which they established residence. Many were scholars who were the conduits of new products and technologies while they served to bring responses from the great Babylonian academies to the halachic questions posed by Jewish communities seeking guidance.

which the route split, one branch leading toward central Asia and the other branch thrusting toward India. Each nexus of the articulated trade system connecting East and West contained a core of Jewish artisans and traders. Among the arts practiced, that of glassmaking is the quintessential manifestation of Jewish presence; wherever a considerable community of Jews was established, the art of glassmaking concurrently appeared; where no evidence of the existence of a sizable community of Jews comes to light, evidence of glassmaking is rarely found. It was an art unknown to the technologically less-advanced peoples among whom fortified caravansaries and urbanized centers were established. It was a trade in which members of the hierarchy of the conquerors of the regions would under no circumstance engage, for it was a sweaty, rigorous, callous-producing, hand-operated activity, relegated to the Jews, the only element among the subject peoples capable of the art.

The cities which Alexander left in the wake of his sweep to the Indus River were socially structured upon the haughty Greek disdain for handwork so succinctly expressed by Aristotle. The Jews, being considered aliens even in their own land, made up a substantial element of the skilled workforce within these military outposts, and were preeminently the glassmakers. Far from decrying engagement in physical labor, the Jews esteemed all creative vocations--physical, mental and spiritual. The sages of the great universities of Babylonia and Eretz Israel proudly labored at various trades to earn their daily sustenance. Teaching was not considered an activity for which compensation was required; teaching *Torah*, Biblical law, was in particular a proud privilege for which remuneration was not accepted. This principle was woven permanently into the body of Talmudic practice: "Torah is not a spade" was the precept practiced by the sages as they eked out a living by creative labor. "God, after all," it was argued, "was the ultimate artisan; it was through His labor that the world was created; He earned a rest on the Sabbath, setting an example for mankind." An ancient and oft-repeated rabbinic maxim placed man within the context of transcendent creativity: "He who is productive so that the world's work might go on has a share in God's creation." The rabbinic sages of the ancient academies dignified their trades:

Abba Joseph was a construction worker; Chiyya bar Abba, a carpenter; Yitchak Nappacha, a smith; Abba bar Zmina, a tailor; Abba Hoshea, a laundryman; and Joseph Zeida made fishing nets. The great Hillel...was a simple woodchopper who peddled his humble commodity on the streets of

Jerusalem before he entered the Academy to lecture. Likewise his famous Rabbinic opponent, Shammai, worked as a land-surveyor; Yochanan ha-Sandler, as his name implies, was a maker of sandals. Abba Hilkiah was a farmhand, and Resh Lakish was a watchman in a vineyard.[39]

The admonishment recited repeatedly in every Jewish household and in every synagogue: "Forget not that we were all once slaves in Egypt," serves as an enduring reminder of the dignity of labor and as a rebuke to those who would set himself above the common laborer.

The Jews were vital to the trade conducted along the route to the East; as artisans they dominated the interrelated trades of weaving and dyeing; as merchants they prevailed over the market for fibers and fabrics. The preeminent involvement of the Jews in these activities evolved from an exceptional knowledge of the provenience of dyes and coloring materials and consequently of their use, a cultural attribute equally true in the case of glassmaking. Jewish involvement in these activities was enhanced as a consequence of their strategic locations at the hub of intercontinental trade. Linen fabrics (byssus) were as marketable in China as silk fabrics were in the West. One of the earliest centers of both weaving and glassmaking was the town of Beth Shean which, the Old Testament informs us, was a Canaanite town which fell to the forces of David. By the third century B.C.E. Beth Shean had achieved world wide fame as a producer of fine fabrics. The Jerusalem Talmud refers to the "fine linen vestments which come from Beth Shean."[40]

Beth Shean was dubbed "Scythopolis" by the Greeks and was one of the first communities overrun when Alexander led his Macedonians and mercenaries across Judah and Mesopotamia as far as the Oxus and Indus Rivers. Its workshops supplied the Greeks, and subsequently the Romans with fabrics and other finished products, with which to redress the balance of payments for merchandise from further east. The exemplary superiority of textiles and clothes produced in Beth Shean was noted by the Roman emperor Diocletian. In 296 C.E., in an attempt to curb runaway inflation, Diocletian decreed fixed ceilings on prices and wages throughout the Empire. The Diocletian statutes entitled the "Edict of Maximum Prices" paid particular notice to the woven produce of Beth Shean. "The textile goods are divided into three qualities: first, second and third. In each group the produce of Scythopolis appears in the first class."[41] The edict also lists only two categories of glassware, Judaean and Alexandrian, which circumstance suggests that the artisans of these two districts were as yet the main, if not the sole, producers of glass at this late date for the Roman Empire.

In a Latin work of the fourth century, *Descriptotus Orbis*, Beth Shean is described as one of the cities which supply textiles to the whole world.[42] The observance of Hebraic law by the community is evidenced by Mishnaic narratives, which, at the same time, serve to illustrate the involvement of the Jews with international trade. One such story records the refusal of Beth Shean Jews to leave for Sidon on a Saturday to conduct business. Sidon was a port through which glass was exported and through which many of the minerals for the production of glass were imported. Glassmaking was a subsidiary industry in Beth Shean and neighboring Tiberias, but a major industry in nearby Beth Shearim, the center of the Galilean glassmaking industry.

The great Halachic sage, Rabbi Chiyya bar Abba, is among those mentioned in the Mishnah who are involved in merchandise shipped to and from the East. While the Mishnah, that vast repository of Jewish tradition and law, does not deal with economic matters as such, we are treated with anecdotes which are cited to point up ethical or legal issues and incidently document the symbiotic relationship between the Jews and the production and distribution of glassware and textiles among other commercial activities. R'Chiyya dealt with three of the basic goods traded along the route into China--glass, silk, flax and the products thereof-- and traveled widely in the conduct of his business.

It is clear that the term "silk route" does not adequately describe its function; the term was coined in the nineteenth century by Baron Ferdinand von Richtshofen from a Western point of view. Without the flow of linens and glassware from the West there would be no return of spices and silks from the East.[43] Joseph Needham, who compiled a most comprehensive and authoritative Western work on Chinese technology, concluded that: "The byssus (fine linen) mentioned as being brought to China by merchants or embassies from the 1st century onward is likely to have come from Scythopolis (Beth Shean) in the Jordan Valley."[44] Glass beads from the Galilee ended up in ancient Chinese tombs along with the linens of Beth Shean.

R'Chiyya had followed his mentor, the great Rabbi Judah Ha-Nasi ("the Prince," 135-219 C.E.) into Palestine from Babylonia. It was a time of trauma; the suppression of the Jews after the crushing of the second revolt and the destruction of the center of Judaic national culture at Jerusalem created a hiatus which Judah ha-Nasi filled; he became the principal architect of the Mishnah. Judah ha-Nasi first resided in Beth Shearim, the glass-making heart of the Galilee, and then in Beth Shean. R'Chiyya's business trips also took him to Beth Shean, to Laodicea (another weaving center), throughout the Galilee and Nabatea. There are references to his dealing in spikenard, a spice imported from the Himalayas whose import was controlled by the Nabatean Arabs.[45] Thus the Mishnah reflects the involvement of Jews like R'Chiyya in all of the elements which composed the China trade. It was this tradition of travel which expanded into a world-girdling network of Jewish trade under the Persian *Radhanites*. "These merchants speak Arabic, Persian, Roman, Frankish, Spanish and Slavonic," wrote Ibn Khurdadhbih in the ninth century. "They travel from East to West and from West to East by land as well as by sea."[46] The Arabic historian might well have added Aramaic and Hebrew to the listing of languages spoken by these intrepid travelers.

Augustus, the first Roman emperor, is said to have commissioned "the original travel guide" from Isidore of Charax, who then wrote *The Parthian Stations*. As the quantity of imports of exotic goods from China and India to Rome increased the trade became a drain on the Roman economy which Rome could not sustain. The emperor Tiberius, alarmed, warned in the first century that precious gold was being drained from the treasury to pay for "articles that flatter the vanity of women; jewels and those little objects of luxury which drain away the riches of the Empire. In exchange for trifles, our money is being sent to foreign lands and even to our enemies." Pliny the Younger later pointed out that the annual drain on the Roman treasury amounted to "55 million Sesterces paid to India and 45 million to Seres (China)." The glassware, metalware and linens produced in the Land of Israel went a long way to ease Rome's balance of trade, but did not resolve the problem resulting from the gluttonous appetite of the Roman hierarchy for exotic and expensive goods.[47]

Antioch became the western capital of the Seleucid kingdom and the main Mediterranean terminus of the silk route, and Seleucia was established as its eastern capital. Seleucia was soon displaced in importance by a town burgeoning within a fortress on the middle Euphrates constructed by Nicanor, one of the generals under Seleucus. It was named Dura (literally, "The Fortress") and was located on the great caravan route which went westward through Palmyra to Antioch. The fortress-city, later called Dura-Europos, sat athwart the center of the Euphraitic section of the busy route.

> [Dura's] walls were erected by the Macedonian Greeks to protect the caravan route at this juncture. Main street, which ran from the desert gate that faced Palmyra toward the river, was twice the width of the side streets and a quarter larger than the secondary arteries. This road must have been the caravan route."[48]

The fort soon grew into a town, a busy center in which the Greek garrison was supported by artisans from the surrounding Parthian environment. Traders from Palmyra settled into the city to accommodate the traffic flowing through Dura and the marketplace was forged into a vital link of the intercontinental commercial chain. The Greek overlords continued to employ Greek, but Persian customs and wives eventually took effect upon Greek language and culture. The Jews of Dura, however, consistently spoke Aramaic and Palmarene Semitic dialects, according to whether they had settled in from the East or the West, and wrote in their own scripts.[49]

Neither the Bactrians nor the Parthians were pleased with the Hellenic presence. A campaign of attrition resulted in the breaking away of small areas of Bactria and Parthia from Seleucid domination early on, followed by the taking of Seleucia in 141 B.C.E. The civil war in Judah also took its toll, and after the Maccabees succeeded in driving the Greeks out of Judah only a small section of the Mediterranean coast, a portion of the desert and the fortress-city of Dura remained in Seleucid hands. In 96 B.C.E. the Parthians came into solid control of the entire Mid-Euphrates area, including Dura. The Romans entered into a treaty in 20-19 B.C.E. in which the border was fixed to the Khabur River, 40 miles upstream from Dura and along which a considerable number of Jewish settlements existed. Invidious Roman incursions, in disregard of the agreements made under Augustus, by Trajan in 115 C.E. and by Verus in 164 C.E., put an end to a 277-year period of Parthian glory.

The magnificent synagogue of Dura-Europos was discovered during the sixth season of excavation under the direction of Clark Hopkins, then with Yale University. The walls of the synagogue were largely intact due to the fact that, being built against an outer wall of the fort, the entire structure had been buried under an inner earthwork embankment created by the Romans in order to reinforce the ramparts against Parthian siege. The walls of the synagogue were emblazoned with huge murals depicting Biblical scenes which were designed and painted by some third-century Michelangelo; the Old Testament scenes covering the entire surface of the four walls of the synagogue composed a magnificent, monumental work of art comparable in size, artistry and impact to that of the Sistine Chapel, allowing only for the difference in artistic development of more than a millennium in time. The discoverer of the synagogue, Clark Hopkins, describes his emotional reaction as it was being brought to light:

> Once, when I was involved in a train wreck, I had no recollection of the moment between the shock when I was thrown from my seat and when I began to pick myself up from the bottom of the overturned car. So it was at Dura. All I can remember is the sudden shock and then the astonishment, the disbelief, as painting after painting came into view....As the full extent of the wall came into view I sent a note to Susan [Hopkins] to come at once. Frank Brown [Hopkin's assistant] came running from his trench. He could not stand the strain of waiting when he saw the bright colors in the distance. We stood together in mute silence and complete astonishment....[50]The devout artist who designed the tremendous scenes of paintings at Dura was a genius who magnificently fulfilled the challenge presented by the bare walls of the synagogue.[51]

The splendid structure uncovered by the archeologists was a two-story affair erected over the remnants of an older, more modestly proportioned synagogue. It was "huge for Dura," noted the astounded Hopkins, and the heart of a vast complex of buildings and rooms which were designed to accommodate the communal needs of a considerable Jewish population; the complex also provided ample housing for Jewish merchants passing through along the silk route.

Glassware was produced at Dura-Europos, of a type which has been recovered from a number of sites along the silk routes. Some of the vessels in use and ostensibly made in Dura-Europus are strikingly similar to certain vessels found in a treasure house at Begram (Kapisa), in Afghanistan, a city astride a loop of the old silk route some 45 miles north of Kabul. The glass vessels are dated to between the first and third centuries[52] and were part of a vast hoard of glass found inside two enormous rooms of the summer palace of the greatest of all the Kushan kings, Kanishka. The rooms were evidently walled up during a period in which an invader threatened to sack the palace, a circumstance which fortuitously preserved the hoard for posterity.[53]

This most fortunate find provides a good cross section of the gamut of goods which were traded along the silk routes, of which glassware was a considerable proportion. The hoard included masterfully carved ivory and bone artifacts from India, exquisitely lacquered bowls from China, porphyry and alabaster bowls from Alexandria, bronze vessels and statuettes from Roman Italy. It was the glassware, however, that was most indicative of the range and sophistication of the trade goods passing between East and West. Among the glass artifacts were numerous masterpieces; an assortment of well-wrought cage cups (diatreta), a two-handled vase made of gold-flecked blue glass, a sculpted skyphos cup depicting in relief the Alexandrian Pharos, the lighthouse atop which stood a statue of Poseidon (one of the seven wonders of the ancient world), and a large vase whose shape and color resembles the ones in the Haaretz Museum of Tel Aviv bearing the inscription in Greek: "Ennion made me." "The egg-shaped body and elegant, ridge-shaped strap-handle resemble so strikingly the blue Ennion-signed vase of the same period...that one cannot avoid the impression that they must have come from the same work-shop."[54] A glass rhyton similar to one found in the heart of the Jewish quarter of Jerusalem together with glassware-making materials, and many other indicative items included in the Begram hoard, add to the conviction that the provenience of this grand collection could only have been the western end of the silk route.

How did this unique treasure arrive at this remote city of upper Afghanistan? The clues to the identity of the traders who passed through emerge from the Zoroastrian literature of the times. The mysterious and historically enigmatic territory now designated "Afghanistan" straddles a critical junction between East and West. The area entered rather late into the written annals of civilization. "The first identifiable mention of the area now called Afghanistan can be found in the *Avesta*, the canonical scriptures of the Zoroastrians plus the teachings (*Gatha*) of Zarathustra, its founder."[55]

Three formidable mountain ranges, meeting tripedally to define the northeastern corner of Afghanistan, determine the character of the country. The Pamirs, the mountain barrier blockading the silk route, conjoin at that point with two other majestic ranges; the incomparable Himalayas, impassable for all practical purposes, spread out majestically from the juncture far into the east; the somewhat more negotiable but nonetheless forbidding Hindu Kush swing out to the west through the heart of Afghanistan. Traders traveling eastward or westward had little choice but to bypass the Himalayas; they were obliged to traverse the passes of the Pamirs; they could then choose to skirt the Kush Mountains westward through Samarkand, or to negotiate the Kush passes southward to or from Balkh and Kabul. The southern route offered the marked advantage of meeting the traffic which flowed into those bustling market centers from India through Taxila, thereby capitalizing on trading from three directions.

The passes of the great central mountain range of Afghanistan, the Hindu Kush, were negotiated by many conquerors, including Alexander, Genghis Khan, Babur and Tamerlane. A main concern of the traders was, however, a political one. In addition to the activities of warriors from outside the area, the distinct tribal entities, separated by the characteristic mountainous terrain, vied for domination over the passes; the state of the relationship between contesting groups often determined which through route was negotiable. The choice of route depended on considerable climactic considerations no less than on geographical and political factors; winter made passes impassable; drought made desert areas forbidding; floods made the rivers gushing down from several-miles-high slopes unfordable.

We Westerners are familiar with history written by or about Western conquerors and somewhat knowledgeable about the murderous movements of such adventurers as Alexander the Great and Genghis Khan; we are ill-informed about equally world-shaping events which the artisans and traders brought about through peaceful intercourse and about the artisans and traders themselves, whose civilizing activity fades into the background. We do not even strike a proper balance between the self-glorification of Western aggressors and that of others in composing history. A. T. Olmstead remarks that "By this time we realize how incomplete was our knowledge of the [Persian] Empire when observed through the eyes of Greek writers only." And again: "Rescripts from Persian kings were cited in Ezra; Old Testament critics had declared them unauthentic, but now there is ample proof that the critics themselves were in the wrong." And yet again: "Most wonderful of all the discoveries was the autobiography of Darius himself, now no longer known only from the inscriptions in the three cuneiform writings, for these Jews possessed a well-worn copy in their own Aramaic language!"[56] The familiarity of the Jews with Persian history was not gained second-hand; it was the result of having lived it, not as warriors but as artisans and traders.

We have yet to recognize how central a role the Jews played in the commercial life and traffic of the area. Evidence of Jewish influence, strangely enough, was rendered by the militant Mauryan Emperor Ashoka (c. 269-32 B.C.E.), who became a Brahman Buddhist after slaughtering (by his own admission) 100,000 innocents. Ashoka marked his conversion of conscience by scrawling a series of edicts on rocks and pillars throughout his empire from the Bay of Bengal clear across the Indian subcontinent into the heart of the Kush Mountains. These pillars proclaim Buddhist principles, exhorting Ashoka's subjects in quasi-commandment form to refrain from evil doings, to desist from disparaging their neighbors, to honor their teacher, father and mother, to treat slaves and dependents with compassion, to kill animals only for food and to abstain from killing animals for sport, etc. These proselyting Buddhist exhortations are remarkable in two respects: they reflect the humanitarianism being promulgated by the Jewish Babylonian sages of the time, and Aramaic is prominent among the languages in which they are inscribed.

Many of the edicts contain duplicate texts in two languages, some in Greek and Aramaic, others in an Indic language and Aramaic. Three Ashoka Rock edicts were found in central Afghanistan near Qandahar; one carries 13 lines of Greek and 8 lines of Aramaic; a fragment of a second edict contains seven lines of Prakit and Aramaic and a fragment of a third edict retains only a few lines in Greek. Fragmentary finds from Taxila,[57] and near Jalala-bad[58] consisted of words in Aramaic and Prakit or Gandhari.[59] "Four new Ashokan inscriptions were found in the Laghman area between Shatalak and Qargha by Jean and Danielle Bourgeois on November 22, 1969 (reported in *The Kabul Times*, January 1, 1970). Three of the inscriptions are reported in an Indic (Prakit?) language, the fourth in Aramaic."[60] Another edict was found at Surkh Kotal, written in Greek characters but not in the Greek language. Other pillars have been identified which are inscribed solely in Indic languages.

Aramaic, the contemporary language of the Jews, had been the lingua franca of the entire Near East for a millennium; it had been carried on as the official vehicle for international communication in Persia by the Achaemenids. Greek had crept into usage during the Seleucid period, but had never succeeded in displacing Aramaic in the eastern areas, as the ubiquitous reappearance of Aramaic in the "Pillars of Morality" (as the proselyting pillars became popularly known), make evident.

The advent of Buddhism into the region provides other clues to the identity of the traders passing through in the early period of the silk route. The impetus to the dispersion of Buddhism into China was given by Kanishka, a soldier who founded the Second Kushan Dynasty and during whose reign Buddhism rose to its apogee in Central Asia. Kanishka was a patron of learning, and the seat of his government, Gandhara, "became a potent and vital center of literary and artistic activity."[61] A great increase in East-West trade occurred during Kushan rule. Begram, the site where the previously mentioned horde of artifacts was found was the summer capital of the Kushan hierarchy.

Gentle Mahayana Buddhism, which had gestated in Gandhara, was uprooted and displaced in India by resurgent militant Brahmanism, but spread along the silk route into Turkestan, Mongolia, China, Korea and eventually Japan. Whereas Buddhism differed fundamentally from Judaism in the acceptance of a panoply of supernatural spirits and deities, it remained tolerant of the Jews who lived, worked and traded peacefully among them. The Kushan empire broke up into independent states, and a remnant of the Zoroastrian Persian tribes came down from the Zagros Mountains to win control over the entire Afghan area under *Ardashir I* (224-241 C.E.), founder of the new Sassanian dynasty and empire (224-651 C.E.). The Sassanians influenced and modified the Buddhist "Gandharan" art, giving rise to the style known as Irano-Buddhist. "Persian influence spread even further east, greatly affecting Buddhist mural art, such as seen at Kizil on the silk road in central Asia. And in China the Persian style was fashionable from the time of the Six Dynasties (220-589) through the Sui (589-618) and T'ang (618-907) Dynasties."[62] It can be readily assumed that it was the traders of the Radhanite types who were the catalysts of this artistic osmosis.

The glassmaking workshops of the Galilee near the caravan city of Beth Shean and the workshops in the desert oases such as Palmyra and Duro-Europus were integral to the trade moving eastward, just as the workshops of the Galilee and Sidon were to the movement of merchandise to the West. In Palmyra an active glass gem and jewelry industry is attested,[63] and is one of the first places where examples of early Chinese woolens and silks was found. The style and technique of these fabrics are similar to fragments of cloth dating from the same period found by Stein at Loulan in the eastern part of Chinese Turkestan.[64] Palmyra's foreign customs were controlled by Rome and managed by Palmyra's own officials,[65] but the conduct of trade was largely in the hands of the Jews.

The trail of the traders is marked along its length by glassware; we have already noted that beads with the same characteristics of those found at Lo Yang have turned up at Caesarea;[66] The three registers of glass inlays on the bronze mirror recovered from the Lo Yang tomb has a close counterpart in a glass plaque recovered some 30 kilometers west of Baghdad from the Kassite palace of Aqar Quf. Eye-beads, characteristic trade goods of the Canaanites around the Mediterranean, are duplicated by those from pre-Han Lo Yang, most probably of a period before production of glass was initiated in the area.[67] The one anomalous, apparently unique characteristic of Chinese glass, the extraordinary amount of barium, turned out to be present in glass found in Khazar (Russian) Georgia of a somewhat later period.[68] The Georgian glass stemmed from a time in which the Khazars of Asia, after installing themselves across southern Russia, became associated with the Jews and converted to Judaism, a relationship which will be dealt with in a subsequent chapter.

Large masses of Jews fled Judah after the Bar Kokba revolt was crushed by the Romans in 135 C.E. The Romans expelled the Jews from Jerusalem, and renamed Judah, Samaria and the Galilee the province of Syria-Palestina, in a vindictive attempt to obliterate the Jews as a national entity. The exodus of Jews into the Diaspora splayed out in all directions along the already well-fixed trade routes; Jews sought refuge in the Jewish communities established along those routes.

During this period the Zoroastrian Sassanians replaced the weakened and fragmented Achaemenian Persians, rejuvenated Parthian power, and undertook the defeat of the Romans. They attacked Dura, invoking the Parthian claim to the city which was being held by the Romans in violation of the Augustan agreement. The Sassanian general, Shapur, destroyed the city in the year 256 to prevent its coming again under the protection of Western power, and desert sands soon covered its ruins. Palmyra, bereft of its vital link to the East, soon followed Dura into oblivion. The Romans themselves leveled Palmyra 16 years later. The silk route was diverted to the west bank of the Jordan River where the city of Gadara kept open the trade route along the rim of the desert which buried Palmyra and Dura.

Over the next five hundred years, thousands of Jews migrated into Persia and Arabia. Part of these continued north into Afghanistan, Balkh, Samarkand and Bokhara, in Central Asia, all on the Old Silk Road. Some, probably about the

7th century, moved overland from there into northwest China, also known as Chinese Turkestan, where they settled, though not in large number. A few advanced further into north China.[69]

Outposts were implanted along the routes radiating out from the Baghdad-Antioch axis into Khazaria, India and China. These far-flung communities served the caravans and functioned as local trading posts. Wherever local conditions and available materials were conducive to the introduction of new technologies, the traders capitalized upon the circumstances by encouraging craftsmen to settle in the suitable areas. The colonies spotted along the silk routes to the Far East added industry to commerce; some became thriving cities which resounded to the sounds of vigorous activity. The shrill cries of venders and the persistent yammerings of the auctioneers were accented by the staccato hammering of the metalsmiths, and the entire medley echoed through the bustling marketplaces of these burgeoning commercial centers. Billowing smoke weaved skyward from the furnaces of potters, metalsmiths and glassmakers. The traditional products of the indigenous pastoral peoples of central Asia glutted the stalls; woolen rugs woven by women, felt and leather trappings produced from the hides and hair of the herds now being pastured around the cities, animal skins regularly unloaded by ranging hunters, cheeses and other herd-based foods, pottery and baskets and woven ware. The stocks of locally produced products adjoined stalls lavishly laded with exotic wares from the Far East and from the Far West, and with the products of the newly introduced industries.

Both Hebrew legends and local lore relating to the Hebrews devolve upon this ancient area of central Asia, materializing substance out of the dimly apparent mists of the past. Many Jews spread out along the silk route from the ancient Jewish community in the Crimea which had separated into two rival factions, the fundamentalist Karaites, and those who followed rabbinate expansions on the oral law. The Karaites remained so strict in their observances that they remained in total darkness on the Sabbath evening and refused to perform any semblance of work, even to the slicing of bread on the Sabbath. Many of the rabbinate Jews from the Crimea and Persia moved to Khiva, where 8000 families formed a congregation, and similar sizable groups gathered in Bukhara, Samarkand, and Tashkent, central to the silk route. These three central Asian cities form a triangle along the silk route whose points lead across southern Russia, down into Persia and India and out to central China. They are among the few cities in which the residence of a significant proportion of Jews remained stable into modern times.

Bukhara is reputed by local legend to be the Biblical Habor to which the ten tribes of Israel were exiled. Living reality reinforces the remnants of truth within these legends; Uzbekistan, one of the Union of Soviet Socialist Republics, presently harbors a population of 103,000 Jews whose records document their ancestry back into the fifth century. Fabulous Samarkand was the hub of this ancient community and in its streets one still hears ancient litanies being circumspectly sung on the Sabbath. The early, most important glassworks of the period were uncovered between and around Bukhara, Tashkent, and Samarkand. The relics of a number of workshops were found in Piandjikent, including bellow nozzles, molds and glassware. Piandijikent lies one third of the way from Bukhara and Samarkand, and was destroyed by the Arabs in the eighth century.[70] Cullet amounting to 500 glass fragments was found closer to Samarkand at Coulder-Tepe, a site which evidently endured the Arab conquest of the area and lasted into the ninth century.[71] By the twelfth century a Jewish population of 50,000 headed by Obadiah was purported to be carrying on a flourishing existence in Samarkand alone.[72]

> Three blocks from a stately minaret on a dusty street called Khudzhunskaya stands a drab brick building with no distinguishing markings where early each morning the sounds of Hebrew prayer break the stillness of the Central Asian Dawn....Here in this synagogue in the heart of the Islamic region of the Soviet Union, as daybreak comes with the shouts of laborers and the blare of truck horns, religious Jews stroll the mosaic floor of their one remaining house of worship murmuring devotions....Twenty men, wearing the characteristic square hats of the region called *tubitikas*, recite from memory prayers as old as the city of Samarkand. They flip through the tattered pages of prayer books and carefully scan the face of each new arrival. When one is recognized he is flashed gold-toothed grins and greeted with the Tadjik welcome: *Salom*....The Jews of the Republic of Uzbekistan trace their roots to fifth-century Persia. For nearly a millennia and a half they have prospered and suffered under the various despots and dynasties that ruled the area and its prized routes.[73]

It was in the fifth century, coincident with the influx of Jews from Sassanian Persia, that glassmaking first appeared in the region of Bukhara, Samarkand and Tashkent. "In central Asia, the art of glassmaking suddenly underwent profound changes and development at the outset of the Middle Age, that is to say, from the fifth to the seventh centuries C.E.," wrote A. A. Abdurazakov of the Archeological Institute of the Uzbekistan Academy of Sciences in the Soviet Union.[74]

Abdurazakov drew this conclusion eight years after he and two of his colleagues had enthusiastically reported on the revelatory results of an intense program of excavation in Uzbekistan; the archeologists had uncovered unmistakable evidence of those "profound changes" in the very area into which masses of immigrating Jews had settled from before the fifth century and through which the silk route passed: "It has recently been established that central Asia was one of the earliest glassmaking centers of the present-day territorial Soviet Union," they asserted,[75] noting that a fellow scientist, Iu. F. Buriakov, had established that "this territory was first settled in the fourth-fifth century A.D.; the formation of urban settlements took place in the following two centuries and its full flowering [took place] in the tenth and eleventh centuries."[76]

> It is precisely during this epoch that one observes...a powerful development of artisanship, including that of glassmaking...in four areas: Afrasiab (Samarkand), Akhisiket, Kuva (Fergana) and Kuju-Saj (Khorezm) glassmaking workshops were uncovered, a direct and incontestable proof of the existence of the art in Central Asia. In addition, indirect evidence appears that a local glassmakers quarters existed in 11 other Central Asian archeological sites....By virtue of circumstantial evidence, at least 9 centers of glass production can be attested to in Central Asia: southern Turkestan, southern Uzbekistan, southern Tadzhikhistan, Samarkand, the Oasis of Bukhara, the Oasis of Tashkent, Fergana, Khorezm, southern Khazakistan and the valley of Chou in northern Kirghizie.[77]

The archeological sites cited by Abdurazakov delineate the central Asian section of the silk route with virtual perfection, allowing for the fact that arid central Asia afforded few wooded areas. Furnaces were located where fuel could be obtained, yet within reasonably close access to the market centers serving the caravans. A startling statistical pattern emerged from a thorough-going chemical analysis of a representative cross section of the forty-odd varieties of locally produced glassware. The composition of indigenous products, reflecting the proportions of materials in the formulas employed, was compared by Abdurazakov to that of equivalent glassware from Assyro--

Babylonia, India, Egypt, Rome, and Byzantia:

| Territory | | | CaO:MgO | Na2:KO |
|---|---|---|---|---|
| Central Asian, (range) 1.24 | 2.0 | | 2.27 | 6.15 |
| " " | (average) | | 1.58 | 4.27 |
| Assyro-babylonian " | | | 1.37 | 5.83 |
| Indian | " | | 2.08 | 5.38 |
| Egyptian | " | | 2.43 | 8.83 |
| Byzantine | " | | 6.67 | 8.65 |
| Roman | " | | 6.78 | 16.48 |

It was readily apparent that the proportion of magnesium to that of calcium oxides in the central Asian ware is consistently comparable to that of Assyro-Babylonian and Indian ware but was radically different from that of European production. The relationship of sodium and potassium oxides was close to that of Assyro-Babylonian and Indian ware, but, again, substantially different from that of Late Roman and Byzantian ware.[78] Egyptian production was entirely in the hands of Semitic glassmakers in Alexandria and Fustat, most if not all of whom were Jews; India, was, of course, the alternative area through which branches of the silk route passed from Assyria-Babylonia.

A reasonable conclusion to be drawn from this and other analyses is that the Central Asian glassware was produced by the same cultural hands as those producing the so-called Persian and Indian ware, and that the slight variation in the percentages of sodium and potassium was due to the variation in the plants from whose ashes those elements were obtained; the plants of central Asia are, perforce, different from those of Mesopotamia. "The glassware of central Asia and that of the Indians and Assyro-Babylonians are neighbors," affirms Abdurazakov, emphasizing at the same time the radical differences of Central Asian glassware to glassware from other areas.[79]

The styles of the Central Asian glassware were largely utilitarian; tableware, vases, toilet articles, cradle urinals, weights, pharmaceutical and chemical containers, and a variety of jewelry such as necklaces and bracelets constitute the bulk of the earlier grave goods found. Not much time passed before more decorative ware appears in the tombs of wealthier persons, some of whom were located at considerable distance from the production centers. It is evident that such purchases were made as soon as the market centers had grown into sizeable merchandizing emporiums to which upper-class Uzbeks as well as the well-off members of all other ethnic tribes of the entire central Asian area came to shop.

The statement that "profound changes and development" took place from the fifth century forward, coincident with the influx of a sizable Jewish population into the trading centers of central Asia, infers that some form of glassmaking existed earlier. The startling discoveries of M. A. Stein as early as 1902 indicate that the art had, in fact, been practiced by itinerant craftsmen along the silk route long before the outlying trading posts of central Asia become bustling cities. Stein successfully completed a campaign of exploration of Chinese Turkestan in which fragments of glass were found in many of the ruins of the oasis' spotted along the northern and southern borders of "that most formidable of deserts" through the Tarim basin, which Stein also described as "nature's true highway from China to the settled lands of western Asia."[80]

It may have been just such craftsmen who produced the remarkable assortment of artifacts found by Bishop White at Lo Yang with locally available barium compounds, and who produced the variety of items that have turned up at Loulan and elsewhere. The heavy use of lead in the Lo Yang glass parallels the similar use of lead in Mesopotamian ware. The emerging facts justify just such a scenario for the development of the art of glassmaking along the silk route and at its terminal, the area around Kaifeng.

Impelled by traumatic experiences under recurrently repressive Christian, Byzantine and Islamic regimes, the Jews filtered out along the byways which seemed to offer reprieve from tyranny, taking their knowledge and skills with them into China and India, and transmitting the knowledge gained in China to the West. Thus Jewish traders in India dealt in the decimal system (including the critical use of zero), translated Indian mathematics into Arabic and introduced the system into Islamic North Africa, thereafter to become known as the "Arabic number system." Jewish traders learned paper making from Chinese prisoners taken in Samarkand in 751 C.E.,[81] and brought the knowledge to Islamic Spain. In the process of servicing the trade routes they colonized important way stations all along the various branches and terminals of the land and sea silk routes. Such communities were integrated into Afghanistan, along the route to India; they were installed in the interior of India itself; they were deployed along the Indian coast. In China, communities were also established in strategic ports at the coast.

The date of the initial establishment of full-fledged communities of Jews in central China has been variously estimated from before the Zhou period (eleventh to eighth centuries B.C.E.) to the time of the Tang, or early Five Dynasties (907-960 A.D.). The earliest date, proposed by Alexei Vinogradov, of the czarist Russian Greek Orthodox Church, derives from a highly doubtful interpretation of an inscription on one of the three tablets recovered from the Kaifeng synagogue, the last synagogue to survive in China, and is based on a highly subjective interpolation of the inscription. The ancient city of Kaifeng was the terminus of the silk route across the vast Asian land mass, and it was at Kaifeng, the very area in which the tombs of Lo Yang are located and from whose relics evidence of wide-ranging Jewish colonization in China has been obtained. The synagogue was built in 1163 to serve the considerable population of Jews at the heart of China and to accommodate the traders who traveled the long and difficult passage across deserts and over mountains. The community of Kaifeng itself was estimated to total some 3000 souls.

The previously mentioned blue-glass lion amulets and a variety of other glass items retrieved from the tombs at Lo Yang, as well from numerous other sites in China and Korea, eloquently testify to the traffic which ended in Kaifeng. Other glass items with peculiar stylistic and chemical composition characteristics point to the possibility of glass production in China as early as the fifth century B.C.E., as does the appearance of ferric technology in bronze-oriented China during this very period. Professor C. G. Seligman notes that "the import of glass into China from the West, and indeed the whole efflorescence of glassmaking in China, was due to that series of foreign influences and contacts that brought iron into the country."[82] The most ancient Chinese glass can be classified into several distinct groups, each of which provide distinguishing information. The most characteristic artifacts found are as follows:

1. Beads, clearly imported from the Near East, of several types typical of the late Iron Age. Seligman states that "similar beads collected East and West were not only of identical specific gravity but also of identical chemical composition."

2. Distinctive eye-beads which are common to ancient Chinese tombs and are of the type ubiquitously found throughout the Mediterranean, Egypt and Europe. Sometimes the eyes are melded into the surface of the core;

at other times the rounded eyes protrude breast-like from the core. A number of "eyes," almost always six, are often clustered around one central eyelet which forms the hub of a sort of wheel of eyes. A single eye-bead or a cluster of eye-beads was also commonly incorporated into other suitable objects of bronze or silver; thus they are found on Chinese robe-hooks, bronze plaques or on the back of bronze mirrors. A famous example of the latter is the "Winthrop mirror," found in the tombs of Old Lo Yang and so named because it is part of the collection of Gertrude L. Winthrop.[83]

Bologna      European or Near Eastern origin      China

COMPOUND EYE-BEADS FROM EUROPE AND CHINA. Eye-beads of the late centuries BCE found in Europe compared with Chinese eye-beads of the same period (pre-Han or Han). The similarity of technique and composition of eye-beads traded entirely across the Eurasian continental span is due to a common Near-Eastern origin. The eventual appearance of the element barium in the Chinese beads suggests the arrival of artisans from the Near East who then employed local minerals in the introduction of glassmaking to China.
*After C. G. Seligman and H. C. Beck,* Far Eastern Glass: Some Western Origins, *The Bulletin of the Museum of Far Eastern Antiquities, No. 10, Stockholm, 1938.*

Segments of rods of a single color (rather than of concentric rings of colors characteristic of the eye-beads), were also clustered into a rosette and employed as a decorative motif. Clay jars of the Late Zhou period (fifth-third B.C.E.) were encircled with such rosettes.[84] Seligman notes that the Eastern eye-bead prototypes "could almost always be distinguished from their Western originals by a somewhat high barium content." Yet the resulting motifs are so much alike that Seligman had to note that "it seems impossible to avoid the conviction that the ornament on the Chinese and non-Chinese specimens has a common origin." It would accordingly appear that the glassmakers who settled in ancient China soon turned to the production of much-favored eye-beads, employing local materials. Seligman's projections were based on his research of the early 1930s. The post-World War II discoveries in northern Iran immeasurably reinforce the bond between Mesopotamian and Galilean glass to the Chinese glass analyzed by Seligman and Beck. Chemical analyses of this new material may even establish further symbiotic relationships between the two groups of glassware.

3. Other glass items commonly found in Chinese graves:

> A. Imitations of bronze swords in glass. A pair of crossed swords were traditionally placed in a tomb with the deceased.
> B. Imitations of jade *Pi*. The Pi are rounded discs or rolls with a central, circular opening symbolizing the sky with a portal through which the deceased can enter into heaven. They are placed under the pelvis of the corpse.
> C. Imitations of jade cicadas. The cicadas represent the power of resurrection, and are placed into the mouth of the deceased. All the items A, B and C were obviously made strictly for the Chinese market, whether they were made in China or not.

4. An object which was characteristic of both India and China was what Seligman designates as capstan beads[85] and Dikshit refers to as an ear-reel.[86] They are cylindrical glass discs, concave around their circumference, either to facilitate the insertion into a perforation of the earlobe and to assure its maintenance therein, or to allow it to be suspended from the ear by a loop which would not slip off the ornament. These interesting adornments, found at two of the eastern terminals of the silk route, are remarkably similar in form; the conclusion can be drawn that they were, initially at least, supplied to both countries from a primary source. The earliest ones are Indian (from Taxila) and date between the sixth and fifth centuries B.C.E., a date earlier than their appearance in China. The India trade was, in fact, considerably older than the China trade. It may be that it was the Indian middlemen who introduced this item to the Chinese before the unification of the silk route through central Asia by the Chinese. In any event, the ear-reels provide a palpable link between the three terminals of that route, the Near East, China and India.

The antiquity of Jewish presence in central China is brought into sharp focus by the information inscribed on the tablets recovered from the Kaifeng synagogue in the three renditions dated 1489, 1512 and 1663 respectively.

THE SYNAGOGUE OF KAIFENG. Substantial Jewish communities sprang up at Samarkand, Bukhara and along the "silk route" from the 4th century CE forward. A great synagogue was constructed in the 12th century at Kaifeng, in the heart of the Chinese Empire, serving a community which grew to some 3000 practicing Jews.
*Copy of a drawing of the Kaifeng synagogue by the French Jesuit Jean Domenge, 1722, from* Jews in Old China *by Sidney Shapiro, Hippocrene Books, New York, 1988.*

Each inscription offers a different date for the arrival of the Jews; the latest of the stone commemorative tablets state that the Jews arrived at the time of the Zhou Dynasty which spans the better part of a millennium from 1056-256 B.C.E., and probably refers to the advent of Jews into China. The 1512 tablet defers to the Han Dynasty (206 B.C.E.-220 C.E.), which may well have been the time at which artisans introduced glassmaking in the area of Kaifeng, the time in which barium appears in the glass artifacts recovered from the tombs of the Chinese portion of the East-West trade routes. The oldest tablet ascribes Jewish settlement into the area to the period of the Song Dynasty (960-1279 C.E.), which was the period in which all three tablets assign the

INTERIOR OF THE SYNAGOGUE OF KAIFENG. Copies of a drawing of the Kaifeng synagogue by the French Jesuit Jean Domenge, 1722, from *Jews in Old China* by Sidney Shapiro, Hippocrene Books, New York, 1988.

**building** of the Kaifeng synagogue.

[Provost] notes that the 1512 tablet in Kaifeng dates the arrival of the Jews as during the reign of the Han emperor Ming Di, who ruled from 58 to 76 A.D. This is within the first to third century A.D...the Jews had a synagogue in Palmyria [sic]. Many of them were merchants. The city was a big trade center between Antioch--which had a population of 600,000 and wove silk from the Orient for the Roman Market--and India and Ferghana, then in the neighborhood of Tashkent and just west of China's Xinjiang province today.[87]

One of the discoveries which attest to such a succession of events is an

A CHINESE STATUETTE OF A SEMITIC-TYPE MERCHANT, 9TH CENTURY CE. The statuette was found in Luoyang; the Luoyang Museum notes that the figurine is one of many semitic types depicted in Chinese sculpture and painting between the Northern Wei and the Song dynasty (4th-13th centuries).
*After* Jews in Old China *by Sidney Shapiro, Hippocrene Books, New York, 1988.*

inscription in a Palmyran Hebrew script on three stone fragments of the second century C.E., found in Lo Yang by Georges Provost. The stone fragments and the rubbings were long considered lost, but they were found in the Museum of History in Beijing by Sidney Shapiro, an attorney who settled in China in 1947, married a Chinese woman and has been resident in China ever since.

A fragment of a business letter written in Hebrew script, a Hebrew prayer written on paper (paper was then unknown in the west) were found by the archaeologists Stein and Pelliot along the "silk route", and the testimony of Marco Polo and others to the presence of Jews upon their arrival reinforce the surviving documentary evidence.

Much investigation remains to be done to document with more precision just when and how glassmaking was introduced into China. The early presence of glass or glassmaking in China is, however, consistent with the presence of Jews, both as merchants and as artisans. The history of glass and that of the Jews appear to be inextricably linked in every area in which each is found, and China is no exception. The proposition: "Wherever glass-making existed, Jews are to be found and wherever Jews are found, the import or manufacture of glassware exists," applies as aptly to China and the silk route as it does elsewhere, and holds almost as true for three other basic ingredients of ancient China trade — silk, flax and spices.

The Jewish population of Sassanian Persia doubled as a result of the struggles with Rome, which ended with the expulsion of Jews from Judah. The Jews continued their role as world-girdling traders and immigrant artisans who spread new goods, ideas and technologies throughout the civilized world, and the Sassanian Jews were prominent among them.

# NOTES

1. A. D. Hirth, *Chinesische Studien*, 1890, p. 65.

2. Herada Yoshita, "Ancient Glass in the History of Cultural Exchange Between East and West," *Acta Asiatica*, 1962. pp. 63-64.

3. Lionel Casson, *Ancient Trade and Society*, 1984, p. 226, quoting I. Low, *Die Flora der Juden ii*, 1924, 108, 113-114; E. Masson, *Recherches sur les plus anciens emprunts se'metiques en grec*, 1967. Casson notes his indebtedness to his colleague, Robert Stieglitz for "invaluable help with the Semitic sources," and notes that: *kinnamomon* first appears in Herodotus 3.107, *kasia* in Sappho, frg. 44 (Lobel Page).

4. Casson, Ibid., p. 256.

5. C. G. Seligman and H. C. Beck, *Far Eastern Glassz, Some Western Origins*, reprinted from the "Bulletin of the Far Eastern Antiquities No. 10," Stockholm, 1938, p. 11.

6. White later became an Associate Professor of Archeology at the University of Toronto and the Keeper of the East Asiatic Collection of the Royal Toronto Museum.

7. William Charles White, *Tombs of Old Lo-Yang*, 1934, p. xii.

8. Takashi Tanichi, "Western Designed 'Composite Eye' Glass Beads Recently Excavated in China," summary in English, *Bulletin of the Ancient Orient Museum*, vol. 5, 1983, p. 323.

9. Tanichi, Ibid., p, 324.

10. C. H. Seligman and H. C. Beck, *Far Eastern Glass; Some Western Origins*, 1938; C. G. Seligman, *The Roman Orient and the Far East*, 1938, pp. 547-568; C. G. Seligman, *Early Chinese Glass*, 1940-1941.

11. Seligman, Ibid., 1938, pp. 40-44; fig. 8.

12. Lionel Casson, *Ancient and Society*, 1984. pp. 254-255.

13. Jean M. James, "Silk, China and the Drawloom," *Archeology*, vol. 39 no. 9, Sept/Oct 1986.

14. C. P. Fitzgerald, *China, a Cultural History*, 1935, pp. 178-179.

15. E. Porada, *Tchoga Zanbil, Mémoires de la Délégation archéologique en Iran*, vol. 4, 1970, p. 42.

16.   Roman Ghirshman, "The Elamite Levels at Susa and Their Chronological Significance," *American of Archeology*, 74 no. 3, 1970, p. 225.

17.  Shinji Fukai, *Persian Glass*, English edition, 1977, p. 16.

18.  Ezat O. Negahan, *A Preliminary Report on Marlik Excavation, Rudbar, 1961-62*, 1964.

19.  Shinji Fukai, Ibid., p. 17.

20.  Axel von Saldern, "Mosaic Glass from Hasanlu, Marlik, and Tell al-Rimah, *JGS*, 1966.

21.  Hayim Tadmor, "The Decline, Rise and Destruction of Israel," *A History of the Jewish People*, ed. H. H. Ben-Sasson, 1969, pp. 133-134.

22.  Tadmor-Sassoon, Ibid., p. 135.

23.  H. H. Ben-Sasson, *A History of the Jewish People*, 1976, p. 135.

24.  Ben-Sasson, idem.

25.  Tadmor, Ibid., p. 136.

26.  Axel von Saldern, "Mosaic Glass from Hasanlu, Marlik, and Tel Al-Rimah," *JGS*, VIII, 1966, pp. 9-24. "The beakers from Hasanlu... combine many elements distinctly Mesopotamian in character." Von Saldern notes the parallels to Babylonian and Assyrian art, "particularly the painted walls and the reliefs found at Aqar Quf." The Marlik beaker exhibits a technique which points to the same general provenience as the glassware from Nuzi, Assur, Hasanlu, Alalakh and Tell al-Rimah. Thus a Mesopotamian continuity is suggested from the mid-second millennium to the ninth century B.C.E., when the art seems to have disappeared as a consequence of a disturbed political period. The Sargon vessel and other such finds, therefore, represent a reappearance of the art with the influx of artisans from the Mediterranean coast.

27.  Ben-Sasson, Ibid., p. 42.

28.  Andrew Oliver, Jr. "Persian Export Glass," *JGS*, XII, 1970. p. 9; A. von Saldern, "Glass Finds at Gordion," *JGS* I, 1959, pp. 27f.

29.  Dan Barag, "An Unpublished Achemenid Cut Glass Bowl from Nippur," *JGS*, vol. X, 1968, pp. 17-20.

30.  Barag, Ibid., p. 20; Paul Fossing, "Drinking Bowls of Glass and Metal from the Achaemenian Time," *Berytus*, IV, 1937, pp. 121-129, Pl. XXIII.

31.  Barag, Ibid., p. 20; A. von Saldern, "Glass Finds at Gordion," *JGS* I, 1959, p. 41; "Achaemenid and Sassanian Cut Glass," *Ars Orientalis*, V, 1963, p. 14.

32.  Barag, Ibid., p. 20.

33.  Aristophanes, *Acharnians*, vol. 74; Mary L. Trowbridge, *Philological Studies in Ancient Glass*, 1930, p. 151.

34. Oliver, Ibid., p. 13; A. D. H. Bivar, "A Rosette Phiale Inscribed in Aramaic," *Bulletin of the School of Oriental and African Studies, University of London*, XXIV, 1961, pp. 189-199; *Sale Catalogue Sotheby*, II, Dec. 1961, lot 22, ill.; D. E. Strong, *Greek and Roman Gold and Silver Plate*, 1966, n. 15, Pl. 25a.

35. Louis Dupree, *Afghanistan*, 1973\1980, p. 286.

36. John Curtis, *Nash-i Jan III, the Small Finds*, The British Institute of Persian Studies, 1984, pp. 42-43; Curtis cites Hasanlu, Dinkha Tepe, Bjalekuti (Dailaman area) Persopolis, Deve Huyuk, Kamid el-Loz, Shapir, Nush-I Jan and gives references.

37. Shinji Fukai, Ibid., pp. 18, 20; E. F. Schmidt, *Persopolis II*, 1957, p. 92.

38. Shinji Fukai, Ibid., p. 21.

39. Nathan Ausabel, *The Book of Jewish Knowledge*, 1964, pp. 234-235. The subject: "Labor, dignity of," is so central to Judaic lore that Ausabel deemed it deserving of a separate heading in his compendium.

40. *Qiddushin* ii, 5-62 c.

41. Th. Mommsen, ed., *Der Maxomaltarif des Diocletian*, 1893, cap. 26-28, as given by Avi Yonah, *IEJ*, vol. 12, n. 2, pp. 128-129.

42. Cf. e.g. E. Schürer, *Geshichte d. Jüdisches Volkes*, II, 1906, p. 77

43. Silk, skins, iron, lacquer, rhubarb and cinnamon are among the products arriving overland from China; and household slaves, pets and arena animals, exotic furs, cashmere wool, raw and finished cotton and some silks arrived overseas from India. Linen and wool textiles, lamps and glassware, carpets, amber and coral, asbestos, bronze vessels, wine, and papyrus were the main products traveling west. Other spices and dye substances such as cochineal and indigo were picked up along the southern route and slaves and animal skins were added on the northern route.

44. Joseph Needham, F.R.S., *Science and Civilization in China*, 1965, vol. 2, p. 192.

45. Anita Engles, Ibid., pp. 11-15.

46. Ibn Khurdadhbih, *The Book of the Routes and the Kingdoms*.

47. John E. Vollmer, E. J. Keall, E. Nagai-Berthong, *Silk Roads-- China Ships*, 1983, p. 29.

48. Clark Hopkins, *The Discovery of Dura-Europus*, 1979, p. 252.

49. Hopkins, Ibid., p. 261.

50. Hopkins, Ibid., P. 131.

51. Clark Hopkins, Ibid., 1979, p. 177.

52. C. W. Clairmont, *The Excavations at Dura-Europus*, Part 5, "The Glass Vessels," p. 56.

53. Rowland, *Ancient Art from Afghanistan*, 1966, p. 25.

54. Anita Engles, *Readings in Glass History 6-7*, 1976, p. 46.

55. Louis Dupree, *Afghanistan*, 1973/80, p. 272; for the document see: E. Wilson, *Sacred Books of the East*, 1945, pp. 55-65.

56. A. T. Olmstead, *History of the Persian Empire*, 1948, pp. ix, xv.

57. Herzfeld, "A new Asoka inscription from Taxila," *Epigraphia Indica*, 1928 xix:251; R. Majundar, H. Rechaudhuri, and K. Datta, *An Advanced History of India*, 1961, pp. 101-102, per Dupree, Ibid., p. 287.

58. W. Henning, "The Aramaic Inscription of Ashoka in Lamaka," *Bulletin of the School of Oriental and African Studies* 13:80-88, (1949--1950), per Dupree, Ibid., p. 287.

59. H. Bailey, "Gandhari," *Bulletin of the School of Oriental and African Studies*, 11:764-976, 1943, p. 46, per Dupree, Ibid., p. 287.

60. Dupree, Ibid., p. 287.

61. W. McGovern, *The Early Empires of Central Asia*, 1939 pp. 251-252, per Dupree, Ibid., p. 300.

62. Shinji Fukai, *Persian Glass*, 1977, p. 22.

63. D. Makay, "The Jewelry of Palmyra and Its Significance," *Iraq,* no. 11, 1949, p. 179

64. Boulnois, 1966, 110, citing Pfister, 1937, 1940, 1951, as given by Anita Engles, *Readings in Glass History*, nos. 6-7, p. 28.

65. F. Stark, *Rome on the Euphrates*, 1966, p. 244, as given by Anita Engles, idem.

66. C. G. Seligman and H. C. Beck, "Far Eastern Glass: Some Western Origins," *British Museum Far Eastern Antiquities* 11, pp. 40-44.

67. Seligman and Beck, Ibid., p. 30.

68. Maria Dekowna, "Etude sur les origines de la verrerie en Pologne," *Annals of the 3rd International Congress on Glass*, 1964, p. 119.

69. Sidney Shapiro, *Jews in China*, 1984, p. x.

70. A. L. Mongait, *Archeology in the USSR*, 1959, p. 295.

71. Anita Engles, *Readings in Glass History*, no. 7, p. 60, quoting B. J. Staviski, *Bulletin de l'Association pour l'histoire du Verre*, 1957.

72. Heinrich Graetz, *History of the Jews*, vol. III, 1894/1967, p. 435; probably deriving from reports by Petachya of Ratisbon, c. 1180.

73. Adriel Bettelheim, *Jews of Samarkand*, in The Jewish Week, Inc., Nov. 1, 1985.

74. A. A. Abdurazakov, *Etude Chimique des Verres d'Asie Centrale, Datant du Moyen Age*, 1971, p. 161.

75.  A. A. Abdurazakov, M. A. Bezdorodov, Iu. A. Zadneprovskii, *Glassmaking in Central Asia in Medieval and Ancient Times*, 1963; and M. A. Bezborodov and Iu. Zadneprovskii, "Ancient and Medieval Glasses of Central Asia," *Abstracts from Papers Presented at Atlantic City*, 1962, p. 94.

76.  A. A. Abdurazakov, "Medieval Glasses From the Tashkent Oasis," *JGS*, XI, 1969, pp. 31-32, citing: Iu. F. Buriakov, *Archeological Data and Historical Topography of Tunkat*, 1962; idem, "New Archeological Data on the Site of Ul'kan-toi-Tiobe (Province of Nikat)," *Scientific Works and Reports of the OON, Academy of Science of the Uzbekistan S.S.R.*, 6, 1963.

77.  A. A. Abdurazakov, 1971, Ibid., p. 162.

78.  Abdurazakov, 1971, Ibid., p. 170.

79.  Abdurazakov, 1971, Ibid., p. 171.

80.  A. Stein, *A Journey of Geographical and Archeological Exploration in Chinese Turkestan*, 1902; *Sand-buried Ruins of Khotan*, 1903.

81.  Vollmer, et. al, Ibid., p. 79.

82.  C. G. Seligman, "Early Chinese Glass," *Transactions of the Oriental Ceramic Society*, 1940-1941, pp. 20-21.

83.  Joseph Needham F.R.S. *Science and Civilization in China*, vol. 4, 1965, plate 11, fig. 294 (after Seligman).

84.  S. Umehara, *Antique Chinese Pottery Decorated with Glass Paste*, Yamato Bunka 15, as given by Engles, Ibid., p. 11.

85.  Seligman, *The Roman Orient and the Far East*, 1938, p. 558.

86.  Dikshit, Ibid., 1969, p. 4.

87.  Shapiro, Ibid., p. 58.

ISLAMIC CARAFE. The styles of Persian glassware and the techniques employed in their production evolved in a direct line from the time of the uprooting of scores of thousands of Jewish artisans from Israel and Judah into Persia through the periods of rule by the Achaemenids, Seleucids, Romans and Sassanians and into the Islamic period. The population of Jews in the agronomic and industrial heartland of the "Land-of-the-Two-Rivers" rose to two million by the end of the Roman period.
*Photograph courtesy of the Israel Museum.*

# CHAPTER 9

# THE SASSANIAN EXPERIENCE

## *The Babylonian Connection*

THE WORD BABYLON CONJURES UP AN ARRAY OF RICH IMAGES. IT WAS IN THE land of Babylon that cuneiform writing was created and literacy spawned, that the pattern for organized society was set by Hammurabi's laws, that ziggurats soared toward the clouds, and that pyrotechnology attained a level of proficiency by which the Bronze Age was born and stone could be transformed into glass. It is written that Babel embraced all tongues, and that by their separation nations were forever parted. It is also written that the progenitors of the Jews departed from the region of Babylon and returned, not once, but again and again and yet again. Each time they returned, they were instrumental in propelling Babylon and civilization to a new level of intellectual and technical achievement.

The advent of the Sassanian Dynasty (224-226) initiated a period in which a great surge of intellectual and commercial achievement took place in Persia. Josephus stated that the Jewish communities of this ancient land of the Diaspora consisted of "countless myriads of which none can know the number."[1] The sudden influx of refugees from the aftermath of the Bar Kokhba revolt and the subsequent immigrations from Christian lands, in fact, swelled Josephus's open-ended estimate; it brought about a doubling of the Jewish Babylonian population from an already substantial 1,000,000 to approach an impressive 2,000,000 persons.[2] They were a literate, skilled people who formed the urban core of Mesopotamian society. No large Babylonian city lacked Jewish merchants and artisans, and many of Babylonia's great cities, "Nehardea, Nisibis, Mahoza and others, were entirely,

299

or almost entirely, populated, maintained and garrisoned by Jews."[3]  The Babylonian Jewish community in this period of the Mishnah and the Talmud stretched from Nisibis to Circesion and Dura-Europus along the basin of the Euphrates down to a thick cluster of flourishing cities crowding the narrow neck between the Euphrates and the Tigris Rivers; Jewish communities continued southeastward from this lush agricultural area from Sura and Nippur, touching strategic points along the passage through Susa and Ahwaz to the Persian Gulf.  From the densely populated heartland of Mesopotamia between the rivers, Jewish settlements crossed the Tigris and strung out toward Turkestan.  The concentration of Jews in the industrial, agricultural and commercial heart of Mesopotamia formed the most dynamic element of Sassanian agriculture, commerce and industry.  River navigation and international commerce were largely in the hands of Jews.  Insurance and banking were carried on by great financial houses, and trade with silk, linen, glassware, wine, grain and spices was financed and promulgated on a scale which approaches that of modern times.

The Mishnah (*Rosh Hashanah*) describes the line of beacons which carried the announcement of the sanctification of the New Moon to the communities in Babylonia; it was a line of communication whose terminal was Pumbadita in the very heart of the Jewish pale of settlement.  The land-based silk route to China and India followed this very line from the Mediterranean into Sassanian Mesopotamia and delineates the pale of Jewish settlement in those regions with perfection.  The two forks of the ancient East-West trade route, one leading from Antioch through Aleppo and the other from Tyre, Acre and Beth Shean through Damascus, conjoined at the Euphrates at Circesion and Dura-Europus.  The main flow of commercial traffic then followed the Euphrates down to the area where it and the Tigris loop close to each other.  The two rivers were connected by the Chobar and a web of other ancient canals which criss-crossed through the narrow neck of The-Land-Between-the-Two-Rivers (i.e., Mesopotamia), one of the most fecund agricultural areas of the ancient world.

It was in that region that the densest population of Jews was installed, a million or more farmers, scholar-teachers and artisans, active at their professions and providers of a major portion of the Sassanian agricultural and industrial products.  The heavy flow of commerce traversed this area directly through Pumbadita, Nehardea and Mahoza, three great centers of Jewish study and leadership; from Mahoza the route crossed the Tigris to Ctesiphon,

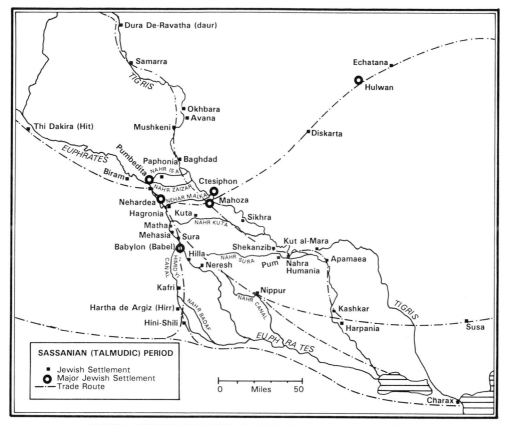

## JEWISH CONCENTRATION IN THE PERSIAN AGRICULTURAL, INDUSTRIAL AND COMMERCIAL HEART OF THE PAN-ASIAN TRADE

The Jewish population of Sassanian Persia ("Babylonia") doubled to 2,000,000 persons as a result of the exodus from *Eretz Israel* after the Bar Khochba revolt was crushed. Great concentrations of the Jews lay at key sites of the rich agricultural Persian heartland, where canals crisscross the narrow stretch between the Euphrates and the Tigris rivers. The centers accounted for 90% of Sassanian industry, and in them flourished the great Jewish universities which drew their student body from throughout the Diaspora. The trade routes connecting the West to China and India radiate out from the Persian heartland and Jewish entrepreneurs were heavily installed in the main cities along those routes.

another prominent Sassanian Jewish population center. At Ctesiphon the route forked out again toward China and India. The Jewish pale of settlement between the rivers was a throbbing heart of the ancient commercial world into which the world's arteries converged and its veins emerged.

Most of the traffic continued from Ctesiphon northeastward toward China, to branch off again beyond the Pamirs and descend into India through the town of Taxila. The alternate, southern route to India from Ctesiphon passed through another important Jewish center at Nippur and descended to the Persian Gulf where the port city of Charax, situated at the mouth of the Tigris, served as the warehouse for and outlet to the sea route to India and the East Indies. Isidore of Charax, who supplied Augustus with a guide to the entire region, came from this strategically situated port.[4] Charax (the name derives from the Aramaic *Kerach* meaning "fort"), was also the terminus of an alternate southern route which connected to Gaza on the Mediterranean through Petra.

The most impressive and lasting work left by the Sassanian Jews to posterity is encompassed in their contribution to learning. Great academies were founded. The universities at Sura, Nehardea, Mahosa and Pumbadita became world famous and their revered teachers created a corpus of *responsa* to inquiries which poured in from throughout the world and which endures to the present day as a fountain of wisdom and knowledge from which scholars take sustenance. The compilation of the Babylonian Talmud remains one of the great works of all time and takes its place along with the Palestinian Talmud at the core of Judaic learning and tradition. The Babylonian Talmud is a compendium of laws and precepts guiding daily life; it is replete with references to farm life and commercial affairs and establishes laws regulating wages and working conditions. Twelve hundred students attended the Sura academy alone in the third century.[5] The Babylonian academies carried on universal education each year during the two *Kallah Months*, and at Pumbadita, "in Ellul, the month preceding Rosh Hashanah, and in Adar, the month preceding Passover, workers and farmers streamed in to the academies. On one occasion they numbered as many as twelve thousand."[6]

There were places in Babylonia that possessed a Jewish tradition which was already ancient in Sassanian times. The Huzal Debei Binyamin near Sura was presumably founded by exiles from the tribe of Benjamin, and it is said of the synagogue of Shaf Yetif near Nehardea that the Divine presence had descended upon it with the arrival of the exiles and had dwelt there ever since.

The Jews who worked the land were settled in Mesopotamia as land tenants of the king and many of the craftsmen were employed in state enterprises.[7] Weavers and dyers, carpenters and smiths, sailors and singers are among the many disciplines mentioned in the Talmud. We also learn from the pages of that great work that those who had no shops or stalls of their own and were seeking employment would gather in the marketplaces where employers would come to engage their service. The wines produced by the Jews of Sura are rendered high praise in poetry quoted by an Arab chronicler of the seventh century. At the end of the fifth century, as a result of disorders which broke out throughout the empire, the exilarch of the Jewish community, *Mar Zutra*, assembled an army and founded a kingdom which endured for seven years. It was a passing phase, but indicative of the importance of the Jewish presence in Sassanian Persia.

Luxury-glass production expanded rapidly in the realm of the Sassanian Empire from the fourth to seventh centuries.[8] The techniques employed in the production of pre-Sassanian Mesopotamian glass relate back to Eretz Israel. "In all the burial grounds of the Parthian period in Mesopotamia we find a range of types connected with the contemporary East-Roman trend," notes Mariamaddelena Negro Ponzi of the Institute of Archeology of the University of Turin in a study of Mesopotamian glass artifacts of the period in comparing them to "Syro-Palestinian" types.[9] A Sassanian style, however, distinguishes itself in the second and third centuries, and reflects the application of some of the carving and abrading techniques which had become common in the production of luxury ware during the Roman period. The changes occur coincident with the influx of Jews from Roman Palestine at this time.

The technique was also employed in Sassanian Persia for the production of expensive ware which only those at the highest social levels could afford, but as time passed the technique was perfected and molds and other means were used to bring decorative ware down to reach a middle range of purchasers. Cut decoration and faceting occurs in glassware of a precedent period at Dura-Europos,[10] as well as in other Roman period contexts. The Sassanian characteristics also point to later Byzantine models and reveal "a point of interaction, not always antagonistic, the Sassanians and Byzantines."[11]

The people who provided the link between the two disparate cultures, Zoroastrian and Christian, were the Jews. A group of vessels which were recovered from Tell Mahuz, near Kirkuk, is representative of a class of glassware which provides the Partho-Sassanian link in the chain of stylistic development between that of Dura-Europus in the northern region, of Ctesiphon at the Mesopotamian center and of Shiraz at the southern section of the Sassanian empire.

Ctesiphon, the capital Sassanian city at the hub of this bustling network of East-West routes, is the site of a vitally important Jewish settlement and the presumed center of Sassanian glass production and distribution. A major production center was identified on the outskirts of that city at Verhardishir.[12] In the first levels of the excavation, dated to the second half of the third century, glassware of a type which became characteristic and definitive of Sassanian ware was recovered. "Judging by the finds in Vehardishir and the [central] position of this town," emphasizes Mariamaddelena Ponzi, "it would seem reasonable to locate [the glassmaking] industry around Ctesiphon, the capital city....The rise of this industry would be connected with the transformation of Ctesiphon from official residence to effective capital, and thus a busy center promoting trade and industry."[13] Tell Mahuz, an archeological site near Kirkuk which lies northeastward toward China along the silk route, provided another link of the stylistic chain whose loop ties the glassware found at that site to that of Ctesiphon and Dura-Europus, and beyond that to the Roman period products of Eretz Israel. The connection of the Tell Mahuz glassware to that of Dura-Europus on the western branch of the silk route and to the Begram glassware on its eastern branch [discussed in Chapter 8] was first noted by Christopher Clairmont in his report on the glass vessels recovered from Dura-Europus.[14] Ms. Ponzi followed up with a detailed study of the Tell Mahuz glassware which expanded on these relationships between and development of the "Sassanian" style.

The parallels of the pattern of the appearance of this and other characteristic types of glassware to that of the centers of Jewish habitation and to the course of branches of the silk route are unmistakable. Other clues to the identity of the artisans and traders of the region derive from the production and distribution of the Chinese product, silk. "In Persia, the silk-weaving industry appears to have been in a flourishing state in the fourth century," writes C. G. Seligman, noting that the art did not arrive further west for another two centuries. "Once silk became common, fabrics bearing typical Sassanian designs were exported eastward in considerable bulk."[15] The demand for this genre of goods was so great that the Chinese proceeded to produce figured silks in typical Sassanian styles. "The most striking evidence of this is the celebrated 'hunter' silk of the seventh-eighth century from the treasury of the Horiuji Monastery at Nara in Japan."[16]

Such silk fabrics were found along the silk route in Chinese Turkestan by Aural Stein, who simultaneously found many fragments of glass in sites posted all along that section of the route.[17] Glass fragments and beads were discovered by Stein during his exploration of the Tarim basin, "nature's true highway from China to the settled lands of Western Asia" along both sides of the periphery of the Taklamakan, "that most formidable of deserts."[18] At the extreme eastern end of the Tarim basin lies the lyrically named town of Lou-lan, a waterless but strategically placed bridgehead of the route unified by the Chinese toward the latter part of the second century. "The bare, wind-eroded ground near the ruined dwellings yielded an abundant crop of small objects of metal, glass and stone." wrote Stein. Most significantly Stein also found a number of documents written on wood and paper in various scripts, including Aramaic.

The two technologies, that of silkmaking and of glassmaking were thus carried by the Jewish-Sassanian traders in opposite directions across the wastelands of central Asia. The ancient civilizations of the Far East had as many or more technologies to offer the newly civilized West at the time, and it was the "Persian" traders who acted as the intermediaries for that cultural transmission. The process of paper making from China and the mathematics of India were among the many cultural gifts borne westward by the "Persian" merchants, who were soon to become renowned as the Radhanites and whose itinerary spanned the entire length and breadth of the Silk Route and continued across Europe.

Early evidence of a branch of this overland traffic to India was recovered in excavations at Taxila and it included the ubiquitous eye-beads. Although there are a few references to glass and in particular to glass beads in Indian literature from the ninth century B.C.E. forward, there are no equivalent Indian legends regarding the advent of the art of glassmaking to those appearing in so many versions in Chinese literature. Until the revelatory results of the Taxila campaign erupted upon the archeological scene it was generally felt that not only glassmaking but glassware was virtually unknown in ancient India. Beads found throughout the Far East in the Malayan archipelago, India and Southeast Asia were regarded as anomalies, or as late introductions. Eye-beads "were in demand throughout Southeast Asia; and there must have been a steady import of these beads from the Mediterranean eastward," reports Alistair Lamb,[19] who raises the possibility that the beads found in south Thailand might have been made locally from "a raw material which contained a high proportion of Middle Eastern scrap....If this conclusion is correct, then it should come as no surprise that so many Southeastern glass beads have an essentially Middle-Eastern composition."[20]

The recovery of glass artifacts from Taxila, and from other West Indian archeological sites previously and subsequently investigated, brought the story of the arrival of glassware and glassmaking in India, as well as that of East-West trade, into focus. Dr. Moreshtar G. Dikshit of the University of Bombay and Director of Archives and Archeology of the Maharashta State accumulated the data in a comprehensive *History of Indian Glass* and noted two facts which resulted from his studies: "(a) that glass was not so scarce in ancient India as was formerly supposed; (b) that indigenous glass came to be manufactured in India at a much earlier date than was hitherto supposed by foreign scholars."[21]

Glass objects from Persia first appear in India at the turn of the sixth century B.C.E., a time which coincides with the release of Babylonian Jewry by Cyrus, the resuscitation of the glassmaking industry in the Galilee, and anticipates the burgeoning of international commerce during the Achaemenid period. The time also coincides with the appearance of glass artifacts among Chinese grave-goods. The earliest strata at Taxila contained an assortment of beads, conspicuous among which were the now familiar eye-beads and a particularly Indian item, an ear-reel. These decorative ear plugs were in the form of thick concave-edged discs averaging somewhat over three centimeters in diameter which could be inserted securely into pierced ear lobes. They were made of diverse costly materials--black jasper, agate, rock crystal, chalcedony etc.--and the introduction of cheaper glass imitations met a need which spurred the introduction of glassmaking. The earliest glass ear-reel known is a single one recovered from a late sixth century B.C.E. level at Taxila; others were found in levels from the fifth century forward, notably at Ujjain, Maheshwar, Nasik and Kaundinyapur. "The large number of such glass discs found indicates the popularity of the glass ornament for more than six centuries in India."[22] Ear-reels found their way to China as well, and their appearance in the tombs of Lo Yang and elsewhere testifies to another link in the trade routes, that which led back from Taxila into China.

The proliferation of glass ear-reels and other characteristically Indian items at numerous sites by the fourth century B.C.E. indicates the existence of indigenous production. Glass seals and sealings impressed with characters and designs of the "Mauryan" or "Pre-Asokan" periods (fourth century B.C.E.) were specifically Indian, and their appearance makes the initiation of local manufacture of such glassware at that time all the more plausible. The probability is that the earliest of these items were produced with raw glass or cullet. The analyses of the early Indian glass artifacts makes central Mesopotamia the probable provenience of such material. "During the Mauryan Period India was constantly in touch with ancient Persia under the Achaemenids, [more than it was with] the Mediterranean area," emphasizes the Indian scholar and glass historian, Dr. Moreshtar Dikshit in his comprehensive study, and reinforces the conclusion that the provenience of the knowledge and materials for Indian glassmaking stemmed from the Aramaic-speaking artisans of central Mesopotamia by placing the emergence of glass-making in India into historical context: "This matter is brought home by the discovery of Ashokan inscriptions in Kabul and Kandahar in the Aramaic characters." Taxila was the seat of the Ashokan hierarchy and was one of the sites at which the edicts issued by the reformed Mauryan emperor Ashoka appear in the Aramaic script. Referring to the stratified eye-beads, Dr. Dikshit adds, "It is ubiquitous that these beads should occur in places like Taxila and Ujjain associated with the viceroyship of Ashoka; and that they should have lingered on at the former place with its influx with the foreigners."[23]

The use of glass and the variety of its artifactual forms increased vastly in India during the two centuries between the first centuries before and after the advent of the Common Era. The variety of types of glass goods which appear clearly resulted from the unification of the silk route, for they run the gamut of the entire catalogue of glassware being produced in Eretz Israel and Alexandria. Lace glass, ribbed ware, marbled "agate" glass, cameo-cut glass, particularly in a white overlay on a blue background, mosaic and millefiore glass, and finally blown glass vessels all make their appearance in India during this period. In the Parthian period other Western innovations were introduced, beads, bangles and bracelets of types to be found elsewhere as far as Cologne. Yet the continuation of the appearance of ear-reels and other characteristically Indian items indicate that much of the glassware appears to have been of local manufacture. At Kopia, in the Basti district of Uttar Pradesh, Dr. Dikshit examined and confirmed the existence of a glassware producing factory dated circa third century B.C.E. to third century C.E. "The mound was literally strewn with thousands of glass fragments and lumps of unworked glass."[24]

Glassware was introduced to both western and eastern Indian coastal cities during the Roman period, and included in the cargos was crude glass. Evidence of glassware-making facilities employing such raw material has been found at a number of such sites, and also in Sri Lanka. Crude glass was unloaded, for example, at Muziris, Neleynda, and Bacare on the west coast in exchange for pepper and other spices.[25] The most ancient community of Jews in India, referred as the "Bene Israel," were settled in this very West Indian area before Roman trade reached the area. One of their traditions holds that they descended from the "lost" ten tribes of Israel, exiled from Samaria by the Assyrian king Shalmaneser in the year 722 B.C.E. Another tradition holds that the ancestors of another group of immigrants escaped by sea from Israel during the reign of Antiochus Epiphanes in the year 175 B.C.E. The forefathers of this group "were shipwrecked and washed ashore on the Konkan coast, south of Bombay." They adopted Indian names and spoke Marathi, the local language, and their descendants survive to the present day.

Glassware and then glassmaking also appeared in Roman times on the southwest coast near Cochin. Here again, a community of Jews appeared, the first of whom are said to have disembarked in the year 72 C.E. at Cranganore, the ancient seaport just north of Cochin, and adopted the local tongue, Malayalam, except for their services, which are conducted in Hebrew. The Cochin Jews were mainly spice traders, and the few Jewish families who are still left carry on a trade in cardamom, pepper, ginger, turmeric and other spices, much as they must have done in the early days of the Common Era. Decorative linens (most probably from such linen-producing centers as Beth Shean) were also prominent among the products shipped overseas to India.

The Jews of India and China never experienced anti-Semitism; on the contrary, they were treated with respect. A Jewish elder of the community, Joseph Rabban, was appointed a prince of the village of Anjuvannam and facsimiles of copper plates which listed the honors and privileges granted the rabbi by King Sri Parkaran Iravi Vanmar are presently sold in the synagogue of Mattancherry, a suburb of Cochin. The Jews did suffer periodically from marauding Moors and Portuguese.

The Portuguese explorer, Vasco da Gama, performed a particularly perfidious act upon arrival at Anchevida, not far from Goa, where a Jewish community had been established long before the arrival of the Spanish and Portuguese adventurers. Da Gama owed much to Jewish science and was well aware of his debt. Da Gama's voyage had been rendered possible by the maps drawn by the Jewish cartographers of Majorca, and especially by tables compiled and the new astrolabe devised by the Jewish astronomer, Abraham Zacuto (with whom Columbus had also conferred). Da Gama demonstrated his appreciation by taking affectionate leave of Zacuto in the presence of his entire crew just before sailing from Lisbon on July eighth, 1497. But events took another turn in India. Da Gama was greeted by

> a Jew from Posen [who] had made his way to India after incredible adventures and had risen to the rank of Admiral of the Viceroy of Goa, whom he had persuaded to treat the strangers kindly. Da Gama's conduct towards the old man was particularly ungrateful....He had him seized and tortured until he consented to be baptised and to pilot the Portuguese flotilla in Indian waters.[26]

The Portuguese later destroyed the Jewish settlement at Shingly (Crangamore) and "the last Jewish Prince, Joseph Azar, escaped by swimming to Cochin, carrying his wife on his shoulders. The Jews then placed themselves under the rule of the Maharajah of Cochin, and in 1568 built their place of worship next to his Palace."[27]

While the Sassanian period was not without problematic periods for the "Babylonian" Jews it was, on the whole, a time of considerable expansion and growing prosperity. The conflicts between the Byzantines, the Persians and the Arabs enmeshed the Babylonian Jewish community in an increasingly complicated web of international intrigues and conflicts by which they were inevitably and adversely affected and which again catalyzed an exodus of its members. The traces of such movements are almost invariably marked by the appearance and disappearance of that exceptional art, glassmaking. The parallel of these events with the state of the art in India is another such remarkable circumstance which cannot be reasonably attributed to coincidence. The "Golden Period" of the glass industry in India came to an end in the seventh century, a period in which records "are so scanty that the period may truly be called the Dark Period in the history of glass in India. The time span is a long one...."[28] Indeed, a long gap occurs, and aside from a few, clearly imported items which show up spottily here and there, it is not for many centuries that some evidence of glassmaking in India can again be acknowledged with any assurance.

The darkness which descended on glass production in India began its dimming during the period of the debilitating struggle of the Sassanians with the Byzantines; it blackened after the bloody massacres which Mohammed inflicted on the Jews of Arabia began a process which ended their Sassanian existence. The Byzantines and the Persians were both drained by a series of encounters. The Byzantines turned to the Khazars, a great and numerous Tatar nation which had established itself across the Caucasus, for assistance, and the Khazars obliged. A mighty force of 40,000 horsemen turned the tide, and the Byzantines were salvaged from ignominious defeat and from a long and bitter struggle from which they may well have not survived. At this very time a new blight began creeping up on the Jews from the deserts of Arabia.

The Golden Period of Indian glassmaking coincided with the wave of Jewish immigration into Persia which followed the crushing of Judah by the Romans after the Bar Kokhba revolt, and reached its apogee during the Sassanian period. The "Dark Period" of Indian glassmaking coincided with the events which followed the *Hegira*, Mohammed's flight to Medina; Mohammed arrived in that thriving city in the year 622, the first year of the Arabian calendar. The Jews had composed fully half of the Medina population at the time of Mohammed's arrival, divided into three tribal communities, the Banu Qaynuga, the Banu l'Nadir and the Banu Qurayza Aws, the tribes occupying three of the five separate sections of the city. Mohammed went to Medina after gaining victory over opponents in Mecca. He turned upon the Jews, selecting as a first target "the weakest of the tribes, the Banu Qaynuga, whose members were mainly artisans and craftsmen." The Jews surrendered unconditionally after a short siege and were permitted to leave Medina with some of their possessions. His power thus enhanced, and needing another boost after suffering reverses elsewhere, Mohammed turned upon the next group, the Banu l'Nadir, demanding their eviction. Resistance proved futile and they were likewise permitted to leave, departing for the Jewish oasis of Khaybar with an impressive caravan of 600 camels.

The remaining tribe, the Banu Qurayza, thus isolated, held out for 25 days against a vicious siege. They did not fare as well as the other two tribes. Upon surrendering, the men were led to the marketplace and beheaded; their bodies were thrown into a large trench dug through the middle of the square. Between 600 and 900 men were slaughtered, the women and children were enslaved and Mohammed's prestige was enhanced throughout Arabia. The booty Mohammed had gained from the property left by the two tribes who were permitted exodus from Medina and from both the property and the possessions of the last tribe who remained, enriched Mohammed and formed the basis of the new Moslem treasury.[29]

Mohammed later led his army against the Jews of Khaybar, who put up a fierce resistance, having learned what to expect from the bitter experience of the fellow-Jews who had been expelled from Medina and the disaster which had befallen those who remained. Jews who escaped the massacre told the embattled Khaybar Jews of the brutality with which the Qurayza men were slaughtered, the callousness with which their bodies were stashed under the sod of the square and of the dire fate of the Jewish women who thereafter swelled the harems. Mohammed bought off the Bedouins, most of whom had been sympathetic to the Jews, and some of whom were their allies. Resistance in Khaybar crumbled; Mohammed prevailed.

The harsh terms of surrender included the forfeiture of half of Jewish produce as an annual tribute. The terms of tribute imposed upon the Jews of Khaybar became the standard model for the terms of tolerance of the Jews throughout Islam. The Jews thus became a major contributor to Muslim conquest. Mohammed went on to similar sieges against Jews in Fadak, and other urban centers which were an essential part of the economy.[30]

The fear of further massacres and the harsh terms under which the remaining Jewish artisans and merchants were permitted to continue their trades spurred an exodus from the Arabian communities into Persia, Yemen, India and China along the now well-established trade routes, and into Khazaria, another haven for Jews in which they could reasonably pursue both their culture and their trades. The Muslims swept up out of Arabia to conquer Mesopotamia, Syria, Egypt and to deliver the coup de grace to a bleeding and enfeebled Sassanian Persia. The Muslims then "surrounded the Byzantine heartland [present-day Turkey] in a deadly semicircle, which extended from the Mediterranean to the Caucasus and the southern shores of the Caspian."[31]

Across the Caucasus the Khazars formed the main bulwark against Islamic expansion into Byzantium. The Arabs first turned their forces against the

Khazars, bypassing the formidable natural barrier of the Caucasus ranges through the defile of Darband, along the Caspian shore. After the year 642 they repeatedly broke through the Darband Gate, but their deep incursions into Khazaria were beaten back each time. In 652 they suffered a disastrous defeat in which "four thousand Arabs were killed, including their commander, Abd-al-Rahman ibn-Rabiah; the rest fled in disorder across the mountains."[32]

The Arabs, frustrated in their attempts to crush the Khazars, turned upon Byzantium, besieging Constantinople again and again by land and sea as fiercely as the Persians had previously done. The Khazars, having meanwhile expanded their state by subjugating the Bulgars and Magyars and consolidating control over the Ukraine and Crimea, reentered the fray in 722. Arab sources speak of armies of from 100,000 to 300,000 men engaging on the battlefield during multiple campaigns waged during this "Second Arab War." It was a war characterized by "death-defying fanaticism [and the] traditional exhortation which would halt the rout of a defeated Arab army and make it fight to the last man: 'To the Garden, Muslims, not the Fire'--the joys of Paradise being assured to every Muslim killed in the Holy War."[33]

In 737 a Pyrrhic victory was won under the future caliph Marwan II. An insidious attack which followed an offer of alliance caught the Khazars by surprise and caused a retreat to the Volga. Marwan extracted a promise of conversion to the "True Faith" from the Kagan, a lip-service given and then forgotten as soon as the Arabian army had retreated to TransCaucasia. It was the last attempt by the Arabs to conquer territory across the Caucasus. Beset by civil war in its rear, "the gigantic Muslim pincer movement across the Pyrenees in the West and across the Caucasus into Eastern Europe was halted at both ends about the same time."[34]

Thus, Khazar initiative again saved the Christian Byzantine Empire from being inundated and possibly destroyed by Islamic hordes. D. M. Dunlop emphasizes that but for the Khazars, "Byzantium, the bulwark of European civilization in the east, would have found itself outflanked by the Arabs, and the history of Christendom and Islam might very well have been very different."[35]

The Islamic policy toward the Jews changed radically as Islamic rule was established over the vast territory they had conquered, albeit they were frustrated in their attempt to complete their encirclement of the Byzantines by crossing the Caucasus. The Jews were a source of immense tribute, the artisans who produced wealth, and the traders whose international contacts and knowledge of languages made their presence invaluable. These world-girdling merchants are exemplified by the Radhanites, the indominable, wide-ranging entrepreneurs who followed in the mainstream of the 3000 year-old Akkadian tradition of personally conducted commerce across the three interconnected continents well into the Middle Ages. Some suggest that the term "Radhanites" stems from a Persian root meaning "those who know the way."[36] Another writer suggests a variant version--*Rahadina*--meaning, "one who sells flaxen and cotton fabrics." Still others postulate that these intrepid travelers stemmed from the district of Radhan near Baghdad (later called Jukha).[37] Whatever be the true origin of the name, the various hypotheses all place the Radhanites at the hub of a tricontinental commercial web and delineate the extensive activity in which they were engaged.

It must be understood that the Radhanites were not mere adventurers; they were learned in languages; they were students of the Talmud; they were the religious, cultural and social liason between widespread Jewish communities; they were entrusted with the collection of communal donations for delivery to the Geonim of Palestine and Babylonia, the spiritual leaders of the Talmudic centers who maintained The Law. The Geonim were Halachic scholars to whom Jews throughout the Diaspora turned for legal and spiritual decisions, teachers who conducted great centers of learning to which all Jews aspired to send their sons and to whom all lent financial support. The Radhanites brought *she'ltot*, queries to the sages on law, ritual and textual exegesis, from the communities through which they traveled; they returned with *teshuvot*, the responsa, to those communities.[38] They were universal scholars of the first order, and were respected and trusted implicitly.

These mercantile Talmudic messengers created the first world wide credit system; they became the conduits of credit through which many nations of the world conducted business through time and space. "Letters of Credit" issued on one continent would be securely honored months and even years later on another continent. The Jews were often the only means by which international trade could be conducted. The tradition of trust was developed as an essential by-product of the spread of Jews through the Diaspora. The Jewish international merchants were worldly-wise; they had entree into royal courts; they were commissioned by kings to carry out royal diplomatic missions and were entrusted by governments to consummate international commercial affairs. They were uniquely accessible to Jews who served the same functions throughout the civilized world.

When Charlemagne sent an embassy in 797 to the Caliph Harun el-Rashid (literally, "Aaron the Upright), the Muslim Caliph of Baghdad, a Jew named Isaac served as interpreter; of all the principals among the envoys, Isaac alone survived the trip home, bringing with him to Charlemagne's court a present from the Caliph--an elephant, until then unseen in Europe. And when Charlemagne wanted exotic foods from the Holy Land, he named a Jew as his imperial purveyor....During the reign of Charlemagne the word "Jew" had taken on a new meaning. Not only did it signify "merchant" to many, but it also meant one who was trustworthy and knowledgeable.[39]

These remarkable traders were accorded extraordinary privileges even during times when Jews in general were otherwise virulently oppressed. They were more than mere merchants in many ways; they were the carriers of a civilized culture which had matured more than two millennia before the young, relatively backward, developing European and central Asian civilizations had appeared, and more than a millennium before Far Eastern civilizations had matured. The Radhanites supplied the energy with which the pulsing heart and arteries of this unique network of intercontinental interchange of both goods and culture functioned.

The Jewish traders left for China laded with Western wares and returned with a variety of exotic Eastern products. A geographic treatise, *The Book of Roads and Kingdoms* written in 846 by Ibn Khurdadhbih, manager of the postal and information service in the province of Media, describes in detail the various itineraries taken and some of the products carried by the Radhanites.

They speak Arabic, Persian, Greek, Frankish, Andalusian and Slavonic. They travel from East to West and from West to East by both land and sea. From the West they bring adult slaves, boys and girls, brocade, beaver pelts, assorted furs, sables and swords. They sail from the land of the Franks on the Western Sea[40] and set out for al-Faruma [a now abandoned port on the easternmost branch of the Nile]. There they transport their merchandise by pack-animal to al-Qulzum [on the Red Sea], which is 25 parasangs away. From al-Qulzum they set sail for al-Jar [Medina] and Jidda [the present supply port of Mecca], after which they proceed to Sind [The Indus River valley area], India and China. From China they bring musk, aloeswood, camphor, cinnamon, and other products as they make their way back to al-Qulzum.[41]

Age-old communities of Jews were rooted along these routes. In the Red Sea, for example, lies the island of Yotabe (now Jijban). In the fifth century Arabia owned half of the island, which was occupied by an Arab prince and his tribe. The other half was a Jewish free state which had been there from time immemorial.[42] Such communities were ensconced upon the entire gamut of routes along which traders traveled, linking the civilizations of the East and the West. Three more of the routes plied by the Radhanites are described by the postal manager turned historian:

> Those of them that set out from Spain....[sometimes] take the route behind the Byzantine Empire through the land of the slavs to Khamlij, the capital of the Khazars. Then they cross the Sea of Jurjan [the Caspian] toward Balkh and Transoxania. From there they continue to Yurt and Tughuzghuzz [an Arabic adaption of *Toghuz Oghuz*, "nine clans" referring to the Turkic confederation of tribes] and finally to China.[43]

It was thus that the adventurous Radhanites linked three continents, a liason evidenced by its effect upon the language and culture of the diverse regions in which they carried on their affairs. The Spanish shawl, for example, was from time immemorial a colorful, characteristic part of women's costume in the Middle East and central Asia. Embroidered shawls were first introduced into China from the Middle East where they became part of the upper class women's dress in the T'ang Dynasty (618-906 C.E.). The highly decorative, Oriental silken versions of the shawl were also introduced into Muslim North Africa and were thereafter adopted in Spain from the eighth through the fifteenth centuries at the time of the occupation of the Iberian Peninsula by the African Moors. "The word 'shawl' derives from the Persian *shal*."[44]

The routes taken by Jewish traders anticipated the movement of Jewish artisans. Jews were kept well informed by their traveling compatriots about the conditions everywhere, and when conditions became intolerable in one area they would establish themselves wherever the environment appeared propitious. The legendary "Wandering Jew" carried his skills and knowledge with him, and became the prime factor in spreading artistic homogeneity, a phenomenon which is most evident in glassmaking. The appearance of glassware and glassmaking in disparate regions with characteristics akin to that found a continent away has confounded glass historians. The solution of the mystery lies in the uniqueness of the manner in which the art was contained and with which it traveled with its practitioners.

315

# THE GLASSMAKERS

The art of Islamic Persia unmistakably evolved from that of Sassanian Persia; so-called "Islamic glassware" was, at first, indistinguishable from that of the Sassanian period which evolved from its precedent Parthian period and which in turn stemmed from the Roman and Achaemenid periods. The continuity of the evolution of the style of Mesopotamian glassware through these periods can be easily attributed to the fact that whatever changes there were of the conquerors who extorted taxes or tribute from the populace, the glassmakers represented a clear and lineal line through successive changes of regime. While this was undoubtedly also true of many of the arts, the spread of particular styles and techniques of glassmaking is peculiar in one outstanding respect. They followed the itinerary of the Jews into the Diaspora. The common denominator of all of these appearances of the art was the presence of newly arrived Jewish immigrants.

The problem of identification of the Jewish artisan lies in nomenclature. Most Jews assumed Greek, Roman or Persian names during the respective periods and thus cannot often be distinguished by tomb inscriptions. The 2,000,000 or so Jews resident in Sassanian Persia at the time of the Mohammedan incursion cannot be accounted for unless their presence is interpolated from other data. The important role the Jews played in the arts of the area is invisible in historiography but can be made visible in the light of the appearance of the art of glassmaking.

At the very time the art disappears from India it bursts into being over the Caucasus in Khazaria.

## NOTES

1. Josephus, *Antiquities of the Jews*, 11.133.

2. Nissim Rejwan, *The Jews of Iraq*, 1985, p. 29.

3. Shmuel Safrei, "The Lands of the Diaspora," *A History of the Jewish People*, 1969, p. 373.

4. W. E. Schiff, *Parthian Stations by Isidore of Charax*, 1914, p. 9.

5. S. Safrei *A History of the Jewish People*, 1976, p. 377.

6. Solomon Grayzel, *A History of the Jews*, 1969, p. 235.

7. Abraham Malamut, *Encyclopedia Judaica*, vol. 6, col. 1036 "Assyrian Exile."

8. Axel von Saldern, *Abstract of the Sixth International Congress on Glass*, 1962.

9. Mariamaddalena Negro Ponzi, "A Group of Mesopotamian Glass Vessels of Sasanian Date," *Bulletin of the 6th International Congress on Glass*, p. 12.

10. Donald S. Whitcomb, *Before the Roses and the Nightingales, Excavations at Qasr-i Abu Nasr, Old Shiraz*, 1985, p. 155.

11. Whitcomb, Ibid., p. 13.

12. O. H. Puttrich Reignard, *Die Glasfunde con Ktesiphon*, 1934, p. 26.

13. Ponzi, Ibid., p. 14.

14. Christopher W. Clairmont, *The Glass Vessels; The Excavations at Dura Europus, Final Report, IV, Part V*, 1963, pp. 56, 57 and note 117.

15. C. G. Seligman, *The Roman Orient and the Far East*, 1939, p. 555.

16. Seligman, Ibid., p. 555 and Pl. 1.

17. M. Aural Stein, *Serindia*, Oxford, 1921, p. 64 and pl. 37; *Central Asian Relics of China's Ancient Silk Trade*, Hirth Anniversary Volume, 1921, pp. 368, 374; "A Journey of Geographical and Archeological Exploration in Chinese Turkestan," *The Geographical Journal*, 1902; *Sand-buried Ruins of Khotan*, London, 1903; *On Ancient Central Asian Tracks*, 1933.

18. Stein, Ibid., 1903, p. 19.

19. Alistair Lamb, "Some observations on stone and glass beads in early South-east Asia," *Journal of the Malaysian Branch of the Royal Asiatic Society*, vol. 38, pt. 2, Dec. 1965, p. 123.

20. Alistair Lamb, "Some Glass Beads from the Malay Peninsula," *Man*, vol. 65, no. 30, March-April 1965, p. 36.

21. Moreshtar G. Dikshit, *History of Glass*, 1969, p. 6.

22. Dikshit, Ibid., p. 15.

23. Dikshit, Ibid., pp. 22-23.

24. Dikshit, Ibid., p. 39.

25. Dikshit, Ibid., pp. 52-53.

26. Cecil Roth, *The Jewish Contribution to Civilization*, 1956, p. 67.

27. Barbara Hansen, "India's Jews Keep the Lamp Burning in Cochin," *Newsday*, Oct. 22, 1989, Travel/17.

28. Dikshit, Ibid., p, 59.

29. Norman A. Stillman, *The Jews of Arab Lands,* 1979, pp. 13-16.

30. Salo Wittmayer Baron, *A Social and Religious History of the Jews*, vol. 3, 1957, p. 79.

31. Koestler, Ibid., p. 27.

32. Koestler, Ibid., p. 27.

33. Koestler, Ibid., p. 28.

34. Koestler, Ibid., p. 30.

35. D. M. Dunlop, *The History of the Jewish Khazars*, (1954), pp. ix-x. Arthur Koestler, underlining Dunlop's prognostication of the dire turn Christian history in particular would have taken "but for the Khazars," the concurrence in that proposition by such diverse historians as Dimitry Obolensky, a professor of history in the University of Oxford: *The Byzantine Commonwealth--Eastern Europe 500-1453*, (1971) p. 172., and by the Soviet archeologist and historian M. I. Artamonov who stated unequivocally that "It was only due to the powerful Khazar attacks, diverting the tide of the Arab armies to the Caucasus, that Byzantium withstood them," *Khazar History*, (in Russian, 1962). English historian A. Toynbee concurs: "Indeed, the Empire may have owed it to the Khazars that she survived."

36. De Goeje, *Bibliotheca Geographum Arabicum*, 5, p. 251.

37. Norman A. Stillman, *The Jews of Arab Lands*, 1979, p. 34.

38. Norman A. Stillman, Ibid., 1979, p. 32.

39. Abba Eban, *Heritage*, 1984, p. 120.

40. Note that the Mediterranean is still called the Western Sea in the ninth century, a designation harking back to Akkadian times of the second Millennium B.C.E., when the Mediterranean was known variously as The Western Sea and The-Sea-of-the-Setting-Sun.

41. Eliyahu Ashtor, *The Jews of Moslem Spain,* vol. I, 1973, p. 282.

42.  Heinrich Graetz, *A History of the Jews*, vol. III, (1967), p. 56.

43.  Norman Stillman Ibid., quoting from Ibn Khurdadhbih, *al-Masalik wa 'l-Mamalik*, ed. M.J. de Goeje (Leiden 1889), pp. 153-155,

44.  Natalie Robinson, "Mantones de Manila, *Arts of Asia*, Jan.\Feb. 1987, p. 65.

# CHAPTER 10

# THE
# JEWISH KHAZARS

## *The Russian Connection*

ON FIVE HISTORIC OCCASIONS, JEWS BECAME KINGS OR KINGS BECAME JEWS. Five times Jews were integrated into an institution which was in contraposition to their culture and repugnant to their philosophy.

Jews became kings in Egypt after the time of Joseph, and boosted Egyptian culture and technology to new heights of sophistication; they became kings in Israel and Judah, where Jewish rulers reigned for a period longer than twice the age of the United States; Judaism was adopted by the royal house of the Yemenite kingdom of Himyar under Yusuf Asar Dhu Nuwas (ruling ca. 517-525); eight North African Berber tribes converted to Judaism and fought bravely under their warrior queen Kahena.

And kings became Jews in Khazaria.

The Khazars were a pastoral people who swept in from the vast, windswept savannahs of Asia onto the steppes of present-day southern Russia in the sixth century of the Christian Era. They were an important part of the ongoing westward movement of a number of pastoral Turkic peoples who fanned out across the vast Russian plains; the Magyars moved on up into what is now Finland and ended up in Hungary; the Avars, Sabirs and Bulgars occupied the Danube basin; the Khazars followed the Kok Turks and spread out along the northern flanks of the Caucasus Mountains, skirting the Aral and Caspian and Black Seas. The tent-dwelling, horse-riding, Khazar herdsmen absorbed some of the peoples of that hilly area, allied themselves with others and became transformed into a sedentary nation.

The derivation of the name "Khazar" is a subject of continued speculation; it is most popularly thought to derive from the Turkic root *gaz*, meaning "to wander," referring to the tribe's nomadic or pastoral subsistence. The Russian word "Cossack" and the Hungarian "Huszar" are among several supposed derivations from the Turkic original. The pejorative German term *ketzer* very likely derives as well from "Khazar"; it is a sneering reference to Jewish heretics, regardless of whether they are of "barbaric" Khazar derivation or not.

The Khazar's growth and expansion was largely peaceful, belying the horrific tales of Tatar fierceness and brutality repeated by Christian apologists. The Khazars formed an amicable alliance with the Alans, a tribe which had inhabited the North Caucasian area from time immemorial, thus securing their eastern flank. A gradual expansion westward around the Black Sea ensued, and the Khazars moved up along the Volga, Don, Dniester and Dniepr Rivers into the Baltics; they spread into the alluvial plain around the lower and central Danube River, an area which now encompasses Bulgaria, Romania and Hungary. The Khazar infiltration proceeded peacefully for the most part; although conflict with the other Tatar tribes did occur, the Khazars generally sought to come to amicable terms with their neighbors. They eventually allied with the Bulgars and settled alongside their allies. Their borders touched upon the belligerent Byzantines to their southwest; they were separated from the Persian Sassanians by a succession of Caucasian ranges to their south; they were in contact with the Finnish Magyars, the fierce Russ and other Celtic and Slavic tribes to the north and northwest.

Studies of glassware of the eighth to the thirteenth centuries found throughout the vast territory from central Asia through Russia, Poland, and the Danube basin, have shown a correlation of style and composition by which the art can be tracked back from the farthest reaches of the area through time and territory to a single source, the Near East. Maria DeKowna, of the Polish Academy of Sciences, expresses her amazement at the phenomenon of commonality. Comparing studies of the characteristics of spherical beads found throughout the territory, the single most prevalent glass artefact, DeKowna demonstrates that, accounting for minor differences which inevitably develop with local production, the beads "exhibit a strong resemblance (form, color, motif and color of ornamentation) which cannot but suggest their influx into this territory from one unique center of production."[1] DeKowna's observations are fully supported by numerous analyses conducted in the past 50 years; the analogous patterns of composition and technique remained inexplicable because they were assumed to be employed by disparate groups, some of whose level of civilization precluded them from the ability to produce glass.

Other studies show that the artisans producing glassware in eastern and central Europe must equally have had a common origin. There is one common factor which rationalizes the considerable universality of technique and composition throughout the region. It is a factor which has heretofore been absent from the historical equations propounded for the dissemination of the art of glassmaking. The peculiar history of the appearance of glassmaking in the vast region under consideration is resolved when it is placed within the context of Jewish and Khazar history. Jews came into Khazar territory from every direction; at various times they coursed in from Persia, from Byzantium, from Italy and across northern Germany. When the patterns of the dispersion of glass technology are placed over those of the dispersion of the Jews, a near perfect match is immediately apparent.

Such a juxtaposition makes abundantly clear the how and why of the deletion of this critical factor must be addressed in order to rationalize both histories, that of glassmaking no less than that of the Jews. The eruption of the art of glassmaking throughout central Europe has seemed inexplicable only because the presence of the Jews (and, incidently of the Khazars) has been erased from the record or ignored. Furthermore, the practice of the art, not merely in Khazar territory but in all of Europe can be linked to the same common factor. The Jews were demonstrably present wherever and whenever glass(ware)making appeared; as soon as that presence is factored into the spread of the art, the enigma is readily resolved.

The mistreatment of the history of the Khazars is a classic case of institutionalized deletion and obfuscation. The Christian Byzantines, the Islamic Mohammedans, the pan-Arabists, the Russian Stalinist ethnocentrists, each in their turn, deliberately and purposefully expunged whatever ruins and records survived the conquest of Khazar territory and the classicophile historians have abjectly turned a blind eye to the effacement.

Literary records of the early Khazar period are sparse, scarcely specific, shrouded in mystery and subject to much dispute. An overlay of mythology and falsehood obscures the explication of Khazar history; the willingness of historians to peel away the veneer has been extraordinarily listless. One Arabist scholar, D. M. Dunlop, proposed that the main reason was neither a lack of intrinsic interest...nor the absence of material, but rather the difficulty of dealing with the existing sources--partly because they are written in a variety of languages, Greek, Arabic, Hebrew, Syriac, Armenian, Georgian, Russian, Persian, Turkish and even Chinese, with which no one can be expected to be familiar at first hand."[2]

Such a problem has scarcely deterred historians from delving into infinitely more obscure languages and histories; philologists were spurred into deciphering languages dead for thousands of years in a concerted effort to reconstruct the historiography of ancient peoples and cultures. Certainly the diversity of living languages in which literature pertaining to the Khazars is written cannot be seriously ascribed to be the prime reason for the dearth of research into a culture which endured for more than a half millennium and whose role in the development of European civilization is far from an inconsiderable one.

A few ancient sources render fabulous versions of Khazar history based on legends which attribute a Biblically related origin to the Khazars. Thus a genealogical table issued by Yossipon in the ninth or tenth century, "depicts the Khazars as descendants of Togarma, a grandson of Noah's son Yaphet, without mentioning that they (at least some of them) had any connection with Judaism."[3] Jehuda Ha-Levi, who translated the *Sepher ha-Kuzari* (the Book of the Khazars) from the Khazar language into Yiddish in the year 1741, states that, according to Arab authors, Kozar, the son of Yaphet and the grandson of Noah, separated from his brothers after they left the ark and built a great city near the Volga River which he named al-Khazar.[4]

There are a number of tendentious pan-Arabic renditions of Khazar history of more recent date, aimed at proving that the Jews stem from a nation of 10,000,000 Asian Tatars to substantiate the argument that since the Jews of Eastern Europe did not originate in the Kingdom of Judah they were not Semites and had no inherent right to Israel.[5] This position found support in the United Nations; Sir Abdul Rahman, representative of India, opposed the partition of Palestine, arguing that Zionist claims to a homeland were invalid because its proponents were racially unqualified.[6] On the other hand there is the ethnocentric Stalinist doctrine which reduces the Khazars to a small "parasitic" group of "bourgeois decadents" who contributed so little to Russian culture and history that they are hardly worth mentioning at all.

Pre-Soviet Russian sources were unequivocal regarding the advanced status of Jewish Khazar civilization and the beneficial influence it exercised on the evolution of the Russian nation. In 1798 Miranovich cited documents which record the ninth century activity of a thriving Jewish-Khazar community in Kiev; they describe the seminal role of the Khazars in the development of industry and commerce and particularly in the importing of big fish, caviar and salt, which were exchanged for furs and other products of the aboriginal northern tribes.[7]

The early Soviet Russian historians likewise credited both the Khazars and the Jews with playing a positive, productive part in pre-Russian and proto-Russian development. Typical of the early Soviet historical renditions is that of Professor Artamonov, whose book expounded on the progressive cultural influence the Jews had exerted upon the uncultivated Northmen, among whom the *Rus* were included. Artamonov expanded on the role the Jews played in the development of the ancient city of Kiev into a great commercial and administrative center, a city which subsequently became the first Russian capital. Artamonov repeated his viewpoint at a session of the Department of History and Philosophy at the USSR Academy of Sciences in 1952. He was immediately subjected to a vicious attack in *Pravda*.

"All these things have nothing in common with historical facts....Only by flouting the historical truth and neglecting the facts can one speak of the superiority of the Khazar culture. The idealization of the Khazar kingdom reflects a manifest survival of the defective views of the bourgeois historians who belittled the indigenous development of the Russian people. The erroneousness of this concept is evident. Such a conception cannot be accepted by Soviet historiography."[8]

A shameful campaign of calumny against Artamonov ensued. His magnum opus, *History of the Khazars*, was apparently in preparation when *Pravda* struck. As a result, the book was published only ten years later (1962), in a revised version and carrying a recantation in its final section which amounted to a denial of all that went before--and indeed, of the author's life-work.[9] Another Russian historian, Krachkovski, was subjected to similar abuse. He reviewed (1939) the documents of *Ibn Fadlan*, written by that Arab traveler about an extended sojourn in Atil (Itil), one of the main Khazarian cities, located at the delta of the Volga River. Fadlan was impressed by the immense city, which consisted of two parts. "In one part live Muslims and in the other the Khazar king and his entourage. The Khazars and their king are all Jews, the Slavs (as-Sakaliba) and their neighbors obey the Khazar king submissively."[10] The mere citation of such historical documents was deemed the fulmination of a renegade flouting the party line.

Not only did Stalinist doctrine propose a revision of the history of the Khazars but made it obligatory. Stalinist doctrine held the Khazars to be the foes of the Slavs. The "idealization of the Khazars" was condemned and the role of the "autochthonic Slavic tribes" (Great Russians) were extolled as "the real creators of the Russian State structure and culture."[11] Any rendition of history which viewed either the Khazars or the Jews as seminal to Russian culture in any form whatsoever became anathematic to the new Russophilic image insisted on by the Stalinist regime. At the thirteenth International Congress of Historians held in Moscow in 1970 Russian critics abjectly objected to statements which merely referred to the previously accepted rendition of Russian history in which the Rus were depicted as subordinate to the Khazar Khaganate in the city of Kiev and elsewhere.[12] The historians who had written on Khazar history were required to write retractions of their "spurious claim" that the Khazars had built the basis for the Russian state and admit that Jewish religion had corrupted the Khazar elite by turning them to trade and parasitic enrichment. The doctrine was termed a "solution of the Khazar Problem."

As Stalinist influence pervaded Soviet Russian culture, Russian ethnography was welded to "Socialist patriotism," a euphemism for the Stalinist party line. While at first it was merely politically expedient to attribute any contribution to Russian cultural and economic development either to the Khazars or the Jews, it soon proved dangerous to even quote such an opinion.[13] The narrowly defined stance required of all researchers had to be adhered to by all who wished to avoid the Siberian Gulag; it had a disastrous effect even upon archeological work, and especially upon the investigations most pertinent to Khazar and Jewish history. The entire corpus of scientific investigation of 70 years of Soviet research must therefore be interpolated with this factor in mind.

How strange and patently ironic is the opposite, no less vehemently vindictive tack taken by American right-wingers, one of whom lamented that communism was the creation of Judaized Khazars, "for the Babylonian Talmud had taught them to accept authoritarian dictation on everything from their immorality to their trade practices," and that the insidious Khazar subversives had infiltrated the Democratic party and were in high positions in the American, British and French governments.[14]

The Jews have become inured to being the butt of extremists from the right, the left and the center; they are regularly condemned with the same breath for being usurious capitalists and radical Communists, for adopting worldly atheism and otherworldly orthodoxy, for being endogamous and internationalists. History suffers thereby, for when the very presence of Jews is ignored and credit for their positive contributions to civilization is denied the resulting historiographical lacuna affects the understanding of such disciplines as that of glassmaking and of the evolution of civilization itself.

It is evident that Khazarian historiography has been subjected to the same obfuscation and deliberate obliteration as has otherwise affected Jewish history as a whole. Truth must be culled out from between the pseudo-historical distortions of the jaundiced pan-Arabist promulgators of a wholly Arabic Near East, the rabid McCarthyite anti-communists and their no less paranoic successors, the bigoted semitophobes epitomized by the Nazis whose professed intent was to wipe out the Jews along with their history. Account must be taken of the crusading Christians as they ravaged through the East, employing the cross to capture treasure and territory, and of the Christian inquisitors who regarded the Jews as the epitome of a devilish antichrist. We must recognize the obscurantism of latter-day Christian apologists who were all too ready to wipe positive Jewish influence from their historical slates. Last but by far not the least are the abject Stalinist conformists who were required to substitute Russian nationalism for scientific objectivity. These contemporary enemies of historical integrity are the most destructive, for it is within Soviet borders that most of the relics of Khazar history lie, and their recovery and explication must be performed under a Soviet doctrine which persists in spite of the passage of its promulgator.

We are able, however, to turn to reports of Arab and Jewish travelers and historians which cast a gleam of light into the darkened corners of Khazar history. We learn from the writings of *al-Musudi* that after the Khazars converted to Judaism they created a tolerant society in which minority rights are respected: "The custom in the Khazar capital is to have seven judges. Of these two are for the Muslims, two are for the Khazars, judging according to the Torah (Mosaic Law), two for the Christians, judging according to the Gospel, and one for the Saqalibah, Rus and other Pagans, judging according to Pagan law."[15]

Rabbi Benjamin of Tudela twice referred to the Khazars, once in describing Constantinople, listing the Khazars among the groups of "all sorts of merchants [who] come here," and mentions them once again in discussing merchants visiting Alexandria.[16] Thus we learn that the Khazars of the twelfth century still had a viable society engaging in international commerce. Petachya of Regensburg, another wide-ranging Jew of the twelfth century, provided another version of the conversion: "Across the river Dnieper is the Kedar country...and an inlet divides the land of Kedar from the land of Kazaria". Petachya then recounts that in the city of Baghdad he came across messengers from that land who related to him that seven Meshekh (Khazar?) kings had been visited by an angel who told them to convert to Judaism. The kings sent a request to the head of the Baghdad Yeshiva (Judaic theological seminary) for "any poor *talmud hakham* (competent rabbinical student) to teach them and their children *Torah* and (Babylonian) *Talmud*. The messenger added that learned Jews from Egypt also went to Khazaria to teach Torah and Talmud.[17] Rabbi Benjamin and Petachya were among the Jewish merchant-scholars who carried on the tradition set by the world-girdling Radhanites of traveling through the length of the three interconnected continents well into the Middle Ages.

It is clear from more or less direct sources that the Khazars were persuaded by the unpretentious precepts of Jewish philosophy, were influenced by the rationality of Jewish religion and appreciated the technological advances wrought by their Jewish advisors. The king, the nobles and many of their subjects demonstrated the deep impression Jewish precepts had made upon them by converting to Judaism and bringing Jews into the government. It was a government whose tenets incorporated the democratic, tolerant teachings of the Jews. They absorbed and profited by the technological and commercial acumen of Jewish artisans and entrepreneurs in their midst. Martin Gilbert notes that about 700 A.D. their king, Bulan, was converted to Judaism, and that a later king, Obadiah, greatly strengthened Judaism, inviting rabbis into his kingdom and building synagogues. Gilbert then repeats the composition of the court as given by al-Masudi: "The supreme court consisted of 7 judges: 2 Jews, 2 Christians, 2 Moslems and a heathen." and adds, "Religious toleration was maintained for the kingdom's 300 years."[18]

The most revealing, and undoubtedly the most accurate, depiction of the process through which the Khazars departed from Shamanist practice and adopted Judaic religion and law comes down to us through the efforts of Hasdai Ibn Shaprut, a youthful Jew appointed by the caliph of Cordova to an important administrative post. Hasdai achieved fame early in life; he was a linguist, a doctor and a scientist who continued important researches while carrying the most delicate diplomatic assignments for the Caliph, achieving notable results, particularly by developing new medicines and rediscovering ancient medicinal formulas. Hasdai was known among the Jews by the title of *Nasi* (prince), for the caliph put him at the head of the Jewish settlement in his kingdom and conferred upon the brilliant scientist the authority to settle the affairs of the communities as he saw fit.[19]

The caliph also assigned the management of the department of customs to Hasdai, a post which was central to the administration of foreign affairs. Hasdai was in touch with the world through his privileged post, and he utilized his position to pursue his passion, which was to assist the Jewish communities of the Diaspora, to exchange information with them, to assemble Jewish history, and to find a refuge for the nation. Hasdai, and beleaguered Jews everywhere, sought desperately to find a realm where the Jews could live and practice their religion in freedom. There were persistent rumors that such a place did exist, stories repeated by merchants who were bringing merchandise back from the Slavic countries. Hasdai pressed them for information, met with Persian emissaries who reported on the mysterious country to their north, and interrogated various other envoys arriving at the court of the caliph. He pieced the information together and obtained a picture of the Jewish kingdom of the Khazars lying beyond Byzantium. Hasdai succeeded in corresponding with the Khazars in spite of a barrier of Byzantine belligerence separating the Khazars from the West.

Hasdai learned that the Khazars had no formal dynasty of kings. A noble who distinguished himself in battle might be chosen to become commander--in-chief, and would usually assume kingship thereafter. Thus it happened that a Jewish commander achieved this position. His wife *Sarah* persisted in urging him to practice Judaism in its entirety. He did so, and many of the nobles followed. The neighboring Moslems and Christians, who had been proselyting their causes within the Khazar realm, angrily protested, sending envoys to attempt to counteract Judaic influence and win the nation over to their respective religions.

A disputation was arranged. Greek, Muslim and Jewish scholars were heard in turn, and since all seemed to base themselves upon the scriptures the Khazar nobles submitted a copy of the sacred books, which had been secreted in a cave in the valley of Tizul, to the disputants. The Jews were able to interpret these holy writings far better than their competitors, and the impact of their convincing performance compelled the nobles to accept Judaism as the true faith. The Khazar Jews who had previously relinquished the faith in part or in whole returned to it, and became the teachers of the Khazars. The nobles declared the Jewish commander their king and chose one of the rabbis to be their judge. The king assumed the name Gabriel, and the subsequent kings were named Benjamin and Joseph.

If it were not for the correspondence carried on by Hasdai and by a miserably few references from Arabic and other sources, the very existence of the Khazars would hardly have been known. This is all the more remarkable since the Khazars exercised control over a considerable part of southern and western Russia, the Baltics and, together with other Asian peoples, over much of the effluvial Danube basin for a period of two centuries and continued as a sovereign nation, albeit in control of a reduced area, for three more centuries. One is left to wonder: "How can the dismal dearth of information of 500 years of the history of a significant portion of Europe be accounted for?"

Investigation of the question soon makes it clear that the history was obscured by the mists the Byzantine Christians, the Arab Moslems and the Russian Stalinists, each in their turn, spewed upon history. Each cult purged the pages of history to suit their purposes and substituted its own obfuscating version of events. Until recently most historians naively accepted the fabrications as fact, scarcely examined the authenticity of sources, and did little to delve into the few records which fortuitously survived. The surviving records suffice to demonstrate to those who deign to delve into them that, in the process of fleeing from repression, the Jews carried civilization across the Caucasus, the Dolomites, the Rhodopes, the Transylvanian Alps and the Carpathians to the Khazars. Thus culturally reinforced, the Khazars made Kiev an important center of commerce and industry and laid the foundation for Russia to become a great nation. The introduction of the unique art of glassmaking region by region provides a tool by which the historical hiatus can be partially filled in. The art can be traced as it appeared across the Caucasus, traveled with the Khazars up along the Volga, Don, Dniester and Dnieper Rivers, penetrated the Slavic heart of Europe and spread across southern Russia and up the Danube.

The Jews first encountered the Khazars when they passed over the Pamirs along the silk route to Kaifeng; they crossed the Caucasus Mountains into Khazar territory in their successive flights from Roman, Persian and Mohammedan persecution; they traversed the Transylvanian Mountains to escape Byzantine persecution; and they passed over the Dolomite Alps in their flight from Aquileia, an area which must be added to the regions to which Koestler refers. Each of these events bears on the history of both the Jews and that of glassmaking, and the best way to examine those remarkable histories is to take them separately and to observe how the pieces fall in place to form a unified whole.

How did the amalgamation of the Jews and the Khazars, two peoples of such disparate cultural, religious and historical backgrounds, come about? On the face of the question it would seem a most unlikely combination. Here were two peoples of disparate histories, one illiterate and one highly literate, whose languages had different roots, one shamanist and the other monotheistic, one nomadic and the other urban, who peacefully mixed and merged to share a common destiny.

The story of the unique relationship between the Khazars and the Jews begins early on. The Jews of the Levant were acquainted with the Turkic peoples of central Asia at least from the fifth century B.C.E. The Asian areas from where the Khazars had come, and the southern Russian areas where they finally settled had, by the fifth century C.E., already been actively traversed for a millennium by caravans treading along branches of the fabulous silk route into central Asia and China. The pastoral peoples of the vast Siberian expanse were the mediums through whom merchants from Assyria and Persia traded with the great Chinese empire. Beads and amulets and other sundry glass artefacts were brought to the area sporadically as far back as the Middle Bronze Age, that is, at the turn of the second millennium B.C.E.; the quantity and types of imported glass artefacts increase during the Hellenistic and Roman times.[20] The pastoral peoples of the vast Siberian expanse were the mediums through whom merchants from Persia traded with the great Chinese empire. The clearing of the passage to the West in the first century B.C.E. by the Han ruler *Ming Ti* (58-77 C.E.) and the securing of the passage between the East and the West by *Pan Chao* in 97 C.E. did not sever the relationship between the traders and the Turkic peoples. On the contrary, intercourse between the Asian pastoral peoples and the itinerant merchants of Persia grew more intimate with the establishment of centers along the routes through central Asia, caravansaries which supplied and serviced the caravans passing through. A bustling business with the local populations converted the trading posts into substantial commercial centers into which artisans settled and markets were established where locally produced merchandise was offered for sale. But it was not until the unification of the land-based silk route to China and the conversion of the caravan-servicing colonies into full-grown towns and cities that evidence of locally made glass shows up at a number of these sites, especially at fifth-century Samarkand, centrally located along that route.

When the Khazars began to filter into southern Russia they were brought into closer contact with long-established colonies of Jews, communities around the Caspian already functioning around the Caspian Sea from the time the Sidonese Israelites and other Sidonese had been deported in 351 B.C.E. In the Crimea documentary evidence shows that both Karaite and Rabbinate Jews had been in continuous habitation at least as far back as the first century C.E.[21] The Caspian communities, the communities of Persia, and the communities along the silk route burgeoned with an influx of thousands of Jews fleeing from Judah after Roman legions crushed the Bar Kochba revolt (135 C.E.). The Roman attempt to obliterate Judah's very existence, the expulsion of the Jews from Jerusalem and the enslavement and exportation of scores of thousands of Jews spurred the exodus to the East.

Until that time the Khazars, a pastoral people, were incapable of producing glassware. The Khazar hierarchy developed a degree of opulence in the process of becoming sedentary and became a natural market for more sophisticated glassware; the globe-traveling Jewish merchants and the artisans who followed in their wake supplied such ware to that new, matured market. Bowls, vases, drinking glasses, dinnerware and a variety of containers and implements of glass were put into production in the areas they had settled. The productivity of these objects reached its height toward the end of the eighth century, coincident with the period of greatest Jewish influence upon the Khazars, the period when the Khazars converted to Judaism.

By the end of the seventh century the Khazar nation had become firmly rooted, had evolved into a vigorous civilization which was self-sufficient enough to become independent of the sovereignty of the Khagans who ruled over the vast eastern Turkic empire. The Khazars thenceforward conducted affairs under their own khans, warrior kings who derived from the same family roots which reputedly produced the powerful, renowned much-maligned Genghis Khan.[22] The development of glassmaking along the silk route through the ninth century was enhanced as the relationship between the Jews and the Khazars crystallized. A flurry of new glassmaking sites were installed in central Asia; workshops of the tenth-thirteenth centuries appear in the south of Turkmany, at Termez in southern Uzbekistan, Samarkand, Achsiket, Kuva, Uzgen in the Fergana Valley, and at Chorezm in the oasis of Kujusaj. The glassware produced at these sites continue almost entirely in the Near Eastern soda-lime and lead-silicon tradition.[23] A notable variation appears in some of the glass found in Georgia: the presence of from 1 percent to 6 percent barium oxide is of particular interest because of the unique existence of that compound in glass produced around Kaifeng. Other samples containing barium have only been found in Caesarea (as was noted in the previous chapter).[24] Jewish glassmakers came into Khazaria from many directions and China was evidently one such direction, reversing the original course along which the art arrived into China from Persia. Persia was again the provenience of the glassmakers who established themselves in the newly constituted Khazar state. It was a natural westward extension of the installations along the route into China.

Waves of Jewish emigration such as that which followed the crushing of Judah by the Romans after the Bar Kokhba revolt recurrently poured across the Caucasus. Although preferable to Christian dominance, neither Sassanian nor Arabic rule were consistently tolerant and many Jews sought respite with the Khazars. The Jews treasured good relations with the Khazars, who were duly impressed with the technical sagacity and cultural acumen of the Jews. The earliest glassworks found in the northern foothills of the Caucasus was at Mecheta-Samtawbro, which seems to date back to the fourth century,[25] a time when the Jews were flourishing in Sassanian Persia (Babylonia) and when Jewish glassmakers were expanding their activities in the colonies established along the routes to the Far East. The Mecheta glasshouse appears to have continued operating into the ninth century, the time in which the Persian Jewish traders (the Radhanites and others) reached the peak of their activity. A significant glass workshop was excavated at Orbeti, dating from the seventh and eighth centuries, the precise period in which the Khazars converted to Judaism and an exodus from Persia took place. The remains of a crucible with glass slag at its bottom, unfinished glass artefacts, bracelets, mosaic pieces, window glass and glassware painted with enamel left no doubt as to the sophistication of the technology and offered a range of comparative items to objects subsequently found as far away as Bulgaria and Kharkov.[26]

The circumstances strongly suggest that the Orbeti glassmakers were Jews from Sassanian Persia where glassmaking had achieved artistic and technical virtuosity. The glassworks were established at Orbeti after the disastrous defeat of the Arab army in 652. They continued firing their furnaces through the period of the consolidation of Khazar control and survived past 737, at which time the Arabs retired permanently from the other side of the Caucasus and posed no further threat. The glassworks was situated directly on the route through the Caucasus which would have been taken by the Jews fleeing Arab terror. This movement of glassmakers from the Levant through Persia is noted by Jindrich Cadik, who made a study of the perfume vessel mentioned in the Gospels (Matthew XXVI, 6:13). Similar tubelike perfume vessels, termed both *unguentaria* and *balsamaria* by the archeologists, have been found throughout Russia, the Crimea and the Bosporus. "The [Levantine] glassworks which survived the fall of the Roman Empire did not disappear with the Arab invasion, before which the artisans of Judea emigrated," Cadik relates, and adds "thus was conserved the continuity of the ancient art for the future European world."[27]

As Jewish presence in Khazaria multiplied, so did the arts. The thick forests of the northern foothills of that mighty range, the Caucasus, provided a plentiful supply of fuel for the ravenous furnaces of glassmakers; quartz and other siliceous stones abounded. Locally made glass artefacts appear in Khazar graves and ruins coincident with Jewish migration across the Caucasus from Persia.

> The numbers [of Jewish immigrants] increased with the streams of migrants fleeing Byzantine and Sassanian intolerance. As elsewhere, the Jews engaged in pioneering pursuits. They taught their rather primitive neighbors more advanced ways of cultivating the soil, and means of exchanging goods among themselves and with foreign nations. They taught the art of writing. A tenth century Arab author states, "The Khazars use the Hebrew script."[28]

Glassmaking production peaked after the conversion of a large section of the Khazar population to Judaism. During this period the art spread with the advancing Khazar influence up the Volga, Don and Dnieper Rivers. The ruins of glassmaking and jewelry workshops were found in the artisan's quarters within the confines of a mighty Khazar fortress defending the great

Khazar city of Sarkal, situated on the lower reaches of the Don. The bastion was built for the defense of the city against groups of marauding Vikings (not an ethnic identification but simply an expression for "north-west European brigands") known as the Rus, who periodically came down the river in great fleets for pillage.

Russian diffidence regarding Khazarian historiography came painfully into evidence when investigation into the site gave way to callous industrial progress. Little protest and no effort at preservation or rescue was made when an artificially created inundation flooded the area and lost forever the opportunity for archeologists to follow through on their promising work. "The famous fortress and priceless archeological site...was submerged in the Timslyansk reservoir, adjoining the Volga-Dan Canal."[29] The Khazar city of Itil and other lesser sites have been almost entirely ignored, but as the limited archeological work progresses, pieces of a vivid picture emerge which require a continuous revision of classical mores. More is the pity that the great commercial metropolis of Sarkal with all its rich evidence of Khazar life lies forever lost under the waters of the reservoir.

The rapid consolidation and development of the Khazar economy impacted on foreign trade and relations. Jewish artisans continued to ply their crafts in their new environment and artifacts of Sassanian-Persian design, now manufactured in Khazaria, were introduced into the north among the more primitive tribes. Persian-style silverware was particularly admired. Persian-style merchandise of the Sassanian period has been found from Baghdad to Sweden. Arthur Koestler points out that "the arts and crafts seem to have flourished, including *haute couture*." Khazar merchants were active in "Constantinople, Alexandria and as far afield as Samara and Fergana."

The marriage of a Khazar princess to a Muslim governor of Armenia was the occasion of a great ceremony, to which the princess arrived in a great cavalcade which "contained, apart from attendants and slaves, ten tents mounted on wheels, 'made of the finest silk, with gold- and silver-plated doors, the floors covered with sable furs. Twenty others carried the gold and silver vessels and other treasures which were her dowry.' The Kagan himself traveled in a mobile tent even more luxuriously equipped, carrying on top a pomegranate of gold."[30] The pomegranate, it will be recalled from previous references, was a favorite motif employed by glassmakers of Mesopotamia and Canaan as far back as the fifteenth century B.C.E., when it was prominent among the very first core-formed vessels ever made. In Armenia, opposite Georgia on the southern flanks of the Caucasus, glassworks of that period were identified at Dwi.[31] It may well be that the establishment of this manufactory came about as a consequence of the marriage of the Armenian governor to a Khazar princess. In any event, the timing constitutes another of a series of curious coincidences.

The favor of the Khazars was as avidly sought by the Byzantines as it was by the Armenians, and a marriage was arranged between the Khazar Kagan's daughter and the future Emperor Constantine V. The dowry she brought with her included "a splendid dress which so impressed the Byzantine court that it was adopted as a male ceremonial robe; they called it a *tzitzakion*, derived from the Khazar-Turkish pet-name of the princess."[32] *Tzitzas* is the Hebrew word for the tassels which are universally strung from garments worn by observant male Jews. The peculiar mixture of Byzantine and Persian designs which characterized the products of the developing Khazarian arts and crafts industry reflect the work of Jewish artisans who arrived into Khazaria from both areas, Persia and Byzantium. The archeologist T. J. Arne points out that just such ornamental plates, clasps (fibulas) and buckles of Sassanian and Byzantine inspiration found as far as Sweden were manufactured in Khazarian territories."[33]

The glassmaking art continued in the Georgian area into the thirteenth century, a fact evidenced by a smaller glass[ware?] manufactory found in Georgia with coins dating from the Khaghanate of 1248-1316.[34] The coins confirm that the glassworks was still in operation just before the Mongol invasion from Siberia put all such activity in Russia at an end. Glass or glassware-making furnaces were also unearthed at Nabagrebi (twelfth-thirteenth c.), at Hasmi (twelfth-twelfth c. ?), at Tbilisi (elventh-thirteenth c.) and at Natbieur (thirteenth-fourteenth c.). The Jewish presence in Georgia continued long after Khazaria, weakened and surrounded by enemies, fell to a new incursion of overwhelming Mongolian forces and consolidated an empire which extended from China to Hungary. Vestiges of the pervasive Jewish presence are still visible in the continued presence of a widespread sect of Sabbath observers, the *Sabotniki* and of the 8000 or so *Dagh Chufuty* ("Mountain Jews") who are still ensconced upon the highlands of the Caucasus under the Soviets.[35]

The Khazars moved eastward and northward up the Danube, Dniester and Dnieper Rivers. They established themselves in Kiev on the middle Dnieper and made it a main center of commerce, trading manufactured goods with the Rus for fish and furs. One of the earliest glassworks of pre-Khazar southwestern Russia harks back to the Roman period, a third century settlement at Komarovo on the middle Dniester. The town came under Khazar control early on and the art continued under the Khazars. The chemical analysis of the glass recovered from this site was compared to the chemical content of glassware from Germany, from the Roman colony of Salonae on the Dalmatian coast and from Zakzhov in Poland.[36] It was evident that "the Komarovo glass and Roman glass from other countries belong to the same type: $Na_2O:CaO:SiO_2$."[37] The Near Eastern provenience of the pre-Khazar glassmakers of Komarovo was thereby postulated. "There has been a common opinion that Roman glass objects excavated in Central and East Europe were imported from the West. This hypothesis will have to be revised in view of the new discovery of the glassmaking center on the Dniester."[38] This conclusion, reached in 1964 by Bezborodov and Abdurazakov, was well substantiated by a continuous series of subsequent discoveries and analyses.

The discovery of this glass manufactory at Komarovo followed a number of other discoveries of glassworks in Greater Russia. The very first glassworks to be uncovered in the region was at Kiev in 1907. Two more glassworks were excavated in the environs of the city in 1950-1951.[39] Locally made window-glass and vessels have been retrieved from near Kiev, as well as from Belgorod, a town located just above Kharkov [Khazar-town], and from Galitch[40] and Vyshgorod. By 1964 eleven glassmaking sites had been confirmed existing in Kievan Russia, "notably at Kiev, Cernigov, Kolodjajin, Kostroma, Novgorod and others". The pattern of their spread can be gauged by the fact that the most ancient of these glass manufactories are those of Kiev (Desjatinna Cerkov), dating from the tenth century.[41] All of these sites lie along established Khazar trade routes. These revelations led to the above-cited conclusion drawn by the Soviet scientists that the Levant should be considered the primary source of both the art and the artisans. The growing body of evidence from throughout Europe, in fact, stimulated a reexamination of the provenience of glassware of western as well as that of Eastern Europe.

The Khazars penetrated as far northeast as Grodno, Lithuania, the Slavic city in which the Khazars established a glass factory in the late ninth or early tenth century. Documentation for that event is contained in the archives of the famous Judaica libraries assembled by the Barons Gunzburg and Polakoff. Both libraries were confiscated by the Bolsheviks soon after their accession to power and are now in the Hermitage in Leningrad. These archival libraries were locked away and made unavailable even to scholars; they contain a wealth of information relating to eastern and southeastern Russia.[42] They were delved into before the Bolsheviks made them inaccessible by the father of David Bezborodko, a glassmaker of a glassmaking family who hails his Khazar heritage with considerable pride.

"My father implanted in me the love of Torah and a love for humanity and science," writes Bezborodko in introducing the subject. David spent several decades researching Jewish-vitric history and was eminently suited for the purpose. "I was born to glass, the third generation in a family of glass producers and mirror manufacturers."[43] The family had established glass manufactories in Poland, White Russia (Leningrad), and Lithuania, starting from 1866, and were active until the Nazi invasion. Confirmation of David's recollection of the information contained in the impounded Jewish libraries has been archeologically confirmed, for an important glassmaking site was indeed found just east of Grodno at Novogrudok. Novogrudok, in fact, has proven to be a center of glass production second only to Kiev. Included in the glassware being produced at the site were "blue, violet, white, colorless and double-layered glasses, some decorated with gilding and white and red enamelling."[44]

The construction of facilities for the production of glass artefacts in Grodno followed the development of a market in the area for imitation gems which was already fully in force by the ninth century. The glass bracelets, beads and other jewelry had become important Khazarian trade goods throughout the Slavic territories. Enameled jewelry with imitation gems of vivid colors were being produced around Kiev in the 10th century, and workshops dating to the eleventh century producing this exotic ware have been excavated in the area of Kiev.[45] The fact that Jewish artisans were among the Khazars who produced this merchandise, and the extent of their influence can be readily surmised from the anti-Semitic writings of the Russian poet and historian Dzierzavin, who crowed with delight over the destruction of Khazarian hegemony over the area, proclaiming that the Khazar *zydy* (the sneeringly derogatory term for Jews in all the Slavic languages), "would no longer be able to exploit our Slavic people by selling them high-priced jewelry which is broken in its first use."[46] The reference is to imitation gems and precious metals being produced in and around Kiev.

A number of centers of glassmaking of the period have been identified in Poland; one of the oldest was uncovered at Wolin, and dates to the first half of the tenth century. That facility was soon followed by the installation of others at Opole, Niemcza Sl. Wroclaw, Kruszwica and at Miedzyrzecz Wielkopolski, their installations ranging up to the mid-thirteenth century.[47] Two glasshouses sprang up during the latter part of this period near Cracow, four others near Gdansk, and another near Poznan.[48] The indigenous Slavic peoples were far from being capable of or knowledgeable about the processes of glassmaking and the fact that foreign artisans, brought the art into the area is undisputed. Only the identity of the glassmakers has heretofore remained a mystery. Although the art has been attributed vaguely to "Byzantine" artisans the Near Eastern connections of these artisans are cited but hardly understood and rarely elaborated on. The Khazar-Jewish presence and influence has been routinely ignored.

A Christian veneer was imposed over the art by the dubbing of a group of glassware collectively as *Hedwig Glasses*. These glasses are decorated with deep cuts (*intaglio*) in high relief (*Hochshnitt*), and have been found as far afield as western Germany, Cracow in Poland, Corinth in Greece and Novogrudok in Russia. Hedwig glassware was also included in the fabulous collection of glassware brought to St. Mark's Cathedral in Venice from Constantinople by rapacious Venetian crusaders, an event which will be dealt with in more detail in the next chapter. The name associated with the glassware derives from a miracle ascribed to St. Hedwig, patron saint of Silesia (1174-1243). It seems that St. Hedwig's husband, Duke Heinrich I, convinced that in practicing self-denial his wife had been drinking water which was making her ill, found to his amazement on tasting the water from her glass that it turned to delicious wine in his mouth. Hedwig died in 1243, was canonized St. Hedwig in 1267 and all the glasses of the genre became associated with the miracle. The glass purportedly belonging to the saint who was so divinely served is preserved in the Schlesisches (Silesian) Museum at Breslau.

The provenience of the Hedwig glassware was variously attributed to Egypt, Byzantium, Germany and Gaul, an indication of the ignorance which attended the subject. As new examples of this distinctive ware surfaced, and knowledge of primary glassmaking in Eastern Europe was gained, it became clear that an eastern provenience had to be considered as most likely.[49] The techniques developed in Sassanian Persia are clearly seen to be generative of those employed in the Hedwig glassware, and were forerunners of the same *Hochshnitt* technology which became characteristic of Bohemian glassmaking. The designs cut into a number of the Hedwig glasses are, ironically, typically Jewish, consisting of stylized motifs used as succoth symbols: palm leaves, crescent and star patterns, and figures used symbolically in ancient synagogues. A good example can now be seen in the ancient synagogue of Sardis, featuring a lion, eagle and griffin. A fragment found at Sabrah, south of Tunis, bears a wheel-cut, distinctly Near Eastern motif of two prancing feline quadrupeds with characteristics similar to that of Novogrudok glass.[50]

An outstanding item of the St. Mark's collection is an eleventh century purple glass cup with a silver/gilt mount inscribed on the inside of its rim in pseudo-Cufic letters. Its principal decoration is composed of seven roundels on which profiled heads appear.[51] The roundel technique and style is of Near Eastern origin and appears in various forms on glassware retrieved from the now-familiar itinerary of Near Eastern artisans. A bottle fragment found in Armenia, for example, is clearly of this type.[52] Fine examples without Cufic lettering but with characteristic friezes of squares or roundels decorated gilt or silver enamelled figured or floral designs have been found at Novogrudok and from Corinth; examples were found in Paphos, Cyprus and a tiny but unmistakable fragment found in England demonstrate the wide distribution of glassware of the type and date. Corinth and Constantinople have been proposed as the sites at which this ware was produced. Dr. Shelkovnikov, of the Hermitage Museum in Leningrad, however, identified the material as having been produced in Novogrudok.[53]

The argument regarding provenience in and of itself delineates the relationship between the glassmasters at those disparate sites. Chemical analysis does not readily resolve provenience inasmuch as virtually all the glassware produced to the tenth century was composed of a similar set of elements, following a consistent Near Eastern formula. It is only during and after that time that potash, lixiviated from the wood, bracken and brush of northwestern Europe forests, takes the place of soda. Until that time soda, derived mainly from marine and swamp plants of the West Asian Mediterranean region, had been employed as the main alkaline constituent of glassware produced throughout Christendom. The technique employed in the production of the Hedwig glassware and the composition of the glass indicates that the style was developed in Sassanian Persia and traveled up the great rivers with the Jewish Khazars to flower in Silesia. The far-flung distribution of Hedwig glassware and of the "roundel" glass is a testimony to the widespread commercial market served by the Khazars and recalls the itineraries of such traders as the renowned Radhanites.

When the Persian Empire began to disintegrate, and Byzantine conquest no longer depended on Khazar assistance, the Byzantines proceeded with a perfidious plan to destroy their erstwhile ally and savior. The plot to destroy the nation which had converted to Judaism was fully outlined early on by Constantine in a dissertation on *How War is to be Made on Khazaria and by Whom.* Constantine expounded on how surrounding peoples as well as dissident peoples within the Khazarian domain could be encouraged to rip apart the Jewish empire. Toynbee, generally an admirer of Constantine, puts this patently devious scheme into historical perspective.

> If this passage in Constantine Portphyrogebitus's manual for the conduct of the East Roman Imperial Government's foreign relations ever fell into the hands of the Khazar Khagan and his ministers, they would have been indignant. They would have pointed out that nowadays, Khazaria was one of the most pacific states in the world, and that, if she had been more warlike in her earlier days, her arms had never been directed against the East Roman Empire. The two powers had, in fact, never been at war with each other, while, on the other hand, Khazaria had frequently been at war with the East Roman Empire's enemies, and this to the Empire's signal advantage. Indeed, the Empire may have owed it to the Khazars that she had survived the successive onslaughts of the Sassanid Persian Emperor Khusraw II Parviz and the Muslim Arabs.[54]

The principle of "divide and conquer" was applied by the Byzantines with consummate duplicity; the Byzantines had no compunction about secretly encouraging the pagan, primitive Rus tribes to invade Khazar territory from the north. The city of Kiev had by that time become a great commercial center, a rich and tempting prize, and it was offered by the Byzantines as bait to the Rus. They were easily persuaded to overrun it. The break of the Rus with the Khazars commenced with the occupation of Kiev by the Rus in the year 862. The bribing of the Rus with the thriving metropolis of Kiev was the first step toward the implementation of the Constantine plan.

Commercial and cultural relations nevertheless continued between the Rus and the Khazars until Prince Svyatoslav of Kiev destroyed Itil, circa 965. An old Russian chronicle relates that a group of Jews arrived in Kiev in the year 986 in an frustrated attempt to convert Vladimir, a dissolute son of the prince who, like his father before him had accepted baptism after a pagan beginning.[55] It can be surmised that their failure was due to an inability of the Jews to counter the rich spoils dangled before the eyes of the prince by the Byzantines. Acceptance of Christianity proved to be a pragmatic tactic which eventually gained the Rus control over all the territory west to the Urals and south to the great inland seas.

After the year 988, the year in which the pagan Russian dynastic rulers adopted the Greek Orthodox faith, relations between the Rus and the Khazars inevitably deteriorated. During that same period the other Slavic and Scandinavian peoples converted to the Latin Church of Rome. The decay of the Abbasid (Persian) Empire during the tenth century removed the Byzantine fear of the Persians and rendered the Khazars superfluous as a buffer state. "Constantinople offered it as bait to the Russians, who promptly seized the opportunity to invade it."[56] The Byzantines welded their duplicitous alliance with the Rus by bribing them with the promise of further spoils, especially by ceding possession of the important Crimean port of Cherson, until then under contention between them. The new era was heralded by a continued encroachment of the Rus into Khazaria, incursions previously discouraged but now fully supported by the Byzantines. In the year 1016, the Byzantine and Rus forces joined in a massive invasion of Khazaria.

Khazarian integrity, already seriously affected by Russian incursions and Byzantine belligerence was further aggravated as a result of a concordance between the Byzantine emperor Leo and the fierce *Magyars*, immigrant Turkic tribes from the east who had absorbed the native Finns. The Byzantines encouraged the ravenous Magyars to assail the Bulgars, allies of the Khazars, from the rear. The Magyars invaded and integrated into the area to become modern-day Hungarians.

The artisans of Kiev now found themselves completely under Russian rule. The conversion of the Rus and Slavic tribal heads to Christianity and the military alliances formed with the Byzantines against the Khazars stemmed the influx of artisans but did not bring the practice of the crafts they had introduced to a halt. The communities of Jews in Kiev, as well as in numerous Jewish colonies in the Ukraine and southern Russia were tolerated, inasmuch as they were essential for bringing wealth into and maintaining the industry of the region. In Perislavl and Cernigov major Jewish communities continued to carry on commerce and crafts. The multiplicity of Khazar and Jewish eponymic names of ancient towns of the western Russian areas testify dramatically to a continuous and pervasive urban Jewish presence: Zydowo, Kozarzewek, Kozara, Kozarzow, Zhydowska Vola, Zydaticze,[57] to mention but a few. The Jews were, however, understandably uncomfortable under the hegemony of the Russians. A movement of glassmakers into Silesia (now Poland) and western Russia ensued; they were enticed by the newly rising feudal noblemen of western Russia and Silesia with forest privileges and sundry other inducements to immigrate into their fiefs.

Julia Scapova, whose valuable research on tracing the origin of Polish glass has added much to our understanding, determined that: "It isn't until near the end of the first millennium of our era that the eastern Slavs achieved its own developed and specialized character." Recognizing the difficulty of fixing the provenience of Polish and Russian glassmaking, Scapova noted that art of the region "found autonomy by a complicated route" and assumed that the art was "incontestably linked to that of Byzantia."[58] The art of glassmaking did indeed arrive by convoluted routes but they were far more tangled than Scapova had envisioned. The advent of the art was linked in the first place to the north-westward movement of the Jewish Khazars up along the great Russian rivers; second to a movement of artisans northward from Byzantium and third to a flow of artisans from Western Europe. The routes are readily recognized when they are set in apposition to those taken by the Jews from the three directions into the Silesian pale of settlement.

Maria DeKowna of the Institute of Material Culture of the Polish Academy of Sciences in Warsaw, another scholar who has delved deeply into the subject of glassmaking points out that the development of the Polish glassmaking industry took place in two stages. During the first stage, which took place roughly from the sixth to the end of the ninth century, the artisans came into Silesia (the future Poland) from Khazar and Byzantine territory. "The principal glassmaking centers were concentrated in the East," principally in Constantinople, Thessalonica on the European continent, Sardis in Anatolia as well as in the still flourishing ancient centers in Eretz Israel, Mesopotamia and North Africa (that is, Alexandria and the Fustat).[59]

Another leg of the complicated route by which glassmaking reached the Slavic peoples, referred to by Scapova and emphasized by DeKowna, stretched across northern Germany, the same route being traversed by the

Jews fleeing persecution during the ninth through the thirteenth centuries. The miserably few glassmakers who remained in Gaul and Germany until the ninth centuries attempted to carry on with their traditional soda-glass formulas, employing soda derived from marine plants of the West Asian region, which had been employed in spite of the difficulties caused by the Teutonic incursions. "There was no real change in glassmaking or in glassmaking ingredients up to the ninth century at least, if not the tenth."[60]

While the Jewish glassmakers of the Cologne region were exempted from conversion and the restrictions the church had imposed upon most other crafts, they found themselves isolated from their co-religionists in the wider Diaspora. Two fifth-sixth century furnaces excavated at Macquenoise[61] near the Franco-Belgian frontier south of Charleroi exemplify the isolated circumstances of such communities. Other traces of furnaces of the seventh-ninth centuries were found at Cordel near Treves, a city which still harbored a sizable Jewish community at the time. The Near Eastern soda-lime formulas were still employed by all the glass manufactories of the region.[62] The glassmakers were bound to the church for a market for most of their products, as is made amply evident by the virtually complete discontinuance of glassware in grave-goods of the period recovered from north France and the Rhineland after those lands became Christian.[63] Two factors impelled these glassmakers to move eastward: the invitation of the Silesian princes to the Jews to immigrate into their domains and the opportune arrival of the Khazars in the Baltics through Kiev.

A community located in Haithabu, north of Cologne in a forested area of the narrows of the Jutland peninsula, provided the material with which the movement of glassmakers to the east could be traced. DeKowna reported on the investigation of the relationship of this community to the Silesian glass-making industry at an International Glass Conference held in 1977.[64] Glassmaking was already flourishing in Haithabu by 800 C.E. and the art continued until 1050 when the site was burned by invading forces. Glassware from the Ardennes, Cologne and Haithabu found its way into Frisia and as far as Sweden.[65] Haithabu was situated on the main commercial land route between Cologne and Kiev and on the sea route which led to Novogorod. The roads connecting Cologne, Haithabu, Kiev and Novogorod delineate the precise routes taken by the Jews in their migrations into the Polish pale of settlement from the East and the West.

The strategic importance of the neck of the Jutland peninsula on that route generated successive conflicts between the Danish, Swedish and German kings over control of the area. "The population of Haithabu was characterized by a great ethnical diversity, reflecting its role as a grand international emporium."[66] Haithabu's situation as a commercial crossroads engendered a proliferation of crafts and industry; in 1913 a glassmaking furnace was identified in an extensive artisan's quarter, and in 1973 the Polish Institute of Science joined the Schleswig Museum in an expedition, one of the purposes of which was to study the relationship of the glassware being recovered from Haithabu graves and workshops to glassware produced in Poland. Important facts emerged from the analysis of the material: potash and natron (natural soda) came into use at the end of this period, a change brought about by the difficulties of importing raw materials from the Mediterranean region; a close relationship existed between the activity in Haithabu and that of the blossoming of the glass industry of the Baltic region,[67] where potash thereafter appears as an ingredient of a fair proportion of the glassware being produced.

The route from Germany across Silesia which potash-glass followed into the land of the Khazars was also one of the important links of the route by which the Jews of the Rhineland and northern Europe kept in contact with the center of Jewish authority in Babylonia. This ongoing relationship had old historic roots. The favorable circumstances which the Jews had enjoyed under Charlemagne enabled them to freely travel and even settle into the Rhineland in spite of the morose attitude of the German ecclesiastics. The towns of Magdeburg, Meresburg and Ratisbon, for example, hosted well-organized Jewish communities of Jews originating from Gaul.[68] The changes of circumstances after the Church re-established repressive policies in Gaul and especially in the ensuing period of the Crusades, however, forced the Jews to flee. Some went eastward over the Oder into Bohemia (now the western portion of Czechoslovakia) and others into Silesia (now the southwestern portion of Poland, contiguous to Bohemia), areas into which the Jews from the East were likewise trading and settling, and into which they were warmly welcomed by the newly constituted noblemen of the area.

The route across northern Germany was one of several the Jews were obliged to establish to meet the exigencies of the period. The sweep of Arab conquest had dropped a curtain between the Mohammedan and the Christian worlds which even Jewish merchants could not always penetrate; the Crusades recurrently made a trip down the Rhineland hazardous; the piracy practiced by Arab ships made the Mediteranean sea lanes insecure. "Even when there was no full-fledged war, the sea was in the hands of Arab fleets. They would capture the ships, seize the merchandise and sell the captives into slavery."[69] Two main land routes continued to be traversed, one leading through Byzantium and Syria and the other across northern Germany (Haithabu) to Prague, Galicia and Kiev and down along the western shore of the Caspian through the Darband gates now secured by Khazar forces. Travel along the Byzantine route to Jerusalem is dramatically illustrated by the assistance given a Jew of Kiev by the leaders of the community at Thessalonica.[70] However, the conflict between the Byzantines and the Khazars precluded passage through Byzantium during certain periods, as was evidenced by the aborted attempt of Hasdai Ibn Shaprut to reach the Khazars and his subsequent reversion to a circuitous route in order to do so.

It was at this time that the Polish nation was formed, and the Jews were central to its formation. Polish, Ukrainian and Russian nobility proffered refuge to Jews escaping Western European persecution and created an environment in which a new organic social structure emerged, the *shtetl* civilization, a fully articulated, organic nation within a nation. A rich store of early Polish legends exists, persistent in spite of being regarded as next to blasphemous by churchmen and as bourgeois Zionist [!] propaganda by the Soviets. Although lacking documentation, these Polish folk tales retain elements which illuminate the significant contribution made by Jews in the formation of the Polish nation. The very creation of the Polish nation is attributed to a legendary Jew, Abraham Prokownik. The Polans were the mightiest of several Slavonic tribes who formed an alliance around the year 962. Having concluded that they needed a king to rule over them all who was capable of creating a viable state, the "Slav backwoodsmen" elected Abraham to that office. "Abraham with unwonted modesty, resigned the crown, in favour of a native peasant named Piast, who thus became the founder of the historic Piast dynasty which ruled Poland from *circa* 962 to 1370."

However sound is the basis for the legends thus circulating among the Poles, the fact is that the princes of the culturally and economically under-developed Silesian region heartily welcomed Jewish craftsmen and merchants of all sorts from Germany, Armenia and Khazaria. The Jews were granted extraordinary privileges, which continued in force into modern times in spite of Christian adherence by the local barons, Byzantine-Russian perfidy and the series of restrictive edicts and proclamations issued by the church bodies and the papacy itself. The Jewish towns, large and small, became industrious craft centers and trading posts from which the people of the surrounding hinterlands, populated by peasants working on the estates of Polish noblemen, obtained locally made and imported products. Fairs were regularly held in which farm products, timber, products manufactured in the towns and in rural cottage industries and imported wares were exchanged. These local trade centers were integrated into a free market network which spanned across the borders of the fiefs of noblemen and nations. The metal working acumen of the Jews had provided them with the obligation of minting coins for most of the rulers of central Europe, a trade which remained in the hands of Jews for many centuries. Polish silver coins of the twelfth or thirteenth centuries bear Polish inscriptions in Hebrew lettering.

> These coins are the final evidence for the spreading of the Hebrew script from Khazaria to the neighboring Slavonic countries. The use of these coins were not related to any question of religion. They were minted because many of the Polish people were more used to this type of script than to the Roman script, not considering it as particularly Jewish.[71]

The economy of the region boomed and the position of the Jews was solidified by King Boleslav the Pious, who issued a charter in 1264 which became a model charter for securing Jewish freedom of opportunity and security from molestation. The terms were reconfirmed and extended by Casimir the Great in 1354, under the influence of Esther, his mistress of ravishing beauty. The Jews were granted the right to maintain their own synagogues, schools and courts; to rent estates, even from the nobility and the priesthood, to hold property in mortgage, and to engage in any trade or occupation they chose. King Stephen Bathory (1575-1586) granted the Jews the right to form a parliament of their own, creating a virtual state within a state; the Jewish parliament met twice a year and had the power to legislate civil law for and levy taxes on their own co-religionists.[72] By the mid-17th century Poland contained a population of more than a 500,000 Jews.

Among the Jews there were those who served the nobles as physicians, managers of estates, accountants, tax collectors and bankers, but by far the vast majority were blacksmiths, silversmiths, tailors, millers, wheelwrights, bakers and candlestick makers; they were scribes who wrote letters for the illiterate; they ran the inns at which merchant/travelers found respite; they were the carters who brought the local goods to market and ranged abroad to barter for goods produced in neighboring *shtetls*; they were bards, itinerant story tellers, troupes of actors and singers; they created a new rich culture which drew from the experiences gained from all the lands from which they migrated or were ejected. Prominent among these artisans were the glassmakers.

The word employed in the Slavic and Romanian (Italic or Latinate) languages for "glass" identifies the artisans who brought the technology to Silesia and to the lower Danube Basin. The Hebrew word, rendered in English as *zakhukhit*, derives from the root *zakhai* (pure, clear) or *zakhit* (purity or clarity). The Hebrew *zakhit* also translates to "frit" and traces back through Aramaic to an Akkadian origin (*zaku*). The Hebrew spelling does not include the vowel "a": it is close in actual pronunciation to its transliteration into the various Slavic vernaculars:

| **Polish** | **Czech** | **Serbo-Croat** | **Russian** |
|---|---|---|---|
| *Szklo* | *Szklo* | *Sklo* | *Staklo* |

The identity of the glassmaking artisans of the Danube Basin is further indicated by the fact that the Romanians, who employ an Italic language, render "glass" as *steklo*, rather than as the Latinate *vitrum*.[73] The fact that the knowledge of glassmaking flowed eastward through Transylvania into Hungary is borne out not only chemically and stylistically but etymologically. The Hungarian (and Magyar) word for glass is *uveg*. This word is not Magyar (of Finnish or Mongolian origin as are the Hungarian people), but is adapted from *avg*, an Ossetian word for glass.[74] The Ossetians were descended from the Sarmatian Alan tribes, allies of the Khazars and whose homeland bordered on Persia. It is noted that "In the Hungarian language many notions are expressed by words of Iranian-Alanian origin, and the word *uveg* has this source."[75] The homeland of the allies of the Khazars, the Alans, was the region into which Jews migrated across the Caucasus from Persia and in which glassmaking first appeared in southeast Russia. The etymological evidence for the introduction of glassmaking into the various regions is thereby fulfilled for the entire Eastern European region which was at one time or another under Khazar control.

The glassmaking industry of Russia, which continued almost unabated after the Russians captured Kiev from the Khazars, was extinguished by the

Mongol invasion which brought about the final demise of the Khazar kingdom as well as the enclaves of glassmakers in that area. "The Mongol conquest of Kievan Russia dealt a crushing blow to the glass industry."[76] After the period of devastation passed the glassmaking industry revived, for the Mongols were tolerant of the Jews, and the Jewish enclaves of such towns as Kiev, Novogorod and of Poland revived as important centers of Jewish commerce and learning. Rabbis of international reputation were established at Kiev and Novgorod, notes Cecil Roth, following "the extension of the area of settlement northwards into what is now Poland."[77] The Polish glassmaking industry was also resuscitated by a fresh influx of glassmakers, mainly from Germany, and remained in Jewish hands until the Nazis massacred its members.

Glassmakers also came to Poland from Samarkand in this later period. The Jewish community of Samarkand survived the Mongol invasion and continued its involvement in glassmaking and in silk horticulture and manufacturing. It was from Samarkand, the bustling metropolis athwart the fabled silk route to China, that Zvi Hillel Bezborodko, a member of that ancient Jewish community, followed the path marked out by the Khazars more than half a millennium earlier across southern Russia and up the Dnieper River to Silesia.[78] Zvi's destination was Slutsk, a small town which lay on the western border of Russia and which harbored a Jewish community of high cultural reputation; it was one of the many centers of Talmudic study in western Russia and Poland to which Jews living at the ends of the earth sent their sons to learn at the feet of great rabbis, teachers whose reputation for profundity and erudition became bywords throughout the Diaspora. It was the ardent desire of Zvi that his son, Chaim, would become the *Chochem Bashi*, the chief rabbi, of the four central Asian districts (Samarkand, Tashkent, Bukhara and Kiva) of which Samarkand was the administrative center.

In the year 1802 Zvi sent his son to complete his studies at the renowned yeshiva of the city of Slutsk. Chaim gained his ordination with honors and fell in love with Pearl, the daughter of his teacher, one of the learned and revered rabbis. Pearl and Chaim were married about the year 1808. Chaim did not return to Samarkand to fulfill his father's dream; he decided to stay in Slutsk. He established a silk business, based partly on the import of velour through Danzig, and soon became successful enough to encourage the entire family to join him in Slutsk. It was a difficult move, for at that time

One of the earliest representations (1023 CE) of a gaffer (glassblower) at work. From Hrabanus Maurus, *De Universo*, Library of the Abbey of Monte Cassino, Codex 132.

the only way one could travel in safety was by joining a caravan. Great assemblages of traders would gather in Samarkand with their goods laded on camels and asses, transferred to river traffic as soon as it was feasible, and ended up in Europe with their goods on the backs of horses. It took a caravan three months to cross Russia from the heart of Asia to the Baltic region.

It was a troublesome time. In 1810 Napoleon's armies tramped through and occupied most of Russia, but the Bezborodko family squeezed through in time to evade the French army. Three of Chaim's brothers were included in the Bezborodko entourage. The name of Zvi's second son was forgotten

Gaffers at the glory holes of a furnace of the 16th century. Note the annealing chamber installed above the fire-pit. From Vanoccio Birincuccio, *De la Pirotechnica*, Venice, 1540.

by the family because he became a renegade writer and philosopher who rejected Jewish values and tradition. The third son, Israel, also became a silk merchant; but the youngest son, who was also named Zvi Hillel, 19 years younger than Israel, was an ambitious young man and wished to become independent of brotherly domination. Having been fascinated by the glassmaking industry as a boy in Samarkand, he looked around for an opportunity to create his own glassworks. Noting that glass lamp bases and chimneys were being imported from Bohemia at great cost he decided to create a facility in Slutsk for their production.

Zvi went to work at a glass factory owned by a Jewish acquaintance in

Bohemia, and returned 15 months later with a few master Jewish glassmakers to set up a glass factory in a thickly wooded area about 70 kilometers from Slutsk. At the time there was nothing more than a railroad station to identify the place as Hancjewicze. It was on the Polish border, and has since passed back and forth under Russian and Polish hegemony. The glassworks at Hancjewicze fired its furnaces in the year 1866 and was the first of seven glassmaking enterprises subsequently established in the former "Silesian" region by the Bezborodko family. The businesses were often registered under non-Jewish names because the proscription against the harvesting of wood from the forests by Jews was strictly enforced during recurrent traumatic periods. The subterfuge of employing a Christian cover was necessary because the vast quantities of fuel required for the operation of the furnaces depended on absolving the noblemen from the responsibility of ignoring the restrictive decrees.

Nevertheless, the Bezborodkos constructed glass manufactories along the Nieman River near Vilna; in Lithuania; in Latvia; on the Finnish border in Jarelia; one outside of St. Petersburg and two in St. Petersburg itself. The tradition of allowing only Jewish masters and their relatives to work at the furnace was strictly observed. It may be that one of the Jewish lads who was allowed to work at the furnace of a Bezborodko glasshouse was a cousin of the author, Chaim Cherches, who was employed at a Jewish-owned glass factory near Vilna in the early 1930s, the name of which he has since forgotten. Chaim made *Aliyah* to Israel just before the Nazi invasion, changed his name to the Hebrew Nachshon, joined the Hagganah and became an accountant.

Chaim Churches leading the celebration parade held immediately after the creation of the State of Israel. He is holding aloft the new flag of Israel before the reviewing stand on which Ben Gurion, Israel's new President, and other dignitaries stand. Chaim left his job in a glasshouse in Poland and made his way to Israel as a Zionist pioneer before World War II and thus narrowly escaped being caught up in the holocaust. Until that time virtually all of the glass manufactories of Poland were still owned by Jews and operated by Jewish masters. Both the owners and the masters disappeared during the traumatic period which followed the Nazi invasion; over 30 of Chaim's closest relations also disappeared.

# NOTES

1. Maria DeKowna, "Remarques sur les Methodes d'Examen de Perles de Verre du Haut Moyen Age Trouvees en Pologne," *Bulletin of the Fourth International Congress on Glass*, 1967, p. 151.

2. D. M. Dunlop, *The History of the Jewish Khazars*, 1954, p. x.

3. David D. Weinryb, "The Khazars, an Annotated Bibliography," in *Studies in Bibliography and Booklore*, vol. XI, 1976, p. 57.

4. Weinryb, Ibid., p. 58, Amelander, *Menachem ben Solomon Ha-Levi*, Yiddish, Amsterdam, 1741, new ed., Hebrew, by Haim Hominer, Jerusalem 1964.

5. Alush Naji, *Al-Masira Ila Filastin* (The Journey to Palestine), 1964; Al-Nashashibi, Nasir al-Din, *Tadhh-karat 'Awda* (Return Ticket), 1962, adds to his argument his assumption that such Eastern European Jews as Ben-Gurion, Ben-Zwi, Dizengoff and Sharret were Khazars.

6. United Nations Special Committee on Palestine, *Report to the General Assembly*, vol. 2, 1947. Sir Rahman argued that the Jew's claim of returning to the land of their ancestors cannot be made by people of the Turco-Finn race who had converted to Judaism about 690 A.D.

7. Ya. Miranovich, *Zapiski o Malorosii*, (Notes on Little Russia [i.e., Ukrainia]), 1789, reprinted in *Regestry i Nadpisi* (Regests and Inscriptions), St. Petersburg, 1913, no. 2450: (Weinryb, ibid., p. 69).

8. *Pravda*, as quoted in the *Times* of January 12, 1952.

9. Koestler, Ibid., p. 94. The abject statements which appear were obviously dictated by the "party line" and written with distaste: "The Khazar kingdom disintegrated and fell into pieces, from which the majority merged with other peoples, and the minority, settling in Itil, lost its nationality and turned into a parasitic class with a Jewish coloration....From the Itil Khazars the Russians took nothing. Thus also by the way the militant Khazar Judaism was treated by other peoples connected with it: the Magyars, Bulgars, Pechenegs, Alans and Polovtsians....Those insignificant eastern elements in Rus culture which were passed down by the Khazars...did not penetrate into the heart of Russian culture, but remained on the surface and were of short duration and small significance."

10. I. Ya. Krachkovski, *Puteshestvie Ibn-Fadlana na Volgu* (The Travels of Ibn Fadlana in the Volga Region), Moscow, 1939; (Weinryb, Ibid., p. 67).

11. *Judaism* 13, (1964), pp. 431-443, "Solving the Khazar Problem. A Study in Soviet Historiography"; (Weinryb, Ibid., p. 74).

12. V. T. Pasuto and Yu. A. Polokov "Voprosi Istorii SSR na XIII mezhdunarodnom Kongrese Istorikov" (Problems of History of the USSR at the Thirteenth International Congress of Historians), *Istoriya SSR*, 1971, no. 1, pp. 9-10; (Weinrub, Ibid., pp. 69-70).

13. "Solving the Khazar Problem. A Study in Soviet Historiography," *Judaism*, 13, 1964, pp. 431-443.

14. John O. Beatty, *The Iron Curtain Over America*, Dallas, 1951, Chapters III, IV, "Russia and the Khazars," and "The Khazars Join the Democratic Party."

15. Al-Musudi, *Muruf al-Dhabad* (Meadows of Gold) II.

16. *Benjamin of Tudela*, edited by Marcus Nathan Adler, reprinted 1964.

17. *Travels of Petachya of Regensburg* (in Hebrew), first edition, Prague, 1595.

18. Martin Gilbert, *Atlas of Jewish History*, who was evidently quoting from al-Musudi, *Meadows of Gold Mines and Precious Stones*.

19. Eliyahu Ashtor, from Abraham B. Daud, pp. 42, 49, 68, 73 (translation pp. 57, 67, 93, 102); *tahkmoni* p. 179. See Luzzato, p. 27.

20. A. A. Abdurazakov, M. A. Bezborodov, Ju. A. Zadneprovskij, *L'arte verrier d'Asia centrale dans l'antiquite et au moyen age*, Tashkent, p. 236.

21. C. de Boor, editor, *Theophanis Chronographia*, 1963, p. 357, and M. J. de Goeje, editor: Ibn al-Faqih, *Compendium Libri Kitab al-Boldan*, 1885, p. 271.

22. D. M. Dunlop, *The History of the Jewish Khazars*, p. 160.

23. DeKowna, Ibid., p. 122; S. A. Trudnovskaja, "Steklo s gorodisca Sach-Senem," *Archeologiceskie i Etnograficeskie raboty chorezmskoj Ekspedicii 1949-1953*, Moscow, 1953, pp. 421-430 (The glass and the ancient fortification of Sach-Senem); A. A. Abdurazakov, M. A. Bezborodov, J. A. Zadneprovskij, *Steklodelie srednej Azii v drevnosti i srednevekov'e*, Tashkent, 1963, pp. 95-106 (The glasshouses of Central Asia in antiquity and the Middle Age); M. A. Bezborodov and A. A. Abdurazakov, Ibid., pp. 64-69.

24. DeKowna, Ibid., p. 119: R. A. Bachtadze, "Kissledovoniju stekol feodal'noj Gruzii;" (Study of Feudal Georgian Glass), *Vestnik Gosudarstvennogo Muzeja Gruzii im. akad. S.N. Dzanasija*, XX.A, 1960, pp. 12-31, in Georgian, summary in Russian.

25. DeKowna, Ibid., p. 117: G.G. Lemmlein, "Ostatki stekloduvnogo proizvodstva v Karsani bliz Mccheta," (Remains of glass production at Karsani near Mccheta) *Soobscenija Akademii Nauk Gruzinskoj SSR*, VI, 1945, no. 9, pp. 751-752, in Georgian, summarized in Russian.

26.  N. N. Ugrelidze, *The Glass of Ancient Georgia*, Tbilisi, 1961 (in Georgian, cited by Bezborodov and Abdurazakov, Ibid.).

27.  Jindrich Cadik, "De l'Evangile de Saint Matthiew a la Russie Medievale," *Annals of the Fifth International Congress on Glass*, 1970, p. 49.

28.  Abba Eban, *My People*, 1968, p. 149.

29.  Arthur Koestler, Ibid., p. 85.

30.  Koestler, Ibid., quoting A. Bartha, *A IX-X Szazadi Magyar Tarsadalom* (Hungarian Society in the Ninth-Tenth Centuries), 1968, p. 184).

31.  DeKowna, Ibid., p. 122;  N. N. Ugrelidze, "Natbeurskaja steklodelatel'naja masterkaja," (The glass shop of Natbeuri), *Materialy po archeologija Gruzii i Kavkaza*, III, 1963, pp. 67-68, in Georgian, summary in Russian; G. A. Lomtatidze, "Rezul'taty i perspektivy archeologiceskoyia izucenija goroda Tbilisi," (The results of the research at Tbilisi), *Sovetskaja Archeologija*, 1959, no. 4, pp. 71-72.

32.  Koestler, Ibid., p. 48.

33.  Dunlop, Ibid., p. 231, quoting T. J. Arne, "La Suede et l'Orient," *Archives d'Etudes*, 1914.

34.  M. A. Bezborodov and A. A. Ardurazakov, "Newly Excavated Glassworks in the USSR, Third-Fourteenth Centuries A.D.," *JGS*, VI, 1964, pp. 67-69.

35.  A. N. Poliak, "The Khazar Conversion to Judaism," (in Hebrew), *Zion*, Jerusalem, 1941 as given by Koestler, Ibid., p. 146, who notes that the data regarding the Mountain Jews appearance in A. H. Kniper's article "Caucasus, People of" in the 1973 printing of the *Encyclopedia Brittanica* is based on recent Soviet sources.  A book by George Sava, *Valley of the Forgotten People* (London, 1946), contains a description of a purported visit to the Mountain Jews.

36.  M. A. Bezborodov, *Glassmaking in Ancient Russia*, Minsk, 1956, p. 80.

37.  Bezborodko and Abdurazakov, Ibid., p. 65.

38.  Bezborodov and Abdurazakov, Ibid., 1964, p. 64.

39.  M. A. Bezborodov and A. A. Abdurazakov, "Newly Excavated Glassworks in the USSR, 32rd-14th centuries A.D.," *JGS*, VI, 1964, p. 64; V. V. Khvoiko, *Early Dwellers of the Middle Dniepr Region and Their Culture in Prehistoric Times*, Kiev, 1913, translator, E. B. Gordon; V. A. Bogusevich, "Archeological Excavations, 1950, in Podolia, Kiev," *Brief Reports of the Archeological Institute of the Ukrainian USSR*, no. 41, 1951; "Glass and Salt Works of Eleventh Century Kiev," *Brief Reports of the Archeological Institute of the Ukrainian S.S.R.*, no. 3, 1954.

40.  V. I. Dovzhenok, "Ancient Village and City Sites near Early Galitch," *Brief Reports of the Archeological Institute of the Ukrainian S.S.R*, no. 4, 1955.

41.  DeKowna, Ibid., p. 122.

42. The documents concerning the glass factory built by the Khazars were examined and attested to David Bezborodko by his father, as related in David's monograph, *An Insider's View of Jewish Pioneering in the Glassmaking Industry*, Gefen Pub., Jerusalem, 1987, p. 63. David traveled throughout central Europe in connection with his family's business. He had an abiding interest in Jewish-vitric history and accumulated two full file cabinets of copies of documents and other information during the 1920's and early 1930s regarding the origin of the glassmaking establishmets, including reports on interviews with the principals of those establishments. The files, stored in his home in Paris, disappeared under Nazi occupation. In 1951 David retraced his steps, only to find that the archives he had delved into had similarly disappeared. His monograph was compiled largely from memory.

43. Bezborodko, Ibid., Prologue.

44. Dan Klein and Ward Lloyd, *The History of Glass*, 1984, p. 53.

45. Klein, et. al, idem.

46. Bezborodko, Ibid., p. 64.

47. DeKowna, Ibid, p. 122; 47.22 J. Olczak, E. Jasiewiczowa, *Szklarstwo wczesnosredniowiecznego Wolina* (The medieval glasshouse of Wolin), summary in English, 1963; J. Olczak, "Stan badan nad sklarstwem wecznosredniowiecznej Slowianszczyzny" (The State of research on the glasshouses of the Upper Middle Ages in Slavic countries), summary in French, *Slavia Antiqua*, XI, 1964, pp. 320-324.

48. Slawomira Ciepela (Musee Historique de la Ville de Varsovie), "La Verre en Pologne a la Fin du Moyen Age," *Bulletin of the Fifth International Congress on Glass*, 1970, citing: A. Wyrobisz, *Szklo w Polsce od XIV do XVII wieku* (Glass in Poland from the fourteenth to the seventeenth century), 1968; L. Olczak, "Warsztat szklarski z XIII-XIV wierku odkryty przez archeologow w Miedzyrezeczu Wielkopolskim," (A glasshouse of the thirteenth-fourteenth centuries discovered by the archeologists at Miedzyrzeczu Wielkopolskim), *Szklo i Ceramica* VIII, 1957, no. 9, pp. 229-231.

49. B. A. Shekkovnikov, "Russian Glass of the Eleventh to the Seventeenth Century," *JGS*, VIII, 1966, pp. 109-112.

50. Rouen, Ibid., p. 95, citing R. H. Smith, *Ars Orientalis*, II, 1957, 98f., fig. A, citing previous publication by G. Marcais and L. Poinssot.

51. Rouen, Ibid., p. 98-100C, citing J. Lamm, *Mittelalterliche Glaser und Steinschnittarbeit aus dem nahen Osten*, 2 vols. 1930, 107f. pl. 34, no. 1; J. Phillipe, *Le Monde byzantin dans le histoire de la verrerie, v-xvi siecle*, 1970, pp. 53-54; A. Grabar, "la Verrerie d'art byzantine au moyen age," *Monuments Piot*, LVII 1971, 90-94, figs. 1-4.

52. Rouen, Ibid., pp. 99-100, citing A. H. Megaw, "More gilt and enameled glass from Cyprus," *JGS*, X, 1968, 97, fig. 16.

53. Rouen, Ibid., p. 100, cites Megaw, Djanpoladian and Grabar as favoring Constantinople, whereas Davidson proposes Corinth. Shelkovnikov ascribes the production of the ware to a Novogrudok factory.

54. A. Toynbee, *Constantine Porphyrogenitus and His World*, 1973, p. 508.

55. Koestler, Ibid., p. 129, referring to *Russian Primary Chronicle*, Laurentian text, translator and editor S. H. Cross and Sherbowitz-Wetzor, Cambridge, Mass., 1953.

56. Abba Eban, *My People*, 1968, p. 150

57. Koestler, Ibid., p. 145. Also mentioned are case histories like that of a Rabbi Mosheh of Kiev who studied in France around 1160, a Rabbi Abraham of Chernigov who studied in 1181 in the Talmud school of London, and Jews who became integrated into Russian culture such as the contemporary Russian poet Kogan (possibly a combination of Cohen and Kagan); S. W. Baron, *A Social and Religious History of the Jews,* vol. IV, 1957, p. 9.

58. Julia Leonidovna Scapova, "Apparition de la verrerie chez les Slaves Orientaux," *Rapports du IIIe Congres Internationale d'Archeologie Slave*, Tome II, 1975, p. 385.

59. Maria DeKowna, "Etude sur les Origenes de la Verrerie en Pologne," *Bulletin of the Third International Conference on Glass*, 1964, p. 116.

60. D. B. H. Rouen, *Ancient Glass*, 1972, p. 87.

61. Rouen, Ibid., pp. 87-88, citing R. Chambon and H. Arbman "Deux fours a verre d'epoque merovingienne a Macquenoise (Belgique)," *Bulletin de la Societa royale des Lettres de Lund*, VII, 1951-1952, p. 199 ff.

62. DeKowna, Ibid., p. 119

63. Rouen, Ibid., p. 91.

64. Maria Dekowna, "Le Verres de Hauthabu," report in *Bulletin of the Seventh International Congress of Glass*, 1977, pp. 167.

65. Patrick J. Geary, *Before France and Germany*, 1988, p. 101.

66. DeKowna, Ibid., p. 168.

67. DeKowna, Ibid., p. 187.

68. Heinrich Graetz, *History of the Jews*, 1978, p. 144.

69. Max Weinreich, *History of the Yiddish Language*, Chicago, 1980, pp. 48-52.

70. Andrew Sharf, *Byzantine Jewry*, 1971, p. 116, citing J. Mann, *The Jews in Egypt and in Palestine under the Fatimid Caliphs*, 2 vols., p. 165.

71. Koestler, Ibid., p. 62, quoting Poliak, *The History of a Jewish Kingdom in Europe*, in Hebrew, 1951.

72. Koestler, Ibid., p. 149.

73. Per Isaac E. Mozeson, author of *The Word*, Shapolsky Publishers, N.Y., 1989.

74. Vernadsky, *Ancient Russia*, p. 244, as given by Anita Engles, *Readings in Glass*, no. 5, p. 32.

75. B. Borsos, *Glassmaking in Old Hungary*, as given by Anita Engles, *Readings in Glass*, no. 5, p. 32.

76. Klein, et. al, idem.

77. Cecil Roth, *A History of the Jews*, 1970, p. 265.

78. The history of the Bezborodko enterprises was recounted to the author by David Bezborodko, a direct descendant of Zvi Hillel Bezborodko, in a series of interviews held in 1987 and 1988. David followed in his family's tradition, taking over the business in 1922. He became an expert glassmaking engineer and inventor. David earned 6 medals and gained 22 patents, including a formula which raised the heat resistance of glass from 500 to 25,000 candlepower, used in lenses which made movie projection possible. Bausch and Lomb employ two of David's patents to the present day.

Mi porto da Muran, e tazze, e goti
Bozze, impolete, e veri d'ogni sorte
E togo anca in barato i veri roti.

51

A VENETIAN GLASSWARE VENDER, 18TH CENTURY. The vender of glassware is depicted in the drawing loudly proclaiming in Venetian dialect that he was also a buyer of broken glass and the woman on the stairs is seen rushing to make the sale. Broken glass was traded to glassmakers for use as cullet or to glassware-makers for remelting into new artifacts. An important document concerning such trade figures in the history of the Republic of Genoa; it registers a group of Jewish glassmakers as the exclusive producers of glass and glassware for the entire Republic. In the mid 17th century, Genoa, seeking to stimulate its faltering economy, invited Jews to settle in the city and granted a group of Jewish glassmakers among them the exclusive rights to "produce or have produced glassware and crystal of every kind in all of the dominions of the Republic." The decree also prohibited the sale of broken glass to anyone but the Jewish glassmakers. (See page 382.)

*After a print of the Correr Library of Venice.*

# CHAPTER 11

# THE BYZANTINES

## *The Balkan Connection*

JEWS WERE RESIDENT IN GREECE, MACEDONIA AND ILLYRIA IN THE HELLENIS-
tic period, having arrived at least as early as the fourth century B.C.E. at the
time of Alexander the Great's thrust into the East. Many of these Hellenic
Jews came from the already ancient communities of Anatolia and others from
Eretz Israel. Direct descendants of these early adventurers into the western
Diaspora are known as the *Romaniots*, and they are still to be found speaking
their own Judeo-Greek dialect in Janina, Larissa, Trikkala, Chalcis, Volos,
and especially in Corfu. The Romaniot community is distinct from the
Greco-Jewish community descending from another, later influx of Sephardic
Jews who speak their own distinct language, *Ladino*. The early Jewish
settlers from the East enjoyed autonomy in communal affairs, including their
own system of jurisprudence. Commercial affairs were likewise controlled
by an *ephorus*, a Jewish overseer, who set and controlled market prices,
weights and measures.[1] These standards were not only applicable to internal
Jewish commerce, but to all trade, and particularly to international commercial intercourse. The Romans, and even the first Christian emperors had to
accept this Jewish quasi-governmental authority because the Jews were key
to the conduct of commerce and crafts.

Glassmaking may have been practiced at Corinth on the Peloponnesian
peninsula during the period of Roman hegemony. The circumstances and time
of the introduction of glassmaking into Corinth from the East is unknown,
but glassware-making, if not glassmaking, was certainly practiced on the
Peloponnesian peninsula during the Roman period. It is clear that the
strategically situated city played a central role in the history of glassmaking

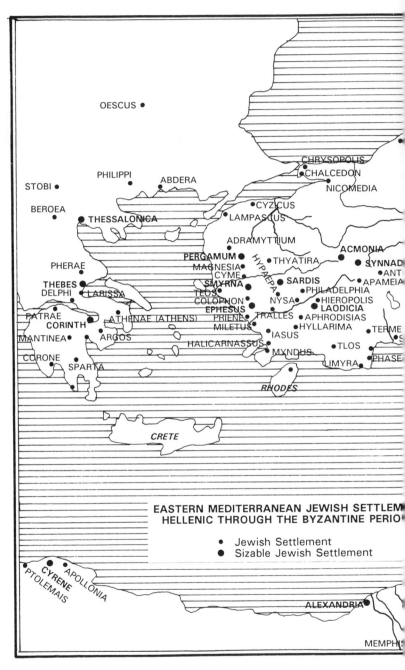

OESCUS •

PHILIPPI •
STOBI •          ABDERA •
BEROEA
        THESSALONICA     CYZICUS •
                        LAMPASCUS •
                    ADRAMYTTIUM •
                                        ACMONIA
        PHERAE •    PERGAMUM •   THYATIRA •   SYNNAD
                    MAGNESIA •                    ANT
        THEBES •    CYME •   SARDIS •    APAMEIA
DELPHI • LARISSA   SMYRNA •  PHILADELPHIA •
                    TEOS •   NYSA •   HIEROPOLIS
        COLOPHON •          LAODICIA
PATRAE •   EPHESUS •   APHRODISIAS
CORINTH • ATHENAE (ATHENS)  PRIENE •  TRALLES   HYLLARIMA
MANTINEA •   ARGOS •   MILETUS •           TERME
CORONE •          IASUS •   TLOS •
        SPARTA •   HALICARNASSUS •       PHASE
                    MYNDUS •   LIMYRA •

                RHODES

            CRETE

**EASTERN MEDITERRANEAN JEWISH SETTLEM
HELLENIC THROUGH THE BYZANTINE PERIO**

● Jewish Settlement
● Sizable Jewish Settlement

CYRENE • APOLLONIA
PTOLEMAIS

                        ALEXANDRIA •

                                MEMPHIS

The Eastern Mediterranean was saturated with a Jewish presence, a sizable portion of the
7,000,000 Jews who populated the Diaspora at the turn of the Common Era.

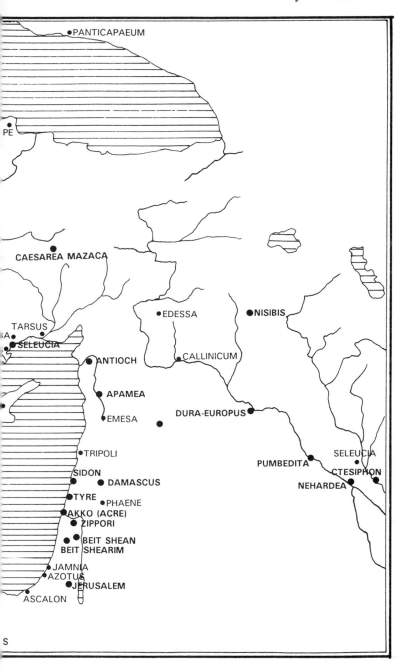

PANTICAPAEUM

PE

CAESAREA MAZACA

EDESSA   NISIBIS

TARSUS
A
SELEUCIA

ANTIOCH   CALLINICUM

APAMEA

EMESA   DURA-EUROPUS

TRIPOLI   SELEUCIA
SIDON   PUMBEDITA   CTESIPHON
DAMASCUS   NEHARDEA
TYRE
PHAENE
AKKO (ACRE)
ZIPPORI
BEIT SHEAN
BEIT SHEARIM
JAMNIA
AZOTUS
JERUSALEM
ASCALON

S

The importance of Jewish communities can be discerned from their concentration at the ports
and industrial centers where they supplied skilled workers and entrepreneurs.

in Greece from the Hellenistic period at a time coincident with the presence of the Jews in the region to the mid-twelfth century, when the Jews were removed by the crusader, Roger II, and the industry disappeared from the peninsula with them.

Rome had been provided with an opportunity to intervene in the area as a consequence of the internecine struggles between members of the Achaean League. Roman pressure spurred Sparta into withdrawing from the league, which precipitated war between the league and Sparta in 146 B.C.E. A force of close to 30,000 Roman soldiers was dispatched under the command of Lucius Mummius, the Roman consul, to assist the Spartans. The league was soundly defeated and Rome was enabled to gain control over Greece and the Peloponnesus. The city of Corinth was of strategic and economic importance; the city controlled the isthmus between mainland Greece and the Peloponnesian peninsula. Julius Caesar designated the city a Roman colony in 44 B.C.E. and renamed it in his honor *Colonia Laus Iulia Corinthiensis*. By this time the devastation wrought by the war had already been erased and Corinth resumed its former central role in the economy of the region. Corinth became the capital of the Roman province of Achaea, which was duly constituted in 27 B.C.E. and placed under the jurisdiction of the Roman Senate; the province included the Peloponnesian peninsula and a major portion of the mainland. Thousands of colonists were thereupon recruited from among the freed slaves of Rome and settled in Corinth; Jewish artisans were a significant proportion of this implanted population. Major reconstruction began and additional thousands of Jews were conscripted from the East by Emperor Nero, who began to dig a canal across the isthmus: "[Nero's] building plans included using as slave labor 6,000 Jewish prisoners captured in the Jewish Revolt in Judea."[2]

The canal would have connected the Adriatic, Ionian and Aegean seas. It was not completed; in fact, it was not until 1893 that a waterway linkage of the two seas was accomplished by the French. Corinth was left with a substantial Jewish population, which, by Roman figures, must have amounted to some 10,000 people. The presence and activity of this community is shrouded in mystery, for the structures in which their affairs were conducted were completely demolished. Pagan and Christian structures were erected with elements torn from these buildings; how much of Byzantine architecture is composed of the elements of Jewish synagogues and other structures will never be known, for Jewish institutions carried few inscriptions and the reused remnants can rarely be identified. Jews erected few monuments and sculpted no statues to God or man. The presence of many communities, even those with a population of thousands of Jews such as that of Corinth are bound to pass unnoted because they cannot be readily perceived in the ancient ruins of pagan buildings, monuments and churches erected with their remnants.

A few identifiable architectural fragments did fortuitously survive to attest to Jewish presence in Corinth. These rare relics were parts of synagogues which served the Corinthian Jewish community into the fifth century, a period in which Jewish structures were destroyed by the hundreds throughout Christendom. On the underside of a marble cornice an inscription in Greek was found: "Synagogue of the Hebrews." A marble impost which "must have also come from a synagogue...is decorated with Jewish ritual objects: three *menorot* (seven-branched candelabra), palm branches (*lulav*) and citron (*etrog*)."[3]

The residential sections of Corinth remain unexcavated. Perhaps, if attention would be diverted from monuments and monumental structures and archeologists were encouraged to delve more deeply into the areas where ordinary people lived and worked, the socio-economic development and demography of the area might be better illuminated, and the critical role played by the Corinthian Jews in the evolution of classic and Byzantine Corinthian civilization might be more thoroughly explicated. As things stand, tantalizing questions are left dangling. What happened to those thousands of Jewish freedmen and slaves, and, we must assume, their families? What were they doing in the four centuries of their residence in the vital Corinthian isthmus? How much of the corpus of "Greek" artifacts can be attributed to the artisans from the East? One fact is clear: primary glassmaking was not among the arts practiced in Greece before the implantation of the Eastern artisans.

Glass(ware)-making disappeared during the succeeding time of turmoil engendered by the creation of the Byzantine entity, but soon after Constantine had become emperor in the East and had designated that city as his capital, Eastern glassmakers were enticed into Byzantium and encouraged to establish furnaces in Constantinople. Constantine exempted *vitriarii* (glassmakers) and *diatretiarii* (glass-carvers) from all public levies in 337 C.E. The Latinized word "Diatretiarii" derives through the Greek from the Hebrew word for "cutter" or "chiseler," referring to the painstaking process of sculpting the outer layer of a thick glass vessel (sometimes of a separate color), then undercutting the design, thereby creating a delicate pattern which is attached at strategic, almost invisible points to the inner, intact portion of the vessel. The word "Diatreton" appears in a Jewish parable of the Midrash which concerns costly and easily broken glass.[4] The technique used in the carving of these labor-intensive vessels (commonly referred to as "cage-cups"), required an application of great skill, meticulous workmanship and infinite patience. They were among the most valuable treasures a rich Roman could boast of possessing, and those Romans who could afford them did in fact publicly boast of their possession.

Byzantium gained another solid core of artisans of the highest quality as a result of the destruction of the synagogues in and the expulsion of the Jews from Alexandria by the patriarch Cyril in the year 415. The Alexandrian holocaust spurred an exodus of artisans and Constantinople benefited from the industrial hiatus created in Alexandria by the fanatical Cyril. Two Alexandrian arts were seriously affected by the drain of artisans: the manufacture of silk and silk products and the manufacture of glass and of glass products. In Egypt the Jewish silk trade had been so integral to the economy that it "fulfilled a function similar to that of stocks and bonds in our own society. In other words, it represented a healthy range of specula-tion, while providing at the same time a high degree of security."[5] The debilitation of the two industries was only temporary, for the destructive measures taken by Cyril were reversed after his passing. In the meantime, however, the burgeoning Byzantine economy was given further impetus by the absorption of a corps of Alexandria's most skilled silkmaking and glassmaking artisans.

The two arts had been practiced side by side in Alexandrian Egypt; they moved together into Byzantine Europe, and remained closely associated thereafter. While silk manufacture was far more visible, since it involved thousands of workers, the production of glass, although also of considerable economic significance, was relegated to a relatively few families who remained privileged with its secrets. The corpus of artisans which actually produced glass and glassware from raw materials always consisted of a tiny proportion of any nation's workforce. Although glassware was being produced earlier in European Byzantium, primary glass manufacture *per se* first becomes visible in Byzantium as a consequence of the immigration of artisans from Eretz Israel in response to Constantine's enactment of liberal laws and as a consequence of a reaction to Cyril's actions against the Jews in North Africa.

Constantinople, Corinth, Thessalonica and Thebes became host to the most productive Jewish communities of the Greco-Byzantine empire. "The Theban Jews were the most skillful manufacturers of silk and purple in the whole of Greece."[6] Benjamin of Tudela later made note of the fact that among the 500 or so Jews at Salonika were many scholars "and they busy themselves in the craft of silk." At Thebes he found "...about 2000 Jews. They are masters at producing silk and purple clothes in the land of the Greeks, and among them are great sages in the Mishnah and Talmud." The estimate refers to two thousand Jewish heads of families and translates to a population of approximately five times that figure.

Thessalonica ran a close second to Thebes as a major silk-producing center and, along with Constantinople and Corinth, boasted of a significant glassmaking industry. Constantinople was home to an additional 500 Jewish Karaite families, who lived in an area separated by a wall from the quarters of the 2000 other Jewish familes resident in the city. The Jewish population of Constantinople therefore consisted of up to 15,000 persons, a sizable proportion of its total population. The many thousands of Byzantine Jews were not the uneducated, unskilled peasants who had flocked into the city from the hinterlands, but were generally the artisans and merchants who had come or were brought to the area because of their technological or commercial abilities. In the heart of the Jewish section of Constantinople was a busy artisan's quarters; its casting and metalworking furnaces gave it its characteristic name, the Brass Market. The quarter surrounded a sizable synagogue. The main body of the community of Jews of Constantinople was thus set in the section of the city where the forges and the furnaces of the metalworkers performed their pyrotechnics, just as the Roman Jewish community was set in the industrial *Trastevere* quarter of Rome. It was from this Roman community, as was noted above, that many of the artisans had been brought to Byzantium.

From the mid-fourth century to the mid-eleventh century the bronze and copper workers of city's fiery industrial district, the *Chalkoprateia*, were thus at work in the heart of a heavy concentration of Constantinople's Jews.[7] The furnaces which spewed smoke into the balmy breezes of the Mediterranean from that quarter of Constantinople adjoined those of the glassmakers, who were ensconced in a separate area allotted to them just outside the walled district. One of the gates through the wall to the port was named after the adjacent glassware factories.

Significantly, no church existed in the industrial area in the early Christian period. It was not until the Jews were expelled from the synagogue by either Theodosius II or Justinius II, and the synagogue itself was seized and converted into the "Church of the Mother of God" that the first significant Christian presence can be discerned in the industrial zone.[8] The Byzantines attempted to throttle Judaism for generations, but in spite of recurrent edicts directed at conversion or expulsion, a highly productive core of Jewish artisans remained in the district throughout the Byzantine period. While waves of emigration inevitably followed each reversal, the glass-makers, metalsmiths, silkworkers and dyers of Constantinople, Thessalonica, Thebes, Corinth and of a number of other smaller communities were essential to the florescent economy of Byzantium, and the attempts to obliterate Jewish heresy gave way recurrently to economic pragmatism.

The juridical precepts of pre-Christian Rome were modified by Theodosius II by a series of restrictions which finally, by the year 438, excluded Jews from all civil and military posts. In contrast to the increasingly severe constraints imposed upon the Jews in all other legal and social aspects, special consideration was given to the glassmakers, similar to the tolerance afforded at the other side of Europe to the glassmakers of Cologne. Theodosius II extended the privileges granted by Constantine to *Vitriarii* and *Diatretarii* by additionally exempting them from personal taxes.[9] The Theodosian edicts were codified under Justinian (527-565) and harsh new restrictions were added. Some glassmakers remained at their furnaces but many left in spite of liberal exemptions and privileges retained by members of their craft. "Jewish glassblowers were settled in Constantinople as early as the reign of Justinian I." writes David Bezborodko, and, to emphasize the continuity of the art in the Byzantine capitol, adds, "and we hear of another Jewish glass-worker in an account dating from a century later."[10]

The gap in production spanned by the two references referred to by Bezborodko was caused by an exodus of glassmakers during that repressive period. Bishop Menas (551-565) attempted to correct the decline in the supply of glassware by again summoning Jewish glassmakers to emigrate from Byzantine-controlled Palestine to the capital of Christendom, offering respite from the restrictive edicts, in effect reinstituting the privileges the glassmakers had enjoyed under the Theodosian code. Glassmakers filtered in from Eretz Israel and glassmaking renewed its tortured existence in Byzantium. The Eastern masters then brought with them the gold-glass technology, wherein gold leaf cut into a design is sandwiched between layers of glass.[11]

Christians pilgrims still, however, turned to the Jewish glassmakers in the Holy Land for mold-blown glassware, *eulogia* (holy oil) bottles, which had become popular and which the glassmakers of Eretz Israel were turning out with Christian as well as Jewish symbols. Hundreds of these small square and round bottles survive; the Jewish types are decorated with a stylized rendition of the temple, *lulav* (palm branches), *menorah* (seven-branched

A BOTTLE WITH JEWISH SYMBOLS, 6TH-7TH CENTURY. The bottle is typical of those produced in *Eretz Israel* for the Christian and Jewish market from the 4th to the 7th centuries. *Photograph courtesy of The Corning Museum of Glass.*

candelabra), *shofar* (ram's horn), the single and double-handed vases employed in the Succoth festival and by crossed torches symbolizing Succoth rites. The Christian bottles carry several types of crosses and lozenges; they were obviously produced by the same enterprising glassmakers of Eretz Israel who had previously supplied the pagan market with glassware for presentation to victorious gladiators and were now satisfying both the Christian and the Jewish markets. "Mould-blown glasses decorated with Jewish and Christian symbols were made in Jerusalem between 578 and the end of the Byzantine period there in 636."[12]

During this period the Byzantines and Persians had been waging intermittent war for a century, and both "seemed on the verge of collapse."[13] The Persians had launched a devastating attack upon Constantinople itself in 617 C.E. and had captured a huge section of the Byzantine Levant, having taken Antioch (611) and Jerusalem (614); in 619 the Persians added Alexandria to their conquests. The Byzantines survived the assaults but were left militarily feeble and fearful of further engagement with the weakened but still menacing Persian forces. They turned to the Khazars for help. The Khazars were endowed with a military force so formidable that in the year 627 the Byzantine emperor Heraclius found it expedient to conclude a strategic military alliance with them against the Sassanians of Persia. Theophanes, in relating the history of the period, reported that "the Turks from the East whom they call the Khazars," under Ziebel, a chief who was rated as "second in rank to the Khagan," passed through the Caspian Gate at Darband and joined the Byzantine emperor at the siege of Tiflis. Theophilus took respectful note of the Khazarian contribution of 40,000 horsemen to the field, fierce fighters who provided overwhelming strength to the campaign and resulted in the crushing defeat of the Persians and the consequent salvation of Byzantium.[14] Other sources confirm that without Khazar help the Byzantines could not have prevailed against the Persians and their Sassanian allies and Christendom may not have survived.

The Byzantines, having been drained by the debilitating war against Sassanian and Persian Iran, looked upon the Jews as a fifth column, especially since the sympathies of many Jews lay with the Persians under whom they had until that time enjoyed a certain measure of national and religious freedom. In the year 632 the emperor Heraclius, in an attempt to consolidate his frayed power, ordered the forcible conversion of the Jews to Christianity.[15] This event took place just six years after the Khazar forces had routed the Persians and had brought Byzantium back from the brink of collapse. The resilience of the Jews prevailed and continued to foil a series of persistent Byzantine attempts to throttle Judaism. The edict was unevenly applied, since the skills of the Jewish artisans were indispensable for many basic trades, and especially for glassmaking. The edicts commanding conversion which had commenced with Justinian I were revived successively in virulent forms under Heraclius, Leo III, Basil and Leo IV and Romanus in the seventh, eighth, ninth and tenth centuries respectively, but the enforcement of the restrictive measures was invariably abandoned almost as quickly as it was applied.

Some glassmakers from Greece are rumored to have migrated to Gaul in the seventh century. It may very well be that they were Jews, although the references to them merely state that they boasted that they "could work glass according to the methods of the Jews."[16] Jewish glassmakers fleeing Byzantine persecution would have had to employ the euphemistic device of assuming Greek identity. They would have been, after all, Greek Jews. There is no way of knowing whether these "Greeks" actually performed such work in Gaul, for no other reference to them has come to light. Perhaps they were in fact Greeks who had observed the Jewish glassmakers at work, but when faced with the necessity of duplicating the necessary skills could not make good on their boast.

The glassmakers of Byzantium were recurrently allowed to continue to work in relative freedom. The period of troubled tranquility which followed the relaxation of the edicts of Justinian I was again roiled when in the years 721-723 the emperor Leo III (Leon the Isaurian) acted upon the precedent set by Heraclius by issuing a new series of suppressive edicts mandating that all Byzantine Jews be baptized. Jews fled in considerable numbers.[17] Other Jews remained and after being forced through the abhorrent experience, expurgated themselves and returned cleansed, clinging to their faith and activities as devotedly as before. Leo was succeeded in the attempt to obliterate Judaism by mass conversion by Basil I (867-886), whose wily directives were more deliberate and longer-lasting. Basil avoided the violence of his predecessors; he offered "high appointments to those who came forward," even enticements such as the granting of "official rank to men of no standing." Nevertheless, as Basil's tenth century biographer bitterly relates, "most of them, when the king no longer lived, returned like dogs to their vomit."[18]

The fact is, however, that not all the Jewish glassmakers fled from Byzantium and the industry continued its erratic course over the period of a millennium. The Cairo Geniza documents make a number of references to a continuing intercourse between the Jewish glassmakers of Greece and those of Old Fustat (Old Cairo). We learn from these documents, for example, that a twelfth century glassmaker from Byzantium, Aby l'Hassan (an Arab transcription of Abraham Cohen), arrived in Alexandria and was on the way to Fustat to conduct business. And our old friend, Benjamin of Tudela, testified to the continuing existence of a colony of Jews in Corinth.

The production of silk and of glass were major industries and tempting prizes which the Crusaders could not ignore. Roger II invaded Byzantium on his "Christian" mission, evacuated thousands of Jewish artisans and peremptorily transported them to Sicily in the year 1147. The glassmaking industry of Corinth and Thessalonica went out of existence immediately thereafter, and virtually disappeared from Constantinople. Glassmakers shortly began to mow down the trees and blackening the skies of Apulia and Sicily. The Italian lands of the Adriatic and Tyrrhenian Seas were not virgin territories for the operations of glassmakers. Glassmakers were established around Spina for a time around the tenth century B.C.E.; some of the earliest examples of gold-glass were recovered from Canosa, Apulia, in the third century B.C.,[19] a date precedent to the implantation of bottoms of vessels (*fondi d'oro*), fabricated in this unique "sandwich" technique, in the Jewish and Christian catacombs of Rome.

The Jews were well rooted around the Adriatic. The Jewish communities at Oria, Otranto and Bari were noted in Byzantine times as great centers of Talmudic study. The great Talmudist R. Anan ben Marinus Ha-Cohen resided at Siponto, a hundred kilometers northwest of Bari.[20] At Oria two well-established Talmudic academies were flourishing in the middle of the ninth century. The great Aaron ben Samuel was a sage from Baghdad who became a member of the Bari rabbinical court and whose decisions "recalled the days of the Sanhedrin."[21] The academies at Oria and at Otranto were famous centers of learning until they were decimated by the persecutions of Romano, and many of their inhabitants fled to Bari. A poignant description of the trauma suffered by the Jews of Oria and Otranto is contained in the correspondence of the Bari community with Hasdai Ibn Shaprut, the administrator of foreign affairs for the Caliph of Cordoba, the same prolific correspondent from whom we learned so much about the Khazars.

Bari boasted of a number of great Talmudic centers. It was said that: "From Bari went forth the law, and the word of the Lord from Otranto."[22] We learn much about the parallel networks in which Jewish learning and commerce conducted dynamic intercourse throughout the Mediterranean world from the numerous references in Talmudic circles throughout the Diaspora to the Bari academies and their distinguished rabbis. That far-ranging record is given vivid expression by a chronicler, Abraham ibn Daud, whose story illustrates "the danger of Mediterranean voyages in the second half of the tenth century: the capture of four rabbis on a voyage from Bari by an Arab captain who held them for ransom." They were seized by this Andalusian corsair on their way around the world to collect money for the semi-annual conference on Talmudic studies (*Kulla*) held at the academies of Sura and Pumbadita, and were separately sold off at four different ports. Rabbi Shemaria was ransomed in Egypt and thereafter became the head of the academy at Fustat (Old Cairo). Rabbi Hushiel was ransomed by the Jews of Kairawan, "at that time the most important Fatimid city after Cairo and Alexandria."[23] Rabbi Moses ben Enoch and his son were ransomed by the Jews of Cordova. It is said that the rabbi found his way to the synagogue in rags where, shabby appearance notwithstanding, his erudition was immediately recognized; he was installed as head of the academy with the unanimous approval of the congregation, a school which "served henceforth as a center for all of the Peninsula."[24] We are not told by Abraham ibn Daud what happened to the fourth scholar, and we must assume the worst.

The Adriatic was a good market for glassware made in the East at the end of the first millennium of the Christian Era. In 1975 the cargo of a vessel sunk off the island of Mljet was found. It included some 30 well-preserved glass vessels, cups, goblets, carafes and lamps, part of a considerably larger collection that had disappeared or is still to be found. They appear to be products of one glassmaking center, although it is possible that they were accumulated at some port for exportation. A comparison of their decorative motifs with others known to have been employed in the latter half of the ninth century provides a likely date for the production of the glassware. The amphoras are similar to those from Sarkal (recovered before the flooding of the site), Kiev and Cherkonese in Russia, in Romania (Dinogetia), Macedonia (Ochride), and Bulgaria (Popina, Pliska, Preslav, etc.). The forms of the other types of glassware, with some exceptions, "conform to common medieval models of the eastern Mediterranean." The

Glassblowing in the late 17th century Germany, as depicted in a work by Kaspar Luyken: *Der Glasmacher* (1695).

exceptions are of "rare and exceptional bicolor glass," known from finds in Egypt and Armenia and "in certain localities of the Trans and Ciscaucasus, one finds samples of containers which exhibit this same combination of color, blue and yellow-green, as on the glass recovered from Mljet."[25] The comparison of the style of glassware thus fortuitously retrieved from the bottom of the Mediterranean to known types and proveniences outlines the itineraries of the Jews and, perforce, of the Jewish glassmakers with perfection.

In the latter half of the twelfth century, glassware manufacture reappears in the Adriatic as a consequence of the previously cited marauding activities of Roger II. Knobbed goblets "of very strong Corinthian affinity" were retrieved from Lucera Castle and other Apulian sites and were also found on the other side of the Adriatic near Dubrovnik.[26] The excavator of the Corinthian glass furnaces, Gladys Davidson, found that several of the Corinthian glassware types derive from Eastern models and become themselves prototypes for the later Italian and northwest European models.[27] Ada Polak notes that traces of twelfth century glassmaking have indeed been uncovered on the Apulian coast and that a modern guidebook describes the Apulian district as "'a mountainous area, covered with forest,'--a typical landscape for glass manufacture."[28] The similarity of the glass made in Apulia with that of glass found in various Yugoslavian sites has led to the theory that its distribution across the Adriatic was "an adjunct to the lively trade in salt which was carried on between the two coasts during the fourteenth and fifteenth centuries."[29] The salt trade was one of the products with which Jewish traders dealt; in fact, Jewish entrepreneurs dominated the traffic in salt in the Mediterranean into the sixteenth century. The Jews were granted royal leases on the salt mines of Poland, for example, as well as exclusive rights to minting, customs and tax-farming.[30] The association between the distribution of salt and glassware has many parallels.

David Whitehouse, of the Corning Museum of Glass, reported in the journal of that renowned institution on two fragments of a bottle found at Otranto, situated at the very heel of Italy, and the site of another significant Jewish community from which it was said, as noted previously, that "The Word of the Lord went forth." The fragments were adorned with a distinctive, unmistakable gilt and enamel ornamentation, typical of "a small but well-known group of vessels... variously attributed to factories in the Byzantine world [Corinth] and the Soviet Union."[31] Associated with the glass were coins of Manfred (1258-1266), which place the deposit of this glass to after 1258. The conclusion drawn by Dr. Whitehouse was the same as that previously arrived at by another scholar, A. H. S. Megaw, that these vessels are so closely related "as to represent the output of a single center."[32] Thus these two small fragments tie together three widely dispersed areas of which the Jews are the factor in common.

Another important find of glassware was made in excavations at *Novo Brdo*, in Serbia, in strata dating between the end of the fourteenth and the mid-fifteenth centuries. Hundreds of bracelet, bead and glassware fragments permitted a comparison to be made to known ware. "The major part of these

A nineteenth century Gaffer, from *The Book of English Trades*, London, 1821.

fragments, by their very fine design and in some cases by their shape, recall those of Roman glass" is a conclusion in an English summary of a report on the finds by M. Corovbic Ljubinkovic of the National Museum of Belgrade, and then goes on to say that: "in any case they are closely related to the Byzantine glass discovered by G. Davidson at Corinth."[33] The apparent lack of differentiation between "Roman" and "Byzantine" glass can easily be rationalized by the realization that both groups of artisans were related and stemmed from the same Eastern provenience.

The rapacious Roger II left the treasuries of Constantinople filled with fine glassware, perhaps because he calculated that, aside from being less fragile, the glassmasters constituted an infinitely greater treasure. The Venetian knights of the Fourth Crusade seized and sacked the city in 1204 and subjected its residents, Jews and Christians alike, to Christian pillage, rape and murder. The Venetian Crusaders confiscated the great glassware collection and deposited it into the treasury of St. Mark's Cathedral, where it is now proudly displayed. The Venetian raiders were not fortunate enough to capture any glassmakers, inasmuch as they had already been removed by Roger II to his domain or had fled to Khazar territory or to Naupolis, Zara and Ragusa (Dubrovnik) and other communities along the eastern Adriatic. The glassmakers of the eastern Adriatic were among the earliest masters thereafter drawn upon by the Venetians to establish an industry which provided it with one of its most valuable products for trade--glassware--a product which made the city famous.

Constantinople, stripped of its treasures and industry, never regained its days of glory under the Christians. The small, impoverished Jewish community was spared from the slaughter perpetrated by the Turk, Mehmet "The Conqueror" when he captured the city in 1453, with the assistance, it is said, of the Jewish "fifth column." Mehmet made the city the capital of the expansive Ottoman Empire, and the Jews prospered under benign Turkish rule. The local rabbis heralded their liberation as a "redemption," quoting Lamentations 4:21, which had prophesied the downfall of the "guilty city." Istanbul is referred to in contemporary literature as a Jewish mother-city, to which Isaac Zarfati, a fifth century rabbi invited, the Jews of Hungary and Austria in an impassioned appeal; many came from throughout the Diaspora.[34] Mehmet constructed the first of the great imperial mosques which give the city its distinguished charisma, and the Jews built a great synagogue, the *Okhrida*, which is still being frequented in modern times. The Jews were encouraged to leave the Ghetto of Pera and settle where they could develop both their own and the city's welfare, and they erected that great synagogue in the working-class district of Galat, on the south shore of the Golden Horn. Glassmaking made its re-appearance in Constantinople and the Jews prospered.

In the meantime, some of the erstwhile Corinthian glassmakers had melded into the glassmaking industry of the Eastern Adriatic, where beads, bracelets and other decorative ware were being fabricated from raw Levantine cullet and supplied to the hinterlands. One of the characteristic products by which the influence of the Corinthian and eastern glassmakers

Glassmakers at work in an 18th century French glasshouse as depicted in the monumental work by Denis Diderot (1713-1784), *L'Encyclopédie ou Dictionnaire Raisonné des Sciences, des Arts, et des Métiers*. The tools and technique employed in glassblowing changed little during 2000 years of practice. A glassblower of the 1st century *Eretz Israel* would find himself perfectly at home in a Muranese *vetreria* or a French or English glasshouse.

can be traced is the introduction of *crown glass*, window panes produced by a method which had originated in Eretz Israel.[35] Crown glass was in use in the Holy Land by the fourth century C.E., as examples from Jerash and Samaria and other sites make amply evident.[36] The technique may have arrived in Byzantium with the glassmakers who responded to the plea of Bishop Menas in the mid-sixth century. The fact that the Corinthian glassmakers were spinning crown glass well before the eleventh century, in any event, appears to have resulted from an ongoing relationship with the Near Eastern rather than the North African masters of the art. The recovered documents from the Cairo synagogue Geniza indicate that the three populations of glassmakers were in continual close contact and exchanged products regularly. The appearances of crown glass in Venice at the end of the thirteenth century, in Normandy in the fourteenth century and in England in the seventeenth century constitute but more of numerous signposts which mark the itinerary of a new complex of westward movements of glassmakers in the last millennium of the Common Era.

Jewish silkworkers, metalsmiths and glassmakers rapidly became an integral part of the Sicilian scene under Roger II. Foreign commerce was also largely in Jewish hands; the industries flourished and the Jews flourished along with them. Emperor Frederick II, greedily unsatisfied with the considerable revenue the industries were producing for his coffers and coveting complete control of the industries, took steps to confiscate and nationalize them. He began the operation in 1231 by driving the Jews out of the silk industry, initiating a process which impelled the Jewish artisans to seek their fortune elsewhere. The emperor first set up a government monopoly over the silk industry in Apulia, pragmatically retaining knowledgeable Jews as operators of the enterprises. Frederick II also suspended all the dyeing operations except those at Capua and Naples, which similarly continued to be maintained under Jewish management.[37] Glassmaking proved more difficult to control, inasmuch as the managers of the industry were also its artisans and it was impossible to substitute for them; the training of Christian workers to take their place could not be affected within the familial confines of the art.

Whatever favorable conditions remained for the Jews in southern Italy eroded further after the passing of Frederick II. In the year 1290 the Kingdom of Naples spurred a massive emigration by forcibly driving the Jewish population into baptism.[38] The Jews who resisted conversion were reduced to poverty and misery and the exodus from the Spanish dominated areas grew to sizable proportions. Obadiah of Bertinoro, for example, reported about 1488 that Palermo "contains about 850 families....They are poverty-stricken artisans, such as copper-smiths and ironsmiths... despised by the Christians because they are all tattered....They are compelled to go into the services of the king whenever any new labor project arises; they have to drag the ships to shore, to construct dykes, and so on."[39]

Many of the emigrants headed for Turkey and China and for other localities outside of Christian control, or relocated in places where the nobility or even the church itself deemed their presence so valuable as to override ecclesiastic scruple. Some Jews returned to Thebes, Salonika and Constantinople, the very cities from which their forefathers had been shanghaied by Roger II. They were eagerly welcomed back in the East inasmuch as the various technologies which had been decimated by the loss of the Jewish artisans and entrepreneurs as a result of the Crusades had never recovered; the robust industries which existed before Jews were removed had almost disappeared. Rome, Genoa and the Venetian Republic pragmatically created enclaves within which the Jews could freely worship and carry on enterprise. Thus the silk, metal, glassmaking and other characteristically Jewish industries were integrated into northern Italy. The artisans first established themselves in Tuscany (in and around Pisa) from whence many moved on to Venice and Genoa.

"The silk art was a new art [in Genoa] in the sense that the development was largely the contribution of foreign immigrants, especially from Tuscany."[40] Mulberry trees were planted by the Jewish residents of various communities within the neighboring Monferrat Marquisate to supply the industry with silk cocoons. The road into Casale Monferrat, for example, is referred to in local folklore alternatively as "Mulberry Road" and as "Jew's Alley." By the middle of the sixteenth century the Genovese industry had grown to employ up to 18,000 workers out of a total population of some 70,000 Genovese.[41] At its peak, the industry employed 30,000 Genovese workers.

The end of the thirteenth century also witnessed a steady influx of glassmakers from Tuscany into Genoa, a fact which led one early chronicler to report that "the first glassmakers in Genova came from Florence."[42] In 1281 a Tuscan glassmaker, "Zino da Firenze" is registered on a Genovese document. The influx of members of that art from Tuscany from that time forward, however, must have been substantial, judging by the preponderance of the names of glassmakers appearing in various documents of the time which identify the provenance of the bearer as Tuscany. Included are glass-masters who are specifically designated as *Conversi*, i.e., Jews who had converted to Christianity--Nov. 29, 1303: Campagno, "conversi glassmaker of Florence"; Oct. 13, 1309: Benagia, "conversi of Florence, who is a qualified glassmaker."[43]

The Jews remained a seminal industrial factor in Genoa until Genoa's policies reflected that of their Spanish overlords; the Jews were officially expelled from Genovese dominions in 1567 but some remained under actual or simulated conversion. The glassmaking industry of Genoa degenerated during the period in which the Spanish influence over Genoa was at its peak, and virtually disappeared after the expulsion of the Jews. By the mid-seventeenth century Spanish treachery against the interests of their supposed protectorate disenchanted some members of the ruling nobility of the republic. Recognizing a new opportunity for re-entering into the affairs of a most important port, a certain *Salamon d'Italia* petitioned the directors of the Banco San Giorgio in the year 1655 on behalf of a group of Jews from Tuscany for the right to resettle into and conduct business from the Republic of Genova. The Banco San Giorgio was an official and powerful branch of the government which acted as a sort of ministry of finance in regard to external commerce for the Republic of Genoa.

Salamon was located at this time at Casale Monferrat, which was under the dynastic rule of the Gonzagas, as was the Universita d'Altare, a commune of glassmakers near Genoa which rivalled Venice for 800 years, and was even more instrumental in spreading the art throughout Europe. The meeting with the "Marinino," as the Banco San Giorgio was locally referred to (reflecting its interest in maritime affairs), led to the first "Statutes of Tolerance," but they were shortly renounced. The effects of a plague served to reopen the issue of inviting Jews to help resuscitate the economy; only three years later, in 1658, Abram da Costa de Leon and Aron de Tovar renewed negotiations with the Banco San Giorgio and succeeded in obtaining the new *Capitoli per la Natione Hebrea* which invited the Jews to "come and settle in the Serenissimo Republic of Genoa" under favorable terms, effective in April 1659.

The Jewish glassmakers among the eager immigrants were granted the exclusive right to produce glass and glassware for the entire dominion of the

Republic of Genoa. Furthermore, to reinforce the successful conduct of that enterprise, and to assure its ability to supply glassware at reasonable prices, these *maestri* were also granted complete control over the market for broken glass which they had petitioned for on the 27th of August, 1659:

> Inasmuch as the Senate of the Republic of Genoa has granted Eliau Bernol and his Jewish compatriots the exclusive rights to produce, and to have produced, glass and crystal of every kind for a period of twenty-five years, it is requested that...the sale of broken glass, which is most necessary for the maintenance of that factory, be made only to Eliau Bernol and his associates and to no one else...and that the prohibition be enforced by such penalties as the Senate deems fit.[44]

A similar pattern appears in the earliest Venetian records. Twenty-nine persons are first denoted as glassworkers in a record of the commune of the year 1224.[45] They were members of the *ars fiolaria*, the glassmaker's guild, of whose existence we are likewise informed by this document. Most of the names are of Semitic origin, of which a number are distinctly Hebraic: Leonardus; Lazarinus; Laurencinus; Marcus; Jacobinus; Symionus.[46] The glassmaking industry was installed at that time in the Rialto district, the center of Jewish commercial activity. It was from the Rialto that the glassmakers were removed to Murano in 1291. The excuse for the removal of the furnaces from the heart of Venice was ostensibly the fire hazard they represented, but it is evident that one of the underlying reasons for the transplanting of the industry was an attempt by the government to gain a control, even a monopoly over the burgeoning industries of the Rialto. The fact that the wool industry, another vocation in which the Jews were predominant (at least, around the Mediterranean), was previously removed to the island of Torcello on August 29, 1272, 19 years earlier than the removal of the glassmakers to Murano, makes the real intention apparent. Documents signed at Rialto attest to the conduct of the art in Venice; it was at Rialto, for example, that a Martino de la Fratina (Martin of Fratina, a town near Padua) contracted for a load of wood to fuel his furnace in May of 1281.[47]

The earliest surviving records of Murano reinforce the implication to be drawn from the predominantly Eastern, even Hebraic, character of the names on that initial listing of glassmakers that a community of Jews existed on the island at that time, and that they were engaged in glassmaking. The first *podesta* (Mayor) of Murano assumed office in the year 1276. His name was

Piero Contarini, a family name which also appears in the earliest surviving *pinkas* (journal) of the Jewish community of Padua, wherein it is recorded that the Contarini family represented the community in many official capacities from the earliest times; a Simon Contarini was one of three persons delegated to negotiate the terms of the establishment of a ghetto in Padua with the Venetian authorities. It was with the assistance of Piero Contarini and the mayors of Murano who succeeded him that scores of *forestieri* were brought in from throughout the Diaspora at the very outset of the development of the industry. Under the aegis of these first few officials of the Muranese community some 30 masters of the art are recorded as having come to the island from the forested areas around Padua from the years 1280-1291. Others came from Tuscany (mainly from Pisa), the Dalmatian coast (Zara, Spalato, Ragusa, and Naupolis), Ancona, Treviso and elsewhere. By the year 1350, taking account of only those whose provenance can be identified by their names or by their application for citizenship, at least 60 such immigrants have been found duly registered in various state documents. These "foreigners" were entitled to Venetian citizenship after a period of 25 years residence in Murano, and the record shows that many of them took advantage of that privilege.

The industry continued to draw its *maestri* from terra firma in an area encompassed by the cities of Treviso, Padua and Ferrara,[48] well into the fourteenth century and Jewish communities were active in each of these cities. Two of the earliest Muranese glassmasters from Padua were Jacobino e Marchesino "de Strata," recorded as owners of furnaces in Murano in the year 1281.[49] In 1310 a Jacobellus a vitrisellis, "resident in Murano," is cited in an official paper, "indicating the existence of a manufacturer of beads and of imitation precious stones"; in the following year Simeone and Menino de Pienega (Pienega is a town near Padua) are listed as *pro laboreriis vitreis;*[50] in the same year, 1311, a Jacobo da Fratina appears in another document which relates the glass industry of Venice to that of Tuscany.[51] In 1310 a Simon Broio cancelled out the distinguishing Jewish name "Simon" on a document and substituted "Benvenutus," and thereafter returned to Simon Broio in 1316 and in several subsequent entries; in 1331 and 1332 Simon was doing business with Bartolomeo Nigro, also the family name of residents of the Padovan and Genovese Jewish communities;[52]

The fourteenth and early fifteenth centuries witnessed a steady movement of *forestieri* into Murano, not only from the contiguous communities but also from the Dalmatian coast, Pavia, Ravenna, Tuscany and elsewhere. Dalmatian cities were particularly important provenances of glassmakers and glass decorators; three Dalmatian coast cities which supplied a number of these artisans were Zara, Spalato, and Ragusa (modern Dubrovnik), all of which hosted important Jewish communities.[53] Glassmaking is attested to in Dalmatian centers as far back as the Roman period; the museums of Zara and Dubrovnik (ancient Ragusa) have significant examples or Roman period glassware, and, although the quantity is not as great as that found in Aquileia and the other centers of glassmaking of the northern Adriatic littoral, and although little evidence of primary glassmaking in those centers has come to the fore, the ancient involvement of artisans in the Dalmatian cities in the vitric arts, whether as primary producers of glass or reprocessors of raw glass supplied to them from the eastern Mediterranean is documented in several contracts preserved in the state archives of Dubrovnik. Such contracts also provide the link between the glassmakers of Dubrovnik (that is, Ragusa) to those of Padua and Venice, In 1312, for example, a deed for property in Ragusa was issued to Mafeus fiolarius de Murano, the owner of a furnace in Murano from at least 1311 to 1316, Mafeus also appears in other papers drawn up between 1325 and 1327 in Ragusa and now conserved in the Dubrovnik archives. In 1332 he is referred to as Mattèo (Maffeo in Venetian dialect) of Pianega (a town near Padua). These transactions point to the existence of a glassworks in Ragusa owned by the patently enterprising Maffeo.[54]

Allegro Schiavo ("Allegro the Slave"), whose descendants became a consequential Venetian family, originated from Dalmatia. The name, while it unmistakably identifies its carrier's descent from slaves, carries no pejorative connotations, inasmuch as many skilled and highly placed individuals were former slaves, people who had been involved in respected activities even as slaves and were proud of their abilities and status as free persons. The name was a common one and recalls that of the Aquileian glassmakers whose similar names are molded into glassware which were produced in the area a millennium before the renaissance of the art in the city of the lagoon. Allegro Schiavo's glassmaking activity first appears in the Muranese records of 1345, and the resident activity of the Schiavo family is amply recorded from then on, continuing in 1360 with that of his sons, who carried on the family tradition and established themselves solidly into the fabric of the Muranese glassmaking industry.[55] In 1415 an active furnace was being operated by a Donato Schiavo, a descendant of Allegro or of one of the other families so distinguished by their surnames. In 1416, "Luca and Donato, father and son, of slave origin, are among the artisans of the eastern Adriatic coast who are attested among the glass-houses of Murano." In 1424 the master-glassmaker Donato "of Murano" designated "the son of Luca Schiavo," concluded a contract in Dubrovnik to produce glassware in Murano for a merchant from Florence![56]

It is important to add the name Balarin, meaning "dancer," a description which refers to the peculiar crippled gait of the progenitor of an important Muranese glassmaking dynasty, Giorgio Balarin. "Balarin" is a name "saturating early Muranese records." Giorgio's descent from slaves is attested in documents of 1456[57] and again of February, 1480: "Giorgio sclavoni dicti Balarin". The relationship between Jewish glassmakers and dealers in glass of the Dalmatian cities and Venice continued unabated into the sixteenth century. In the year 1512, for example, a dispute arose in which a nobleman of Dubrovnik, Marinus Paul de Goze, is accused by Simon de Ragnina of skimming off some of the "glassware and crystal" consigned to another "Simon," Simon de Venise, in a shipment of glassware which Marinus was supposed to deliver to the Venetian Simon.[58]

Jewish presence in Venice became compromised towards the end of the fourteenth century when the Venetian Republic reversed its more or less tolerant stance. The Jews were expelled from Venice, including those of the well-established community on Giudecca; they were forced to join the communities on nearby terra firma or move out of the area. The state finally secured its monopoly over the local glassmaking industry through a statutory control of the guild. It was, however, dependent on knowledgeable and skilled artisans, so the settlement of *forestieri* from the neighboring cities on Murano continued to be encouraged. Resistance to a succession of punitive edicts intended to complete the absorption of the industry from the surrounding areas continued to the end of the sixteenth century.[59] Squeezed by the restrictive statutes which affected the entire area, some glassmakers from the neighboring cities accepted the invitation; others moved westward to join the Universita d'Altare, where they were made welcome; still others began to filter further out into the Diaspora. It was during this period that, despite the threats of dire consequences for daring to disobey the series of edicts designed to prevent the exodus of skilled glassmasters, such a movement did take place.

The economic loss engendered by the expulsion of the Jews led the Venetian senate to reconsider its previous actions and to permit the Jews to dwell and conduct their affairs in Venice, on condition that their dwellings be physically separated from the Christians and that they be confined at night to their assigned quarters. On April 22, 1515, a return to Giudecca was first proposed. *The Jews made a counter-proposal that they be allowed to establish themselves on the island of Murano!*[60]

This pointed request is explicable only within the context of either an ongoing Jewish community on the cluster of islands devoted to the one industry, glassmaking, the islands collectively known as "Murano," or at the very least, as in the case of the Universita d'Altare, the existence of a community which made Jews, practicing or covert, welcome. The proposal of the Jews to establish communal residence on Murano or alternately on Giudecca was rejected; the first ghetto was established in neither of the two proposed districts but on the island of San Geralomo at what was then the northern boundary of the city. In 1516 the Jews, essential for the continuation of commerce and banking, but considered expendable for the trades, were allowed to return to Venice but were ensconced within the confines of a huge, fortress-like, defunct cannon-producing foundry, termed a *Geto*, in the Venetian lingo; its name became the eponym of restricted Jewish quarters from that time forward. The Jews were walled into the area with a single door to the outside world. A curfew was imposed and the door was shut tight all night, guarded by Christian guards at the expense of the penned Jews. Thus began a new phase of segregation in which the Christian world, having driven the (practicing) Jews out of most means of making a living as artisans, continued to make use of the Jews as bankers, doctors, merchants, international correspondents and credit custodians. The decree of the *Signoria* of March 29, 1516, indicates 'that in spite of the presumed prohibition against dwelling within Venice, many Jews, in fact, continued to reside throughout the island complex. The decree demands that the Jews "who live in the various districts of the city go immediately to live in the houses of the Geto."

Within a few months 700 Jews were permanently housed within the walls of the erstwhile foundry, forming the core of a continuously expanding Jewish, mainly mercantile, population in the lagoon. A much larger Jewish artisan population continued to reside in the contiguous communities of the mainland. An influx of Sephardic and Levantine Jews were accommodated in the year 1541 with the addition of an area adjacent to the *Geto*; still another additional area was allotted in 1603. By that time Polish and Western European Jews could also be counted among those who joined the walled-in community; the population of permanent residents of the ghetto grew to an impressive 2500 people, to which must be added a considerable influx of transitory Jewish merchants and travelers.[61] By the end of the century the Jewish population of the ghetto alone had risen to over 5000.[62] The Jewish communities of Mestre and Padua had similarly expanded during this period as a result of the significant, even massive scale of Jewish industry and commerce which had developed. Many trades were represented; ironsmithing was important among the arts stimulated by artisans who had been driven out from the southern Italian regions under Spanish control, as were the arts of silk production, weaving and dyeing.

The Jewish community of Padua, although it did not suffer expulsion, did undergo a traumatic period. The records kept by the community have disappeared; that they existed is evident from the fortuitous survival of 42 resolutions from what is designated therein as "the old *pinkas*" of the Paduan community. The minutes book containing the resolutions passed by the Paduan Community Council between 1577 and 1603 and subsequent minutes books were, fortunately, preserved. The dates of the missing centuries and the date of the appearance and preservation of a new set of community records match the similar period of darkness in the Universita d'Altare and in the capital of the Montferrat dynasty, Casale Montferrat, where the hiatus ended with the initiation of a new set of journals by its Jewish community.

The Paduan *Pinkasim* reflect a parallel pattern of names and origins to that of the names of the *forestieri* who flooded into Murano in the early period. In addition to numerous entries of the names of families common to both Venice and Altare cited above, many other Hebraic names with indicative regional origins appear in documents recorded in the journal: Iseppe Dalva d'Ancona; Salamon di Zara; Simon da Coneglian (Conegliano is a town just north of Treviso); Mandolin Trevese; Jseppe Mantoan; Lion de Napoli (Naupolis of Dalmatia); Isach Ferarese.

On the 25th of June of the year 1615, eight representatives of the Jewish community of Padua appeared before the ruling body of Padua to come to a compromise concerning the payment of unbearable taxes fixed in the terms of their permission to remain in Padua.[63] The names of five of these representatives, Simon Cantarin, Giacob Moretto, Moise Moretto, Aron de

Salom and Finea di Negri, pertain to families which are also indigenous to the glassmaking industries of Genoa, Altare and Murano. Other family names which relate importantly the history of glassmaking appear in the earliest of the Paduan community records in the persons of Simon Pisano and Daniel Ferro.

From 1287 to 1478 the Negri family operated a *fornace* in Murano, after which the family emigrated to Altare and became one of the original 16 *nobile* families of the Universita d'Altare, coat of arms and all.[64] A most noteworthy Abram Salom resided in the ghetto of Genoa, the same community cited previously which had received the exclusive rights to the production of glass and glassware throughout the dominions of the Republic of Genoa. Salom was registered as a "dealer in lead oxide used for the production of glass" in the same year that a patent was taken out in England for lead glass. The formula was obtained by George Ravenscroft from a glassmaker from the Universita d'Altare, Giacomo da Costa, a branch of whose family was a neighbor of Salom in the Genovese ghetto at the time. Cantarini, as was noted previously, is the name of a family whose history in Murano goes back to the year 1276 when Piero Contarini became the first *podesta* (mayor) of Murano in that year, an event which took place 15 years before the glass-making industry was removed to that island and five years after the first statutes concerning the glassmaking industry were passed. It was Piero Contarini who was instrumental in gathering in the *forestieri* from throughout the Diaspora during the propitious period of Venetian tolerance, the masters who were responsible for the development of the industry on that island. The Pisanos and the Ferros were important families in both Venice and the Universita d'Altare, and were active among the glassmakers who spread the art ever wider into the Diaspora.

The paths through the Diaspora intertwine tortuously, cross, form nodules, disengage and reengage in country after country, finally fading into oblivion. The first course of the odyssey of the glassmakers carried them from Akkadia into Canaan and from thence into Egypt where their art suddenly appeared and just as suddenly disappeared as the pharaohs chose plunder over progress. Greek Alexandria drew the artisans back into Egypt to create a center in which the art became the envy of the classical world. The glassmakers followed the Roman legions into Italy, Spain and Gaul, were driven out by Christian intolerance, and took their art with them. Linen and glass and silk and spices were borne back and forth over the

Persian passes into China and India; the glassmakers crossed the mountains from the Galilee, Judah, Byzantium, Persia, and Transylvania, gathered in the Danube basin, and were pushed by Byzantine perfidy through Bohemia and Bavaria into France where they achieved noble status as the *gentils-hommes verrieres*; the artisans were thereafter swirled around in an eddy of intolerance and were cast off by its spume into England and America; Crusaders transplanted the artisans from Eretz Israel and Byzantium to the Adriatic and southern Italy, from whence they were forced to make their way to Tuscany and Venice and Genoa. Wherever the Jews went on their desperate odyssey through the Diaspora, the art of glassmaking went with them, and their descendants finally forgot from whence they came.

The latter courses of that long, involved journey must remain the subject of another book.

# NOTES

1. Heinrich Graetz, *History the Jews*, vol. III, 1967, p. 27.

2. Victor Paul Furnish, "Corinth in Paul's Time," *BAR*, May/June 1988, vol. XVB no. 3, pp. 16, 18.

3. Furnish, Ibid., p. 26.

4. *Midrash Exodus Rabba*, trans. Dr. S. M. Lehrmann, Chapter XXVII, 9, p. 330.

5. S. D. Goitein. *A Mediterranean Society*, I, 1967, p. 223.

6. Heinrich Graetz, Ibid., p. 425.

7. Andrew Sharf, *Byzantine Jewry*, 1971, p. 16; ref. A Galante, *Les Juifs de Constantinople sous Byzance*, 1940, pp. 23-25; cf. C. Emereau, "Constantinople sous Theodore le Jeune," *Byzantion*, 2, 1925, p. 112.

8. Graetz, Ibid., p. 26.

9. Theodosian Code, 13, 4.2.

10. Bezborodko, Ibid., p. 41.

11. Dan Klein, Ward L. Loyd, eds. *The History of Glass*, 1984, p. 53; James Fowler, *Archeologia*, vol. XLVI, 1881.

12. Klein et. al, Ibid.

13. Arthur Koestler, *The Thirteenth Tribe*, 1976, p. 25.

14. Theophanes, *Chronographia*, ed. De Boor, 1883, p. 72; *Encyclopedia Judaica*, 1972, "Khazars," p. 944.

15. Norman A. Stillman, *The Jews of Arab Lands*, 1979, pp. 22-23; Sharf, Ibid., p. 43.

16. A. Kisa, *Das Glas in Altertume*, I, 1908, pp. 99-100. This watershed work on the history of glassmaking makes numerous references to the influx of glassmakers into Gaul, Jewish and otherwise, but does not always offer sources. The Jewish glassmakers of Gaul had been driven out of the Guilds in the fifth and early sixth centuries and the resulting deterioration of the art would have impelled noblemen to seek replacements.

17. Eliyahu Ashtor, *The Jews of Moslem Spain*, vol. 1, p. 196.

18. Sharf, Ibid., pp. 83-84, quoting from *Vita Basilii XCV* = Theoph. Cont. pp. 341-342 and other sources.

19. Vose, Ibid., p. 55.

20. Andrew Sharf, *Byzantine Jewry*, 1971. p. 164, citing H. J. Zimmels, "Scholars and Scholarship in Byzantium and Italy," *The World History of the Jewish People*, second series, vol. 2, 1966, pp. 180, 182.

21. Sharf, Ibid., p. 164.

22. Max L. Margolis and Alexander Marx, *A History of the Jewish People*, 1927, p. 299.

23. Sharf, Ibid., p. 167; the report comes from *Book of Tradition*, pp. 63-72 (translation); pp. 46-73 (text).

24. Cecil Roth, *A History of the Jews*, 1970, p. 172.

25. V. Han and Z. Brusic, "Une Decouverte sous-Marine du Verre Medieval dans l'Adriatique," *Annals of the Seventh International Congress on Glass*, 1977, pp. 280-281, citing: G. Gambatchidze, *Raskopki Thaba-Erdi (Ingutvhetia), Dekorativnoe iskusti SSSR*, 7 (152), 1970; [Bulgaria]: I. Cangova, "Srednovekovni amfori v Blgarija," *Isvestija na Archeologiceski Institut*, XXII, 1959, pp. 250-254; [Macedonia]: B. Aleksova, "Srednovekovna kermika od crkvata Sveta Sofija vo Obrid," *Glasnik na Institutot za nacionalna istorija*, 1-2, 1960, pp. 202-204; [Rumania]: I. Barnea--E. Comsa, *Dinogetia I*, 1967, pp. 250-254; [Russia]: A. L. Jakobson, "Srednevekovie amfori severnogo pricernomorja," *Sovietskaja Archeologija*, XV. 1951, pp. 333-336.

26. D. B. H. Rouen, *Ancient Glass*, 1972, p. 101, citing Gladys R. Davidson, "A Medieval Glass Factory at Corinth," *AJA*, XLIV, 1940, pp. 297-397.

27. Gladys R. Davidson, "A Medieval Glass Factory at Corinth," *AJA*, XLIV, 1940, pp. 308-310; *Corinth XII. The Minor Objects*, Princeton, 1952.

28. Ada Polak, *Glass*, 1982, p. 49.

29. Polak, Ibid.

30. Nachum Gross, et. al, *Economic History of the Jews*, 1975, pp. 125-126.

31. David Whitehouse, "Medieval Glass in Italy: Some Recent Developments," *JGS*, no. 25, 1983, citing Gladys R. Davidson, "A Medieval Glass Factory at Corinth," *AJA*, 44, 1940, pp. 297-324; A. H. S. Megaw, "A Twelfth Century Bottle from Cyprus," *JGS*, 10, 1968, pp. 88-104; B. A. Shelkovnikov, "Russian Glass from the 11th to the 17th Centuries," *JGS*, 8, 1966, pp, 95-115.

32. Whitehouse, Ibid., p. 120; Megaw, Ibid., p. 100.

33. M. Corovbic Ljubinkovic, "Fragments de verres medievaux trouves a Novo Brdo," *Annals of the Seventh International Congress on Glass*, 1965, p. III., 22.244.1.

34. Gabe Levenson, "From an Istanbul balcony," *The Jewish Week, Inc.*, Dec. 4, 1987.

35. "Crown glass" is produced by first producing a large bubble of glass (*parison or paraison*), to which a metal rod (*pontil*) is attached opposite the blowing (*gaffing*) tube. The parison is separated from the gaffing tube and the opening is spread wider with a

tool resembling a large forceps. The resultant vase-shaped parison is then spun rapidly at the end of the pontil, and centrifugal force causes the still-molten glass (*metal*) to flare out into a great disc which is placed face down on a flat plate and separated from the pontil. The center of the disc is left with a characteristic crown. Flat sections cut away around the crown are for use as window panes. Sometimes the center portion, or even the entire assembly, is employed as a pane in which the crown is a decorative motif.

36. Klein, et. al, Ibid., p. 57.

37. Attilio Milano, "Vicende economiche degli Ebrei nell'Italia meridionale ed insulare durante il medioevo," *La Rassegna Mensile di Israel*, no. 6, 1954, p. 220.

38. Cecil Roth, Ibid., 1959, p. 5.

39. *Iggorot Erez Israel*, ed. A. Yaari, 1943, p. 104.

40. Claudio Constantino, *La Repubblica di Genova*, 1986, p. 34.

41. Constantino, Ibid., pp. 155-156.

42. A. Ferretto, *Codice diplomatico delle relazioni fra la Liguria, la Toscana e la Lunigiana ai tempi di Dante (1265-1321)*, 1921, p. XI.

43. Guido Malandra, *I Vetrai di Altare*, 1983, p. 36. Malandra cites a series of Tuscan glassmakers who appear in records of from 1279 through 1314.

44. Archivio di Stato di Genova, *Hebreorum*, Archivio Segreto.

45. Bertolomeo Cecchetti, *Monografia della vetreria veneziana e muranese*, 1875, p. 7.

46. Cecchetti, Ibid., footnote pp. 7-8, quoting from *Liber plegiorum Communis*, carte 64, May 1224.

47. Luigi Zecchin, "I Primi 'Atti dei Podesta di Murano," *GE*, no. 2, 1966, p. 748.

48. Thorpe, 1929, Ibid., p. 73.

49. Luigi Zecchin, "Cronologia vetraria Veneziana e Muranese fino al 1285," *RSV*, no. 1, 1973, p. 22.

50. Luigi Zecchin, "Gli 'Atti' del Podesta' di Murano dal 1291 al 1343," *GE*, XX, Venice, 1966, p. 1109.

51. Luigi Zecchin, "Cronologia vetraria Veneziana e Muranese dal 1302 al 1314," *RSV*, no. 3, 1973, p. 124.

52. Luigi Zecchin, "Gli 'Atti'...," 1966, pp. 1108-1109.

53. F. Hamilton, *The Adriatic; The Italian Side*, p. 6.

54. Luigi Zecchin, "Cronologia vetraria Veneziana e Muranese dal 1332 al 1345," *RSV*, no. 5, Sept.-Oct., 1973, p. 213.

55. Luigi Zecchin, idem; see also "Decoratori di Vetri a Murano dal 1280 al 1480," *RSV*, no. 1, 1977; also: "Nicolo di Biagio, vetraio a Murano dal 1459 al 1512," *RSV*, no. 6, 1983.

56. Verena Han, "Les Relations Verrieres entre Dubrovnik et Venise du XIV au XVI siecle," *Annals of the Sixth International Congress on Glass*, July 1973, p. 163; Luigi Zecchin, "Vetrerie Muranese dal 1401 al 1415," March-April 1972 and "Verrerie Murane dal 1416 al 1425," *RSV*, May-June 1972.

57. C. A. Levi, *L'arte del vetro in Murano nel Rinascimento e i Berroviero*, Venice, 1895 (reference to a document of 1456 appears in which Giorgio is identified as "Georgius sclavonus famulus ser Menegin Caner").

58. Verena Han, Ibid., p. 161, ref. *Mobilia 25.141*.

59. Luigi Zecchin, "Vetrerie padovane fra il XIII ed il XVI secolo," *RSV*, no. 5, Sept.-Oct., 1980.

60. Carla Boccato, "Licenze per altane concesse ad ebrei del Ghetto di Venezia," *LRM*, March-April 1980, p. 106.

61. Boccato, Ibid., p. 110.

62. Milano, Ibid., p. 648.

63. Daniel Carpi, editor, *Minutes Book of the Council of the Jewish Community of Padua 1603-1630*, Jerusalem, 1979, p. 437.

64. Malandra, Ibid., p. 71.

# BIBLIOGRAPHY

**ABBREVIATIONS**

*AA*: Antichita Altoadriatiche (Aquileia).

*AASOR*: Annual of the American Schools of Oriental Research.

*AJA*: American Journal of Archeology.

*AN*: Aquileia Nostra (Aquileia).

*BA*: Biblical Archeology.

*BAR*: Biblical Archeological Review.

*BASOR*: Bulletin of the American Schools of Oriental Research.

*GE*: Giornale Economico della Camera di Commercio (Venice).

*IEJ*: Israel Exploration Journal.

*JAOS*: Journal of the American Oriental Society.

*JGS*: Journal of Glass Studies.

*JNES*: Journal of Near Eastern Studies.

*JPS*: Jewish Publication Society of America.

*LRM*: La Rassegna Mensile di Israel (Rome).

*RSV*: Rivista della Stazione Sperimentale Vetro (Murano).

Abdurazakov, A. A., *Etude Chimique des Verres d'Asie Centrale, Datant du Moyen Age*, report to the Ninth International Congress on Glass at Versailles, 1971.

Abdurazakov, A. A., M. A. Bezborodov, J. A. Zadneprovskii, *Steklodelie srednej Azii v drevnosti i srednevekov'e*, (Central Asian Art of the Ancient and Middle Ages), Tashkent, 1963.

Abdurazakov, A. A., "Medieval Glasses From the Tashkent Oasis," *JGS*, XI, 1969.

Adler, Marcus Nathan, ed., *The Travels of Benjamin of Tudela*, J. Kauffman, Frankfort am Mainz, 1903-1904, reprinted by P. Feldheim, New York, 1964, and by J. Simon, Malibu, California, 1983.

Aharoni, Yohanan, *The Archeology of the Land of Israel*, 1978, English translation, Anson F. Rainey, Westminster Press, Philadelphia, 1979\1982.

Aharoni, Yohanan, "Khirbet Raddana and Its Inscriptions," *IEJ*, 21, 1971.

Albright, William Foxwell, *The Proto-Sinaitic Inscriptions and Their Decipherment*, Harvard Theological Studies, Cambridge, 1966.

Al-Nashashibi, Nasir al-Din, *Tadhh-karat 'Awda* (Return Ticket), Beirut, 1962.

Ahlstroh, G. W. and D. Edelman, "Merenptah's Israel," *JNES*, vol. 44, no. 1, Jan. 1985.

Ahmad, Jama ad Dom, *Muthir al Gharam*, 1351.

Aldred, Cyril, *The Egyptians*, Thames and Hudson, London, 1961/1984.

Aleksova, B., "Srednovekovna kermika od crkvata Sveta Sofija vo Obrid," *Glasnik na Institutot za nacionalna istorija*, 1-2, Skopje, 1960.

al-Mvsudi, *Muruf al-Dhabad* (Meadows of Gold [and Golden Stones]) II; Mvsudi, *Les Prairies d'Or*, text and translation C. Barbier de Meynard and Pavet de Courteille, 9 vols., Paris, 1861\1877, 2: 9-12, 15, 18-25; 3: 61-65.

Amelander, *Menachem ben Solomon Ha-Levi*, (Yiddish), Amsterdam, 1741, new ed., (in Hebrew), translated by Haim Hominer, Jerusalem, 1964.

Angelos, Leopoldt, *Das Judische Goldglas*, Berlin 1928.

Archivio di Stato di Genova, *Hebreorum*, Genoa, Archivio Segreto.

Aristophanes, *Acharnians*.

Aristotle, *Politics*.

# Bibliography

Arne, T. J., "La Suede et l'Orient," *Archives d'Etudes Orientales*, 8 ov. 8, Upsala, 1914.

Artamonov, Mikhail Illarionovich, *History of Old Russian Culture*, in Russian, Akademiya Nauk. Institut Istorii Materialisnoi Kultur, 1962; translated "Geschichte der Kultur der Alten Rus; die Vormongolische Periode," by Walther Biehahn, Akademie-Verlag, Berlin, 1959-1962.

Ashtor, Eliyahu, *The Jews of Moslem Spain*, vol. I, *JPS*, Philadelphia, 1973.

Ausabel, Nathan, *The Book of Jewish Knowledge*, Crown Publishers, New York, 1964.

Avigad, Nahman, "Excavations in the Jewish Quarter of the Old City of Jerusalem," *IEJ*, 22, 1977.

Avigad, Nahman, *Beth Shearim; Archeological Excavations from 1953-1958*, in Hebrew, Jerusalem, 1971.

Avigad, Nahman, *Discovering Jerusalem*, original Hebrew, Shikmona Publishers, Israel, 1980; English editions: T. Nelson, Nashville, 1983; Basil Blackwell, USA, 1984.

Avigad, Nahman, *The Upper City of Jerusalem*, in Hebrew, 1980.

Bachtadze, R. A., "Kissledovoniju stekol feodal'noj Gruzii, *Vestnik Gosudarstvennogo Muzeja Gruzii im. akad. S.N. Dzanasija*, XX.A, 1960, (Feudal Period Georgian Glass), in Georgian, summary in Russian.

Bailey, H., "Gandhari," *Bulletin of the School of Oriental and African Studies*, 1943.

Barag, Dan, "Mesopotamian Vessels of the Second Millennium B.C., Notes on the Origin of the Core," *JGS* IV, 1962.

Barag, Dan, *Bulletin of the Ninth International Congress on Glass*, Section B II, Versailles, 1971.

Barag, Dan, "Recent Epigraphic Discoveries Related to the History of Glassmaking in the Roman Period," *Annales du Tenth International Congress on Glass*, Madrid-Segovie, 1985.

Barag, Dan, *Ancient Jewish Glass in Modern Research*, Museum Haaretz, Tel Aviv, Jerusalem, 1972.

Barag, Dan, "Cosmetic Palettes from the Eighth-Seventh Centuries B.C."

Barag, Dan, "Glass Vessels from the Cave of Horror," *IEJ*, vol. 12, nos. 3-4,

1962.

Barag, Dan, "An Unpublished Achemenid Cut Glass Bowl from Nippur," *JGS*, vol. X, 1968.

Barag, *Ancient Jewish Glass in Modern Research*, Museum Haaretz, Tel Aviv., Dec. 1972.

Barag, Dan, *Catalog of Western Asiatic Glass in the British Museum*, vol. I, The Magnes Press, Hebrew University, Jerusalem, 1985.

Barnea I. and E. Comsa, *Dinogetia I*, Bucharest, 1967.

Baron, Salo Wittmayer, *A Social and Religious History of the Jews*, revised and enlarged editions: *JPS*, Philadelphia 1952; Columbia University Press, New York, 1952-1983.

Baron, Salo W., Arcadius Kahan and other contributors, ed. Nachum Gross, *Economic History of the Jews*, Keter House Ltd., Jerusalem, 1975.

Bartha, A., *A IX-X Szazadi Magyar Tarsadalom* (Hungarian Society in the Ninth-Tenth Centuries), Akademisi Klado, Budapest, 1968.

Bass, George F., "The Nature of the Serce Limani Glass," *JGS*, vol. 26, 1984.

Bass, George F., "Civilization Under the Sea," *Modern Maturity*, (Journal of the American Association of Retired People), April-May 1989.

Bass, George, "A Bronze Age Shipwreck at Ulu Burun (Kas): 1984 Campaign," *AJA*, 90, 1986.

Beatty, John O., *The Iron Curtain Over America*, Dallas, 1951.

Berliner, Abraham, *Geschichte der Juden in Rome*; *von der altesten zeit bis zur gegenwort (2050 jahre)*, vol. I, M. J. Kaufmann, Frankfort-am-Main, 1893.

Bertacchi, Luisa, "Nuovi mosaici figurati di Aquileia," *AN*, Anno XXXIV, 1963.

Bertacchi, Luisa, "Il mosaico Teodoriano scoperto nell'interno del campanile di Aquileia," *AN*, Anno XXXII-XXXIII, 1961-1962.

Bertacchi, Luisa, "Nuovi elementi e ipotesi circa la Basilica del Fondo Tullio," *AN*, Anno XXXII-XXXIII, 1961-62.

Bertacchi, Luisa, "Due vetri paleocristiani di Aquileia," *AN*, 1967.

Bettelheim, Adriel, "Jews of Samarkand," *The Jewish Week*, Nov. 1, 1985.

Bezborodko, David, *An Insider's View of Jewish Pioneering in the Glassmaking Industry*, Gefen Pub., Jerusalem, 1987.

# Bibliography

Bezborodov, M. A., *Glassmaking in Ancient Russia*, Minsk, 1956.

Bezborodov M. A., and A. A. Abdurazakov, "Newly Excavated Glassworks in the USSR, Third-Fourteenth Centuries A.D.," *JGS*, VI, 1964.

Bezborodov M. A., and Iu. Zadneprovskii, "Ancient and Medieval Glasses of Central Asia," abstracts from papers presented at Atlantic City to the American Chemical Society, 1962.

Bickerman, Elias J., *The Jews in the Greek Age*. Harvard University Press, Cambridge and London, 1988

Bivar, A. D. H., "A Rosette Phiale Inscribed in Aramaic," *Bulletin of the School of Oriental and African Studies*, University of London, XXIV, 1961.

Blancourt, Haudicquer Jean de, *The Art of Glass*, 1697; "Printed for Dan. Brown etc.," London, 1699.

Bluestein, Dott G., "Storia degli Ebrei in Roman." P. Maglione and C. Strini, Rome.

Boccato, Carla, "Licenze per altane concesse ad Ebrei del ghetto di Venezia," *LRM*, March-April 1980.

Bogusevich, V. A., "Archeological Excavations, 1950, in Podolia, Kiev," *Brief Reports of the Archeological Institute of the Ukrainian USSR*, no. 41, 1951.

Bogusevich, V. A., "Glass and Salt Works of Eleventh Century Kiev," *Brief Reports of the Archeological Institute of the Ukrainian S.S.R.*, no. 3, 1954.

Boulnois, L., *The Silk Route*, London, 1966.

Brand, *Glass Vessels in Talmudic Literature*, Jerusalem, in Hebrew, 1978.

Breasted, J. H., *Ancient Records of Egypt*, vol. 2, University of Chicago, Chicago, 1906-1907.

Brill, Robert and John F. Wosinski, "A Huge Slab of Glass in the Ancient Necropolis of Beth She'arim," a paper submitted to Section B of the Seventh International Congress of Glass, Brussels, 1965.

Brill, Robert H., "A Great Glass Slab from Ancient Galilee," *Archeology*, vol. 20, no. 2, April, 1967.

Brill, R. H., "Preliminary Notes on the Analysis of Some Egyptian Glasses from Malkata and Lisht," submitted to the Egyptian Department of the Metropolitan Museum of Art, March 26, 1982.

Brown, J. P., *Lebanon and Phoenicia*, I: "Beirut."

Brusic, V. Han and Z., "Une Decouverte sous-Marine du Verre Medieval dans l'Adriatique," *Annals of the Seventh International Congress on Glass*, Brussels, 1977.

Brusin, Giovanni, "Orientali in Aquileia romana," *AN*, XXIV and XXV, 1953/1954.

Brusin, Giovanni, "Grande edificio culturale scoperto a Monastero di Aquileia," *AN*, Anno XX, 1949.

Brusin, Giovanni, "I mosaico paleocristiani di aquileia e il libro di un Parocco inglese, *AN*, Anno XXXIV, 1963.

*Bulletin of the Metropolitan Museum of Art II*, 1907.

*Bulletin of the Museum of Modern Art*, 1908.

Buriakov, Iu. F., *Archeological Data and Historical Topography of Tunkat*, Tashkent, 1962.

Buriakov, Iu. F., "New Archeological Data on the Site of Ul'kan-toi-Tiobe (Province of Nikat)," *Scientific Works and Reports of the OON, Academy of Science of the Uzbekistan S.S.R.*, 6, Tashkent, 1963.

Burgoyne, Ian, "The Evolution of Glassmaking Techniques," *Journal of the Pilkington Glass Museum*, June 1980, vol. 80, no. 1.

Cadik, Jindrich, "De l"Evangile de Saint Matthiew a la Russie Medievale," *Annals of the Fifth International Congress on Glass*, Prague, 1970.

Caley, Earle R., *Analysis of Ancient Glasses 1790-1957*, Corning Museum of Glass, 1962.

Callaway, Joseph A., "A Visit with Ahilud," *BAR*, Sept.\Oct. 1983, vol. IX, no. 5.

Calvi, M. C., "The Roman Glass of Northern Italy," *Bulletin of the Haaretz Museum*, 8, 1966.

Calvi, M. C., *I Vetri Romani del Museo di Aquileia*, Aquileia, Associazione Nazionale per Aquileia, 1969.

Calvi, M. C,, "Il miracolo della fonte nel vetro dorato del museo di Aquileia," *AN*, Anno XXX, 1959.

Cangova, I., "Srednovekovni amfori v Blgarija" *Isvestija na Archeologiceski Institut*, XXII, Sofia, 1959.

Carlini, Antonio, "L'epigraphe Teodoriana di Aquileia," *AN*, Anno LV, 1984.

# Bibliography

Carpi, Daniel, ed., *Minutes Book of the Council of the Jewish Community of Padua, 1603-1630*, Israel National Academy of Sciences and Humanities, Goldberg's Press, Jerusalem, 1979.

Cassel, D., "Juden," *Allgemeine Encyclopadia*, XXVII, eds.: Ersch und Gruber.

Cassola, F., "Aquileia e l'Oriente Mediteraneo," *AA*, 1977.

Casson, Lionel, *Ancient Trade and Society*, Wayne State University Press, Detroit, 1984.

Cecchetti, Bertolomeo, *Monografia della vetraria Veneziana e Muranese*, Murano, 1875.

Chambon R., and H. Arbman, "Deux fours a verre d'epoque merovingienne a Macquenoise (Belgique)," *Bulletin de la Societe Royale des Lettres de Lund*, VII, 1951-1952.

Charleston, Robert J., "Glass Furnaces Through the Ages," *JGS* vol. 20, 1978.

Cicero, *On Duties*.

Cicero, *Pro Rabirio Postumo*.

Ciepela, Slawomira, "La Verre en Pologne a la Fin du Moyen Age," *Bulletin of the Fifth International Congress on Glass*, Prague, 1970.

Clairmont, C. W., "The Glass Vessels," *The Excavations at Dura-Europus*, Final Report IV, Part V, Yale University and the French Academy of Inscriptions and Letters, Duro-Europus Publications, New Haven, 1963.

Classon, *Ancient Trade and Society*, Wayne State University Press, Detroit, 1984.

Constantino, Claudio, *La Repubblica di Genova*, Genoa, 1986.

Cowley, A. E., *The Sinaitic Inscriptions*, reprinted from *The Journal of Eastern Archeology*, vol. XV, Parts II and IV, 1929.

Curtis, John, *Nash-i Jan III, the Small Finds*, The British Institute of Persian Studies, 1984.

Davidson, Gladys R., "A Medieval Glass Factory at Corinth," *AJA*, XLIV, 1940.

Davidson, Gladys R., *Corinth, Results of Excavations Conducted by the American School of Classical Studies at Athens, XII, The Minor Objects*, Princeton, 1952.

De Boor, C., ed.: *Theophanis Chronographia*, 1963.

De Goeje, M. J., ed.: Ibn al-Faqih, *Compendium Libri Kitab al-Boldan*, Leiden, 1885.

De Goeje, M. J., ed.: *Bibliotheca Geographum Arabicum*, 5.

DeKowna, Maria, "Le Verres de Hauthabu," report in *Bulletin of the Seventh International Congress of Glass*, Brussels. 1977.

Dekowna, Maria, "Etude sur les origines de la verrerie en Pologne," *Annals of the Third International Congress on Glass*, Damascus, 1964.

Demsky, Aaron and Moshe Kochavi, "An Alphabet from the Days of the Judges," *BAR*, Sept.\Oct. 1978, vol. IV, no. 3.

Dikshit, Moretshwar G., *History of Indian Glass*, University of Bombay, 1969, (a compilation of the Pandit Bhagwanlal Indraji Endowment Lectures, 1967).

Dothan, Trude, "In the Days When the Judges Ruled--Research on the Period of the Settlement and the Judges," *Recent Archeology in the Land of Israel*, co-published by the IES, Jerusalem, 1981; Hebrew edition edited by Benjamin Mazar, and the *BAR*, Washington, 1984; English edition edited by Hershel Shanks.

Dovzhenok, V. I., "Ancient Village and City Sites Near Early Galitch," *Brief Reports of the Archeological Institute of the Ukrainian S.S.R*, no. 4, 1955.

Dunlop, D. M., *The History of the Jewish Khazars*, Princeton University Press, Princeton, 1954.

Dupree, Louis, *Afghanistan*, Princeton University Press, Princeton, 1973\1980.

Dussaud, R., *Un Nom Nouveau de verrier Sidonien*, 1920.

Duval, Yves-Marie, "Aquilee et la Palestine entre 370 et 420," *AA*, 1978.

*Encyclopedia Judaica*, Jerusalem, 1972.

Eban, Abba, *Heritage*, Summit Books, 1984.

Eban, Abba, *My People*, Behrman House Inc., (Random House), 1968.

*Egypt's Golden Age*, catalog of the exhibition of "The Art of Living in the New Kingdom 1558-1085 B.C.," of the Museum of Fine Arts, Boston, 1982.

Emereau, E., "Constantinople sous Theodore le Jeune," *Byzantion* 2, 1925.

Engles, Anita, "Who Were the Early Glassmakers?" and "3,000 Years of Glassmaking," *Readings in Glass History*, no. 1, Phoenix Publications, Jerusalem, 1973.

# Bibliography

Engles, Anita, "The Elder Pliny and the River," *Readings in Glass History*, no. 3, Phoenix Publications, Jerusalem, 1974.

Engles, Anita, *Readings in Glass History*, 6-7, Phoenix Publications, Jerusalem, 1976.

Engles, Anita, "Glassmaking in Ancient Jerusalem," *Readings in Glass History*, No. 18, Phoenix Publications, Jerusalem, 1984.

Farnsworth M. and P. D. Ritchie, "Spectographic studies in ancient glass, Egyptian Glass, mainly of the Eighteenth Dynasty, with special reference to its cobalt content," *Technical Studies*, VI, 1938.

Ferreto, A., *Codice diplomatico delle relazione fra la Liguria, la Toscana e la Lunigiana ai tempi di Dante (1265-1321)*, 1921.

Finley, M. I., *The Ancient Economy*, University of California Press, Los Angeles, 1973\1985.

Finley, M. I., *Ancient Sicily to the Arab Conquest*, Viking Press, 1968.

Fitzgerald, C. P., *China, a Cultural History*, D. Appleton-Century Company, edited by C. G. Seligman, 1938; revised edition, London Cresset Press, 1954.

Forbes, R. J., *Studies in Ancient Technology*, vol. 5, Leiden.

Fossing, Paul, *Glass Vessels Before Glass-blowing*, Copenhagen, 1940.

Fossing, Paul, "Drinking Bowls of Glass and Metal from the Achaemenian Time," *Berytus*, IV, 1937.

Fowler, James, *Archeologia*, vol. XLVI, 1881.

Frankfort, H., *Third Preliminary Report of the Iraq Expedition of the Oriental Institute of the University of Chicago at Tel Asmar*, 1934.

Froehner, William, *La Verrerie Antique, Description de la Collection Charvet*, Le Pecq, 1879.

Fukai, Shinju, *Persian Glass*, Tokyo, 1973, English edition, New York, Weatherhill/Tankosha, 1977.

Furnish, Victor Paul, "Corinth in Paul's Time," *BAR*, vol. XVB, no. 3, May/June 1988.

Gadd and Thompson, "A Middle-Babylonian Chemical Text," *Iraq*, iii, first part, 8/1928, 1936.

Galante, A., *Les Juifs de Constantinople sous Byzance*, Istanbul, 1940.

Gambatchidze, G., *Raskopki Thaba-Erdi (Ingutvhetia), Dekorativnoe iskusti SSSR*, 7 (152), Moscow, 1970.

Gardner, Sir Alan, *Egypt of the Pharaohs*, Oxford University Press, London; Oxford, New York, 1961/1979.

Geary, Patrick J., *Before France and Germany*, Oxford University Press, N.Y., 1988.

Gersprach, E., *L'Arte de la verrerie*, Bibliotheque de l'Enseignement di Beaux-Arts, Paris, 1885; A. Picard, Paris, 1908.

Ghirshman, Roman, "The Elamite Levels at Susa and Their Chronological Significance," *AJA*, 74, no. 3, 1970.

Gilbert, Martin, *Atlas of Jewish History*, Dorset Press, USA, 1969.

Ginsberg, L., *Legends of the Jews*, vol. 3.

Ginzberg, L., *Serdai Talmud Yurushalmi*, in Hebrew, Jerusalem, 1936.

Goldstein, Sidney Merril, *A Preliminary Study of the Glass Manufactured at Jalame in Israel*, Cambridge, 1970.

Goodenough, Erwin R., *Jewish Symbols in the Graeco-Roman Period*, Pantheon Books, 1953, vols. 2, 5 and 12.

Gordon, Cyrus H., *The Ancient Near East*, third ed., W. W. Horton & Co., New York, 1965

Gottwald, Norman K., "Were the Early Israelites Pastoral Nomads?," *BAR*, vol. IV, no. 2, June 1978.

Gottwald, Norman K., *The Tribes of Yahweh: a Sociology of the Religion of Liberated Israel, 1250-1050 BCE*, Maryknoll: Orbis, 1979.

Gottwald, Norman K., Review of John Bright's New Revision of *A History of Israel* in *BAR*, July\Aug. 1982, vol. VIII, no. 4.

Grabar, A., "la Verrerie d'art byzantine au moyen age," *Monuments Piot*, LVII, 1971.

Gracco-Ruggini, Luila, "Ebrei e Orientali in Aquileia," *AA*, 1977.

Graetz, Heinrich, *History of the Jews*, JPS, Philadelphia, 1967.

Grayzel, Solomon, *A History of the Jews*, JPS, Philadelphia, 1969.

Grose, Frederick David, "The Hellenistic Glass Industry Reconsidered," *Annals*

# Bibliography

*of the Eighth International Congress on Glass*, 17-25 Sept. 1979.

Hall, Haray Reginald Holland, *A Season's work at Ur, al-Ubaid, Abu Sharain (Eridu) and Elsewhere; being an unofficial  account of the British Museum Archeological mission to Babylonia, 1919*, Methuen & Co., London, 1930.

Hall, Haray Reginald Holland, *The Civilization of Greece in the Bronze Age*, Methuen and Co., London, 1928.

Halpern, Beruch, *The First Historians*, Halpern and Row, San Francisco, 1988.

Hamilton, F., *The Adriatic; the Italian Side*, 1966.

Han, Verena, "Les Relations Verrieres entre Dubrovnik et Venise du XIV au XVI siecle," *Annals of the Sixth International Congress on Glass*, Cologne, July 1973.

Han, Verena and Brisic, Z. "Une Decouverte sous-Marine du verre Medieval dans l'Adriatique," *Annals of the Seventh International Congress on Glass*, Brussels, 1977.

Handcock, Percy, S. P., *Mesopotamian Archeology*, Macmillan and Co., Kraus Reprint, New York, 1912/1969.

Hansen, Barbara, "India's Jews Keep the Lamp Burning in Cochin," *Newsday*, Oct. 22, 1989.

Harden, D. B., *Ancient Glass I: Pre-Roman*, 72, p. 46, reprinted from the Archeological Journal, vol. CXXV, 1968.

Harden, D. B., *Ancient Glass*, Royal Archeological Institute, London, 1972.

Harden, D. B., "Syrian Glass from the Earliest Times to the 8th Century A.D.," *Bulletin des Journees Internationales du Verre*, no. 3, 1964.

Harden, D. B., *Study and Research on Ancient Glass: Past and Present*, presented at the Twenty-Third Annual Seminar on Glass, Oct. 21, 1983, rep. *JGS*, vol. 26, 1984.

Harden, D. B., *Catalog of Greek and Roman Glass in the British Museum*, vol. I, London, 1981.

Hasson, Rachel, "Islamic Glass from Excavations in Jerusalem," *JGS*, 25, 1983.

Havernick, T. Te., "Beitrage zur Geshichte des antiken Glases. III Mykenishes Glas; IV Gefasse mit der Masken; V. Kleine Beobachtungen technischer Art," *Jahrbuch des romisch-germanischen Zentralmuseum Mainz*, VII, 1960.

Hemmy, A. S., *Journal of Egyptian Archeology*, XXIII, 1937.

Henning, W., "The Aramaic Inscription of Ashoka in Lamaka," *Bulletin of the School of Oriental and African Studies*, 1949-1950.

Herzfeld, "A new Asoka inscription from Taxila," *Epigraphia Indica*, 1928.

Hirth, Frederick, *Chinesische Studien*, Munchen, G. Hirth, 1890.

Hoffman, Michael A., *Egypt Before the Pharaohs*, Routledge and Kegan Paul, London and Henley, 1980.

Homer, *Iliad*.

Hopkins, Clark, *The Discovery of Dura-Europus*, Yale University Press, New Haven and London, 1979.

Israeli, Yael, "Ennion in Jerusalem," *JGS*, no. 25, 1983.

Jakobson, A. L., "Srednevekovie amfori severnogo pricernomorja," *Sovietskaja Archeologija*, XV, Moscow, 1951.

Jackson, F. Hamilton, R.B.A., *The Shores of the Adriatic*, "The Italian Side; the Austrian Side," John Murray, London, 1906.

James, Jean M., "Silk, China and the Drawloom," *Archeology*, vol. 39, no. 9, Sept. Oct. 1986.

Jastrzebowska, Elizabeth, "Les Origines de la Scene du Combat entre le coq et la Tortue dans les mosaics chretiennes d'Aquilee," *AA*, VIII, 1975.

Josephus, Flavius, *Against Apion*.

Josephus, Flavius, *The Wars of the Jews*.

*Judaism*, 13, 1964, "Solving the Khazar Problem. A Study in Soviet Historiography."

Keller, Warner, *The Bible as History*, Translated from the German by William Neil, revised edition, William Morrow and Company, New York, 1981.

Keller, C. A., "Problems in Dating Glass Industries of the Egyptian Kingdom: Examples from Malkata and Lisht," *JGS*, 25, 1983.

Khurradadhibh, Ibn, *al-Masalik wa 'l-Mamalik*, edited by M. J. de Geoje, Leiden, 1889.

Khvoiko, V. V., *Early Dwellers of the Middle Dniepr Region and Their Culture in Prehistoric Times*, translated by E. B. Gordon, Kiev, 1913.

Kisa, Anton, *Das Glas in Altertum*, 3 vols. K. W. Hirsmann, Leipzig, 1908; also issued in 5 parts by W. Spemann, Berlin and Stuttgart, 1905-1907.

# Bibliography

Klein Dan and Ward Lloyd, eds., *The History of Glass*, Orbis Press, London, 1984.

Kniper, A. H., "Caucasus, People of," *Encyclopedia Brittanica*, 1973.

Koestler, Arthur, *The Thirteenth Tribe*, Hutchinson, London, 1976.

Koldewey, Robert, *Das Wieder Erstehende Babylon*, J. C. Ilnrichs, Leipzig, 1913, English translation, London, 1914.

Krachkovski, I. Ya., *Puteshestvie Ibn-Fadlana na Volgu* (The Travels of Ibn Fadlana in the Volga Region), Moscow, 1939.

Lamb, Alistair, "Some observations on stone and glass beads in early South-East Asia," *Journal of the Malaysian Branch of the Royal Asiatic Society*, vol. 38, pt. 2, December 1965.

Lamb, Alistair, "Some Glass Beads from the Malay Peninsula," *Man*, vol. 65, no. 30, March-April 1965.

Lamm, Carl Johan, *Mittelalterliche Glaser und Steinschnittarbeit aus dem nahen Osten*, 2 vols., D. Reiner, Berlin, 1929-1930.

Landsberger B. and H. Tadmor, "Fragments of Clay Liver Models," *IEJ*, 1964, no. 14.

Langdon, *PBS.x*, no. 4, p. 342.

Layard, A. H., *Nineveh and its remains*, vol. II, J. Murray, London, 1849; G. Putnam and Co., New York, 1852.

Layard, A. H., *Discoveries in the Ruins of Nineveh and Babylon*, J. Murray, London, 1853; G. Putnam and Co., New York, 1853.

Lemmlein, G. G., "Ostatki stekloduvnogo proizvodstva v Karsani bliz Mccheta," (remains of glass production at Karsani near Mccheta), in Georgian, summarized in Russian, *Soobscenija Akademii Nauk Gruzinskoj SSR*, VI, no. 9, 1945.

Lepsius, Karl Richard, *Die Metalle in den Aegyptischen Inschriften*, Berlin, 1872; *Les metaux dans les inscriptions egyptiennes*, F. Viewag, Paris, 1877.

Le Strange, Guy, *The Noble Sanctuary at Jerusalem*, J. Royal Asiatic Society, 1887.

Levenson, Gabe, "From an Istanbul balcony," *The Jewish Week*, Dec. 4, 1987.

Levey, M., *Chemistry and Chemical Technology in Ancient Mesopotamia*, Elsevier Publishing Co., Amsterdam, New York 1959.

Levi, C. A., *L'arte del vetro in Murano nel Rinascimento e i Berroviero*, Venice, 1895.

Livy, *The Early History of Rome*.

Ljubinkovic, M. Corovbic, "Fragments de verres medievaux trouves a Novo Brdo," *Annals of the seventh International Congress on Glass*, Brussels, 1965.

Lomtatidze, G. A., "Rezultaty i perspektivy archeologiceskoyia izucenija goroda Tbilisi, (The results of the research at Tbilisi), *Sovetskaja Archeologija*, 1959, no. 4.

Low, I., *Die Flora der Juden ii*, Vienna, 1924.

Lucas, Alfred, *Ancient Egyptian Materials and industry*, E. Arnold and Co., London, 1926; Longmans, Green and Co., New York, 1926.

Lucretius, *De Rerum*.

Luzzatto, Moshe Chaim, *Derech haShem* (The Way of God), translated by Aryeh Kaplan, Jerusalem, 1983.

Mackay, Ernest and Langdon, Stephen, *Report on Excavations at Jamdet Nasr*, 1931.

Majumdar, Ramash Chandra, H. Rechaudhuri, and Kalikinkar Datta, *An Advanced History of India*, and edition, Macmillan, London, 1961 (1950\1967); St. Martin's Press, New York, 1967.

Makay, D. "The Jewelry of Palmyra and Its Significance," *Iraq*, no. 11, 1949.

Malandra, Guido, *I Vetrai di Altare*, Cassa di Risparmio di Savona, Savona (Italy), 1983.

Mann, J., *The Jews in Egypt and in Palestine under the Fatimid Caliphs*, 2 vols., Oxford University Press, London.

Margolis Max L., and Alexander Marx, *A History of the Jewish People*, Atheneum, USA, 1927.

Masson, Emilia, *Recherches sur les plus anciens emprunts sémetiques en grec*, C. Klincksieck, Paris, 1967.

Mazar, B. and I. Dunayevsky, "En-Gedi: The First and Second Seasons of Excavations 1961-1962," *Atiqot V*, English series, Jerusalem, 1966.

Mazar, Amihai, "On Early Cult Places and Early Israelites: A Response to Michael Coogan," *BAR*, July\Aug., vol. XV, no. 4, 1988.

# Bibliography

Mazar, Amihai, *IEJ*, 14.

McGovern, W., *The Early Empires of Central Asia*, Chapel Hill, 1939.

Megaw, A. H. S., "A Twelfth Century Bottle from Cyprus," *JGS*, 10, 1968.

Megaw, A. H. S., "More gilt and enameled glass from Cyprus," *JGS*, 10, 1968.

Meiggs, Russell, *Roman Ostia*, Clarendon Press, 1960, second edition 1973, reprinted 1977, Oxford University Press.

Mentasti, Rosa Barovier, "la coppa incisa con 'Daniele nella fossa dei leoni,' al museo Nazionale Concordiese," *AN*, Anno XIV.

Mian, Franca, "La Vittoria di Aquileia," *AA*, VIII, 1975.

*Midrash Exodus Rabba*, trans. Dr. S. M. Lehrmann, Chapter XXVII, 9, p. 330.

Milano, Attilio, "Vicende economiche degli Ebrei nell'Italia meridionale ed insulare durante il Medioevo," *LSM*, no. 6, 1954.

Miranovich, Ya., *Zapiski o Malorosii*, 1789, reprinted in *Regestry i Nadpisi* (Regests and inscriptions), St. Petersburg, 1913, no. 2450.

Mongait, A. L., *Archeology in the USSR*, translated from the Russian by David Skvinsky, Foreign Languages Publishing House, Moscow, 1959.

Moorey, P. R. S., *Materials and Manufacture in Ancient Mesopotamia*, Corning Museum, 1985; *BAR* international series 237, Oxford, 1985.

Mulhy, James D., *How Iron Technology Changed the Ancient World*, *BAR*, vol. VIII/6, Dec. 1982.

Naji, Alush, *Al-Masira Ila Filastin* (The Journey to Palestine), Dar al-Tali'a, Beirut, 1964.

Needham, Joseph F.R.S., and Wang Ling, Ph.D., *Science and Civilization in China*, Cambridge University Press, 1954-1965.

Negahban, Ezat O., *A Preliminary Report on Marlik Excavation, Rudbar, 1961-62*, Teheran, 1964.

Nesbitt, Alexander, F. S. A., *A Descriptive Catalogue of the Glass Vessels of All Ages in the South Kensington Museum*, Eyre and Spottiswoode, London, 1878.

Frederic Neuberg, *Ancient Glass*, trans. Michael Bullock and Alisa Jaffa, Barrie and Rockliff, London, 1962.

Nolte, Birgit, *Die Glasgefasse im Alten Agypten*, B. Kessling, Berlin, 1968.

Oates, D., "The Excavations at Tell al Rimah," *Iraq*, XXX, 1968.

Obolensky, Dimitry, *The Byzantine Commonwealth--Eastern Europe 500-1453*, Praeger Publishers, New York, 1971.

Olczak, J., "Warsztat szklarski z XIII-XIV wierku odkryty przez archeologow w Miedzyrezeczu Wielkopolskim," (A glasshouse of the thirteenth-fourteenth centuries discovered by the archeologists at Miedzyrzeczu Wielkopol skim), *Szklo i Ceramica* VIII, 1957, no. 9.

Olczak, J., E. Jasiewiczowa, *Szklarstwo wczesnosredniowiecznego Wolina*, (The medieval glasshouse of Wolin), summary in English, Szczecin, 1963.

Olczak, J., "Stan badan nad sklarstwem wecznosredniowiecznej Slowian szczyzny," (The State of research on the glasshouses of the Upper Middle Age in Slavic countries), summary in French, *Slavia Antiqua*, XI, 1964.

Oliver, Andrew Jr. "Persian Export Glass," *JGS*, XII, 1970.

Olmstead, Albert Ten Eyck, *History of the Persian Empire*, University of Chicago Press, Chicago, 1948.

Oppenheim, A. Leo, "The Cuneiform Texts" in *Glass and Glassmaking in Ancient Mesopotamia*, revised edition, University of Chicago Press, Chicago, 1970.

Orlinsky, Harry, *Ancient Israel*, Cornell University, Ithaca and London, 1960\1977.

Panciera, Silvio, *Vita Economica di Aquileia in eta Romana*, Aquileia, 1957.

Pasuto, V. T., and Yu. A. Polokov, "Voprosi Istorii SSR na XIII mezhdunarodnom Kongrese Istorikov" (Problems of History of the USSR at the Thirteenth International Congress of Historians), *Istoriya SSR*, 1971, no. 1.

Perkins, Ann, *The Excavations at Dura-Europus*, 1963, Final Report IV.

Petachya B. Jacob of Regensburg, *Travels of Petachya of Regensburg* (in Hebrew), (from Ugolini Thesaurus, vol. 6), first edition, Prague, 1595.

Peters, John Punnett, *Nippur, or Explorations and Adventures on the Euphrates*, New York and London, 1899.

Petrie, William Matthew Flinders, *Tell-el-Amarna*, London, 1894. Transactions of the Society of Glass Technology, 38, 1954.

Petrie, Sir Flinders, *Researches in Sinai*, J. Murray, London, 1906.

# Bibliography

Pettinato, Giovanni, *The Archives of Ebla*, Doubleday and Company, New York, 1979/1981.

Pettinato, Giovanni, *Ebla, nuovi orrizonti della storia*, Rusconi, Milano, 1986.

Phillipe, J., *Le Monde byzantin dans le histoire de la verrerie, v-xvi siecle*, Bologna, 1970.

Phillips, Phoebe, *The Encyclopedia of Glass*, William Heinemann Ltd., London, 1981.

Philipson, David, *Old European Jewries*, JPS, Philadelphia, 1894\1943.

Philo, Judaeus, *Quod imnis Probus Libus Sit*.

Pliny, *Natural History*, Loeb Classical Library, translation by Eichholz.

Polak, Ada, *Glass*, Weidenfeld and Nicolson, London, 1974.

Poliak, A. N., "The Khazar conversion to Judaism" (in Hebrew), *Zion*, Jerusalem, 1941.

Polo, Marco, *The Travels of Marco Polo*, translated by William Marsden, Doubleday and Co., New York, 1948.

Polybius, *The Rise of the Roman Empire*.

Ponzi, Mariamaddalena Negro, "A Group of Mesopotamian glass vessels of Sassanian date," *Bulletin of the Sixth International Congress on Glass*, Cologne, 1973

Porada, E., *Tchoga Zanbil, Memoires de la Delegation archeologique en Iran*, vol. 4, P. Geuthner, Paris, 1970.

Pritchard, James B., *The Ancient Near East*, vol. I, Princeton University Press, 1958/1973.

Pulak, Cemal, "The Hellenistic Shipwreck at Serce Limani, Turkey; Preliminary Report," *AJA*, 91, 1987.

Pulak, Cemal, "Excavations in Turkey: 1988 Campaign," *Institute of Nautical Archeology Newsletter*, vol. 15, no. 4, College Station, Texas, December 1988.

Rahman, Sir Abdul, *Report to the General Assembly*, United Nations Special Committee on Palestine, vol. 2, Lake Success, N. Y., 1947.

Reignard, Oswin H. Puttrich, *Die Glasfunde von Ktesiphon*, Kiel, 1934.

Rejwan, Nissim, *The Jews of Iraq*, Westview Press, Boulder, Colorado, 1985.

Riefstahl, Elizabeth, *Ancient Glass and Glazes in the Brooklyn Museum*, Brooklyn Museum, 1968.

Rich, Claudius James, *Memoir of the Ruins of Babylon*, London, 1815.

Rinaldi, Giovanni, "I tre quadri di Giona nel mosaico dell'aula Teodorina," *AA*, VIII, 1975.

Robinson, Natalie, "Mantones de Manila," *Arts of Asia*, Jan./Feb., 1987.

Roth, Cecil, *The Jewish Contribution to Civilization*, Horovitz Publishing Co. Ltd., London, 1956, p. 67.

Roth, Cecil, *A History of the Jews*, 1954, new ed., Schocken Books, 1970.

Rouen, D. B. H., *Ancient Glass*, London, 1972.

Rowland, *Ancient Art from Afghanistan*, 1966.

Ruggini, Luila Cracco, "Il vescovo Cromazio e gli ebrei di Aquileia," *AA*, VIII, 1975.

Safrei, Shnuel, "The Lands of the Diaspora," *A History of the Jewish People*, [see Sasson], 1969\1976.

Saggs, H. W. F., *The Might That Was Assyria*, Sidgwick and Jackson, London, 1985.

Sasson, H. H. Ben, *A History of the Jewish People*, English translation, George Weidenfeld and Nicholson Ltd., Tel Aviv, 1969; also Harvard University Press, Cambridge.

Sava, George, *Valley of the Forgotten People*, London, 1946.

Scapova, Julia Leonidovna, "Apparition de la verrerie chez les Slaves Orientaux," *Rapports du IIIe Congres Internationale d'Archeologie Slave*, Tome II, Bratislava, 7-14 September, 1975.

Sharff, *Byzantine Jewry*, 1971.

Schiff, W. E., *Parthian Stations by Isidore of Charax*, Philadelphia, 1914.

Schmidt, Erich F., *Persopolis II*, University of Chicago Press, 1957, (1953-1970).

Schumacher, G., *Tel el-Mutesselim I*, Leipzig, 1968.

Schurer, E., *Geshichte dem Judische Volkes*, II, Leipzig, 1906.

Schwab, M., and A. Reifenberg, extract from *Rivista di Archeologica Cristiana*, 1939.

# Bibliography

Schwarz Leo W., ed., *Great Ages and Ideas of the Jewish People.*

Seefried, M., "Les Pendentifs en verre faconnes sur noyau du Musee National du Bardo et du Musee National de Carthage," *Karthago*, XVII, 1973-1974.

Seligman, C. G., and H.C. Beck, *Far Eastern Glass, Some Western Origins*, reprinted from the "Bulletin of the Far Eastern Antiquities," no. 10, Stockholm, 1938.

Seligman, C. G., *The Roman Orient and the Far East*, reprinted from The Smithsonian Report for 1938.

Seligman, C. G., "Early Chinese Glass," *Transactions of the Oriental Ceramic Society*, 1940-1941.

Shanks, Herschel, "Should the Term Biblical Archeology Be Abandoned?" *BAR*, May\June 1981.

Shanks, Herschel, "BAR Interviews Yigael Yadin," *BAR*, vol. IX, no. 1, Jan./Feb. 1983.

Shanks, Herschel, "Dever's 'Sermon on the Mound'," *BAR*, Mar.\Apr. 1987.

Shapiro, Sidney, *Jews in China*, Hippocrene Publications, New York, 1984.

Sharf, Andrew, *Byzantine Jewry*, Routledge and Kegan Paul, London, 1971.

Shelkovnikov, B. A., "Russian Glass of the Eleventh to the Seventeenth Centuries," *JGS*, VIII, 1966.

Singer Charles Joseph et al., *A History of Technology*, vol. 1, (Weights and Measures) Clarendon Press, Oxford, New York, 1954\1958.

Smith, Ray W., *Glass from the Ancient World, The Ray Winfield Collection*, Corning Museum of Glass, 1957.

Smith, Ray Winfield, "Mediterranean Glass from the Beginnings to the First Century B.C.," *Bulletin of the First International Congress on Glass*, Liege, Aug. 1959.

*Sotheby's Sale Catalogue* II, Dec. 1961.

St. Jerome, *Comm. in Exekiel*, xxvii, in *Pat. Lat.* 25, 313, "Orbe, Romano Occupato."

Stark, F., *Rome on the Euphrates*, 1966.

Starr, Richard F. S., *Nuzi, Report on the Excavations at Yorgan Tepa, 1927-1931*, Harvard University Press, 1939.

Stech-Wheeler, T., J. D. Muhly, K. R. Maxwell-Hyslop, R. Maddin, "Iron at Taanach and Early Iron Metallurgy in the Eastern Mediterranean," *AJA*, vol. 85, no. 3, July 1981.

Stein, M. Aural, "A Journey of Geographical and Archeological Exploration in Chinese Turkestan," *The Geographical Journal*, London, 1902.

Stein, M. Aural, *Sand-buried Ruins of Khotan*, 1903.

Stein, M. Aural, *Serindia*, Oxford, 1921.

Stein, M. Aural, *Central Asian Relics of China's Ancient Silk Trade*, Hirth Anniversary Volume, 1921.

Stein, M. Aural, *On Ancient Central Asian Tracks*, London, 1933.

Stern, Ephraim, *Material Culture of the Land of the Bible in the Persian Period 538-332 B.C.*, Hebrew, Bialik Institute and the Israel Exploration Society, Jerusalem, 1973; English edition by Aris and Phillips, Ltd, Warminster, England, 1982.

Stillman, Norman A., *The Jews of Arab Lands*, *JPS*, Philadelphia, 1979.

Strabo, *Geographica*.

Strong, D. E., *Greek and Roman Gold and Silver Plate*, 1966.

Tacitus, *The Histories*, translation by Kenneth Wellesley.

Tacitus, *Germania*.

Tadmor, Hayim, "The Decline, Rise and Destruction of Israel," *A History of the Jewish People*, [see Sasson] 1969.

Tamaro, Bruna Forlati, "Ricerche sull'aula teodoriana nord e sui Battisteri di Aquileia," *AN*, 1963.

Tamaro, Bruna Forlati, "Iscrizioni greche di Siriani a Concordia," *AA*.

Tanichi, Takashi, "Western Designed 'Composite Eye' Glass Beads Recently Excavated in China," summary in English, *Bulletin of the Ancient Orient Museum*, vol. 5, Tokyo, 1983.

Theophanes, *Chronographia*, ed. De Boor, 1883.

Theophrastus, S.IV: III.

Thompson, R. Campbell, *A Dictionary of Assyrian Chemistry and Geology*, Clarendon Press, Oxford, 1936.

Thompson, R. Campbell and C. J. Gadd, "A Middle-Babylonian Text," *Iraq*, no.

3, 1936.

Thompson R. Campbell, *On the Chemistry of the Ancient Assyrians*, Luzac and Co., London, 1925.

Thorpe, W. A., *English Glass*, A. & C. Black Ltd., London, 1935\1949.

Toynbee, A., *Constantine Porphyrogenitus and His World*, Oxford University Press, New York, London, 1973.

Trowbridge, M. L., *Philological Studies in Ancient Glass*, Urbana (USA), 1928/1930.

Trudnovskaja, S. A., "Steklo s gorodisca Sach-Senem," *Archeologiceskie i Etnograficeskie raboty chorezmskoj Ekspedicii 1949-1953*, Moscow, 1953.

Turner, W. E. S., "Studies in Ancient Glass and Glass-making procedures, Part I: Crucibles and Melting Temperatures Employed in Ancient Egypt about 1370 B.C.," *Transactions of the Society of Glass Technology*, 38, 1954.

Ugrelidze, N. N., "Natbeurskaja steklodelatel'naja masterkaja, *Materialy po archeologija Gruzii i Kavkaza*, (The glass shop of Natbeuri) III, 1963, in Georgian, summary in Russian.

Ugrelidze, N. N., *The Glass of Ancient Georgia*, (in Georgian), Tbilisi, 1961.

Vandiver, Pamela, "Glass Technology at the Mid-Second-Millennium B.C. Hurrian Site of Nuzi," *JGS*, 25, 1983.

Vattioni, Franceso, "I nomi Giudaici delle epigrafi di Monastero di Aquileia," *AN*, XLIII, 1972.

Van Seeters, John, *The Hyksos*, 1966.

Vermeule, Emily, *Greece in the Bronze Age*, University of Chicago Press, Chicago and London, 1984/1972.

Vogelstein, Hermann, *The Jews of Rome*, translated from the German by Moses Hades, Philadelphia.

Volkmar, Fritz, "Conquest or Settlement," *BAR*, June, 1987, vol. 50 no. 4.

Vollmer, John E., E. J. Keall, E. Nagai-Berthong, *Silk Roads-- China Ships*, Royal Ontario Museum, Toronto, 1983.

Von Bissing, F. W., "Sur l'Histoire du Verre en Egypte," *Revue Archeologique*, serie 4, XI, 1908.

Von Saldern, Axel, *Glas von der Antike bis zum Jugendstil*, Philipp von Zabern,

Mainz am Rhein, 1980.

Von Saldern, Axel, "Mosaic Glass from Hasanlu, Marlik, and Tell al-Rimah, *JGS*, VIII, 1966.

Von Saldern, Axel, "Glass Finds at Gordion," *JGS*, I, 1959.

Von Saldern, Axel, *Abstract of the Sixth International Congress on Glass*, Cologne, 1962.

Von Saldern, Axel, "Achaemenid and Sassanian Cut Glass," *Ars Orientalis*, V, 1963.

Waldbaum, J. C., "From Bronze to Iron," *SIMA*, Goteburg, 1978.

Weinberg, Saul, "Tel Anafa," *Encyclopedia of Archeological Excavations in the Holy Land*, vol. I, Prentice-Hall, Inc., New Jersey, 1975.

Weinreich, Max, *History of the Yiddish Language*, University of Chicago Press, Chicago, 1980.

Weinryb, David D., "The Khazars, An annotated Bibliography," Cecil Roth, editor, *Studies in Bibliography and Booklore*, vol. XI, Gregg International Publishers, Farnborough, England, 1976.

Wilson, E., *Sacred Books of the East*, 1945.

Whitcomb, Donald S., *Before the Roses and the Nightingales, Excavations at Qasr-i Abu Nasr, Old Shiraz*, Metropolitan Museum of Art, New York, 1985.

White, William Charles, *Tombs of Old Lo-Yang*, Shanghai, 1934.

White, William Charles, *Chinese Jews*, University of Toronto Press, 1942\1966 (distributed in the USA by Paragon, a subsidiary of Paragon Book Gallery Ltd., N.Y.).

Whitehouse, David, "Medieval Glass in Italy: Some Recent Developments," *JGS*, no. 25, 1983.

Woolley, Sir Charles Leonard, *Abraham*, Faber and Faber Limited, London, 1936.

Woolley, Sir Charles Leonard, *Ur Excavations II*, Oxford University Press, London, 1934 (1927-1955).

Woolley, Sir Charles Leonard, *Alalakh; an Account of the Excavations at Tel-Atchana in the Hatag 1937-1949*, (Oxford) printed at the University Press by Charles Baleg for the Society of Antiquities, Burlington House, London, 1955.

# Bibliography

Wright, G. Ernest, *Biblical Archeology*, the Westminster Press, Philadelphia, 1957\1979.

Wright, G. E., "The Archeology of Palestine from the Neolithic Through the Middle Bronze Age," *JAOS*, no. 91, 1971.

Wyrobisz, A., *Szklo w Polsce od XIV do XVII wieku* (Glass in Poland from the Fourteenth to the Eighteenth centuries), Wroclaw-Warszawa-Krakow, 1968.

Xenophon, *Oecinomicus*.

Yadin et al, *Hazor II*, Jerusalem, Magness Press (Heb. Un.), 1960.

Yadin, Yigael, *The Art of War in Biblical Lands*, McGraw-Hill, London, 1963.

Yadin, Yigael, *Hazor*, Random House, London, 1975.

Yadin Yigael, et al, *Hazor II*, Jerusalem, Magnes Press, Hebrew University, 1960.

Yadin, Yigael, "Is the Biblical Account of the Israelite Conquest of Canaan Historically Reliable?" *BAR*, V. VIII, No. 2, Mar./Apr. 1982.

Yaari, A., ed., *Iggorot Erez Israel*, 1943.

Yoshita, Herada, "Ancient Glass in the History of Cultural Exchange Between East and West," *Acta Asiatica*, 1962.

Zecchin, Luigi, "I Primi Atti del Podesta di Murano," *GE*, 1966.

Zecchin, Luigi, "Gli Atti del Podesta di Murano dal 1291 al 1285," *GE*, XX, 1966.

Zecchin, Luigi, "Vetrerie Muranese dal 1401 al 1415," *RSV*, no. 2, March-April 1972.

Zecchin, Luigi, ""Vetrerie Muranese dal 1416 al 1425," *RSV*, no. 3, May-June 1972.

Zecchin, Luigi, "Cronologia vetraria Veneziana e Muranese fino al 1285," *RSV*, no. 1, 1973.

Zecchin, Luigi, "Cronologia vetraria Veneziana e Muranese dal 1332 al 1345," *RSV*, no. 5, Sept.-Oct. 1973.

Zecchin, Luigi, "Decoratori di Vetri a Murano dal 1280 al 1480," *RSV*, no. 1, 1977.

Zecchin, Luigi, "Vetrerie Padovane fra il XIII ed il XVI secolo, *RSV*, no. 5., Sept.-Oct. 1980.

THE GLASSMAKERS

Zecchin, Luigi, "Nicolo di Bagio, vetraio a Murano dal 1459 al 1512," *RSV*, no. 6, 1983.

Zimmels, H. J., "Scholars and Scholarship in Byzantium and Italy," *The World History of the Jewish People*, second series, vol. 2, Tel Aviv, 1966.

Zovatto, Paolo Lino, "Architettura e decorazione nella basilica Teodoriana di Aquileia," *AN*, 1980.

# INDEX